Rounders 3

Also by Max Evans

THE HI LO COUNTRY
SUPER BULL
BOBBY JACK SMITH, YOU DIRTY COWARD
XAVIER'S FOLLY

MAX EVANS

Rounders 3

A DOUBLE D WESTERN
DOUBLEDAY
New York London Toronto Sydney Auckland

A DOUBLE D WESTERN
PUBLISHED BY DOUBLEDAY
a division of Bantam Doubleday Dell Publishing Group, Inc.
666 Fifth Avenue, New York, New York 10103

DOUBLE D WESTERN, DOUBLEDAY,
and the portrayal of the letters DD
are the trademarks of Doubleday, a division of
Bantam Doubleday Dell Publishing Group, Inc.

"The Rounders" was originally published by the Macmillan Company.
"The Great Wedding" was originally published by Houghton Mifflin.
"The Orange County Cowboys" originally appeared in the Winter 1987 issue of
  South Dakota Review. Copyright © 1987 by South Dakota Review.
All reprinted by permission of the author.

Library of Congress Cataloging-in-Publication Data

Evans, Max.
  Rounders 3/Max Evans.
    p.   cm.—(A Double D. western)
  Contents: The Rounders—The great wedding—The Orange County cowboys.
  1. Western stories. I. Title.
PS3555.V23R7   1990
813'.54—dc20   89-38622
                                                                      CIP

ISBN 0-385-26723-1
Copyright © 1960, 1963, 1990 by Max Evans
All Rights Reserved
Printed in the United States of America
April 1990
First Edition

To my wife, Pat, for the years of faith and acceptance

CONTENTS

Rounders 3

AUTHOR'S NOTES TO THE READER
also being the account of
SEARCHING FOR THE ROOTS
OF THE ROUNDERS TRILOGY

IF THERE'S ANYTHING to genes and heritage then *Rounders 3* started in Lynn County, Texas, approximately twenty miles southeast of Lubbock, before I was born. My Evans grandparents had a modest-sized cattle ranch there along with six sons and one daughter. One son, W.B., would later become my father.

It was the winter of 1918, the last year of the first World War. The eldest son, Elbert, had just been killed in combat in France. Before the family could overcome that shock, a terrible blizzard ripped down from the north. A great, black, rolling cloud stretched across the flat plains from horizon to horizon, leaving the family barely enough time to pen the chickens and open gates to corrals and haystacks. The horses and mules made it to these enclosures and survived. The cattle, scattered over many sections of land, turned their tails to the screaming wind and freezing snow, trying to move away from it. When they hit the long drift fence, they stopped and died.

The family huddled helplessly inside the shivering frame house for two days. Then it was over, and they moved out into the drifts to see what had survived. Most of the cattle were buried, frozen. The few that made it through the fence alive were found later in such pitiful condition that they had to be shot.

My Uncle Lloyd, of Levelland, Texas, recalls that the snow was piled so high in a plum thicket that they could walk right over the top of it. As the huge drifts melted and were dug away, they salvaged what they could—mostly cowhides. They split the hide properly, then finished peeling it off with a team of mules. It was a terrible struggle to save so little. Lloyd (who was ten years old at the time) remembers digging out what he thought was a cow and finding to his surprise a neighbor's hog standing upright, frozen solid, as if it had stopped to rest.

My Uncle Bernard, presently of Dallas, Texas, was five years old and the baby of the family. He said, "If I live a thousand years, what I'll remember most vividly of that storm is a fence covered with cowhides as far as I could see."

My grandparents sold the land, the few surviving cattle, the cowhides, and moved their family to Ropes, Texas. They bought a section of land right out of town, put in a mercantile store and started over.

My father met and married my mother, Hazel Swafford, whose family had recently moved to Ropes from the Indian Territory near Fredrick, Oklahoma. A short time later the newlyweds, driving a wagon and team, were instrumental in organizing Hockley County. My grandfather, J. R. Evans, was soon the first elected judge of the new county.

The Evans family pioneered many other things in West Texas and eastern New Mexico. My mother was the first postmistress at Ropes. My Uncle Elbert was the first soldier killed from Hockley County in World War I.

One Evans son, Robert (a.k.a. Slim, Tex, and Ion) would, many years later, contribute considerably to the *Rounders 3* stories. He was a cowboy all the way down to his liver. He broke and trained horses for anyone who would hire him—and some who wouldn't.

He rode West to punch cows and ride rough strings from Mexico to Canada. He was eighty-three and working cattle the old, Spanish Vaquero way—horseback with the help of cattle dogs—when he died in the High Sierras of California.

My father traded for a modest-sized piece of ranch land just north of Hobbs, New Mexico, and set about establishing a town there. He moved his widowed sister, Pearl Nettles, and her children there to take care of the cattle on the east end of the land—the rest was turned into a town he called Humble City (and was it ever). The drought and depression both came right after he promoted a school and post office. My mother was a postmistress again.

I'll never know how my mother did it, poor as we were and busy as she was, but she acquired some books and taught me to read. By the time I started school I could read almost as well as the teacher. I will be eternally grateful for this most precious of gifts.

It was a great place and time for a boy to grow up in. I loved the vast, unplowed prairies. They were full of all sorts of small game which I harvested and brought home for our lean supper table. I had a horse named Cricket and several dogs. When I wasn't herding my Aunt Pearl's cattle, I was hunting with my dogs or visiting my grandparents back in West Texas.

Farmers were just beginning to plow up all the Ropes area. The temporary exception was the famous Spade Ranch west and north of town. I resented them ruining those natural prairies, then and now. Some of it might have been fine, but *all* of it? No!

I remember when the hot winds of the drought blew the furrows barren and almost level. I wasn't too dismayed. I told all the local kids who would listen, "Don't worry, this drought is the best thing that ever happened. They'll never be able to raise a cotton crop again, and it's all gonna turn back to grass."

Well, in spite of my optimistic enthusiasm, my folks lost it all at Humble City—but it's still on the map. They moved to Lubbock, Texas. I was coming on ten years of age.

My father went into business with his Uncle Pit Emery, an auctioneer. The day came when he asked me to saddle and ride Cricket to an auction location just out of Lubbock. He told me to really rein the horse out and show him off for the crowd. We sold Cricket that day. It hurt for a while, but I learned, and accepted, that sometimes it's necessary to sacrifice one thing in order to get another. This particular transaction would lead to a string of adventures that were to change my life and partially guide me towards *The Rounders*, the first story of this trilogy.

My father and his uncle took the proceeds from this sale and bought a string of half-starved horses way down south at Jal, New Mexico. Then he introduced me to a one-eyed, extremely bowlegged cowboy named Boggs, gave us three dollars and directions into and across West Texas all the way up north to Guymon, in the Panhandle of Oklahoma. He told us to get there on an exact date with the horses in *better* shape. That was almost a cinch because I half expected the buzzards to start tearing at their bone-stretched hides while they were still walking.

There was a problem, to wit: we only had one saddle and it was mine. On the fourth day Boggs talked me out of it by demonstrating how saddles had bowed and ruined his legs permanently. He didn't want to see me disfigured in this manner. I rode several hundred winding, twisting miles bareback with a hind end raw as fresh ground hamburger meat.

Boggs was truly a drifting, hobo cowboy. But in the following weeks I found out that he had survival instincts as strong as a coyote's.

We zigzagged across Texas, "borrowing," as he so carefully explained, patches of grass, weeds, remains of old feed stacks, grain from many bins. We twisted rabbits out of holes with forked barbed wire, rescued chickens from locked henhouses and did some midnight seining of catfish from privately stocked ponds. The horses ate. We ate.

We survived flash floods, great thunder and sandstorms, and arrived at a stock farm three miles out of Guymon the morning before the 1 P.M. start of the sale—and the horses *were* in better shape than when we'd left. It was a roaring success and gave our families a new start in the recently battered West.

I wound up with a tough ass, soft brains, and an uncommon craving to go to the mountains. Boggs had told me so many entrancing tales of his adventures across the deserts and mountains of Colorado, Arizona, and New Mexico, that nothing could keep me from "experiencing" some of my own. Another key step on the road to The *Rounders* had been taken.

About this time I, my parents, and Glenda, my baby sister, were moving to the ranch and oil town of Andrews, Texas. When everything was settled in, I talked my parents into letting me go to Lamy, New Mexico, a tiny village a few miles south of Santa Fe, in search of my Uncle Slim. He was supposed to be in that area. I promised to return to Andrews in the fall for school.

It was a long bus ride to Lamy, over dirt and dippy gravel highways, but I could see the mountains ahead. I got off Wednesday morning at the railway station where, not too many years before, Mabel Dodge Lujan had met D. H. Lawrence, his wife Frieda, and the artist Lady Dorothy Brett. So many internationally famous people—Georgia O'Keefe, Witter Byner, and scores of others—had entered the world of the West from this little spot, and chosen to stay. I didn't know or care about any of them at the time.

I walked over to the nearest business establishment, the Lamy Bar. The only customers were two local Hispanics and a gringo wino. The bartender was a thin, fragile, pale man. He saw my one bag and asked who I was looking for. I told him my uncle, Slim Evans.

He grinned and said, "Sure, he's working for Pete Coleman. They come in most Saturday afternoons."

I was relieved, scared, and excited all at once. He let me sleep on a cot in a back room, and took me to the Harvey House next to the train station for all our meals.

On Saturday, Uncle Slim and the cowboys came. The very next morning they were moving Coleman's herd of cattle to a new ranch at Haney Springs on Glorieta Mesa. I was given the "honor" of riding a half-broke bronc on the three-day drive up on the mesa.

After a few weeks at the Coleman place, Uncle Slim decided I should try out for a job on Ed Young's Rafter EY Ranch. He said, "There's never been any kids make it on his outfit. He's hard, but fair. If you could hang in there, Max, you'd learn a lot."

I really didn't have much choice; jobs with pay were scarce. No one could afford to hire all the hands they needed, so everyone loaned and borrowed cowboys like coffee and sugar.

Ed did hire me. I made a fair hand mainly because I was naturally pretty good with a rope, but it took several seasons. Ed introduced me to a couple of "borrowed" cowboys as the new horse wrangler. What that actually meant was, I was the one who got up at daylight, saddled ole P. Nasty, a silly-looking bay night-horse, and headed out to gather everybody's mount for the day.

When I found them, they whirled and took off in a dead run towards the corrals. Hell, this was going to be easy; these horses were trained like circus seals. Ole P. Nasty laid his ears back and stormed after the remuda. About a hundred yards from the corral, before the horses entered the open gate, P. Nasty ducked his head and violently changed gears. He started bucking.

I can still remember thinking that this horse's head must have fallen off because all I could see was a black, flying mane in front of and below me. His forelegs seemed to be dropping into holes deep enough to strike oil. I was bucked completely loose on the third jump, but I couldn't fall off. Ole P. Nasty was miraculously bucking back under me. He came to the corral, bucked along the fence, then whirled back. All parts of my anatomy, from my hip pockets on down, were taking a hell of a beating as I came down and met nine hundred pounds of horse coming up.

I remember Ed Young running beside me waving his hat to keep the horse from hitting the corral posts and yelling encouragement. "Ride the son of a bitch, Max. Stay with the bastard. Spur hell out of him, son."

My balls were mashed; the breath had been knocked out of me several jumps back. The world was spinning faster than eyes could follow. What seemed like hours later, I was finally standing there clinging to the corral fence, when one of the cowboys presented me with Ole P. Nasty's reins. I took them like I'd been handed a blazing cow turd.

I knew I was doomed when Ed said flatly, "The horses turned back. Go get 'em. We're running late."

Somehow, I remounted, gathered the horses again, then rode twenty miles that day through rocks and brush, helping move cattle from a winter pasture to a summer one. It wasn't so bad. I changed to a good, gentle horse named Ole Snip, who knew what we were both supposed to do.

It was just like Boggs had said it would be—multitudes of long rides and endless new adventures. There were wild horse chases and sometimes capture; many wrecks out in the rocks and brush; the roundups and brandings; the rare trips into town. The good and the bad in abundance were here on the mesa.

Ed Young kept me working. Each fall I commuted back to Andrews for the football season. Some of the late winters on Glorieta Mesa made the high, sandy winds of the Andrews country seem like Hawaii.

Sometimes we'd have three or four extra "borrowed" cowhands around and other times I was loaned out all over the country. I looked forward to being temporarily transferred to the San Christobal outfit just south of Lamy. That eighty-thousand-acre ranch was covered with the first black Angus cattle I'd ever seen, Indian ruins, petroglyphs, great white and red bluffs, and a wonderful winding stream that gave the ranch its name and life.

Ed Young's wife was known as "Mother" Young. The term was used with enormous respect. I never knew why I started helping her after supper, but thanks to any and all great spirits for the privilege. I'd chop and gather wood for the next day and fill the hot water reservoir on the side of the huge wood-burning cook stove, fill all the water buckets for drinking, washing, and cooking, help clear the supper table, and then—the real treat—stand and dry dishes for her. We talked, and talked—even about books, paintings, and sissy stuff like that.

Her contributions were everywhere. She made the rag rugs that covered the floors, built the lamp stands from tree cactus or wagon hubs, painted the pictures that hung on the walls, cooked, cleaned, doctored, washed, ironed, and in true essence held the whole damned outfit together, as thousands of others like her did, and still do.

I have slowly realized that those tough, old ranchers would have been helpless without the Mother Youngs of the world. I know, because my wife, Pat, is a lot like that. Without her keeping a strong loop around our little art-addicted family, we would have long ago been lost in thick brush.

It is sad that back in those days, working cowboys seldom had a chance to meet the kind of woman they would, or could, marry. There were those they held in awe and respect, like Mother Young, and there were the other kind.

There usually would be three or four local dances held a year, but working cowboys seldom had transportation or money to properly date a girl, even after he met her. The old legend of a simple cowboy marrying the boss's daughter was extremely rare. It was nobody's fault. That's just the way it was. It has changed enormously, as you'll see in the stories of *Rounders 3*. In the beginning stories I wrote the women as they were viewed by working cowboys, and I end by describing the long-overdue respect they hold now. Any other way would have been false.

The first winter I spent on the mesa, Mother Young put a box of books on a little homemade shelf. There were three Balzacs in the bunch. I started reading them and couldn't quit. I was mighty impressed that anybody could take these varied characters and make me know them, see them, feel their loves and hatred, their fears, and occasional gallantries. It was a magic, different world the little potbellied Frenchman gave me here in this enchanted land of New Mexico. I could see the colors and smell the perfume.

Balzac's largesse carried over to Andrews. Income from new oil made this school one of the richest in Texas. They built a fine library where I spent hours and hours engrossed in its treasures.

Years later, after the first volume of *The Rounders* had been published, they put a picture of me in the Andrews High School Hall of Fame. It'll never be known if this was because of my work as a writer, an artist, or because of running so fast with the football. I was offered two athletic scholarships, to small colleges, but declined and became a rounder instead.

My Uncle Slim was on the lower Pankey Ranch gathering wild cattle that had been missed during several roundups. Naturally, he asked Ed Young if he could borrow me to help him. Ed agreed.

I rode down to the line camp on Ole Snip. He was the other favorite horse of my life after Cricket. Horses and catch ropes are just about the most important things in the cowboy's world. He will talk about horses he's known even more than the women in his life.

We worked the brush and rocks checking for tracks in openings, trails, and water holes. Slowly we dragged or drove the gather into a holding pasture.

Slim was having some trouble with a four-year-old roan horse. Everybody put their spoiled horses and rough string off on Slim because they knew he could handle them.

The roan bucked Slim off at a water hole. It took me a spell to run the horse down and bring him back. Slim mounted and spurred the roan out. The sucker acted as if nothing had happened. He reined around like a champion cutting horse.

Several days later, Slim was riding this same roan. He dismounted to open a gate. We passed through and Slim closed it. The roan jumped, trying to jerk free. Slim hung on to the reins until the roan kicked him in the belly and ran off.

I knew he wasn't dead because he gasped, "Go get that mean son of a bitch."

We were racing down the edge of a twenty-foot-deep gully. The fence line and the arroyo formed a V. As the space narrowed, I thought Ole Snip and I would be cut to pieces by barbed wire; instead, we all three went off into the arroyo. The roan had more wind knocked out of him, in the wreck, than Snip or I.

We all scrambled up in the clouds of dust: I climbed back on Snip and continued the chase. He charged out of the arroyo into a fence corner. I threw the loop. It went out so far that I couldn't believe the roan had stuck his head into the tiny circle left at the end—but he had.

I returned the outlaw to Slim. He led the roan into the corral, took his catch rope off the saddle, doubled it, and tied him to the snubbing post. Silence. He stood over by the corral and rolled a smoke, staring at the half-sleeping critter. He lit the cigarette and stared. He puffed. He stared. More silence. Then his long legs propelled him across the corral in about three strides and he kicked the roan in the belly so hard it went "Whooommp." The horse humped up like he'd swallowed a cactus. Slim repeated the performance.

I made the mistake of opening my mouth and even worse I asked a question: "What did you do that for?"

Slim snarled through grinding teeth, trying to ignore the pain of his hoof-imprinted belly. "The son of a bitch just shouldn't have been a horse."

Take three guesses and see if you can come up with who was *honored* to ride "Ole Son of a Bitch" the rest of our time at the cow camp. You got it!

This continuing education damn near killed me, but here's where I got the name and a lot of the personality for the satanic horse in all *Rounders 3* stories. I always thought this particular horse's name really was Son of a Bitch, because that's all Slim ever called him; but now and forever on the hard, rocky ground and the soft paper of the stories I'd write, he would be known as Old Fooler.

The drought and the depression were slowly going away. Hitler's war was spreading in Europe and other parts of the world. I was seventeen and in my senior year at Andrews High School.

My maternal Aunt Fay was a lady with real class and flair in whatever she did. I called her my "marryin' aunt." She had three deceased husbands. She was currently married to an M.D. from Oklahoma City. In lieu of a bad debt, he had taken in a small ranch, fourteen miles east of Des Moines in northeastern New Mexico. They hadn't even seen the property, but she sold it to me on easy payments.

I borrowed money from Mr. F. H. Chilcote, at the Farmers and Stockmens Bank in Clayton, to buy some cattle. Then I married my high school sweetheart, Helene Caterlin. We had a baby named Sharon. Life was really "whuppin' up" for me. All these things happened faster than the movements of a short-order cook.

Even though I was a lousy bronc rider, I took on stings of raw broncs to break and did day labor for neighboring ranchers to make a living.

Hitler's war was gaining momentum, so I sold all the livestock, sent my new family off to the kinfolks in Texas, and joined the army.

Naturally, since I had a horse background, they put me in the walking infantry. There was, in concentrated time, basic training, shipment overseas, landing (DI), France, on Normandy Beach. Shortly after the Saint Lo breakthrough, I was blown into the basement of a bombed-out building by an artillery shell at Vire, France, and survived for several more months of combat all the way into Germany—by way of the Battle of Brest—then, back to northeast New Mexico to start painting pictures.

While I let the ranch slowly go to hell, I had lots of excitement and education in living—dancing, fistfighting, playing poker, and sundry other fun items.

In this readjustment period, I decided to change careers. I sold the

ranch and moved into town. I bought a few acres just outside of Des
Moines—still in New Mexico—with two houses on it. My close friend,
woodcarver Luz Martinez, moved into one of them. I continued with
even more dedicated oil painting and hell-raising.

Then came the divorce. I sold everything and moved to Taos—a
mystical, savage and loving spread of land with lush mountains and
high, dry desert; so beautiful that no writer or painter has ever completely captured it.

I planned to become rich and famous here as an artist. (I was poor
and infamous within a year.) As soon as I moved there I bought, and
paid for, a house with twelve subirrigated acres near the mesa three
miles west of Taos. There was plenty of room to keep the horses
necessary to maintain my serious hobby of calf roping. This kind of
security, for most artists of any kind, might be a luxury; to me it was a
necessity.

I was in Taos about four months when I met my future wife—artist
and artist's model Pat James. After our marriage, we continued painting and I started writing. We didn't have much materially, but we had
a lot of other things more important.

My artistic and spiritual mentor and friend, Woody Crumbo, the
great Pottowatime Indian artist, gave us advice on selling art as well as
painting it. Our sales and prices both increased.

Then Woody Crumbo and I became partners in the mining business.
We climbed mountains over several western states, prospecting. We
opened up scores of old tunnels, some that had been caved in for
nearly a hundred years. We promoted mills and mines all over. We got
rich. Then in one hundred and twenty days the price of copper
dropped from forty-eight cents to twenty-four cents. We were broke.

Pat and I had twin daughters, Charlotte and Sheryl (both have become accomplished artists), as well as debts of eighty-six-thousand dollars below nothing. We were out of money, credit, paintings, and
everything else but desire.

Even during the years of mining and other things, I continued to
write. I had two published books: *Southwest Wind,* a collection of short
stories, and *Long John Dunn of Taos,* a biography. Some of my maga-
zine articles and short fiction sold. This was not enough—I needed to
work on a novel. About what? War? No, I wanted to forget that.
Hunting? Possibly, even though by now I couldn't stand to shoot
anything but a tomato can. Nature? I knew so much about coyotes that
I loved them more than most humans.

What else did I know something about? Cowboys! I'd write a novel based on all those old-timers who were born in the 1890s—the ones who had raised me (kicked me up would be more accurate) and the younger ones who had worked and raised hell with me.

The Rounders was on its way. No steady paychecks were ready for me to pick up weekly, but we did have some western lithographs I had printed earlier at Woody Crumbo's suggestion. These were lifesavers.

I'd work on *The Rounders* a few days and then, when groceries became scarce and overdue bills plentiful, I'd take off for Taos plaza, or to Santa Fe, and peddle the prints. We managed fairly well, and I finally finished the novel.

My agent, Henry Volkening in New York, was enthused by what he called "a new kind of western." He had the power to get it straight to the senior editors at the major publishers. Eleven of them in a row turned it down, saying it was a superior, but too-different, western.

Finally, on the twelfth run, Al Hart, Jr., the editor-in-chief of MacMillan, took it on with enthusiasm. His judgment proved to be right—the reviews were all tops. Some called it the funniest tragicomedy western of its time. It made several best-seller lists; was published overseas and in braille for the blind. The U.S. Army libraries ordered a thousand hardback copies. It was made into a fine little movie starring Henry Fonda and Glenn Ford. Noted film critic Judith Crist rated it one of the top films of the year. It was also made into a TV series for ABC.

The novel has been written up over the years in many academic books and journals, and taught in a large number of high schools and colleges. It finally paid off all the soul-bending debt from the mining days.

In Hollywood, director Burt Kennedy discovered a prepublication copy of the manuscript. The movie possibilities grabbed him; so he took it to Fess Parker. Fess was world famous at the time, starring in the Davy Crockett TV series. The title song blasted out everywhere, and millions of youngsters played wilderness in coonskin caps.

Fess Parker called me in Taos. He wanted me to come out to California so we could talk about an option. Pat and I went.

I sat on vast grassy slopes, just below Fess's semi-castle at Hope Ranch in Santa Barbara, looking down on the enticing blue-green of the Pacific Ocean. He sat next to me speaking in a voice as sincere and believable as God's. He told me not to have a single worry. He would never let anything injurious happen to my book. I was delighted and comforted to hear this.

I'm sure Fess meant all this at the moment, but in truth I'd just heard my first line of Hollywood bull and had failed to recognize it. In the many months of many years I spent out there, dozens of producers, directors, and just plain "script-packers" would lay this sort of thing on me. No bother. It's all part of the great poker game of illusion.

Fess got the writer who had done most of the Davy Crockett scripts, Tom Blackburn, to do a screenplay on *The Rounders*. Then Fess pulled off a miracle and later let it all slip away. He actually got director William Wellman to come out of retirement to work on this project. Wellman, a great World War I hero, had joined the Lafayette Escradille and flown combat missions for the French. When he came home, he directed for the great financier, Howard Hughes, *Wings*, and other classic pictures such as *The High and the Mighty, Battleground,* and *The Ox Bow Incident.* He was now retired with wealth and world fame assured. Everyone was offering him lucrative deals to come out of retirement to direct. He refused all offers until he read *The Rounders.*

Not only did he agree to direct it, he sat with Blackburn almost daily, working on the script. He also traveled around the country talking to working cowboys; even crawling down in the chutes with rodeo hands.

The finished work was the truest screenplay, in the sense of authenticity and the use of its humor (which is the only survival mechanism that salvages life for working cowboys), that I have ever read—or believe I ever will. I was ecstatic.

Then the casting and the eternal meetings with United Artists started. All details but one were agreed on. Wellman and someone else had a clash of egos and wills on the casting. Wellman walked. Even though it hurt, I didn't blame Wellman a particle. In fact, his monumental efforts on behalf of *The Rounders* has brought only the feeling that I've been mightily honored.

We sold five options on the novel in the next five years. Ironically, Burt Kennedy and MGM came back into the deal and got it made. It has become a minor classic, having been shown on TV scores of times in recent years.

The Great Wedding was inspired, in part, by Old Santa Fe—all its art, its social life, my friends who were there, and the interesting strangers from everywhere in the world who came to soak up its unique charms. I have loved and visited this ancient city for over half a century. It seems like many lifetimes. I made a lot of trips there peddling art, books, mines; whatever I had. However, I have also spent a great part of my life writing about the little-known dignity of the coyote, and now Santa Fe artists and craftsmen have made so many wood, iron, or ceramic cartoon-type models of this wonderful creature they have cheapened his honor. My mind forgives the insult to my heart and to those noble animals.

The early Hollywood years, associating and partying with such wild and wonderful actors as Brian Keith, Lee Marvin, Slim Pickens, Warren Oates, and Morgan Woodward, and directors Tom Gries, Sam Peckinpah and his entire family, helped keep me in keen spirits to write *The Great Wedding*. Even though the time period in the book is the late 1950s and the early '60s, the book seems surprisingly, and almost exactly, up to date now.

All of the above, and many more, tried to get a film made from this book. Again, we sold a lot of movie options. Scripts were written, producers hired, money and emotions spent. In fact, our old family friend, Sam Peckinpah, was trying to get it made when he died in 1985. He loved the plot—one cowboy trying to get the other married to a rich woman for honorable purposes. He loved the concept of throwing two real working cowboys into the Santa Fe social structure and watching the explosion.

While *The Great Wedding* was intentional, the third story, *The Orange County Cowboys*, was triggered into action by an incident experienced by two California friends, Ed Honeck, an advertising writer and sports columnist, and Al Johnson, an international manufacturer. They told me of a little incident they experienced while relaxing at Al's "play" ranch up north. They had accidentally found a neighboring rancher's lost calf where it had fallen into a big hole. Their amateur efforts at saving the creature struck me as funny. They both hoped I would be inspired to use this as a basis for a short story. I agreed. Then it took on a different shape thanks to writer Joe Lansdale, who said I should write it as a novella.

Well now, novellas are my favorite form of both reading and writing. I decided to wind up the *Rounders* trilogy, bringing the continuing characters right up to date, including their dealings with the Japanese. So everyone was happy. It even won a 1988 Western Writers of America Spur Award.

As the novels have progressed with the changes of time, so have the women. They are more at the forefront in *Orange County Cowboys* than they were in the other two books, which reflects their progress in reality over the last couple of decades. This is especially true in the business world.

A working cowboy must be a veterinarian, a part-time mechanic, an engineer, a tracker, a teacher, and much more. It is a complex, dangerous, and demanding profession. By the time he learns all the things he has to know to be a top hand, he is usually too old and too crippled to do all of them.

When I was a young man the word "cowboy" was only used as a point of great honor. One of the favorite sayings from these top hands was, "I may not be a cowboy, but I can take one's place till he gets here."

Now the title is insulted every time a group of corporate executives or high government figures get caught plundering or warring; they are called—and call one another—"cowboys." Or "Presidential cowboys." Or "savings-and-loan and corporate-merger cowboys." Even motorcycle and patrol car cops, along with grocery store butchers, are often called "cowboys."

Well, the old, open-range days are long over except in mostly mythical entertainment forms, and I give thanks for their continuance in this way. The contemporary days of transition combining cowboying with both the horse and pickup truck are about complete. The most glorious reflection of America's history may shortly be gone. Past.

Recently I read the following in America's largest daily newspaper: "Cowboy crisis grips West. Cowboys aren't home on the range anymore. Ranchers are having trouble finding workers."

Yes, they are becoming scarce. What a pity there are not enough monetary benefits to entice young people to the profession. It's true that most cowboys spend their last years in stifling poverty. Sad.

Yet, the wonderful western myth of the cowboy is the one constancy of admiration the rest of the world holds for America. This is only fitting; the American cowboy developed from every imaginable nationality. That myth has been spread to other nations by films, writings, songs, clothing, and uncountable other manners. Massive fortunes have been made based on the sweat and blood of these hardworking men. Careers have been born, world fame and worship enjoyed by many, while those whose guts, perseverance, and solid sense of humor had created the source of such success were being paid a pittance for labor that few have the courage and skill to perform.

I wish the public could be made aware that there is a vast difference between the big greedy, destructive ranchers and the other ranchers who are dedicated to caring properly for their land and its creatures. The cowboys who work for both kinds do the best they can under mostly adverse conditions.

It has been a long, bone-breaking, hide-splitting, joyous journey through the contemporary West for me. I've written it down, as I lived it, felt it, and loved it, the best I could. There are boozers and bankers, hookers and heiresses, merchants, artists, and practicers of many other professions throughout this trilogy. I genuinely hope the reader enjoys the trips half as much as I have.

The Rounders

ONE

JIM ED LOVE is a very funny name for a man who likes nothing better than to see a cowboy get what little brains he's got kicked out by a rawboned, walleyed, bucking, ground-stopping bronc. Just the same, that's the way he is. Me and Wrangler listened to the same old story we'd heard ever since we'd started working for Jim Ed and the JL outfit.

"Now, boys, this ain't goin' to be no trouble a tall. Half of them ponies is broke already. Just look at the blaze-face roan standin' there like a milk-pen calf. Why, I bet he's been rode a thousand miles, and all it'll take to gentle him down is one or two saddlin's."

I could see from where I was standing, with the sun square in my eyes, that there was healed-over spur marks in that old pony's shoulder. That could mean just one thing. Trouble. I had worked for outfits that gave spoiled horses like that one away just to keep from crippling up good cowboys.

"Now, boys, that roan has got the makin's of a real rope horse, and after you get the tallow melted a little I'll probably want him for the old lady and kids to ride," Jim Ed went on.

One thing for sure, there ain't nobody going to catch Jim Ed riding one of them broncs and taking a chance on getting his tailor-made western suit dirty. I don't know whether he is too smart or too clean for it. He's the cleanest feller I ever saw. Stays shaved all the time, keeps his sixty-dollar boots shined, and that shirt, stretched so tight across his big belly, is starched like a priest's collar. He wears a big gold chain across his big belly with a gold watch on it that must weigh as much as a baby calf. His hat is whiter than a scared bronc's eyeballs.

You don't never see him out among his cows unless he is there to count them and see how many pounds they have gained and how many dollars he can put in the bank come shipping time. He ain't no cowboy, this Jim Ed Love, but he is a cowman. He don't never over-stock his pastures and he always has plenty of hay up when a blizzard strikes. He can dicker for six days and nights for one-fourth cent a pound more for his beef. He can get more work from and give less pay to a cowboy than anybody I ever saw. Like right now, for instance. He was going to expect us to break horses and work cows both at the same time, either one of them plenty for one man.

Wrangler snorted through his little flat busted nose, and then before Jim Ed could see the grin on his face he ran out and forefooted a two-year-old black. The pony hit the end of the rope, and Wrangler dug his heels in the dirt. That colt went up and over and down right smack dab on the back of his neck. While this was going on, I decided to rope the roan.

Well sir, he went trotting around the corral like a workhorse on a hot day. I rolled that loop out in front of him, and he stepped in it like one of them trick horses you see at a fancy rodeo. I jerked the slack out of the rope and braced for the spill. Hell, that old pony just stopped and stood there.

"See there, boys?" Jim Ed yelled. "Just like I said—gentle as a milk-pen calf."

I had to admit that the roan acted mighty gentle, and began to think maybe I was wrong. Well, Jim Ed turned and climbed over the corral and crawled in his pickup and drove off toward town, leaving me and Wrangler to our rat killing.

I decided to catch a heavy-quartered bay three-year-old before I worked on the roan. I forefooted him and spilled him several times. He came up kicking, falling, snorting, and raising hell until I set back on that rope and piled him again. He finally caught on to the fact that when the rope pulled tight, unpleasant things happened to him. Pretty soon he just stood there trembling, and rolling his eyes.

I turned him loose and then I took another whirl with the loop and fit it around his neck. This was something else. Now we went barrel-ing around the corral with my boot heels plowing two uneven tracks in the dirt.

I yelled at Wrangler, "Ear him down, ear him down; the son of a bitch is settin' my heels afire!"

Wrangler came sailing in looking like a bowlegged hog crossed with a short-shanked bear. He finally got that ear in his mouth and held on till I got a hackamore on the bay's head. We snubbed him up to a big post out in the middle of the corral. While he was fighting his head and stretching his neck ragged against that stout cedar pole, I went over and earred a brown bronc for Wrangler. I turned the rest of the horses out so there wouldn't be so many to kick at us.

Now, I ain't never figured how that ugly short-legged little devil could get up on a bronc, much less ride him, but once Wrangler was in the saddle he stuck like he was nailed there. Now me, I like to take a little more time about it. While the bay and Wrangler went sailing around the corral, I tried to keep out of their way long enough to get me a gunnysack.

I yelled, "Wrangler, get down and tie that brown to the corral fence while I sack this bay out." Well, every time I rubbed that sack on him he fell back and kicked and pawed right straight up in the air. After a while he quit and stood spread-legged and trembling, just like he'd done with the rope.

It don't take a smart horse too long to catch on to what's right and what's wrong. Now take that roan . . . wait a minute. I'll get to that skunk-hearted bastard later. Anyway, I finally got the saddle blanket over that bay's back and then the saddle. He romped around a little bit, but when I jerked the cinch up he farted like an overloaded pack mule and started bucking right up against the snubbin' post. While he was sort of around on the other side I got the cinches drawed up tight. Then Wrangler chewed on his ear again while I untied the hackamore reins.

I gathered that heavy mane up in my left hand with the reins drawed tight. With my right hand I held the reins and the saddle horn at the same time. I held him this way so if he tried to pull away from me he wouldn't have a chance to kick me in the belly. He'd be forced around toward me, and about the worst he could do was step on me with both front feet.

"Turn 'im loose," I yelled. Wrangler did just that and let out a yell that sounded like a choked coyote. That old bay didn't know how to buck very hard but he was sure trying to learn. He crashed into the corral until I reached over and whopped him across the nose with a loaded quirt. It took several whops before he quit trying to tear my leg off against that pole corral. Now, I never was much of a quirt man, but there's times if you'll apply it good and hard right where the colt sucks you'll discourage a lot of bucking. This was one of those times. The bay soon settled down and either balked or sort of crow-hopped around, making a very feeble effort to buck.

Wrangler rode the brown with his spurs in his neck, yelling and

kicking hell out of him every time he left the ground. The brown
bucked out ahead and then turned back and went up again, coming
down with all four legs stiff as a bunch of fence posts.

This kind of thing went on for three days except for some of the
time we had been riding outside. Now, to make horse breaking easy
you need two cowboys—one on the bronc and one on a gentle, well-
broke horse. This way if the bronc tries to cut your leg off on a
barbwire fence or jump off a bluff, your partner can ride in front of
him or gather up your hackamore reins and wrap them around his
saddle horn. That is the sensible way and the safest way to break
horses. Do you think that's the way we did it for Jim Ed's outfit? Hell
no! That was too slow. He wanted both his horse breakers riding in
different directions at once, just bucking and raising hell. I think when
he was off in town, checking in at the bank to count his money, that he
could picture all this in his mind. I know damned well he kept himself
laughing all the time just thinking about what was going on back at the
ranch.

On the fourth morning I stood there with my rope in my hand and
looked first at the roan, then at Wrangler. He looked just like a
groundhog coming up for air when he crawled out of his bedroll in
the morning, and he didn't look a hell of a lot better now except that I
stood so far above him I couldn't see much but the brim of his hat and
his potbelly hanging out over his droopy britches. What his britches
was hanging on I don't know. They looked like they would drop right
down around his knees any minute, but that was as far as they would
have gone. His legs was bowed so bad that if you was to straighten
them up he would be twice as tall.

"How old you think that roan is, Wrangler?"

"I reckon he's about seven or eight."

"Jim Ed says he's a fiver."

"If Jim Ed says he's a fiver, time has been passing a hell of a lot
faster than Jim Ed thinks."

"I bet he's nine if he's a day," I said.

"Look at his teeth and see," said Wrangler kind of funny-like.

"Well, now," I said, "I figured I'd let you take him over, seein' as
how that brown has been givin' you so much trouble. It'll give you a
chance to rest up and get the soreness out of your bones."

"Naw, I reckon I'll just let you go ahead with him," says Wrangler
real kind, like I was his baby sister. "Seein' as how Jim Ed wants a

fancy pony made out of him and you're so much better at reinin' a
horse out than me."

We stood there and jawed back and forth for a spell. I could see
there wasn't a thing to do but take in after the roan. Maybe he wasn't
spoiled. Maybe them marks in his shoulder was put there to stop some
good honest bucking. Maybe he'd quit then and settled down to make
a good, gentle cow horse. Maybe.

Well sir, I pitched out the catch rope, and the roan turned to me
kinda quiet-like and looked right down that rope like he was staring
down a gun barrel. He didn't wiggle a hair. I put the hackamore on
him and tied him to the corral fence. Hell, I didn't need the snubbing
post, as gentle as the old roan was. Besides, Wrangler had that bucking
brown tied up to it.

Wrangler was acting kind of peculiar. He'd rear back on them
squatty hocks of his and kick that brown in the belly just as hard as he
could. The brown would hump up so the saddle looked like it had a
big watermelon under it. Then Wrangler would look at the ground
under his belly, step back, and kick again. When he stopped to look at
the ground under the brown for about the fifteenth time, I just plain
had to go see what the hell he was doing. I saw what he was after, all
right. There was a wet foamy spot there in the corral dust. Wrangler
seemed satisfied now and mounted the brown for about the twentieth
time and started reining him around the corral. Seems like that kidney
action kind of gentled the brown down some.

I rubbed my hand across the roan's shoulder, feeling all them spur
scars. "You must of been a mean son of a bitch when you was a colt," I
said. The roan looked like he had gone to sleep on me. I crawled
under the hackamore reins kind of careless-like to get around on the
other side and see how bad he was scarred up over there.

"*Ouch!*" Good Lord a'mighty, a bear must have reached through the
corral poles and bit about half my back off! I whipped around hollering to beat hell. Right there in the same spot stood the old roan with a
patch of my shirt hanging out of his jaws. I felt up my back where
there was a big chunk of meat missing.

"Wrangler," I yelled, "this goddam roan is a cannibal!"

Well now, about half mad and still hurting, I saddled that horse up. I
jerked the cinch so tight it almost cut him in two. He didn't even
grunt. I took my catch rope and flipped it around the saddle horn and
threw my hat under him and hollered as loud as I could. He walked
off like he was carrying the Queen of England to a church meeting.

Sometimes if you are in a hurry to get someplace and don't want to dirty up a new shirt or something, you can buck an old pony out with just the saddle on his back, then mount and ride off about your business. It didn't work this time.

I led him over in the corner of the corral so if he tried to pull away from me the posts would stop him. I eased up in the saddle and turned him out in the corral. Now I'm saying right now that this old roan had the best rein on him I ever saw. Just start to turn him and he was already around, swinging smooth and quick with his head down like a good cutting horse.

I told him, "Roan, I don't mind you bitin' hell out of me, but I wish you hadn't tore my shirt."

Just when I was beginning to feel proud of this good cutting horse he let a big windy and took a run straight at the corral. As easy-mouthed as he was a minute before, you would think I could have turned him back, but it didn't turn out that way. I was busting a gut trying to turn him, but he just gathered speed and jumped right up on top of the corral. Over he went, smacking the ground like a ton of dead beef and knocking the wind out of both of us. I fell free and jumped up before he did. I had a lot more air than I could handle. My lungs were bouncing around like a hog's belly.

When the old roan stumbled to his feet I was on him. He took off in a run again. His legs was still wobbly when he started bucking. Now I had the jump-go on this bag of bones. I had my right hand around that saddle horn like it was the doorknob to heaven's gate, and my right elbow was crimped down over my hipbone like a vise.

I was pulling up on them hackamore reins like I was dragging a pot of gold out of a deep well. But it just didn't do any good. That son of a bitch bogged his head and jumped way off out toward the Arizona border and came down hard on his front legs, driving them in the ground plumb to bedrock, the way it felt to me. The next jump was just as high and just as long, but when he drove into the ground again he was headed toward the Texas border, and in between that old roan horse was sure tearing hell out of the state of New Mexico.

I stayed till I lost my hat. I stayed till I lost a stirrup. I stayed till I lost both stirrups, and a while longer after that. It just didn't do any good. The world was jumping around and going in crazy circles, and eleven hundred pounds of horseflesh was pounding my behind to pieces. Then I flopped around in the pure, clean fresh mountain air like a baby bird and came down on my back right where the roan had bit me. It was a very poor feeling.

I rolled over and looked around. The roan was in a dead run headed back for the corral. For a minute I thought he was going to jump back in, but he came to a sliding halt and looked back at me with his head up high.

I shook my fist at him and yelled kind of weak-like, "I'll make you as gentle as a milk-pen calf if I have to kill you doin' it."

I could see Wrangler off about a quarter of a mile trying to rein the brown back toward the corral. He was having his own troubles. I got up and hobbled along toward the roan. Wrangler beat me there. He set on the brown holding the roan's hackamore reins.

"Hell's fire, he sure fooled hell out of me," I said. "That's what I'll call him. Old Fooler."

"Bucks harder'n I figgered," said Wrangler, glancing sideways at Old Fooler.

"You never know what a dog's eaten till he shits," I said, grabbing the reins. I mounted that Fooler horse and dug the spurs in his shoulders—hard. He wouldn't buck a jump—just moved out, flinching a little now and then from the steel.

Wrangler tried to follow, but he made several figure eights and a back track on the way. Now things were looking up. Wrangler had got his horse to where he could turn him around inside a hundred acres, and Old Fooler was moving out in the prettiest running walk I ever seen. I had him reining again, and I began to perk up. Well, there is where I learned something basic about that horse. Not that it did me much good, but I had the pleasure of the knowledge just the same. When things looked best he was at his worst. He broke into a run, circling like we were on a racetrack. I reared back on the hackamore, jerking and cussing.

We came to a little gully about twenty feet deep and ten feet across. By God, I damn near died right then! It looked like he was going to jump right in it. He was running with his ears laid back and legs stretching for strange country. Hell's fire, he sailed up and out and across that gully like he was one of them fancy horses military men jump around at horse shows. He came down on the other side and wheeled, running parallel to the gully as fast as he could move his legs.

I could see old Wrangler up ahead and I yelled, "Rope the son of a bitch before he falls into the canyon!"

I didn't know if he heard or not. I kept imagining Old Fooler was running with both feet on the left side hitting nothing but clean, pure fresh mountain air out over the gully and two feet on the right side lapping about halfway over the brim. I saw Wrangler throw a big loop at us, turn the brown, and spur him away from the gully.

When I could see again, I gazed upon a very strange sight. I could see the bellies of two horses. The roan was stretched out a few feet in front of me. A little farther on, the brown was lying in the same position. There was just one thing wrong. That brown had six legs and two of them was real short and had high-heel boots on the ends.

I stumbled up, limped over to the roan, and got him on his feet. Then the brown got up, shaking his head and looking over at the roan. He wasn't paying any attention to poor old Wrangler laying there so peaceful and quiet. I looked down at Wrangler, expecting to have to say some prayers over him. He was turning blue, and I figgered that if he was dead he wouldn't have started turning so fast. So I got ahold of his arms and started pumping them up and down. Pretty soon he made a noise like a turkey gobbler makes that has the croup. I kept pumping. The noise got louder.

I said, "You all right, Wrangler?"

He finally said, "Yeah, but tell the bartender to quit servin' that cheap whisky."

It was a day or two before Wrangler got his right mind back, what there was of it. But he got up and helped me untangle the rope from around the broncs. I got back on the roan and Wrangler got back on the brown. We didn't really want to, but it was a three-quarter-mile walk back to the corral. I sat kinda stiff-like with my hind end screwed right down into solid leather. Old Fooler moved out smooth and easy, just fox-trotting to beat sixty. Just as gentle as a milk-pen calf . . .

TWO

THREE DAYS LATER I crawled out of my bunk. I felt like I had been beat across the back by a ten-foot giant swinging a brand-new wagon tongue. Sore? I reckon I was.

If it hadn't been for the smell of Wrangler making coffee and cooking up some sowbelly and biscuits, I would have quit right there. I can't remember when a boot was so hard to pull on, considering how skinny I am. Seems like that boot had shrunk and my foot had swelled. Finally, though, I got upright. Then the hard part commenced. One hip was hanging about two inches lower than the other and my knee joints was just plain locked solid.

I was hoping Old Fooler was in the same condition.

"Wrangler," I said, "if that Old Fooler horse don't slack off before long, I am goin' to take a sharp ax and hit him right between the eyes."

"Ain't no use ruinin' a good ax," Wrangler said, reaching into the oven and pulling out a pan of brown hot biscuits.

"Maybe you're right," I said, pouring me some coffee in a big tin cup. I finally got settled down at the old splintery table and washed about a quart of coffee down my gullet. It limbered me up enough so I could slice off a chunk or two of sowbelly and eat about two thirds of them biscuits.

"Now ain't that just like that goddam Jim Ed to take all the other hands over east for the fall roundup and leave me and you here by ourselves with that pen full of spoiled horses?"

"Just like him," said Wrangler. "Sometimes I wish I was back wranglin' dudes."

"How come you ever quit and took a job on a underpaying, overworked outfit like this?" I asked.

Now old Wrangler is usually making a long speech if he grunts twice, but once in a while he will bust loose and you can't hardly shut him up. He swallowed a biscuit whole and squinted out of a face that looked like a bulldog that had run headfirst into a big mule's hind foot and said, "A woman."

"A what?" I said.

"A woman by the name of Toy Smith," he said.

"Mighty pretty name," I said.

"Mighty pretty woman," he said.

"Well, god a'mighty, quit wastin' all this time and *tell* me about it!" I yelled.

"I was workin' for that Castle Rock outfit over near Phoenix," he said. "You heard of it, ain't you?"

"Yeah," I said, wanting to kick him in the belly for holding up the story.

"Well," he went on, "it's one of them fancy outfits caterin' to all them rich people from back East and out in California. They have these here hot springs all around the headquarters, and they got 'em rocked in like a regular windmill tank."

"You mean like a swimmin' pool?" I asked.

"You might say that," Wrangler agreed. "Anyway, there wasn't nobody there that wasn't rich or aimin' to be soon. I had this job of takin' these dudes out for a moonlight ride among the cactus and cookin' up a meal over the campfire. Then I'd play a git-tar and sing somethin' or other."

This last pretty near ruined my breakfast because I have never seen a cowboy that could play a guitar worth a damn, much less sing so you could stand to listen. Least of all Wrangler, who had a voice like a rusty hinge.

"What in the hell did you sing?" I asked.

"Oh, I don't know," said Wrangler, "I just run a bunch of words together and beat on them guitar strings. But that's what started all the trouble with Toy Smith," he went on. "Seems like she thought I was a great primitive singer."

"What's that?"

"How in the hell would I know?" said Wrangler. "Just the same, at nights when we got back and I got the horses unsaddled and fed, there would be Toy Smith hangin' over the corral gate waitin' for me to go for a swim in them hot-water tanks. She sure was a swimmer," said Wrangler. "And float! Hell, she looked like a whole mountain range lyin' out there on her back."

"Was she big?" I asked.

Wrangler looked at me and snorted through his flat nose. "Big? Why, Dusty, you couldn't get her in a hay barn without widenin' the doors."

I figured he was stretching it a little, but I got the drift that this Toy woman was on the generous side.

"She got to where she follered me every place I went except the toilet. Ever' time we'd have a dance for the cowboys and dudes, she just grabbed little old me and waltzed all night. I couldn't see past her for all that belly and there weren't no use lookin' up, for there was about forty pound of bosom hangin' over my head. There was just one thing to do and that was hold on tight and pray. She was all right as far as that part goes, but I began to get that crowded-in feelin'. You know, like you get in a cave with just one way out and a mama bear blockin' your trail. She kept tellin' me how much she loved me and that if I hitched up with her I'd never have to work another day in my life."

"You crazy damn fool," I said. "She was rich and you passed up your chance to tie on to her?"

"I didn't just exactly pass it up," said Wrangler, sort of sad-like. "It's just that things happened to alter the course of true love, as them dudes say. She got me to comin' over to her room ever' night after our swim."

"Naturally," I said.

"But seems," said Wrangler, "that she wasn't the only one that liked my cookin' and this er . . . uh . . . prim—primutive singin'. This other gal was about half as big and twice as purty. One night I told Toy to go on to bed—that I had to shoe a horse and would see her somewhat later."

"Whoever heard of shoein' a horse at night?" I said.

"Well, Toy Smith did," Wrangler said. "I went for a little ride and a little swim with this here other little tender thing. I never figgered that Toy would get up and check on me."

"You just can't tell about true love, can you?" I said.

"Naw, you sure cain't, Dusty," he said. "Anyway, 'long just before daybreak I come sneakin' into Toy's room as quiet as a country kid in a new suit of clothes. I eased down on the bed and pulled one boot off. Then I felt something hard and cold sticking out from under her piller."

"What was it?" I asked, my mind having jumping fits.

"It was a ball-peen hammer," Wrangler said, as if that was the end of the world. "I eased my boot back on, listenin' to Toy breathe heavy as a foundered mare. Then I sneaked out of there and headed for the barn. I got my horse and saddle and loaded them in the pickup, expectin' any minute to feel that ball-peen hammer drove plumb to the handle in my skull. When I started that pickup it sounded like seventeen water barrels rollin' off a steep mountain. I lit out for Phoenix and hunted me up a bar. Well, I found one where I had made some friends before, and stayed there watchin' the door for Toy Smith. About two or three days later one of the hired hands came in, knowin' where I might be. He said he had a message for me. I called him off in a far corner and a deep booth and ordered two double shots and said, "Shoot." He said to me, 'Wrangler, Toy is kinda mad. She said her branch of the Smith family didn't lie and they didn't steal and when she says she aimed to kill Wrangler Lewis, that is exactly what she meant.'

"Now," Wrangler went on, breathing kind of heavy, "knowin' how set in her ways Toy was and how honest this cowboy was, I decided it was time to move on."

"Well, that explains how come you went to work for a sorry outfit like this," I said.

"Yeah, sometimes I wish I'd of faced old Toy instead," he said. "By the way, how come you're workin' on this no-good ranch?"

"Now, Wrangler," I said, "you know damn well it's because I'm so dumb. Ain't it right plain that any cowboy who'd ride that Old Fooler horse more than once is just plumb ignorant?"

"Reckon you're right," he said.

I hated to face it, but knew I couldn't stall it off much longer. Old Fooler was out there in the horse pasture waiting for me to come and get him. I finished off what biscuits was left and rolled me a smoke. Wrangler poured us both another cup of coffee.

"Just think," I said, "of all the fun the rest of the boys are havin' down there gatherin' those cattle and cuttin' out the calves and all the ropin' and brandin' and no tellin' what else is goin' on. It makes me kinda sick to think about it. That cockeyed Jim Ed Love don't have no consideration for horse breakers a tall."

"Don't nobody else, neither," said Wrangler.

"Reckon you're right," I said. "If it's all the same with you, I'll go wrangle the horses while you clean up this mess."

"Whatever suits you just tickles me plumb to death," said Wrangler.

Well, I saddled the night horse and loped out into the horse pasture.

It wasn't long till I had that Roman-nosed, walleyed, spur-marked bunch of critters back in the corral. That mean-ass, bald-face roan led them in. By the time I unsaddled the night horse I'd limbered up somewhat. Pretty soon Wrangler came out. We roped us a couple of mounts, snubbled them up, and turned the rest out.

Wrangler looked at me kinda queer. "You ain't goin' to take on that roan again today, are you?" he asked.

"Got to," I said. "He's gainin' on me now."

Well sir, it was a day to remember for a long time to come. Me and Wrangler rode out of there on what was beginning to look like a couple of old-time ranch horses. He had his little black working the reins good and was even getting him used to the bits. I was still using the hackamore on the roan, trying to get his nose as raw and sore as I could.

We strung out across the half-mile down to a section line fence. That roan rolled along so smooth a man was tempted to forget what he really was. I guess I did for a minute. I got down to open the gate, pulled it back and let Wrangler ride through. Just as I stepped back to hook the wire loop over the gatepost, I felt something jerk at the reins, then something heavy hit me in the belly. The son of a bitch had pulled loose and kicked me all at the same time. I was bent over trying to get rid of excess wind.

"Wrangler," I croaked, "let me have your horse."

He stepped down and I crawled on. Old Fooler had run off a ways and then stopped to graze peaceably, as if nothing had happened at all.

"I'll be back in a minute," I yelled at Wrangler. Old Fooler had got himself in a jam this time. He'd gone too far. Here is where I would fix him once and for all. Off to the right a fifty-foot-wide arroyo cut in toward the fence, making a triangle. It had a ten- to twenty-foot drop-off, so I figured Old Fooler wouldn't try to jump it, and I didn't think he was crazy enough to jump *into* it. I spurred the black toward him, undoing the leather thong from around the catch rope, flipping the honda over the saddle horn, shaking out a loop and cussing Old Fooler all at once.

He threw his head up and took off for the far corner. The dust was boiling up and the triangle was getting more pointed all the time. I could feel the black stretching to beat hell under me, but I still spurred for more. Old Fooler was glancing over at the arroyo, wondering what he had overlooked, when I rode up on him.

I didn't get to use my rope this go-round. The first thing I knew I

was riding stirrup leather against stirrup leather. The arroyo was
crowding Fooler on one side, and the barbwire fence was scratching at
me from the other. And it wasn't getting any wider. If I kept going I
would lose a leg on the wire. If Fooler kept going he would fall off
into the arroyo. I just couldn't make myself stop. Pretty soon that
triangle came to a sharp point and there was just one place left to go.
We all went down over the side, and I mean down. I don't know how
it happened but I landed on my feet still holding the reins, right in the
middle of a bunch of kicking horseflesh.

When the dust cleared, the black was struggling to his feet. He was
real shook up. I could see Old Fooler's tracks in the soft bottom of the
arroyo. The black got his wind back in a dead run because I climbed
back aboard and spurred him down the arroyo, gathering up my rope
at the same time.

It seemed like we ran down that hot, dusty washed-out ditch for a
long time. Finally, Old Fooler found a place to get out, and he did. I
spurred the sweating black right up after his tracks. All I could see
when we topped out was a long streak of dust heading for some low
cedar-covered hills about a mile away. It's a fool thing to do to try to
catch a loose horse out in the open from the back of another. There is
just too much difference in what they're carrying. Besides, Old Fooler
could run like a rabbit dog. But then, like I told Wrangler, I was
stupid anyway, and on top of that I was mad.

We just kept going and when we finally hit timber I started tracking.
Old Fooler, not knowing this part of the country, was headed into a
barbwire corner. This corner set out in an opening, and if I could get
my rope on him I would drag him to death.

Sure enough, there he was. He charged down the fence to the right
and I cut across, swinging a big loop. The black was so tired I could
feel him wobbling under me. It looked like Old Fooler was going to
get away this time, too. He was a long way out.

I threw the loop anyway. It seemed like the slowest loop in the
world. It just floated and shrunk the farther it went, and then Old
Fooler ran his head into what was left of it. The black had already set
up, not from experience but from being so tired. This gave us the
advantage.

Old Fooler went up and over and around and down. Just as he
scrambled to his feet, I spurred hard sideways and jerked both of us
down. Well, it wasn't much of a fall because there wasn't much speed
left in any of us. When me and the black got up, Old Fooler did the

same. He was about half choked, but he trotted right over to us just like he was going to apologize and love us to death. Of course, the old devil simply wanted to loosen the rope from around his neck. Just like a house dog, he followed me back to Wrangler.

Wrangler was lying in the shade of a post, asleep. He sat up, pulling his hat back down on his head. "I thought you said you was just goin' to be gone a minute," he said.

"Time flies," I said.

I took the rope from around Old Fooler's neck and handed Wrangler the reins of the black. Then I walked up and yelled just as loud as I could and kicked Old Fooler in the belly. He jumped straight up with all four feet and I set back with all I had on those hackamore reins. You talk about hitting the ground—well, that old pony jarred the world right down to the deep-water level. He got up. I hollered and kicked him again. He just stood there this time, humping up a little. I kicked till I couldn't lift my sore leg anymore. I hollered till nothing but a sick whisper came out of my throat. He wouldn't budge.

I got my breath and said to Wrangler, "Now what you goin' to do about a horse like that?"

He didn't have an answer. I didn't have one either.

I was beginning to wonder if Old Fooler was going to break me before I did him. In fact, I felt right then that one of us would just plain have to kill the other.

THREE

THE BOYS CAME BACK from the fall roundup. They had delivered the stock to town, loaded it into cattle cars, and Jim Ed had gone to Denver to see to the final delivery. In a few days he would be back with another bankful of money to his credit. The boys kept going on about what a time they'd had in town, telling one big lie after another.

I got so disgusted about missing out on all this that I just went out to the corral, saddled Old Fooler, and rode off by myself. Now wasn't that a dumb thing to do?

This horse had me slightly boogered. You would figure that most horses would come nearer bucking downhill than up. You would be right, except for Old Fooler. I don't say he bucked uphill exactly. It amounted to the same thing, though. I learned this a very hard way.

I was watching him real close as I rode across the ripened grama-grass-covered hills. We moved down into this little draw and started up the other side. Just as we topped out, he fired. Naturally, the saddle slips back a little when a horse is pulling upgrade, but the way Old Fooler jumped it had lapped right over his rear end. He lunged way out and kicked back with both hind feet. It snapped my head back like the tip end of a bullwhip. My teeth chipped enamel at every jump.

Well, I made one mistake I would never make again with Fooler. If you can use a loaded quirt, that's fine. It will take a lot of sass out of some pretty mean horses. I raised it up high and took a hard swing, aiming to hit Old Fooler right between the ears. I didn't much care if he did fall on me. I figured this might help us both. I should have kept my right hand on that saddle horn where it belonged, though, for all I hit was air. I smacked the ground like a dead buzzard.

It was about three miles by bird travel to the gate opening into home pasture. That was where Old Fooler was headed. He was still bucking, and I could see them stirrups clanging together above his

back. Then he disappeared over a rise and there wasn't a thing to keep
me company but one little white cloud about a thousand miles off over
the northern mountains. I saw that cloud when I looked up at the sky
and asked the Lord to please not let me kill myself and to give me the
wings of an angel so I could fly after that horse and break his goddam
neck.

Well, the Lord answered the first part of my prayer, for in about an
hour and a half I'd forgot all about killing myself. I was hurting so bad
I figured I would die anyway. I walked and walked, and a big blister
grew on one foot. I pulled off my boot to ease the pain. When I tried
to put it back on she just wouldn't go. That foot had swelled up bigger
than the hole in the top of that boot. I started to take my pocket knife
and make that hole bigger. Then I thought this over and decided
against it. My foot would mend—the boot wouldn't.

I walked and I walked. I cussed and I cussed. I hoped that black-
hearted Fooler horse heard some of the things I called him. He would
be ashamed of himself or awful proud, one. A hole wore in my sock.
The sweat ran from under my hat and down into my eyes, and the
bottom of my foot proved to be softer than the ground I walked on.

Pretty soon I limped about a yard deep on the barefoot side. The
boot I was packing got heavier and heavier no matter which hand I
carried it in. The sock wore plumb off the foot. There was a little bit of
it hanging around my ankle to remind me what color it had been. If I
just hadn't reached for that quirt I might have been sitting a horse,
ready to get down and open the gate into headquarters right now.

I got back just before sundown. There stood Old Fooler at the gate,
looking back at me with his head up high as if he was sure enough
glad to see me.

I felt kind of embarrassed riding into camp with one boot off. The
boys all laughed and wanted to know if I'd felt sorry about my horse
carrying such a big load. They acted like I had just got down and
walked on purpose. It would have been easy to have killed the whole
bunch, including Old Fooler, right on the spot. I was just too tired to
do it.

It took two days of soaking that foot in hot water before I could get
the boot back on. On the third day I was back with Wrangler working
the horses. But I can tell you for sure I was going to lay off that Fooler
horse the first day.

We had topped out the whole bunch by now. Most of them were
reining good and beginning to stop with their hind feet tucked up

under their bellies like good horses should. They didn't buck more than once or twice a day now, and then not very hard. I had one big bay that I could tell was going to make a real working cow horse.

Just when everything was going our way and it looked like we might make a few head of good horses, Jim Ed showed up. He had plans. These plans concerned me and Wrangler. Now me and old Wrangler hadn't been to town since the Fourth of July, and we were beginning to get mighty thirsty for some of that high-powered town water with maybe two or three high-stepping females thrown in. Do you think that's what Jim Ed had in mind? Hell, no!

Jim Ed says in that purry voice of his, "Now, boys, I'm goin' to give you the chance of a lifetime. Down at the lower camp there is around a hundred and fifty, maybe a hundred seventy-five, strays that's gone wild on us. I want you boys to go down there and spend the winter gatherin' this stuff. It's a lot lower in elevation there. The snow don't hardly stay on the ground a tall. Why, it'll be a regular vacation for you."

I was just itching to tell Jim Ed where to go and how long he could stay for his vacation when he put the clincher on the argument.

"Boys," he said, rearing back and grinning so all the gold in his mouth glittered, "there is five dollars a head bonus for every head you gather. Cows, calves, steers, it don't make no difference. Five dollars a head! Did you ever hear anything like it?"

Just as he said this he threw a whole stack of five-dollar bills on the floor in front of where me and Wrangler stood staring bug-eyed. It worked.

We said, "Yeah, that sounds all right." I never knew of a couple of dumber cowboys than us.

We got in a couple of pack mules and slung the pack with sow belly, dried peaches, beans, flour, the works. We got in the string of broncs, too.

Jim Ed said, "Boys, this will give you a chance to work your horses like they need to be worked. Sore backs and tender hoofs is what makes gentle horses." Then he walked over and picked up a whole armload of brand-new catch ropes. For a minute I was fooled into thinking Jim Ed was being considerate, but a little later, down at the lower camp, I realized different. We would need every one of those ropes before we got those wild cattle out of that wild country.

Well, we strung out with me riding lead on Old Fooler. I led the pack mules till they got used to following. Wrangler rode behind on the drag with the string of half-broke broncs in between.

If we kept going steady and didn't stop to admire the scenery, we could make it to Vince Moore's outfit for supper. I sure was anxious to see old Vince. It had been a long time. He was a good feller to my notion. Besides, he made the best bootleg whisky in New Mexico.

Old Fooler didn't act up at all that day. He even moved out like he knew where we were going. I watched him careful and close, figuring he was just shoring up his energy.

The sun was still warm at midday, even though it was November. Along about the shank of the afternoon she began to cool down, but we rode hard, keeping a little sweat breaking out on the flanks of our mounts. Just before sundown I spotted Vince Moore's windmill. Then we saw his old wooden, unpainted, run-down shack. It looked like the one we would be living in down at lower camp.

When we got about a hundred yards of the house, the dogs started barking—hound dogs, collie dogs, and just dogs. I bet there wasn't a rabbit in five miles of Vince's outfit. Damn if he wasn't up on the crow's nest working on his windmill. He yelled down, "Well, I'll be. Where in the hell did you boys come from?"

I said, "Vince, I hope we are just in time for supper."

"The woman'll have it ready in about half an hour," he said. "Say, why don't one of you boys get down and help me with this here windmill. It'll only take a minute."

Now, if there is one thing I hate worse than a diamondback rattler, it's a windmill. That is the only thing I could figure in Jim Ed's favor. his whole ranch was watered by springs—not a windmill on the whole place except at headquarters.

I yelled back, "Vince, you get down and ride out two or three of these old ponies, and I will climb up there and fix your windmill."

Vince didn't say anything more about the windmill. "Go ahead and turn your horses loose in the corral, boys. Pitch 'em some hay out of the stack and I'll be done here directly."

This we proceeded to do.

Then Vince yelled, "Go on over to the house, boys, and wash up. Don't use too much water, though. Been kinda short ever since this windmill's been givin' trouble." Well, he had been kind of short of water for at least thirty years.

We walked over toward the house. Marthy, as Vince called her, met us on the porch. Four or five little kids and big kids were peeking

around her. She was sort of sagging all over like a swaybacked mule.
Her dress wasn't quite clean. Her hair hung straight down in little
wads like a horse's mane that's full of cockleburs. But she was glad to
see us and that made her beautiful like she'd been before the hard
times had worn her down.

"Why, howdy, boys. Haven't seen you in a long time. Where you
headed?"

I said, "We're goin' to winter down in the lower-camp country,
Marthy, and try to pick up a few strays for Jim Ed."

"Yeah, he's starvin' to death," said Wrangler.

"Like a fat hog," said Marthy. "Come on in and wash up, boys. You
young-uns get out of the way now and let the gentlemen clean up."

"God a'mighty, Marthy, that ain't little Bobby, is it?" I asked.

"Yeah, that's him."

"He's growed a foot since I saw him summer a year ago. And look
at Christine and Sally. Why, they're pretty near grown-up young ladies."

The kids just stood and twisted around and grinned, not saying a
word. Vince believed in doing most of the talking in his family.

I know one thing, the Moores might not eat very fancy but they eat
a whole lot. Marthy put the biggest pot of beans I ever saw on the
table and about four pans of corn bread and some homemade butter.
A gallon bucket full of coffee steamed on the stove. It got kind of
hungry-like thereabouts.

Vince came in talking to beat hell, washed up, and everybody sat
down at the splintery old homemade table and started lapping it up.
Vince could eat faster than any of us and still keep on talking at the
same time.

"How's Jim Ed?" he asked.

"Fine, I reckon," I said.

"How much did his calves weigh out this year?"

"They did right well, Vince," I said. "Weighed out right at four
hundred pounds average."

"Man, that's good," Vince said. "I didn't have any to ship this year.
Business ain't been too good."

I knew he was talking about his whisky business because this little
old one-man starvation outfit of his wouldn't make anybody a living. I
knew too that before Jim Ed bought up just about every little outfit
around, Vince had had a lot more customers.

We ate and talked and pretty soon we got down to the smoking and coffee-drinking stage. Vince was bragging on one of his hounds and telling how that hound could run right up beside a coyote and latch on to its throat and kill him all by himself. I knew this was mostly a big yarn, but I enjoyed it.

Pretty soon Marthy and the kids went to bed, and Vince said, "Would you boys care for a little snort?"

"Don't mind if I do," I said.

Wrangler said, "Whatever suits you just tickles me plumb to death."

Vince got up and went outside and came back in with a gallon jug. He got some tin cups and poured us all a big slosh.

"Well now, I reckon some fellers know how to make store-bought clothes, and some fellers can patch up an old wreck of a pickup so it runs like new, and some fellers can make lots of money like Jim Ed, but there ain't nobody makes better whisky than you, Vince Moore," I told him.

That stuff rolled down my gullet just as smooth and warm as milk to a titty baby. Old Wrangler just kinda closed his eyes and leaned back against the wall, and that busted nose of his was flared out like a wolf in a henhouse. It was sure enough good.

"More?" Vince asked.

"Believe I will at that," I said.

"Yeah," said Wrangler.

Well sir, it was a fine evening, and after about four or five more cups of Vince Moore's special it got finer.

I asked Vince, "Did you see that good-looking blaze-faced roan I was a-ridin'?"

"First thing I noticed," said Vince.

"Did you ever see a runnin' walk like that?"

"Did seem like he moved easy and sure," said Vince.

"Listen, Vince," I said, kind of warming to my pitch, "that horse has got the best rein of any animal I ever rode. Ain't that right, Wrangler?" I said.

"He's got that if nothing else," said Wrangler.

"Nothing else?" I said, half sore-like. "Listen, he can run faster than a slim jackrabbit and stop before you even get the reins pulled back half tight. Vince, how about some more of that wonderful juice?"

"Sure, boys, just say when."

Vince filled them cups right up to the brim. I had to go into action quick to keep any of that precious liquid from spilling over and going to waste.

"Now, that Old Fooler horse was just made for a nice little outfit like yours, Vince," I went on. "You can work cattle on him, for one thing. And just to ride him is a pure pleasure, what with that runnin' walk you yourself noticed."

Vince was staring kind of red-eyed, and every once in a while he wiped the long gray hair back from where it was falling down over his ears.

"Now, Vince," I said, "you know how it is when one of them old hound dogs of yours, especially the one that can kill by hisself, gets in hot and heavy after a coyote."

"Yeah," Vince said, wiping his mouth with a creased, rough hand. "Yeah, I know."

"Well," I said, "you want to get in on the kill worse than anything else in the world. Ain't that right?"

"Yeah," he said, scratching his chin and blinking them little pig eyes that was something like Wrangler's, only redder.

"You haven't got any more worries about being there when you ride Old Fooler."

"He ain't my horse," said Vince.

"Now that's where you're dead wrong," I said. "For just a small consideration and just to show you how much we appreciate your hospitality to us here tonight, I'm goin' to let you have him."

"I ain't got a dime to my name," said Vince, moving that big rusty hand back up to his hair. "Not a penny."

"Good Lord, Vince, you didn't think I was wantin' money, did you? Here, hit me another slug of that wonderful stuff. All I want would be eight jugs of this stuff. It's gonna be a long winter down at the lower camp."

"Yeah, and dry," Wrangler said.

"Jim Ed said it was dry as a snuffbox down there. The snow don't stay on the ground a tall," I raved. I could see them little red eyes just strainin' with the effort to think.

"Well, I don't know, boys," he said.

I had one of them sinking feelings like I had been fell on by a thousand-pound bronc. I knew if I waited till morning, and Vince sobered up, he would never agree to the swap. I was a desperate cowboy. Just then nature lent me a kind, helping hand. About a mile to the north a coyote let out a howl, and all the dogs jumped up and went to barking and raising hell. I saw quick-like that Vince's blood was really pumping and singing him a song. Yes sir. The old coyote fever was on him.

That's when I put the clincher to him. "Vince, you can catch that yappin' son of a gun an hour after sunrise tomorrow and be right there when the old red dog puts the big bite on him." For a minute the red eyes went blank. Then they shone out real bright.

"It's a deal!" he said. Then he shook our hands and poured some more of that wonderful stuff all round.

After a while Vince said it was time to turn in, and slumped forward with his head on the table and went to sleep, the proud owner of one hell of a piece of horseflesh. Me and Wrangler stumbled out to our bedrolls and said good night to the stars.

It was a good breakfast Marthy served up about daylight the next morning, but she had a tough time getting anybody but the kids to eat. Finally, after a lake of coffee, we got the packs back on the mules. On each pack hung four jugs—two on each side. I was anxious to get the hell out of there before Vince decided to try Old Fooler out.

"It shore has been enjoyable," Wrangler said, trying to sound fancy.

"Mighty hospitable of you folks," I said, trying to sound even fancier. I reined the bay out front and we got out of there. I will admit that Old Fooler looked a little lonesome standing there with his head up over the top of the corral watching us ride off. I didn't tell him good-bye. My stomach felt like I had swallowed a bunch of snapping turtles mixed with rusty barbwire. Wrangler must have felt the same, because after a while he called for me to stop. He said he had something he wanted to tell me.

I stopped and said, "What is it you want to tell me?"

"I'm thirsty," he said.

I agreed that this was a very important announcement. We both got down and had a drink.

Wrangler said, "What you goin' to tell Jim Ed about Old Fooler?"

"I don't know yet," I said, "but if I ever see that mean son of a bitch again I am goin' to kill him and tell God he committed suicide."

We rode on down toward the lower camp but we didn't make very good time. Seems like we had made the mistake of taking our first drink out of the same jug. It seemed unfair to make a mule carry a lopsided load, so we had to stop every now and then to make sure things was kept evened up.

FOUR

THERE IT WAS—Jim Ed's lower camp. Someone had homesteaded it long ago, but now it was lonesome as hell. The corrals and the dirty wooden shack needed fixing. It's a hell of a big country out there. You could look for a hundred miles in almost any direction except west. There the view was blocked by a long, rocky, piñon-covered mesa. I knew it was there we would find the wild cattle. Gathering them would be something else. There were hundreds of brush-covered canyons for them to hide in, and the rough country was going to be hard on men and horses.

We moved on down, turned the horses out to pasture, keeping one up for a night horse. We unpacked the mules and started straightening up the shack. It was in a hell of a mess. Two windows were out and dust was thick over everything. The last boys there had left dirty dishes all piled about. The rats had built nests all over the three rooms and the birds had roosted in the broken windows. The rotten shingles on the roof had blown away, leaving several holes you could have thrown a tomcat through.

I got tired of messing around the house. So I packed in about a dozen buckets of water and told Wrangler, "I reckon I better go get you some firewood and cut it up since you are goin' to do the cooking around here."

Wrangler just grunted and I sneaked out to saddle the night horse. I rode out a ways and threw a loop over a fairly good-sized dead piñon tree. Then I spurred the other way. It was about all the little sorrel bronc could do to drag it in.

I turned him loose in the corral again and collected the ax we had packed. I don't like chopping wood worth a damn, but it's better than keeping house. I lit into that tree, and about three hours later, just before sundown, I had enough wood to do Wrangler for a week or two.

I was sure surprised when I got back up to the house. Wrangler had everything in place and about half clean. Water was boiling on the old four-hole iron range and the coffee was hot. He had a pot of beans on that would simmer for several days and was frying hell out of a bunch of sowbelly. Besides that, he had started some sour dough bread. He looked comical as could be standing there with that flour sack tied around his middle. The sack dragged on the floor and you couldn't tell whether he was walking or rolling.

I said, "Wrangler, you're goin' to make somebody a hell of a fine wife one of these days."

"I hope she's rich instead of so damn good-lookin'," he said, dishing up the grub.

It was a fine supper, considering the condition of everything when we got there. We crawled in our bedrolls that night feeling almost at home.

The next day we were anxious to get back up in the hills and start locating the cattle. That bonus on each head didn't have anything to do with it, of course—we are just naturally industrious cowboys. However, we decided we'd better work around the place for a few days first. The holding pasture was in bad shape. It wouldn't do us any good to gather the stock if we couldn't hold it. We took a heavy set of wire pliers, wire stretchers, and staples and went to work. Every so often we would stop and pull four wires tight as a slopped hog's gut. Then we would clamp her down solid with staples. We patched up the water gaps by tying heavy rocks to the wire so the spring rains wouldn't wash them out so easy. We put up a wing about a hundred yards out at an angle from the gate. We set the posts deep and stretched the wire tight. We would have to pen the wild stock here, and this wing would help get them through the gate.

We checked the snubbin' post in the corral. It was cedar and still stout as a yearling bull. We reworked the corral by adding new poles here and there. It would do now to work the broncs in. Then we took a couple of rusty shovels, that didn't fit our hands at all, and cleaned out the spring in the gathering pasture. It had filled up with black mud. After a couple of days of this degrading labor the water ran fresh and clear.

I said, "Well, Wrangler, I reckon we're set for the winter. I don't know but what that Jim Ed didn't pull a fast one on us. Do you realize we'll just barely get out of here in time to make the Fourth of July rodeo in Hi Lo?

"I'd given that a little thought," said Wrangler. "It will be exactly a year since we went to town last."

I thought on this a spell and it made me feel kind of cut off from the rest of the world. I tried to cheer us up by saying, "Yeah, but think of all the back wages we'll collect and that big bonus from gatherin' this wild stock. Why, Wrangler, we'll pitch one that will make history even in a wild town like Hi Lo." But it just didn't do any good.

We saddled up a couple of the rawest of the broncs and rode toward the mesa. We didn't aim to try any gathering for a couple of days. Our idea was to scout out where the main bunches were running. Then we would move in and get after them.

It was one of those days that makes a feller feel good whether he wants to or not. The birds were singing to beat sixty and the wind had died down so you could feel the warm fall sun. The grama grass was up almost stirrup high, and I was thanking my lucky stars that I didn't have to be worrying about Old Fooler. Then I wished I hadn't thought about that son of a bitch. It gave me a uneasy feeling right where I buckle my belt.

Well, in one sandy wash we found traces of fifteen or twenty head. We didn't see them, but we could tell by the droppings and the way the grass was tromped down that they were ranging in there. We rode damn near to the top, finding tracks crossing tracks of steers, bulls, and old mother cows with calves. About the fourth day we figured we had done enough tracking.

"Wrangler," I said, "how many head you gonna guess is here?"

"Over two hundred," he said.

"Well, Jim Ed guessed a hundred and twenty-five to a hundred seventy-five. Maybe they ain't all his."

"He wouldn't care. Look what he did to Vince Moore. Bought out all his customers. Why, it's got to where a honest bootlegger like old Vince cain't hardly make a living anymore."

"I sure know it," I said. "The country is goin' to hell in a hurry. If these ranchers keep buying these pickup trucks, there ain't goin' to be no use for horse breakers like us."

We had been reining the broncs over rocky ridges until my hands were sore and set like an eagle's claws, but every time one of them swallowed his head to buck I went down after those hackamore reins like they were made of velvet.

Like I said, I was sure enough glad I didn't have to ride Old Fooler with these sore hands, and was about to say so to Wrangler when damned if Vince Moore didn't come riding up on a little brown horse leading the bastard.

I swallowed my tongue and felt like all my blood had run right out through the soles of my boots. He was right up in front of the shack before I could speak.

"Why, hello, Vince. Sure nice to see you again so soon. Get down and tie your horses. Wrangler's putting a bunch of sourdough in the oven. How's the wife and kids? I reckon you got the windmill fixed. How's business? Gettin' any new customers for that wonderful product of yours? How's Marthy and the kids? Looks like it's goin' to be a long, dry winter, don't it? Seen Jim Ed lately? How's your hounds gettin' along? Specially that one that kills a coyote by hisself. How's Marthy and the kids?"

"Howdy," said Vince, sort of sour. He got down off his horse. Then he took Old Fooler out and turned him loose in the corral with the night horse. I stood there with my mouth still moving but nothing coming out.

Vince walked back up and says, looking me straight in the eye, "There's your goddam outlawed horse. I want my whisky back. That is, if there's any left."

I said, "Whatever do you mean, Vince? You must be kiddin' old Dusty Jones."

"I am like hell," he says.

"What happened?" I asked, wishing I could go deaf before he answered.

"Well, in the first place, I went coyote huntin' on him the mornin' after you left. The first thing that happened, we jumped a big coyote not a half mile from the house."

"That's good," I said.

"No, that' ain't good," Vince says. "I lined out on him like you told me, right behind the hounds."

"That's good," I said.

"That ain't good a tall," Vince said. "That son of a bitch can run, all right. He ran right on past where the dogs had that coyote down and he kept runnin' for about three miles. I didn't even have time to glance at the fight. We went by so fast I couldn't have seen nothin' but a blur anyway. When I finally got him turned around and headed back, the dogs had tore that coyote into so many pieces he looked like a fresh cow turd in a cyclone."

I opened my mouth but decided I might catch cold or something, so I shut it and listened to Vince rave on.

"The next mornin' I saddled him up in the corral and walked around pretty as you please, and just when I was feelin' like the day before had been a accident, it happened."

Wrangler rolled up to the door in his flour-sack apron and was fool enough to ask, "What happened?"

Vince did not need any urging. He said, "He bucked off about a mile and stopped and went to eatin' my good grass."

"A spirited horse like him gets hungry," I said.

Vince didn't pay any attention to this. He had other things on his mind. "Well, that made me so damn mad I figgered if I couldn't ride the ornery bastard, maybe I could plow with him. I been wantin' to put in some winter wheat anyway."

"How did he work?" that foolish Wrangler asked.

"Work!" Vince screamed. "He ran off with the plow and got it hung in a fence and tore down at least two hundred yards of good stout posts and barbwire and then he broke up all my harness. I've been several days and nights tryin' to get the whole damn place stuck back together." He stopped and choked a minute, then said, "I want my whisky back."

There wasn't a thing to do but give it back. Howsomever, I talked him into leaving one jug for medicine, seeing as how we were so far from a doctor. He went on cussing Old Fooler until I was downright embarrassed. So I made the mistake of saying, "Vince, I'm sure sorry this turned out like it did. But I think it was just one of those things, you know. Some people, good people, too, just can't get along with each other. I think that's the way it is with you and Old Fooler. Why, he never gives me a bit of trouble."

"That so?" says Vince. "Let's see you saddle him up and kick him into a dead run, then."

Well, I felt just like a dog caught sucking eggs. I was trapped. I moseyed out to the corral trying to act like my guts wasn't tying themselves in big sheepshank knots, and threw the rigging on Old Fooler. I said to him, "Now, you old bastard, just this once, please don't buck. Please."

Old Fooler stood there half asleep, his eyelids drooped down. He didn't even bother to switch his tail at a horsefly that was trying to swallow him whole. In fact, he was leaning so heavy on one side it looked like he might just fall over. I untracked him and stepped aboard. He walked around the corral easy and slow. I could feel the sweat running down my back.

"Well," says Vince, "you ready for me to turn him out?"

"Yeah," I croaked, just above a whisper. What I had in mind was to ease him out when Vince opened the gate, then get him into a lope and make for the nearest timber, where I could hide out, as quick as I could. It didn't work out. Vince had barely got the gate undone when Old Fooler went rocketing out through it.

He was bucking like mad but running at the same time. Vince was knocked six ways from Sunday and I was milking hell out of that saddle horn. Away we went. I could see he was headed for another arroyo. That goddam horse must have had one of them arroyos for a mother, the way he liked to fall in their laps. I decided to change the act and started digging my left spur up in his shoulder and bending them hackamore reins to the right. It worked. Slow but sure.

There was a deep bog off a ways to the right. If there's anything that will slow down a bucking horse and take the flint out of him, it's a deep bog. Old Fooler jumped smack dab in the middle of it and came to a sudden stop. *Boy*, I thought, *I've got you at last!* I knocked about two pounds of hair out of his shoulders and sides. He didn't even twitch. I reckon I could have killed him and he would have fell over dead before he would buck. Old Fooler had been there before.

I spurred and spurred. The horse hair was in my eyes and my mouth, and my legs were getting heavy and numb. It just didn't do any good. Finally I quit spurring, and cussed till I couldn't think of anything else to call him. This took quite a bit of time. Then I gently reined him out of the bog like I was helping my crippled grandmother to a rocking chair and rode back toward the house. I turned him out in the pasture. He threw up his tail and ran off looking for the other horses just like he owned the outfit.

"I'll get you yet if I have to run you off a thousand-foot bluff onto a bunch of sharp rocks," I yelled, waving my fist at his rump. I walked back to the house. "Where's Vince?" I asked Wrangler.

"He got his wonderful stuff and left while you was out in the bog."

"I hope he wasn't mad," I said.

"Naw," said Wrangler. "He just said he hoped Old Fooler kicked your eyeballs right out between your ears."

"Oh," I said.

FIVE

EVERYTHING WAS READY. The serious work started. Me and Wrangler was mighty earnest about that five-dollar-a-head bonus. It could be one hell of a big Fourth of July if we even made a 50 percent gather.

First we jumped three mother cows and a four-year-old steer. They tore through the brush like a dose of salts. The broncs plowed right in after them, with me and Wrangler setting aboard ducking limbs, reining around boulders, feeling the brush pull and drag at us like the devil's own claws. That's why cowboys wear heavy leather chaps. Without them, there wouldn't have been enough meat left on our leg bones inside of ten minutes to feed a dying sparrow hawk.

When we couldn't see stock we could hear them. For a while it didn't look like we were going to get anywhere. The big steer cut back and I cut back with him. The brush was so thick and the rocks so big that I either had to let him go or risk losing the cows and calves. I turned back and went in after Wrangler. We had them headed downhill in a dead run. If we could keep them that way till we hit the flats we had a good chance. We made it.

One old cow turned back again and again. The half-bronc sorrel I was riding didn't know what to do. I just had to whip him in the side of the head with my hat and spur hell out of him, all the time working them hackamore reins like they were a steering wheel to head that ornery cow.

Finally I got mad, and when she turned back for the tenth time I spurred up and dropped a loop around both horns. I kept spurring one way and she headed the other. It was quite a shock to her when all the slack pulled out of the rope. She came back and over and my little old bronc damn near went down. I threw my weight over on one side, ramming the spurs to him at the same time. He stayed up and held, turning to face down the rope like I'd been training him to do. It was all over quick-like. I had the rope off the cow's horns and was back on my horse before she got her wind back. From then on she headed the way I wanted her to.

There was no slowing up now. We came downhill in a long hard lope. Three cows, three calves—thirty dollars on the hoof. That's a lot of money to a working cowboy.

They hit that wing we had built and whirled around looking for an opening, but we crowded in just right and got them through the gate. I got down and slammed it shut, grinning all over. While the sweat dried on our horses, me and Wrangler had us a smoke and got a little clean, fresh pure mountain air into our lungs.

I said, "God a'mighty, thirty dollars in one day. This ain't never happened to me before."

Wrangler said, "Me neither."

I said, "I wish the Fourth of July was just next month."

Right then we figured we would have been the two richest cowboys ever to make a country rodeo. However, there was a whole long cold winter between us and the Fourth of July.

We went four more days before we penned another head. But little by little, one, two, three at a time, we gathered the stock out of the brush. We were sure enough doing what Jim Ed wanted. We were gathering his stock and putting sore backs and tender feet on the broncs at the same time.

The mother cows came first. They were easier to gather than the wild fat dry cows and the big, longer-legged steers. When we got to these last, things would really get wild on the mesa.

Finally, though, we had quite a bunch. We decided to pen what we had and hold a branding. These calves weighed in at between four and five hundred pounds and were as fat and slick as wagon grease on a peeled limb.

We penned them at the corral. Then we cut the mother cows out and checked the branding irons in the fire.

Wrangler said, "Just a little while more and they'll be ready."

I got the blackleg vaccine in the needle and sharpened my knife, getting ready to make a lot of little steers out of a lot of little bulls. Ever since I can remember I've liked a branding.

I remember when I was back home with Pa on his little leased outfit. We used to invite all the neighbors over for the brandings. The women brought something cooked, like chicken, hogside, pies, and cakes. We made a real to-do out of it. There was plenty of hands to help. The women and little bitty kids watched from on the corral fence while the bigger kids like me and the old hands went to work.

There were two fires and always one old boy who was good at heelin' calves. He took great pride in this. A calf is lots easier to handle with the rope around his heels instead of his neck. Two of us would go down the rope just as the roper dragged the calf close to the fire. We jerked in opposite directions, one on the rope, the other on his tail. Down he would go. While one man jumped on his heels, the other gathered up a foreleg with his knee in the calf's neck. We would hardly get him down before a cowboy was there burning a brand on him and another was cutting his testicles out if he was a bull, and at the same time he would earmark him and reach for the needle to shoot the blackleg vaccine to him. The same thing would be going on at the other fire. We would brand a whole herd of calves in one day and have a big time doing it. After a while everybody would eat and drink some water or something. You just couldn't beat it.

Me and Wrangler were going about it a little bit different. These were big calves—wild and mean. We were shorthanded and had only a bunch of raw broncs and an outlawed roan son of a bitch to rope off of.

Wrangler said the irons was ready. He went out and fit a loop on a big whiteface calf. Then he fought his bronc around and started dragging him to the fire. I went down that rope and reached over his back with one hand in his flank and the other on the rope. The calf jumped straight up and kicked me in the belly with both feet. While he was up I heaved and down he went.

Wrangler bailed off his horse and came to help. In the meantime the calf had got one foot in my boot top and tore the bark off my shin. Then he kicked me in the mouth with the other foot. I had only one tooth in front that hadn't been broke, and now I didn't have that.

Wrangler pulled the calf's tail up between its kicking hind legs and held on while I tied all four feet with a four-foot piggin' string. Now, in rodeo they just tie three feet, but out here where we were you tied all four.

Wrangler went after the branding iron and started burning Jim Ed's JL brand on the calf's hip. I reached down and pulled the testicles as far out toward the front of the bag as I could. Then I split the bag and cut out the balls. I cut the fat off because that can cause infection, and swabbed the bag with pine tar. Then I cut a big chunk out of his ear called an earmark, which is part of a brand on every ranch. I cut off the little nubbin' horns and swabbed a little more pine tar on the holes. I shoved the needle in the loose folds of skin at his neck and pushed the plunger. The hair was burning and getting in my eyes and up my nose, but I could see that red-colored brand would stay there as long as that calf hide was in this world.

Wrangler went back and got on his horse and rode him up to give me slack in the rope. I took the loop off his head, undid the piggin' string, and turned this young ex-bull loose into the world, all fixed up so the black leg wouldn't kill him and branded so some cattle thief couldn't make off with him. He now belonged to Jim Ed Love for sure.

Well, we handled about three more like this and I had all the wind kicked out of me and half my hide was peeled loose here and there. My mouth was swelled up and I was already missing that broken tooth.

I said to Wrangler, "I wish we had a good heelin' horse. We could sure save lots of work and wear and tear."

I decided I would try Old Fooler. It was a crazy notion, but strangely enough it worked. I never rode a better heelin' horse in my life. Old Fooler had been to lots of brandings. Wrangler would throw his loop around a calf's neck and start toward the fire with him. Then I'd ease Old Fooler in close, riding in the other direction. At just the right spot I would let my loop drift slow and easy under the calf's belly, letting it lay up against his hind legs, then just as he moved out I'd pull it up around his heels, holding the slack out of the rope and riding on. The calf would hit the ground stretched out nice and tight between those two ropes. It made branding a lot faster and a lot easier.

I just couldn't believe that Old Fooler had ever tried to kill me. He really enjoyed this branding and settled down and did his job just like the rest of us. The way he worked that rope was sweet as a baby's dream. He held it just tight enough but not too tight, and when you wanted slack he gave it to you. Those little short ears of his worked back and forth, and he watched every move out of those dark mean eyes. I still couldn't believe it when it was all over.

We turned the calves out to their mothers who were standing outside the corral. They trotted off together, all bawling, with the mother cows licking the calves like they had just been born.

I stared at Old Fooler standing out there looking so proud it showed right through the roan horsehair.

"I just can't figger that horse out," I said.

Wrangler said, "You never will. He's just like a woman."

"No," I said, "he may act like one but there is some little difference in the way they are built. How many mountain oysters we got?"

"Enough," he said, "for a good supper."

We went to the house and washed up. I brought in some wood for the cookstove. Wrangler set about mixing up a bunch of batter to cook them calf balls in. I got out the jug Vince Moore had left and we took a big slug apiece.

I said, "Wrangler, maybe I'm gettin' the best of that Old Fooler horse after all."

He didn't answer.

I hunted up an old stub of a pencil and sat down at the table to see how much our bonus was. It was just too much to add up in my head.

"Let's see, eighteen mother cows and calves, three dry cows, and two steers." It took a lot of hard figuring, but I finally come up with the right answer.

I jumped up and took another slug out of the jug and yelled, "Wrangler, we've already made one hundred and fifteen dollars besides our regular wages."

"You don't mean it," he said, and sat down and figured it for himself. He never could get anything but a hundred and ten, but we decided as rich as we were that he was close enough.

I said, "Get back over to that stove. Them oysters is about to burn."

Pretty soon he took a pan of sourdough out of the oven browned just right. We poured us a big tin cup of coffee and sat down to consume a whole pan of crisp mountain oysters. It was the end of a hell of a fine day.

SIX

EVERYTHING WAS GOING ALONG about as good as could be expected. We spent a lot of time, between runs on the mesa, trying to put a finish on some of the broncs. We kept three or four on a stake rope all the time. There is nothing better for a horse than that. Let an old pony get tangled up in that rope and peel all the hide from his hocks right down to the frog of his foot, and he learns not to fight a rope anymore. First he gets respect for it, then he overcomes his fear. If a horse won't work with a rope, he ain't fit for a thing.

I was teaching them to turn at the slightest pressure of the knee and the feel of the rein on their necks. If you have to turn a horse by force and pressure from the bits only, you are going to ruin his mouth. He will get high-headed and start slinging his head. That kind of horse is a disgrace to any cowboy. I like to train a horse to back, too. There are lots of places you get with a cow horse that you will need to back out of. Another thing we worked hard on was stopping. A horse should stop with his hind legs well up under his belly and his tail jammed almost in the ground. This way is lots smoother, and leaves both the horse and rider ready to turn and move out. He has to be trained this way to keep him from overworking the livestock. I put a good stop on them by throwing my weight back in the saddle just as I pull up on the reins.

Jim Ed was not only going to have a lot of lost cattle found and gathered, he was going to have a top string of cow ponies by the Fourth of July.

Now maybe that's going too far. There was one big exception—Old Fooler. The thought caused my gizzard to cloud over. I felt a lot better about him after the branding, but I knew if I got overconfident the son of a bitch would try to kill me again. Just the same, I caught myself feeling pleased with him.

We had penned just about all the mother cows and calves. Now the rough part was starting. Those old thousand-pound steers and big fat dry cows were wilder than outhouse rats. We had jumped one huge steer about ten times, but we never even got him bent down the mountain toward the flats, much less had a chance to fit a loop over them long sharp horns.

We were riding along tracking him. I was on Old Fooler. Wrangler was on his favorite black. We saw where he had gone into a big thicket of oak brush and topped out on a steep point.

I said, "Wrangler, he's still in there. You stay up on this point so I can skylight you and I'll mosey over on the other side and go in after him."

"Whatever suits you just tickles me plumb to death," he said.

"Now if he comes out where you can get a run at him," I went on, "just yell and I'll know what you mean. If he comes out where you can't, but I can, just point at the spot and I'll go after him like Jim Ed does to money."

I rode around and reined Old Fooler into the brush. He didn't like it but went in just the same. I heard something move. Then it sounded like a whole herd of hydrophobia buffalo had broke loose. It was just that one big steer.

I looked up and saw Wrangler pointing. He yelled, "To your left! There he goes!"

The steer had cut right back out not twenty feet away. I turned Old Fooler and that's all I had to do. Out of there he sailed with his head down and his ears laid back flat. I caught a glimpse of the steer and knew we had him going at an angle downhill. It was up to Old Fooler now. He really put out. I could feel that smooth running power of his building up at every stride and pretty soon we could see that old steer's flying tail most of the time. Another half minute and I was actually thinking about undoing my rope and getting a loop ready. *Cowboys, what a horse!* I said to myself. I was sure glad Vince had brought him back. I was going to have to figure some way to trade Jim Ed out of this fine steer-gathering old pony.

Well, the steer hit a bunch of scattered piñons. I could see a big opening just past. I jobbed the steel to Old Fooler and he gave it all he had. Things were looking up. The next thing I knew I was too, but I couldn't see much.

We had started around this piñon tree, and I had leaned over just enough so Old Fooler would know which side to go on. He acted like he was doing just what I wanted, but when we got to the tree he whirled back the other way at full speed. So there I was trying to go around one side, and him going around the other. My chest whopped into hard bark and off I went.

I was laying on my back trying to find the sky. My breath was gone and every move I made I could feel them busted ribs scraping against one another. It hurt so bad I tried not to breathe at all. I reckon that's why old Wrangler thought I was dead when he first rode up. But he soon found out different because as bad hurt as I was I could still think up new names for that double-crossing Fooler horse.

As soon as Wrangler figured I had at least a fifty-fifty chance of living, he rode on down and gathered Old Fooler and led him back. I would have taken a piñon limb and beat him to death right then and there but it was all I could do to hold myself together long enough for Wrangler to help me up on him. I couldn't have picked up a broken matchstick at that moment.

It was a long ride in. I laid around in my bedroll, for four or five days, moaning and groaning. Finally Wrangler took some strips of ducking canvas and tied them around me and it helped hold the ribs in place.

I asked him, "Ain't you got an old .44 pistol in your war bag?"

Wrangler looked at me out of them pig eyes and pulled at his drooping britches.

"Yeah," he said.

"Will it shoot?"

"I don't know," he said. "I never shot it."

"Well, let me see it," I said. I pulled the hammer back and shot right up through the ceiling. It went off like a wet firecracker.

"Wrangler," I said, "if you'll go down and shoot that son of a bitch I will give you all my bonus from this wild-cow gather."

"Naw," he said.

"Why not?" I asked.

"Hell, he belongs to Jim Ed and we'll have to pay for him. Jim Ed will charge us double and be makin' a big profit."

Well, this thought hurt me just as bad as that tree did. I couldn't stand for Jim Ed to profit by that horse's death instead of me.

"Wrangler," I said, "there are times you amaze me. You actually show faint signs of intelligence once in a while."

Wrangler did not think this was funny and he made a noise like a fat bay mule that has just jumped a five-wire fence.

"I am goin' to stay here and get well and then I am goin' to go out and kill him in the line of duty."

When Wrangler asked, "How?" I gave him the same kind of answer he'd given me.

When my ribs healed to where I could take a deep breath, I told Wrangler, "Get that horse up for me, will you?"

"What horse?"

"You know what horse," I said.

He brought Old Fooler up. I limped out and stood and stared. Then I brushed him down nice and gentle-like, taking my time. I talked as sweet to him as I would to my old crippled grandmother. I bragged on that horse and told him that if only I had any sugar cubes I would give him a whole sack. I mean to say, I spread it on like honey on a hot biscuit. Then I got on him and rode easy and slow out toward the hills, not even touching him with my spurs and still bragging on him like he was my favorite animal in all the world.

I got off up there a ways and my ribs was aching to beat hell, but they still held together. Then I ducked my head like I had just found a fresh track. It was at least two weeks old. Then I threw my head up and made out like I had spotted a thousand head of unbranded steers. I didn't have to do anything but lean over, and away we went. You could build a fire on a jackrabbit's tail and he would look like he was going backward compared to the way Old Fooler ran. I could almost feel that rascal laughing plumb through the saddle leather. What a fool he thought I was. This time he would really get me.

The ground was rolling away under us so fast it made me dizzy. Right out ahead was another bunch of piñon. I spurred him straight at them, leaning over just like I did before. Old Fooler was already bunching his muscles to jump the wrong way and break my crazy neck once and for all. Just as he thought it was time, I straightened up and pulled one foot out of the stirrup, yanking my leg up behind the cantle of the saddle. Then I jerked him into that tree at full speed.

There must be a lot more wind in a horse than in a man. The air that came busting out of his lungs would have blown a Stetson hat around the world three times. That old horse staggered and fell. I stepped off, taking care not to make any sudden movements and snap a rib. A cowboy in my condition has got to be careful and not take any chances.

I hadn't killed him, though. He got up, and his eyes were rolling around in his head like a couple of gallstones in a slop jar. He wobbled on his legs.

I fancy-stepped all the way back to camp with Old Fooler stumbling along behind, just barely able to make it. That was the only time I ever took a walk I enjoyed.

Wrangler came out on the porch and asked, "What happened?"

I said, "You know what? That is the tree-lovingest horse I ever saw. He just can't pass one by without runnin' over it."

I knew that I had cured that pony of at least one bad habit. It probably wouldn't do any good, though, as I figured he would die before morning.

I was wrong again. Not only did he get well in a couple of days, but he was doing better than I was. This made me so mad I decided to keep the lessons going. With a short piece of rope I necked Old Fooler to the biggest pack mule we had. Old Fooler didn't like this one bit. He looked at me with those dark, evil-thinking eyes of his and I could just feel ribs and bones snapping all over me.

It didn't make any difference. The mule led him off out into the pasture acting like he didn't even see Old Fooler coming along. That is one of the best ways a cowboy can use to gentle and teach a bronc to lead.

A couple of days later I was sitting on the porch having a smoke and wondering if my ribs would hold together for another set-to with the wild bunch on the mesa when up rides Onofre Martínez on a scraggly-looking bay. Old Onofre is a friend of mine. He has a little place over east of us a ways—twenty-five or thirty head of sheep, about ten cows, five goats, four hound dogs, and eight or ten kids.

"Howdy, Onofre, you old son of a gun. Get down and tie your horse," I said.

He got down and tied his horse to a post holding up the rickety porch.

"Hello, my friend," he said, sticking one dark paw out at me. "What are you doing down here?"

"Me and Wrangler are down here on a vacation," I said. "Good-hearted Jim Ed thought the north part of the JL would be too cold for a couple of tender-skinned boys like me and Wrangler."

"A considerate boss, this Jim Ed," said Onofre.

"Yeah," I said. "When is the last time you been into town?" Meaning the town of Hi Lo, New Mexico.

"Just last week, my friend," said Onofre. "Had a nice little pitch game over at Moon's Bar."

Onofre went on to tell me about the pitch game, then the poker game, then the big drunk, then how pretty his young sister was who lived in town. It made me nervous, all this talk. Then it made me thirsty. And hungry.

I said, "Onofre, how would you like a slug of some of Vince Moore's wonderful stuff?"

"I could think for days without conceiving a better thought," said Onofre.

I got the jug out. It was still half full.

"Where is Wrangler?" Onofre asked, wiping his mouth.

"He's up in the hills lookin' for cows."

"You boys must have done a good job already," said Onofre, motioning out into the gather pasture where the herd had grown pretty sizable.

"Not bad, Onofre. We get five dollars a head bonus."

"Calves and all?" he asked wide-eyed.

"Calves and all," I said.

"Whoooeee, there's goin' to be a big Fourth of July in Hi Lo, no?"

"Sí, hombre," I said.

We rattled on for a while, going over some of the good times we had had together, when I happened to think of Old Fooler. I was just going to light in and cuss him when I saw that mule leading him in toward the spring out by the corrals. They were coming slow but would make it in the next fifteen or twenty minutes. I started handing that jug to Onofre so fast he didn't hardly have time to get one swallow out of the way before another was right on its tail.

I got to looking at that sorry single-rig saddle of his. Now there is a big difference of opinion about the flank cinch on horses. I like a double-rig outfit because you can rope bigger stock without jerking your saddle off. When an old pony is really ducking his head and turning it on, it helps to have the rear end of your saddle tied down so it isn't whipping you in the rump at every jump. The other side thinks that with a single rig your horse won't do near as much bucking in the first place. All I know is, I always feel sorry for those single-rig boys. And them bits that Onofre had on his bridle—short-shanked and light as a gnat's whiskers. Just the kind of bit to ruin a horse. No wonder that little ugly bay of his had his head up in Onofre's face, slinging it around like a duck in a dry pond. He had iron stirrups instead of wooden. If a horse fell on him, those stirrups would more than likely bend over his foot and his horse would drag him to death. What a rig! I got to thinking that all this sorry equipment was just what Old Fooler deserved. I passed the jug to Onofre again.

After he'd lowered the jug for about the twentieth time he spotted Old Fooler and the mule. "What you got that roan horse necked to that mule for?"

It was exactly what I wanted him to ask.

"It's the other way around," I said. "That is the worst spoiled mule I ever saw—just kicks and tears up everything he gets close to. We have to keep him necked to Old Fooler all the time. He's the only thing around that can handle him."

"I be damned," said Onofre.

About that time the mule stuck his muzzle in the water and took a long pull. Old Fooler started to do the same. The mule ran backward bending hell out of Old Fooler's neck. The mule came back to drink. So did Fooler. The same thing happened. That mule simply was not going to let Old Fooler drink. I wondered what in the hell Old Fooler had done to that mule to make him so mad.

"Look," I said. "Look at that goddam mule. Ain't even goin' to let that good old roan horse have a drink of water. Now, ain't that the meanest damn mule you ever saw?"

"He sure is," said Onofre, swaying just a little and squinting his eyes to see better.

"I tell you what, Onofre, if you'll go pen them animals I'm goin' to turn that mule out to himself. That roan is the best horse on the whole outfit. We just can't take any more chances of the mule ruinin' him."

Onofre got up and climbed on his horse. He rode out and drove them in the corral.

I untied Old Fooler from the mule. He actually gave me a half-grateful look.

I saddled up Old Fooler and pointed out to Onofre how still he stood. How gentle he was. Onofre sagged against the corral, and agreed. Then I got up on him and rode him around the corral.

"Did you ever see a horse rein like this one?" I asked.

"That's the best I ever saw," said Onofre.

"Look what a stop he's got," I said, kicking Old Fooler into a run and leaning back and showing off his brakes.

"Never saw anything like it, my friend," said Onofre. "What you pulling so hard on that saddle horn for?" he asked.

"It's the rein he's got," I said. "So fast he might turn out from under me."

"Oh," said Onofre.

I got off, unsaddled, and led Old Fooler up to the house, watching every move. I didn't want to take any chances on him running off into the timber with me. Onofre followed, stumbling along, figuring this was the day for walking.

We sat down on the porch and I handed Onofre the jug. He really took a slug. That Adam's apple of his was jumping around like a barefooted kid in a red-ant bed. I helped myself to an outsized drink and said, "Onofre, ain't we always been the best of friends?"

"Sí, amigo."

"Ain't we played poker, fist-fought, run women, raised hell together?"

"Sí, sí, mío amigo. Sí, sí."

"Ain't you been just like a brother to me and me to you?"

"That is right, my friend," he said, reaching for the jug of wonderful stuff.

"There ain't nobody in the world that I have had more fun with, Onofre. Remember the time we got in jail over at Hi Lo for breaking up the poker game with them crooked Madison brothers?"

"How could I forget, my friend?" he said.

"Well, now, out of appreciation for all we've been through together and for this here long and everlasting friendship, I am goin' to do something for you."

Onofre was silent. He looked at me out of them big soft black eyes of his and waited, almost breaking into tears.

I said, jumping up and grabbing him by both shoulders, "Onofre, I'm goin' to make you the greatest gift one man can make another!"

The tears squirted out of his eyes at that, and if I hadn't been holding him up he would have fell on his face right on the ground.

"You goin' to kill yourself for me?" he asked.

"No, better than that," I said. "I am goin' to give you that beautiful roan horse. The greatest piece of horseflesh in New Mexico!"

Onofre just couldn't hold back any longer. The tears ran down his cheeks like a whitefaced cow taking a piss on a flat rock. He shook my hand until I thought it was a water pump.

"Gracias, my friend," he said. "My friend, my old amigo, my compadre."

"Now, get on your pony," I said, "and lead this here wonderful animal home to show your wife and kids."

I had to help him on his horse. All the time he was blubbering and telling the saints to send me straight to heaven without holding court over my soul. He rode out of there swaying in the breeze like a baby cottonwood.

A few days later me and Wrangler were out in the corral saddling some ponies, fixing to head for the hills. I was bragging about getting rid of Old Fooler once and for all.

I said, "If old Onofre can't ride him he will kill him and eat him, as many kids as he's got to feed."

I felt my horse throw his head up and look around. There was something coming toward the corral in a cloud of dust. It ran right up to the gate in a dead run and came to a sliding halt. That's right. It was Old Fooler. The saddle was up on his withers, and the one cinch was stretched like thin skin around a snakebite. The reins were broken off at the bits, and one of Onofre's boots was still dangling from a stirrup.

"Reckon Onofre's all right?" Wrangler asked.

"If he ain't, we'll hear about it in a few days," he said.

Wrangler said, "Wonder what happened?"

"Old Fooler just didn't like that sorry single riggin'," I said.

SEVEN

IT MIGHT HAVE BEEN two or three degrees warmer at lower camp than it was at headquarters, but it was still colder than a well-digger's ass in Alaska. It wasn't because of the snow either. Down around the shack it would mix up with the sand and gravel and blow around in circles until it just plain evaporated. Up in the shade of the rimrocks you could sometimes find drifts two or three feet deep. The ground was frozen in the shade and it made tracking hard. The gather slowed down. We had to ride twice as far and rub saddle leather twice as long to get half as many head. The wind whistling around the mesa top was freezing cold and it never seemed to let up.

Me and Wrangler wore heavy sheep-lined coats. Just the same our eyes watered and our noses ran like leaky water troughs from the cold. The hair grew out long and shaggy on the horses and cattle. The wind bent and broke the dried-out grama grass. The stock got thinner and so did our horses.

At night the wind howled around that little old shack, shaking hell out of it and shoving that freezing cold through every crack. I kept thinking it was a long long time to the Fourth of July. I thought about Jim Ed and cussed him out to Wrangler, swearing that I was going to quit his chicken outfit in the spring.

We were sure as hell giving the broncs a workout up on those half-frozen slopes. They were gentling down fast, but like all horses in cold weather they had a tendency to want to buck a little when first saddled in the morning. We were used to this, but I never got used to Old Fooler. I was forced to saddle him once in a while, riding all the time with my guts right up in my throat and feeling that cold sensation in my belly that had nothing to do with the winter wind. I was beginning to wonder if my nerve was breaking on me and if that goddam horse would kill me before spring. I was just as nervous as a whore at a convention of Sunday-school teachers.

The winter wore on, and me and Wrangler sort of wore with it. Somehow, by staying on guard every single second, I had kept from getting hurt by Old Fooler for quite a spell. I kept thinking I should knock him in the head and get it over with, but at the same time I kept kidding myself into thinking I might win out.

The winter slacked up just a little. In the middle of the day, where the sun could hit, the ground thawed. It got to where we could do a little decent tracking again. I kept seeing the tracks of that big old outlawed steer, and something started eating at me. Seems like for a while I thought almost as much about catching that steer as I did about breaking Old Fooler. It was just about the same amount of problem. I jumped him out a half-dozen times by myself and with Wrangler along. He just showed us his tail and ran off, tearing hell out of the thick brush. It got kind of embarrassing.

"A couple of fine cowboys we are," I said to Wrangler.

"That steer is going to be the cause of me going to work in a gas station," said Wrangler.

Then I had an idea. Now most cowboys get the skull ache if they try to think overly much, but this was such a brand-new idea that I couldn't help but feel good about it.

"Wrangler," I said, "you know that Jim Ed told us to butcher whatever beef we needed to winter on."

"He did," said Wrangler.

"Well, I am goin' to shoot that goddam steer," I said, looking at Wrangler and expecting him to jump right through the side of the shack yelling, "Hooray for Hurrah!"

He looked at me, pulled his britches almost up on his hips, snorted through his busted nose, and said, "Hell's bells, no better than you can shoot, you'll never get close enough to hit the same mountain he's on."

"Bullshit carver!" I said. "Without a rope hangin' and draggin' me back in the brush I can spur right on up to him."

"Maybe you could on Old Fooler," he said, looking way off out the one little dirty pane left in the west window.

I never said a word. I just walked over and got Wrangler's six-shooter out of his war bag and went out and gathered in the horses. Old Fooler kept rolling his eyes around, half expecting me to fit a loop around his wicked neck. Somehow there was a gleam in his eye that made my loop sail over him and settle gentle-like over the neck of the big bay that had turned out so good. It was the horse I knew Jim Ed would pick out for his own. It wasn't very long till I had him saddled. I turned the other horses out and rode for the hills.

It was cold but warming some as the sun moved toward the middle of the sky. My heavy sheepskin coat was breaking the wind pretty good except for a few leaks around the collar and sleeves. My breath was frosting out in front of me and the bay's was doing the same.

I rode up and around through the open spots looking for the steer's tracks. I didn't find them. That six-shooter was setting there in my coat pocket all loaded and ready to go. I was about to give up when I felt the bay bunch up under me and throw his head up and his ears forward. Right across a little draw stood the big red steer. He snorted and whirled, heading for some oakbrush a quarter-mile to the north. I leaned over on the bay and he lit out of there in a dead run. The wind was blowing to our backs, but it was left far behind. I didn't feel it at all.

That bay was a natural-born cow horse. He judged just the angle to cut that steer out of the brush. It was close all right, but just the same we headed him back and down through a bunch of piñons. Well, I leaned over as low as I could in the saddle to duck all those low-hanging limbs and jobbed the steel in the bay's sides. We moved up fast.

Pretty soon I could see a glimpse of the steer at every jump. Then we hit this clearing going what seemed like about ninety miles an hour. I hit the bay again with the spurs, letting out a yell and pulling the pistol out of my pocket at the same time. The hammer got kind of hung in my pocket lining, and it looked like the steer would make it to the brush before I could get a shot in. I finally got the damned gun out and there we were, right on top of the steer. I pulled the trigger. Then me and the bay were rolling through that clean, pure fresh mountain air. Down we went. The world sure did seem big and hard where we hit. It jumped around for a while. Then it settled down to where I could see. I was flat on my back, and eleven hundred pounds of horse-flesh was laying on both my legs almost up to my knees. That horse-flesh wasn't moving. I had blown that bay horse's brains right out his ears. The very bay horse that I knew my boss, Jim Ed Love, wanted for his very own.

I strained, I pulled, I pushed, I clawed at the ground like a fat tomcat with the thin dirties. I couldn't budge an inch from under that horse. I cussed. I prayed. I rolled and moaned. It just didn't do any good. I was stuck. Pretty soon the sun would set and it was going to get plenty cold. If I stopped moving I would freeze. I wondered how long it would be before Wrangler missed me and came looking. There was an awful lot of country I could be in besides where I was.

It was not a nice place to be. I was ashamed to be found in such a position even if I died. It took about four or five days for the sun to set. The cockeyed coyotes started howling. I always kind of liked to hear this noise before, but now it was an unpleasant sound. I could see a lot of stars up above but I didn't consider them very pretty. I kept moving my arms and tried not to think about sleep. I knew damn well I had to stay awake and moving or else join a lot of other good cowboys in another camp. I didn't know what time of night it was, but a hell of a lot of owls had hooted and gone to roost.

For a minute or two I was sort of discouraged with the carefree life of a cowboy. What had ever made me take up this calling anyway, that could put a man out here by himself in the mountains on a cold winter night with a dead horse for a blanket?

Seems like the first thing I could remember was Pa leading me around on an old ranch horse of his called Shorty. I wasn't old enough to go to the toilet by myself but I was old enough to get up on that horse. I reckon that's what you call being born in the saddle. A few years later I remember Pa telling me I looked like a big fat wash-woman the way I was getting on my horse.

"Look here," he said, "get that mane and reins in your left hand and the reins and the saddle horn in your right and stick your left knee in that horse's shoulder. This way he's got to turn toward you when he moves out—otherwise he'll turn away from you and kick your belly button off."

Later on: "Good Lord, boy, don't you know better than to put your spur buckles on the inside of your boots? You're really asking for trouble that way. Keep them buckles on the outside so they can't get hung in the riggin'. . . . Look at that leather thong holdin' the top of your chaps together. Why, that's way too strong. What if you was to get throwed up over the saddle horn and that leather wouldn't break? Why, that horse would buck you to death. . . . Here, boy, don't never get on a horse without untracking him. You can tell a whole lot about what mood a horse is in just by untracking him. . . ."

Day after day, year after year, it seemed like all I got was an ass-chewing.

"Here, boy, you gone crazy? Don't never get down off a horse when he's drinkin'. He'll run backward with you every time. Keep your left trigger finger between the reins. You can handle a horse better that way and have the feel of every move he makes. . . . Man alive, boy, you are goin' to lose your catch rope. Don't you know to never put less than three wraps around your rope with the horn string? If you don't, your rope will come loose and fall under your horse."

It never let up.

Then I remembered one morning in particular when I was riding with Pa. It was a good day. We had plenty of rain on our little two-by-four outfit. The green grass was pushing up out of the ground thick and fast. The cows were full and lay around in the sun chewing their cuds. The tongue marks in their thick hair showed they had been licking themselves—a sure sign they were doing good.

The calves reminded me of a bunch of kittens, the way they jumped around playing. Their faces were clean and pure white compared to the darker, grass-stained ones of the mother cows.

Out of pure habit, Pa counted the cows and said, "That ole muley cow, the one that went dry, is missin'."

I looked at him and said, "Maybe she's in the bog."

"No, it ain't likely," Pa said, "since we fixed that good pole fence around it."

"Yeah," I said, "but you know how that old black cow was we used to have? She'd tear down the fence just to get hung up in the bog."

"Well, we'll ride over and see," Pa said.

Riding over to look at the bog I was feeling kind of proud of Pa in spite of all the eating-outs he had given me, and I was remembering some of the things he had taught me.

I had finally learned when driving a bunch of cows to tell if one really meant to bolt the herd or was just running a bluff. This saves lots of wear and tear on both horses and cowboys.

I knew when unsaddling a horse to always undo the flank cinch first. Otherwise I might forget and pull the saddle off with the flank cinch still buckled. When that happens a horse was sure to buck and kick the saddle to pieces. I knew that a horse should work with his head down close to his withers for best results. A high-headed horse blocks a cowboy's view and is a shame on any working cow ranch. I had been taught all this and a hell of a lot more.

"Look, Pa," I yelled, "I told you that old cow was in the bog."

We pulled out to where she had knocked the poles down. The cow was struggling deep in the mud, sinking inch by inch as she strained.

"Now, don't that beat you," said Pa. "All this green grass out here and the old son of a bitch breaks in there to get a bite of grass she ain't supposed to have."

Pa took down his rope and spurred up as close as he could, just out of the mud. He tied one end to the saddle horn and took the coils in his left hand and the loop in his right.

"Sure wish she had horns," he said. "This is goin' to be rough on the old fool. I'll have to rope her around the neck, and that's goin' to choke her."

Pa whirled the loop. It floated out and circled around the cow's neck. He jerked the slack and spurred old Shorty away from the bog. The rope tightened. Shorty lowered his head and lunged against the rope. Still the old cow was stuck tighter than a new boot on a big-footed kid. Her eyes bulged as the rope pulled tighter. Shorty hit the rope again, hard and steady.

The old muley cow struggled. Her breath was grinding in bursts out her nostrils. Then she was out six inches, then to her belly, then her hocks. At last she was on dry ground.

I spurred up and threw a loop at her heels. I missed.

Pa turned back, dragging the cow, and yelled at me: "Here now, boy, use a slow loop. A fast loop is no good for heelin', except in a rodeo arena."

The next time I caught. We spurred in opposite directions. The old cow stretched out flat on the ground. Pa rode up to give the rope slack around her neck. I kept mine tight. Pa jumped down and took the rope off the cow's neck. He yelled, "Give me slack, boy!" I spurred up. He jerked the rope off the cow's heels. She got up and made a run at Pa before he could get to his horse. But I was watching and rode between them, heading her out toward the rest of the herd.

We fixed the pole up and rode back toward the ranch house with me wondering why that old cow was so mad because we had saved her life.

Well sir, while I was laying there thinking back about these things and telling myself what a fool I had been to ever learn anything at all about horses, the night wore on. But it didn't warm up any. My arms were getting kind of tired from slinging them around, and it seemed like from my ass down I was already froze solid to the ground.

It might have been all right just to be a plain old cowboy, but to be a horse breaker along with it was the sad mistake. If I hadn't of showed off back there on the Diamond-2 that day when I was just a big-butted kid, maybe it would have been easier.

An old blue horse had unloaded Cliff Hadley, the top rider for the Diamond-2. He came limping back up to the corrals where the blue stood and waited for him. It was sure griping Cliff to take that walk. Besides, we all stood and watched him coming. Finally he got close enough so we could hear him talking.

"Lead that son of a bitch out in the corral. I'm goin' to feed him a bellyful of steel." Hadley didn't last past the third jump. The blue went up, turned sideways and sucked back in a spine-twisting, gut-jarring leap that drove Cliff face first into the corral dust. Now, Cliff was a bronc rider and he got right back on. First his hat went, then he lost a stirrup, then off he sailed again, whomping into the ground like a sack of wet meal.

"When a horse can buck my hat off, cain't no man ride him," he said.

Well, I just couldn't help but have a try at it. At first the blue walked around easy and gentle-like, reining good—something like Old Fooler. Then he ducked his head low, squealed like a schoolgirl running through the brush, and leaped right straight up with all four legs in the air. He came down with his legs like four wooden stilts. The jar loosened every bone in my body. The next jump my hat went, then a stirrup. I was pulling that saddle horn out by the roots. Somehow I got the stirrup back. Then he flew high and to the right, and as his front legs hit the ground his hind end swung around in an arc. Then he went into a long straight forward leap, kicking back hard. At every kick I felt my head snap back. I was sure my neck was broke in at least ten places. I held on to the horn, jamming my right elbow down over my right hipbone. Just as I knew my insides were squeezing out between my ribs and every joint was ground to powder, I felt him weaken. The blue was squealing like a dying rabbit and all I could see was a flash of mane and I was thinking that I was setting right up on the tip end of a blue tornado.

He hadn't weakened much. Everything started looking gray as my head was flung back harder and harder. I didn't know it right then, but a long streamer of bright red was running down out of my nose and across my shoulder. Then the blue roan slowed fast. With all my might I swung the spurs out and into his belly. He was slowing and I was sitting solid in the saddle. I could see his neck now and out of the corner of my eyes the corrals and the cowboys standing there yelling. Then it was over.

I crawled down all weak and wobbly but I tried not to let anybody know it. The blue roan was plumb black with sweat and stood spread-legged with his head down, breathing hard. He was beat.

When the boys began to tell me what a ride I'd made I said, feeling kind of smart-like, "All you got to do is keep them between your legs."

Well, I've only got hold of one horse since that could buck as hard —another roan it was. That bastard of an Old Fooler is the one I mean. From that day on, the word spread and I always drew the rough string. Oh, for the life of a cowboy!

It seemed like it had been around two or three years since that bay had rolled on top of me. I wiggled my arms and hands every once in a while. There wasn't a whole lot of feeling left in them.

The stars were gone and over there somewhere the sun was making a stab at coming up. If I could just last till it got high enough to thaw me out, Old Wrangler might accidentally find me. There wasn't much of a chance, but it was all I had to keep me company.

Well, the sun came up and I couldn't hold my eyes open any longer. I just let them shut and away I went. It was late that afternoon when Old Wrangler found me. He was riding his favorite black and leading Old Fooler. It had been Old Fooler that had thrown his head up and kept looking through the thick brush toward the opening where I was taking it easy. Wrangler told me all this later while he was tying a splint around my right leg. He made it from some boards out of the floor of our shack. But when he woke me up and told me he was going to drag that bay off me, all I could see was the horse he had brought for me to ride home on.

"Why, you dirty bastard," I said, "if you ain't a good friend bringin' that outlawed son of a bitch with you. Hell's fire, just leave me here!"

EIGHT

I KEPT THAT BUSTED LEG propped up in front of the fire most of the time. It had been about ten days since Wrangler had tied the splints around it. A piece of cowhide covered the hole in the floor where he had torn up the boards to make the splints. I was setting there looking at that hide, thinking that old Wrangler was having all the fun. He had gathered three dry cows and a lone yearling all by himself since I got fouled up.

"Wrangler," I said, "do you reckon Jim Ed will take it out of my pay for shooting that bay horse?"

"You know goddam well he will," Wrangler answered.

"If he does I'm goin' to tell him to go to hell with a downhill run. I'm goin' to quit the JL and go get me a job wranglin' dudes," I said.

"You better think a long time about that," said Wrangler.

"About what?" I asked.

"About wranglin' dudes. Remember what happened to me?"

"Yeah," I said, "that *is* right. Well then, maybe I can do like you said you was gonna do. Get me a job in a gas station."

Setting around with this busted leg gave me the gripes, so I lit in on Jim Ed.

"Now, Wrangler, I think I *will* quit this outfit, anyway. All the other hands got to make the fall roundup. We didn't. They ride the gentle, easy workin' horses me and you break out. And what do we ride?" I asked. "Nothing but the rough string. I can't remember when I've rode anything but a bunch of outlawed horses."

"That's the way it is," Wrangler said.

"I bet you the other hands have been into town two or three times a month, and here we set down here a half mile from hell and thirty-five miles from town. It just ain't right," I griped. "Now, it ain't long till Christmas. Ever'body else will be in Hi Lo havin' a big turkey dinner and passin' out presents and havin' themselves a sure-enough fine time. Do you think Jim Ed Love will give a damn about us settin' off down here all by ourselves? Hell, no! Then New Years there'll be a big dance and lots of good music to go with it. I bet Jim Ed gives all the rest of the hands a whole week off."

"Yep," said Wrangler.

"Besides," I went on, "that Jim Ed Love is the meanest bastard in nine counties. I'll bet half my wages he charges me forty dollars for that bay horse."

"More than that, I reckon," said Wrangler.

I wished Wrangler hadn't of said that. It upset me somewhat. "Well, if he does he just lost a horse breaker for good. Can you imagine a man that would charge a cowboy for killin' a horse in the line of duty?"

"Well," said Wrangler, "there ain't many cowboys kills a good, well-broke horse by shootin' his brains out in a dead run."

I reached for a piece of stove-wood, planning to knock Wrangler in the head. Then I got to thinking about what a good cook he was and let it go.

"This is the coldest goddam winter I ever saw," I said. "And the longest. Seems to me like we been down here for a whole year already."

"Been quite a spell," said Wrangler, and shoved a pan of sourdough in the oven.

"I had rather live like a blanket-ass Indian than the way we are livin'," I said.

"Did I ever tell you that I was part Indian?" asked Wrangler, setting down and rolling a Bull Durham.

I could see he was about to go over his two-grunt and one-sentence limit. "Everybody I ever talked to," I said, "claims to be part Indian."

"Them Indians gets around," he said. "It was my grandpa that was full blood," he added.

"How much does that make you?" I asked.

"I don't know," he said. "I have tried to figure it fifty times but it's just too much addin' and subtractin' for me. He was married to a squaw as big and fat as that Toy Smith woman I was tellin' you about. Seems like us Lewis folks always draw fat women. You think this is a cold winter," Wrangler said. "Let me tell you about the one my grandpa spent in Montana."

I could tell Old Wrangler was fixing to bear down on some wild-eyed story. So I looked up like I just couldn't wait to hear it. "Grandpa was just a young buck then. A hunter. It was in a February, and Grandpa, three more bucks, and a squaw was camped out huntin' game for the rest of the tribe. Grandpa said this buck's squaw was a way fatter than his old woman. In fact, he said she was the fattest woman he ever saw. The reason was that she was an expert skinner—they had her along to skin the animals—and she was always sneaking tastes of raw meat. Claimed she could tell if it was goin' to make good jerky or not that way. She and her Indian was in one tepee and Grandpa and the other Indians was in another."

Wrangler was really warming up now. "Talk about a winter. They hadn't no sooner got set than the snow commenced to fall. It set in and snowed two foot the first day and it never stopped. Pretty soon they had eaten up all the grub they had brought along and they commenced to get a little lank in the middle. It just kept gettin' worse. Grandpa said his belly was as thin as a well-honed knife blade and it looked like they were done for.

"Finally they got to thinkin' about that fat squaw over in the other tepee. Ever' once in a while they would break out and go over and take a look at her. The snow was so deep they could climb right up and look down in the tepee from the top. Grandpa said that old squaw was sure doing good. She was like a hibernatin' bear—enough fat to last her a long time.

"Now her buck was in bad shape but he thought a lot of this squaw. After Grandpa spent about thirty minutes just lookin' down in that tepee with his mouth waterin', the buck looked up and saw him. He decided to slip his squaw out of camp, snow or no snow. Grandpa and the other buck were watchin, though, and they hadn't hardly left when Grandpa was after them. It was hard goin' in all that fresh snow, and they were so weak they could hardly walk."

"Did they catch 'em?" I asked, getting pretty interested in the outcome of this story about Wrangler's ancestors.

"Well," said Wrangler, "you see, the squaw's husband was just as weak as Grandpa, and the squaw wouldn't walk off and leave him."

"Yeah, but what I want to know is, did they catch 'em?"

"Wait a minute," said Wrangler. "Let me tell you. Grandpa and his runnin' mates took a shortcut, figgerin' just about where they would come together."

I couldn't wait any longer if I had to get up and throw Wrangler through the wall. "Goddammit, did they *catch* 'em?"

"Yeah, they sure did," he said. "Grandpa had figgered it just right. They all met in a little openin' with a lot of thick brush all around for a windbreak."

"What happened then?" I asked, feeling my sore leg starting to pound.

"Well, I don't rightly know. Grandpa wouldn't talk much about it but he did say that four sets of tracks came together in the fresh snow, and a few days later only three walked away."

"Oh," I said, feeling in the stomach something like I did every time I climbed on Old Fooler's back and also realizing that this present winter was a lot warmer than I'd thought.

"Wrangler, do you reckon if I was to catch that big red steer that Jim Ed might not charge me for killin' that bay horse?"

"Somethin' to study about," Wrangler said, not helping a bit.

"Why, that steer must weigh in the neighborhood of a thousand pounds," I said. "That's a lot of beef on the hoof."

I had already settled my mind to the fact that if I was going to catch that steer it would have to be on Old Fooler. It was an uneasy thought to live with.

Well, I sat around the fire and griped for a couple of more weeks. Christmas Day came around and we didn't have a decorated tree. We had run through them trees after wild stock until we couldn't stand the thought of having one in the house. But old Wrangler did the best he could. He took some dried apricots and cooked up the best-tasting pudding you ever wrapped your gums around. We butchered a beef and had us some steaks as thick as a two-by-four. It was all mighty good. We didn't give each other presents and we didn't sing carols, but we crawled in our bedrolls pretty well pleased all the same.

On New Year's Eve I couldn't sleep at all. Seems like I kept hearing that music all the way from Hi Lo, and I cussed Jim Ed till almost sunup.

My leg felt pretty good now, and I couldn't stand it any longer. Like I said, Wrangler was having all the fun. He was up in the hills somewhere when I took the splint off. It wasn't bad. I got Old Fooler up and decided I would take a ride out on the flats instead of up in the rocky country where he might fall on me.

I wasn't a mile from the shack when I saw this coyote watching me from behind a soapweed. Them two ears of his was sticking up like the back sights on a thirty-thirty. I rode along easy, keeping an eye on Old Fooler and the coyote both. I made out like I didn't see the coyote and kept riding in a circle—getting closer all the time. I had tried all my life to rope a coyote horseback but had never been on a horse fast enough to give him a loop. Once I almost caught one right after he gorged himself on a dead cow. He was so full I figured I would have caught him except that my horse stepped in a prairie-dog hole and rolled over about nine times. When I got to where I could see, the coyote was gone.

I started breathing harder the closer we got. Then all of a sudden I reined Old Fooler straight at him. I had already slipped the leather thong from around my rope. The coyote took off in a hard run, and Old Fooler really lit out after him. I shook a small loop out, knowing I would never be able to jerk the slack on a big one. The coyote was headed for some malpais breaks about a mile to the north and we were right on his tail.

For a while I didn't think Old Fooler was gaining; then I saw the coyote start switching his tail from side to side. That meant he was putting out all he had. Old Fooler must have known it too, because he laid his ears back and ran like a greyhound.

I could see them malpais breaks getting closer every heartbeat, and Old Fooler was gaining all the time. Then I could see the coyote glancing back and I whomped the spurs into Old Fooler's belly and there we were. This was it! There wouldn't be another chance. I leaned over and whipped that twine out and I saw the little loop lay right over that coyote's ears and across his nose. The coyote slung his head—and he was caught like a horse thief at a public hanging!

I rode right on by, and that coyote must have thought he was a big-ass bird because he sure did fly through the air. It wasn't near over yet. I still had to keep Old Fooler from taking off when I got down to kill the coyote. He sure surprised me. He worked that rope like a regular roping horse. I went up and took hold of the rope about three feet from the coyote and whirled him around in the air; then I brought him down hard. It didn't take but a minute more to stomp a boot heel into his ribs, and *that* coyote would never steal another chicken.

Old Fooler was snorting and raring back on the rope but he stayed put. I think the son of a bitch enjoyed it more than I did. For a minute, before I had time to reflect, I was real proud of Old Fooler. He had helped me do something I had wanted to do all my life. Something I had just about given up on.

Three or four days later I was riding Old Fooler along with Wrangler. We had just hit the foothills and I was bragging about catching that coyote. Wrangler wasn't saying word one. I'm not even sure he was listening.

Now, it ain't very often that a man can brag on a horse like Fooler. I had just said, "Wrangler, he worked that rope like the gentlest kid pony you ever saw. He may come out of it yet. What do you think?" Wrangler just humped up in the saddle and grunted. This was not his day for talking.

"Yes sir, wouldn't that be something if Old Fooler gentled down and turned into a lady's horse after all?"

About the time I said this a big bobcat jumped up out of a little clump of brush and loped across a clearing. You hardly ever see a bobcat in the daytime and you hardly see a cowboy try to rope one. But after the coyote I was what town folks call "flushed with victory." If I was going to be hung on my wedding day, I couldn't have helped myself. Undone came that rope. Untracked came Old Fooler. A bobcat ain't half as fast as a coyote. It wasn't ten jumps till Old Fooler had me right on him. Fellers, it was easy. I was getting to be quite a roper. I never saw a loop fit around anything so clean in all my life. Just like the coyote. I rode right on by him, spurring to beat hell.

Well, I learned one new thing then and there. A bobcat's neck is made out of rubber. When that cat hit the end of the rope he went up in the air all right, but it was straight at Old Fooler's hindquarters. He was yowling to beat hell and he must have sunk them claws plumb to the bone in Old Fooler's hind end because that horse snorted and started bawling and bucking at the same time. I never had much chance after that to check up on the bobcat. It was all I could do to stay on Old Fooler. He took off through the brush, then bucked through the middle of a bed of sharp rocks. He was looking for a big hole to jump in, and he didn't care where he found it. I figured right then that if I ever wanted to teach a bunch of rodeo horses to buck, I would hire me a pen full of bobcats to train them. There wouldn't be enough riders left in a month to put on a show anywhere.

The next thing I knew I felt something digging in my back. It felt like an eagle with claws six inches long, but it was that bobcat. I couldn't turn loose of the saddle horn to knock him off, and if I did I wasn't sure I could get the job done. About that time Old Fooler ran under a low-hanging limb. I didn't see this limb. I don't know if the bobcat did or not. I never had a chance to ask him because Old Fooler just kept going with that rope stringing out behind and that bobcat meowing on the other end. I kind of sat up and waited for the world to come to an end. About that time Wrangler spurred by. He was after Old Fooler, but it looked to me like he was going to laugh himself to death before he caught him.

I sat down, rolled a smoke, and waited. I could still hear the brush crackling and Wrangler hee-hawing up the other side of the mountain. I failed to see what was so goddam comical.

About half an hour later Wrangler came back. He was leading Old Fooler. That horse was in one hell of a shape. He was brush-marked all over, and that bobcat had dug furrows in his hind end that looked like a fresh-plowed field. It took some time to find out how Wrangler had caught him so quick. Every time he would start to tell me he would slap those little old chap-covered bowlegs of his and just plain howl with laughter. It was a disgrace the way he carried on.

Finally, though, he told me. "Old Fooler ran that rope through a big forked stump. The fork was too narrow for the bobcat to get through."

"Oh," I said. "Didn't you bring the hide back with you? A bobcat hide is worth about ten dollars."

"Not this bobcat hide," he said. "There ain't a place on it the daylight wouldn't show through."

Well, we went on trying to gather more cattle. They were getting few and far between now. The wind was still blowing, but it wasn't near as cold. The drifts had started melting up around the rimrocks. And every once in a while in an out-of-the-wind spot we could see a few sprigs of green grass. The stock had scattered out all over hell trying to run down a decent bite or two. It made it hard to find them.

One day I was mounted on Old Fooler and riding by myself. Somehow me and Wrangler had got separated while tracking through the rocks. It was snowing a wet, cold snow up high, but down in the lower breaks it was drizzling a fine rain. I was really hunting for the big red steer, hoping I might make up for killing that good bay horse. I couldn't hardly stand the thought of all the ribbing I was going to get about that.

Then I jumped him—or rather Old Fooler jumped him. I felt him leap out and I thought, *Here we go again.* While I was gathering in the saddle horn I saw that Old Fooler had headed the steer downhill and that there wasn't anything but a few little patches of cedar between us and the flats. Now, I want to say here and now that I have rode some fairly rough country and some damn fast horses, but the way Old Fooler built to that steer would have made the greatest racehorse man in the world just jump right straight up and holler till he keeled over in a dead faint.

I got that rope down and shook me out a great big Mother Hubbard loop and it wasn't but a minute till I was almost close enough to throw. That loop looked like it never would settle down, but when it did that steer was in it!

I'd waited a long time for this. I put them spurs to Old Fooler and he went by that steer like it was standing still. I threw a trip on the way by. That is, I pitched the rope over on the steer's right side, wrapped it around and under his tail. When the slack came out of the rope with all of us going at full speed, there was a stack-up to remember. That steer was whipped around and up. When he came down it looked like he was trying to go to China headfirst. He got up shaking his head and turned back for the hills. Me and Old Fooler repeated the performance twice more. By then that steer was ready to go horn the devil, but he sure didn't want any more trouble out of *us*. We headed him for the gathering pasture at lower camp in a long trot with the catch rope still tied between us.

Now I was really proud of Old Fooler. I was a little proud of the way I had been roping lately, too. Sometimes you go for a month and no matter how hard you try, you just can't make that loop fit over anything. Either a figure eight comes in your loop or you hang it on a limb or just plain miss. But the last few times I'd thrown it, something would run its head into the circle.

It was a great day. Now maybe old Jim Ed wouldn't be so mad over me killing that bay horse. The rain was getting heavier. The lightning and thunder were really mixing it up. The ground turned slick as owl grease and shone like a big mirror every time the lightning flashed. That old steer was running along out ahead of us with his head down, his tongue lolled out to one side, slobbering like a mad dog. Me and Old Fooler came sliding along behind. *Let 'er rain,* I thought.

Finally we hit the gathering pasture fence and were only about a quarter of a mile from the gate. I was feeling mighty good. Then one of them bolts of lightning knifed down and hit the fence right between us and the steer. Blue sparks shot out in every direction, and when they bounced off my boots it felt like my legs had been pulled out by the roots. The steer went down, Fooler went down, and I went down with him. I was dizzy as hell but managed to stand up.

For a minute I thought Old Fooler was dead, but when I kicked him in the side he struggled to his feet. The wires along the fence were melted in two, and one post was black and splintered. That steer's horns were split like a drunk Apache had been swinging at them with a chopping ax. He was stone dead.

It was a long wet ride into lower camp, even if it was just three quarters of a mile. But as the feller said in the song, "Spring is just around the corner."

NINE

THE GREEN GRASS came up in bigger patches. The wild stock up in the hills was pretty thin, and they ran off a lot more weight chasing after the green stuff. A really hard blizzard this time of year could have killed a lot of cattle, but it didn't come. What we had caught and held down in the gathering pasture was in good shape. The thick cured grass in the subirrigated pasture had kept them in the winter, and there was lots of green stuff mixed with it now. The long hair was shedding off in patches. The horses were shed off almost slick and had begun to pick up weight.

The snowbanks up high melted during the day and became smaller all the time. Me and Wrangler had rode all day without jumping a thing. We were still about five miles from camp when we stopped to water our horses at a big spring. I kept spurring Old Fooler up to the edge and he kept running backward. It had been a long hard ride and I just knew the old rascal was thirsty.

"What in the hell is the matter with you now?" I said as I jabbed at him again.

Wrangler's horse had his head down drinking long and deep. I hit Old Fooler with the spurs again. Now, this spring was still iced over just a little bit from the cold nights. Old Fooler let out a snort you could have heard all the way to Hi Lo, and jumped right out into the middle of the pond. I have had horses do a lot of things with me, but this was something new.

He went under and I went under with him. Then I came up and he came up, choking and strangling. He went down again. By then I was out of the saddle but still holding onto the saddle horn. The third time he went down I quit him. If I was going to drown I was going to do it my own way. Old Fooler came pawing at the thin ice and snorting water out of both nostrils. It looked like a windmill with twin pipes

running wide open in a high wind. There was only one thing wrong. I
can't swim. I kept going down and coming up, pawing just like Old
Fooler at the thin edge of ice. It kept breaking off. I thought, *What a
hell of a way for a cowboy to cash in his chips.*

Then Wrangler roped me. It was not a clean loop. It went around
my neck and down under one arm. He turned around and spurred off
like he was trying to jerk down a yearling bull. I came out of there like
a catfish hooked right in the jaw. He drug me a ways before he turned
around and let some slack in the rope.

I yelled, "God a'mighty, stop! I'd rather drown than be drug to
death!"

Now, spring was easing up on us, but the middle of it was not here
yet. That ride home that evening after the sun had set was not one of
great comfort. The wind wasn't blowing too hard, but as wet as I was I
could have felt the breath of a prairie dog from twenty feet under-
ground.

I said, "Well, this son of a bitch has now tried everything in the
world to kill me. He has run through corrals, barbwire fences, jumped
off a bluff, rolled over me, kicked me in the belly, bit me in the back,
run me into a tree, bucked me off and left me afoot, and now he's
tried to drown me! You know what I am goin' to do to this dirty
bastard, Wrangler? I am goin' to take him into town and sell him to a
soap factory. Then I am goin' to buy the first bar of soap they make
out of him. I am goin' to waller around in cow-shit for a week. Then I
am goin' to bathe with that dirty son of a bitch. And ever' time I wash
my hands from then on I am goin' to laugh like hell. That's what I'm
goin' to do."

By the time we got into camp my clothes was froze so stiff I couldn't
hardly get off of Old Fooler. I walked up to the house as stiff-legged as
a man with the jake-leg. I had not enjoyed the afternoon, and I meant
what I said about selling that terrible horse to a soap factory. If I had
to go to work for the company myself.

When I was about half thawed out, Wrangler asked a stupid question. "How you feelin'?" he asked.

I said, "I feel just like that old boy that had been sleepin' out under
the chuck wagon durin' a rainy spell: 'I am tired, wet, and hungry,
busted, disgusted, and can't be trusted.' " There was more to this but
Wrangler don't hold with dirty words.

It was hard to believe, but spring did come. Everything turned
green and started growing. The does was having fawns, the coyotes

was having pups, the cows was having calves, and me and Wrangler was about to start having fits if the Fourth of July didn't hurry and roll around. We gathered the winter's catch in and branded all the new calves. Then we counted our gather. A hundred head in all! Lord-a-mercy, a five-hundred-dollar bonus and all that back pay coming!

"Wrangler, we will go to town and celebrate gettin' rid of Old Fooler for a month," I said.

"That horse belongs to Jim Ed Love," Wrangler said, lowering my spirits.

"I will buy him if it takes half of what I've got," I said.

"You cain't let him know you want him," said Wrangler. "If the cheap bastard knew that, there ain't enough money in New Mexico could buy him."

"I won't let him know," I said. At the same time I was wondering how I was going to explain about shooting that bay horse.

Everything seemed to be coming out of the ground, even the snakes. I was riding out among our gather on a little sorrel gelding when he snorted and jumped sideways. It was a rattlesnake. He was behaving kind of funny. Then I saw what was going on. There was a rat squatting, paralyzed, not six inches from his hole in the ground. That snake was looking him straight in the eye. The rat wasn't moving. He was hypnotized.

At first I didn't think the snake was moving either. Then I saw he was. You couldn't actually see it—it was like the way the wind blows. You can feel it but can't see it. After a long time he was real near the rat. Then with a quick dart he had him. That rat came un-hypnotized long enough to make one squeak, and that was all.

I got down and picked up a big stick. The snake dropped the dead rat and coiled, sticking that little black forked tongue in and out at me, and shaking his tail a mile a minute. I had a hard time holding my horse and killing that snake at the same time, but I did.

I rode on down to the pasture. One big old cow stood with her head down, her jaw swelled twice its regular size. That snake had bit her. She was breathing hard in the warm June sun, and I knew if I didn't do something quick the swelling would choke her to death. I fit a loop around her horns, got down and pulled out my knife. That old cow made one run sideways against the rope and then stopped. Seems like she knew she was a goner if I didn't do something for her. I opened the knife blade wide. Then I cut deep. The blood spurted out all green and black. By the time I got the rope off her the blood was running red and I knew she would live. Not everything that comes up in the spring is all to the good, I decided.

I rode on out and made another count of the cattle. The little calves were getting plenty of milk from their mothers and were gaining weight and feeling good. I reckon the prettiest sight in the world is a young calf when its mother is giving lots of milk. As long as me and Wrangler had been away from town, though, I imagine a woman would have run a mighty close contest with the calves. Any woman!

It was getting to where I couldn't hardly sleep at night for thinking about it. And lots of times while I lay awake in my bedroll I could hear Wrangler murmuring, "Irene. Irene." That little potbellied bastard had never told me about any Irene. I never asked him, either, because that was probably the one he had really cared about.

Well, it didn't get any better. I was craving to get into town so bad I could feel it plumb to my toenails.

I wanted me and Wrangler to get bathed and shaved, get us some women, get drunk, get in the rodeo on the Fourth, and last but not even close to least, get that goddam Fooler horse to that soap factory.

It was the twenty-eighth day of June and I was telling Wrangler, "Here we've come down here and spent a hell of a long winter makin' the best gather on this wild stock anybody ever made. We've made Jim Ed a lot richer, and now look what he's doin' to us. If he don't send some cowboys on down here to help us move this stuff into headquarters, I'm just goin' to turn 'em all loose back in the hills."

Now Wrangler knew I wasn't going to do this, and I knew I wasn't. We had to have that bonus and that paycheck or there wouldn't be no Fourth of July as far as we were concerned. Just the same my nerves was cracking and popping like a stick of frozen wood in a hot fire.

Then three hands rode up. If seventeen angels from heaven had stopped by for supper and each one of them had donated a pot full of gold for the Fourth of July, I couldn't of been any happier to see them. All the same, Jim Ed had squeezed every damn hour of time out of us he could. The least little thing and I was going to quit this chicken outfit. And I meant it, just like I meant about Old Fooler and the soap.

Well, we got the horses in and packed the mules and gathered the stock and started moving the herd toward headquarters.

I told one of the hands, "It's a good thing you boys showed up when you did because me and old Wrangler just had one catch rope left between us, and we would have had one hell of a fight to see which one got to use it to hang himself with."

I was in charge of the herd, so I worked it so that we moved past
Vince Moore's outfit too late for breakfast and too early for lunch. I
didn't feel like discussing Old Fooler in front of the other cowboys.
The herd moved slow because we had so many young calves that tired
easy on us. We spent half the time carrying them on the swells of our
saddles. Two and a half days later I could see the big gate into headquarters. A horseback rider was setting there waiting.

I rode over by Wrangler and said, "Now take three guesses who
that is up there waitin'."

Wrangler looked through them little pig eyes of his, humped his
shoulders, and kind of scrooched his rump around in the saddle.
"Why, I bet it's Santie Claus," he said, "just sittin' out there waitin' to
pay us our bonus."

"That's right," I said. "Jim Ed Santie Claus Love."

Jim Ed reined back from the gate a ways, and I could see his hand
moving up and down as he counted the cows and horses coming
through. Now I had already made a bet with myself about what his
first words would be. I was right.

"Hello, boys. Have a good winter?" And then, "Where's my bay
horse?"

I didn't answer right away. I didn't want the other hands to hear. I
told him we'd had a fine pleasant winter. No trouble a tall. The horses
was broke out nice and gentle and we had made a good gather on the
wild stuff.

"Where's my bay?" he asked again.

I told him about how we had only lost one head of stock and the
lightning did that.

"Seems to me," he said, "that roan horse is scarred up somewhat
worse than he was last fall."

"Oh, we had a little trouble with him," I said. "He's the sorriest son
of a bitch I ever saw in my life. He ain't fit for nothin'—can't run, and
won't work a rope," I lied.

"Can he buck?" Jim Ed asked. But before I could answer that question he hit me with another. "Where's my bay horse?" It was like an
obsession, as they say.

I couldn't dodge it any longer. So I told him. He didn't say a word,
but one of the other hands heard and yelled ahead to the others. They
were all laughing. Even the cows was laughing. I could swear every
damn one of them had a big grin on its face, baby calves, bulls, steers,
and all.

Well, Jim Ed had crowded me just as far as he was going to. Just one more little thing and I was through.

We got on into headquarters, and just as nice as pie Jim Ed says, "Go get cleaned up. I know you boys will be wanting to head for town and the Fourth of July celebration."

Wrangler snorted through his flat nose.

Jim Ed went on: "Soon as you're all cleaned up come over to the house and I'll pay you off. You boys are going to need a little money over the Fourth."

The way he said it he made it sound like he was doing us the biggest favor on earth. We got all shaved and cleaned up slick as a judge on election day. Then we went over to see his highness.

"Come in, boys," he shouted. "Come on in here and set down. Amantha," he yelled out into the kitchen, "bring us that bottle of whisky out of the cupboard."

Mrs. Amantha Love came in speaking to us like she wished to hell we would get out of her house and not track it up. I kept looking down at my boots to see if I had left any cow dung on them.

Jim Ed poured us a nice stiff drink. We downed her, then he let us have it. He picked up the money and said, "Now, boys, in all I owe you a five-hundred-dollar bonus. Five dollars a head for every one you gathered. Right?"

"That's right," I said. "What about the calves that was born this spring?"

Old Wrangler wiggled around on the edge of his chair trying to get his bowlegs on the floor.

"Well, now, that wasn't part of our deal."

"We gathered them," I said. "They was right there in their mother's bellies when we penned them."

"It ain't quite the same thing," said Jim Ed. "There wasn't no trouble a tall to them calves. They just went along for the ride and there wasn't a damn thing they could do about it."

Well, I thought, *there went an extra hundred or so dollars.* Now where was the next cut coming from?

"I figured that bay horse was the best horse in the bunch," Jim Ed said. "He was worth at least sixty dollars." So, then and there Jim Ed counted sixty dollars out of our pile.

"That's it!" I said. "That does it! I quit! You can take the JL and shove it all the way back to that sorry Andrews, Texas, ranch you're always braggin' about owning. What about you, Wrangler?" I gathered up our money.

"Whatever suits you," he said, "just tickles me plumb to death."

Just as we hit the door, Jim Ed said, "Wait a minute, boys. I am goin' to give you that good Old Fooler horse in the place of that sixty dollars."

Well, I was so damn mad I was halfway to the bunkhouse before this soaked in on me. At least I would have the pleasure of getting even with that outlawed son of a bitch.

We threw our bedrolls and war bags in the old pickup. Then we loaded Old Fooler and jumped in. The goddam battery was dead! We had to push to beat hell to get it going downhill before it would start.

Jim Ed was standing on the porch waving and grinning like a cat eating a whole pile of it. He had a look on his face like he knew something we didn't.

I gave that old pickup all the gas she could take, and we went barreling out of there headed for Hi Lo, New Mexico. I wanted to get as far away from Jim Ed Love and the JL just as fast as I could. I knew Wrangler felt exactly the same.

TEN

WRANGLER HUMPED UP over that steering wheel, frowning fierce over the top of it like he was fixing to pull the trigger on something or other. He sat on the edge of the seat so his crooked legs could reach the gas pedal. His little potgut lay out in his lap.

"Wrangler," I said, "have you ever seen anything like that Jim Ed?"

Wrangler grunted.

"I cannot think of one single goddam thing in his favor," I went on.

Wrangler grunted.

"He is without a doubt the lowest-life son of a bitch in the world."

Wrangler grunted and stepped on the gas. The old pickup jerked and sputtered. Then she took hold and we really started to put ground between us and the JL.

About eight or ten miles off I could see the little Mexican village of Sano. It stuck right up out of the ground like a bunch of little square mud mountains. The adobe houses looked kind of lonesome and dried out from where we was.

I knew my good friend Telio Cruz ran one of those places just made to cure the thirst of dry-throated cowboys.

"Faster," I said to Wrangler.

"That's all she'll do," he said.

Sano crept closer, and I could see the rocky foothills beyond where in the old days a bunch of gold mines had operated. And on past that about a hundred miles I could see a long blue stretch of mountains. I figured that me and Wrangler could find an outfit over there that would appreciate a couple of dumb cowboys like us. Maybe we could get a half-decent job over there. Anyway, as soon as the Fourth of July was over we would sure as hell find out.

"God a'mighty, Wrangler, I'm goin' to die of thirst before we get to

Telio's. Can't you speed this cockeyed heap up? If I didn't hate to walk so bad, I would just bail out of here and save time."

"If you're in such a big hurry," said Wrangler, "why don't you ride Old Fooler?"

I said, "I had just as soon have my head tied up in a sack full of feverish rattlesnakes! But even that would be better than dying of thirst."

Well sir, it seemed like forever but we finally got there. I spotted old Telio looking through a dirty window to see who was driving up. Wrangler pulled the pickup on around past the one gas pump and let her coast to a stop. The brakes needed adjusting or something, so he didn't have much choice.

Telio met us at the door, grinning out of that big fat face of his and smoothing his long black hair. When Telio smiled it was like a whorehouse chandelier. He must of had fifty teeth on the top side alone. Now, Telio ain't what you would call stupid. He could see that we was all cleaned up and he knew that meant we was going to the Fourth of July in Hi Lo. It also meant we had a pocket full of back pay.

"Come in, friends," he said, smiling like a million watts. "Long time no see. Welcome home. The first drink is on Telio."

While he was pouring her out I smelled that bar like a bird dog smells a covey of quail. It smelled like as much beer, wine, and some little whisky had been spilled as had ever been drunk. It made my eyes sort of glaze over. Wrangler was stretching up as high as he could, trying to get his elbows comfortable on the bar. For a minute I thought he was going to jump right on over and help himself.

"How about a double shot to start with?" asked Telio.

"That's mighty nice of you, Telio," I said, knowing how little business he had.

"How did you boys winter?"

"Well, I reckon we wintered mighty fine," I said, not wanting to spoil the mood of things.

"How's Jim Ed?" he asked.

Me and Wrangler didn't answer but just throwed our heads back and downed that double shot. Well, it burned somewhat going down and settled in my belly like a hot rock in a cold pond. My eyes smarted, and the naked girl on the beer calendar hanging behind the bar kind of blurred. Then things straightened up and got better.

"Give us another one," I said.

Down she went like a bolt off a tall windmill.

"Give that old boy over there a drink," Wrangler said, pointing to an old white-headed wino sitting in one of the high-backed booths across the room.

"Yeah, and another all around—only this time make it water on the side," I said.

The old man got up and walked over. He had a big hump on his back and his eyes was just oozing Dago red.

"He don't drink nothing but wine," said Telio.

"Give him all he wants," I said.

The old man smiled at us and without a word downed the whole glass. Then, polite-like, he nodded about five times, saying, "Gracias, señors, gracias."

Well sir, things got better all the time. I got to telling Telio what a great horse that was out there in the pickup, and he let me rave on for a while.

Then he went out and looked at him and said, "Shorty Wilson over at Hi Lo buys outlaws like that for fifteen dollars apiece."

This kind of set me back on my hunkers, but I asked, "What does he do with them?"

"He sells them to the dog food company up in Colorado."

"That's it!" I yelled. "Wrangler, did you hear that! That's a whole lot better than soap. I am goin' to sell him to them dog food people and buy the first can made out of him and feed that son of a bitch to the mangiest old cur of a hound dog I can find."

This made me feel so good that I sang out, "Give everybody in the house another drink."

Now somehow or other you can start a party in one of these Mexican bars with nobody around but the bartender, and pretty soon everybody in town is there. We now had six people in tow. Five Mexican-Americans and an Apache Indian, also a gringo salesman we didn't count.

Everybody kind of slipped up to the bar, and the first thing you know Telio was washing glasses just as fast as he could fill them up, and there was wine and beer running all over the cracks in the bar. Telio would take a quick swipe at it and grab up a bunch of empty glasses. Before he could get that bunch clean, we was hollering for a refill. Pretty soon he joined in by taking a drink now and then himself. Then he threw the bar towel on the floor and just left the same glasses out on the bar top. He was short on water anyhow, seeing as how it took so much for me and Wrangler to wash down his cheap whisky.

Now, I'm telling you this place really filled up fast from there on in. I never saw so many amigos in all my life. And that's what they called us—shaking hands about every two or three seconds until I felt like my arm was going to fall right off. The old wino had gone over and fell asleep in one of the booths. Every once in a while he would raise his head, mumble something, and go right back to sleep.

Then this long tall old gringo with more whiskers than a porcupine has quills got me off to himself and started telling me about his gold mine.

He said, "Looky here." And sure enough, there in a little bottle was a half-dozen nuggets of gold about the size of a shriveled-up piñon nut. "I know where there is a vein of this ten feet wide," he said. "It assays eight hundred dollars to the ton in gold and one hundred and ninety dollars in silver."

"Well, I'll be damned," I said, trying to add this up in my mind. I didn't have any luck—just too many zeros at one time.

He looked at me out of little bitty watery blue eyes and pulled his greasy hat loose from around his ears and started bearing down on me.

"Them old-timers didn't have any modern machinery, and when they got to a vein like this they would all go crazy anyway. I know personally of twenty-five men killed over this very vein of gold. I am the only one left that knows about it."

"Well, I'll be damned," I said.

"All I need to bring out ten tons a day is some good powder, drill steel, and enough money to hire two good miners for a week. And of course some grub and hay for the burros. Do you realize how much profit a day that would be at ten tons?"

"Well—" I started to answer.

"Well," he interrupted, getting kind of excited-like, "let's figure it at only five tons. Let's be conservative. 'Course a vein that wide," he said, "you can really break a lot of rock. Figure it up," he insisted, looking me in the eye and breathing like a sheepherder at a beauty contest.

"It's a whole lot," I said, trying not to appear ignorant. "How much money would it take?"

"A hundred dollars," he said, "and half the profit's yours."

I got that hundred dollars out so fast you would have thought it was a tarantula in my pocket instead of cash.

"Here," I said, "write me General Delivery in Santa Fe, New Mexico. Make out the checks to Dusty Jones."

Well sir, that old prospector—name was Adams—felt so good about that grubstake that he ordered everybody in the house a drink of pure whisky and paid for it out of the hundred.

Now the place was getting fuller. So was me and Wrangler. He had finally give up trying to get his elbows on the bar and instead was setting right up on top with his thick arms in the air telling a big lie to a bunch of drunk amigos. It was plain to see that he had got past the grunt and one-sentence stage.

All of a sudden, right out of nowhere—you might say right out of the clean, pure, fresh mountain air—a guitar and fiddle appeared. Two Spanish fellers with kindness in their hearts was going to furnish the music. It was the best I ever heard. The music got faster and louder. I never did know what they were playing. All I know is it was the best I ever heard.

Every once in a while Wrangler would throw his hands in the air and open his mouth and howl like a lobo with a belly full of sheep. Old Telio would pull his mouth around that head full of teeth and do a fancy jig behind the bar. Everybody was laughing, hollering, raising hell, and having a real good time. There was just one thing missing. A woman!

I was staring hard at the naked gal on the beer calendar, thinking that I would give all my interest in that gold mine (getting my pardner's agreement, of course) to have her for just one whole night. Then I got to thinking that I was bragging to myself a little maybe. I decided I would settle for ten minutes.

Then Wrangler let out a yell like a young bull in a pasture full of two-year-old heifers. He jumped off that bar top and was running before his feet hit the floor. There it was, standing inside the door. A woman! Now, she didn't have no teeth and her nose swung down almost to her chin. Her hair wasn't black and it wasn't gray either. It was sort of in between. She was kind of wide and drooped in the hunkers like a hen laying an oversized egg, but the main thing is, she was a woman!

Wrangler gathered her up and got her over to the bar so fast it looked a little greedy on his part. Telio introduced her as Sophia and said she was the *seester* of the old wino sleeping over in the booth.

"A fine girl," he said.

We started buying her drinks just as fast as she could get them

down. Sophia might not have been much for looks, but she sure could
apply herself to them drinks we bought her. She'd run her tongue out
when she set her glass down and lick her chin so's not to waste a drop.
Pretty soon Wrangler had her out in the middle of the floor and they
were doing a "Folsom Stomp." (Folsom is a little town in northern
New Mexico where they don't do much dancing but a hell of a lot of
stomping.)

Finally I just couldn't stand it any longer and I ran out and jerked
her loose from Old Wrangler and she really bellied up to me. Things
got better all the time. Them two old boys played the prettiest music I
ever heard in my life. Yes sir, the best I ever heard. The more we
whirled around, the more beautiful Sophia looked. Why, I never saw
such lovely eyes, as them town fellers would say. And that hair . . . it
shined like a fresh-brushed mane of a slick sorrel mare. I decided that
the girl on the calendar couldn't hold a candle to my Sophia. Now
there was one place I was wrong, and that was this *my* business. As it
turned out, Sophia was *ours*.

Old Wrangler waltzed in there and shot me out of the saddle as slick
as axle grease. He waltzed right on around by the door and slipped
outside. It was just getting dark. His timing was right on the money. I
hobbled back up to the bar. Old Telio winked at me and threw his
head back and laughed. "Shut up, you drunken bum," I said, "and
give me another drink." I stared at the girl on the calendar and decided she wasn't so bad after all.

After a while Wrangler came in grinning like a jackass eating briars
and proved his friendship right then and there. He snuck up beside
me. I could tell he wanted to speak quiet-like. I bent my ear down and
he said, "She's waitin' for you out in the pickup."

Now, I never was no hand at taking seconds on anything. Howsomever, this was no time to argue principles. I ducked my head and
tore on out.

After a little spell me and Sophia decided we needed another drink.
We moseyed back inside. Hardly nobody paid any attention to us.
Some of them was asleep at the bar. Two more was laying in the
booths, and one was under a table in the back of the room. The rest
was either struggling like hell to hold the bar up or was out in the
middle of the floor jigging and hollering.

The party went on. A little priest came in and motioned for Telio to
give him a glass of port wine.

"Wine, Father?" Telio asked. "Sure, Father, sure. It's on the house.

92 ROUNDERS 3

Our dear Father is leaving us soon," he said to me with tears brimming out of his eyeballs and leaking down on the bar top. "After all these years," he said, "they are taking him away from us."

"Well, I'll be damned," I said. "When you leaving, Reverend?"

"Father!" Telio yelled at me.

"Father," I said, trying not to show my ignorance.

"The day after tomorrow," the Father said, shaking his head sadly.

"How come?" I asked. "How come they are doin' this thing to you?"

"I have been called elsewhere, my son," he said, gritting his teeth and bucking up. "My duty has called and I must answer."

"Not enough money in this parish," Telio said. "Not enough people. No funds to fix the church."

"I must go tomorrow and gather the Santos from our blessed little church on the hill," the Father said.

"Have another drink," I said.

He did. "Thank you, my son," he said.

"Well, if there is anything we can do to help, just call on us," I told him, feeling downright religious.

"There might be," he said. "You could help me move the bell."

"The bell!" yelled Telio. "That's my bell. Father, I want that bell back. You know I am a good Catholic," he went on, "and I pray to the saints. I go to mass. I am steady at confession but I will not let them take the bell. It is bad enough that we lose you, Father," Telio said, pouring another glass of port. "A good priest like you is hard to find. But the bell! I traded three sheep, a goat, and a suckling pig for it."

"Do not anguish yourself, my son," said the Father, shaking his empty glass under Telio's weeping eyes. "We will return your bell."

Telio filled his glass.

It came a time when I could not stand to hear Telio yap about his bell any longer. "Let's go get the goddam bell," I said.

"I cannot leave the bar," said Telio. "Look." He waved a fat arm around.

"I can see that," I said. "Well, me and Wrangler will go with the priest and get your bell."

"You will have my undying blessing to follow you across the earth," said Telio.

I said, "Well, I sure appreciate that. Come on, Father," I said, "let's get goin'."

"Yes, my son, let's do. We must not keep from Telio what is his any longer."

It seems we was having quite a time keeping Wrangler from what was *ours*. He was out in the pickup again with Sophia.

I got a bottle from Telio, telling him the drinks were on us till we got back. Me and the Father strolled out of there and climbed in the pickup with Wrangler and Sophia. It was a little crowded, but we all kind of scrounged up together and made room. Old Fooler was snorting and eyeballing around in the back end. For a little while I had forgotten about him and Jim Ed. It had been a good feeling.

I drove off up toward the little rundown church on the hill. Wrangler was snuggling up to Sophia, telling her what a great woman she was. Me and the Father was taking a little slug out of the bottle to keep from hearing all them gooey words Wrangler was using.

We pulled up in front of the church. There the bell was, hanging up there in the steeple. The moonlight was shining so bright, for a minute I thought the sun was coming up.

We all crawled out and took a little slug out of the bottle so we wouldn't catch cold. I let ol' Fooler out of the truck and walked him around about three minutes before reloading him.

"How we goin' to get up there?" I asked.

"Well, my son," the Father said, "that does pose a problem."

Wrangler had one of his rare ideas then. He pointed to an elm tree that was growing beside the church and hung out over it.

"You are showing signs of intelligence again, Wrangler," I said and commenced to climb the tree. I made it all right for a while and crawled out on a limb like a big-ass bird.

Every time I would bend over to reach for the bell the limb would get to swaying and I would damn near fall off. I could hear my three friends down below cheering me on and passing the bottle back and forth. It was just what I needed to hear. I leaned way on out and reached for the bell. The limb broke. I fell. I kept falling for a long time, it seemed like to me. When I kind of came to, I thought I had died and was at my funeral. Then I saw a streak of light, and a match flared.

There I was setting right smack in the middle aisle of the church and there was the bell where it had come through the roof with me. The bell had gone right on through the floor. I got up slow, wondering if I had busted my leg again. It felt all right.

I said, "Wrangler, strike another match."

He did. It took all of us to get that bell up out of the floor, ringing to beat hell all the while.

I said, "I'm sure sorry, Father, about tearing up your church."

"It does not matter, my son," he said. "It will go back to dust now just as you and I." He had me kind of rattled for a minute. Then he said, "It is a courageous thing you have done this night. I am sure Telio's prayers will follow you forever."

That sounded mighty good to me, and also it meant that Fooler horse might not be going to kill me after all, if I was going to be around that long.

ELEVEN

SOMETHING WOKE ME UP. Whatever it was, it was prizing my jaws apart. I sat up in my bedroll and saw my prospecting pardner, Adams.

"You got my teeth?" he asked.

"Hell, no!" I yelled. "I've had these ever since I was a kid."

"I lost my teeth," he mumbled through his beard. He got up and stared around kind of helpless-like.

I said: "Why don't you go find Sophia? She's a smooth mouth. Maybe she's usin' them."

"I lost 'em," he said, and stumbled off down the road toward Sophia's place. I was sure hoping he'd find them so he would get on up in the mountains and dig for our gold.

Wrangler raised up in his bedroll, pushing his tangled hair out of his eyes. I don't think it made any difference about his hair. His eyes was so swelled up and red that he couldn't see anyway. They looked like two burnt holes in a saddle blanket.

"Good morning, glory," I said.

Wrangler was not on one of his talking spells. He didn't even grunt.

Then I saw the bell hanging on the pickup and Old Fooler tied around to the side with an empty oat bucket by him. I didn't remember hanging the bell, and I didn't remember letting Old Fooler out of the pickup.

Old Fooler nickered and looked back over his shoulder.

I could tell he wanted a drink. I got dressed and led him across the street to a horse trough. I washed my face and combed my hair while Old Fooler drank. The sun was just coming up and the roosters was all through crowing.

Then I heard the door to the bar slam and here came Telio. He had not bothered to comb his hair or even push it out of his eyes. He looked like a bareheaded Indian in a cyclone.

"Come on over to my house and I will get you some breakfast," he said.

"Naw," I said. "We'll drive on over to Hine's Corner. It's on Highway 202 and we can whip right on into Hi Lo from there. We can get breakfast there and maybe a drink."

I knew that according to New Mexico law the bars was not supposed to open till nine o'clock. It was about six now.

Telio said, "Come on over, I will get you a drink. There is no law here," he added, reading my mind.

Wrangler had his head plumb under water. I thought for a minute he was trying to drown himself. Then he came up for air. We stumbled over to Telio's and got us a drink. It was as hard to get down as a bucket full of mud, and when it hit bottom I was sure it would bounce.

I didn't think Old Wrangler could look any worse than he did just natural, but after swallowing his shot he made a face that would have caused his own mother to hang herself. I doubt if he had a mother anyway. I don't think he was born at all. I'm pretty sure Wrangler just hatched out from under some old bear droppings.

By the time we had a couple more, things were beginning to look up. I said, "Wrangler, you ready to pull out to Hine's Corner and get some grub in our bellies?"

"Whatever suits you just tickles me plumb to death," he said.

We did up our bedrolls and loaded Old Fooler back in the pickup. Then I noticed the bell again. I also noticed where my hide was peeled in several places.

I yelled at Telio, "Come out here and get your bell!"

"It ain't mine," he yelled back. "It's yours. You gave me twenty-five dollars for it last night."

"Well, I'll be damned," I said. I decided I had better tie something around that bell to keep it from ringing. Old Fooler must have had a fit when we drove down from the church last night. Telio brought me a gunnysack and I tied it around the bell.

We crawled in the pickup and took off. The clapper swung back and forth but it didn't make much noise, which was a damn good thing, the way my head was hollowed out from the sporting activities of the past night.

It wasn't long until we hit the pavement. It was mighty nice riding and the first time we had been out of the sand, timber, and rocks for a long time. Before we hardly knew it, there was Hine's Corner. It was a big restaurant and bar as well as a curio store selling Indian trinkets to the tourists. Highway 27 crossed with Highway 202 and Hine's Corner joined them both. It was a welcome sight.

We crawled out of that old pickup and walked into the restaurant part. It was still too early for the bar to be open.

Well sir, another sight to make a man sling his head and wring his tail like a bronc on the first saddling stood right there behind the counter—a little old brown-haired, blue-eyed gal built like a registered quarter horse. She smiled at us as we came in.

"Sit down, boys, and make yourselves at home," she said. She handed us a menu. It was a low counter, and Wrangler didn't have no trouble at all getting his elbows on it. He wasn't reading the menu but was aiming out over the top of it at this gal. I don't think he can read anyway.

I took over for both of us, seeing as how he was so "enamored," as the town fellers say. "Give us three eggs apiece, a stack of hotcakes, a big chunk of ham, and about a half a gallon of coffee," I said.

"How do you want your eggs?" this toothsome thing asked.

"Just cooked," I said.

Well now, it came as sort of a shock to look up and see another one just as pert stick her head out of the kitchen stall and take the order. She looked out at us and she smiled too. Old Wrangler just spun around on the counter stool and started pawing the floor. It looked for a minute like he was going to run back there and ear her down right on the cook stove.

It was a right good breakfast. One of the best I ever had. Wrangler took out a five-dollar bill and went back to tip the cook. He stayed quite a while, even after three or four truck drivers had stopped to order breakfast. I just kept drinking coffee and eyeballing the waitress.

Come to find out these two gals had leased this place about three months back. The cook was named Kate and the waitress was Mary.

It surprised me to hear this because I had once worked a team of mules by the same names. Of course, I didn't mention this to the girls.

Mary looked at me out of those blue eyes and said, "You boys heading for the rodeo at Hi Lo?"

"Yeah," I said. "Why don't you and Kate come along?"

"Sure wish we could," she said, and slung her head kind of sad-like.

Time flies, and it wasn't long till Mary opened the bar. Another waitress stopped in and took her place in the kitchen. I told Wrangler to come on in the bar and we would have a bottle of beer to wash our breakfast down.

He didn't much like leaving Kate. I reckon, though, that salty ham had made him thirsty.

"It must have been a bigger breakfast than we thought," I said to Wrangler. "We have already had six bottles of beer apiece and I'm still thirsty."

"Give us anothern," he said, peering around the bar, trying to see into the kitchen.

"Have a drink, Mary," I said.

"Can't now, boys. Against my rules. Too early. Now, if you boys were to be around here about nine tonight when Kate closes the restaurant . . ."

"It's a long time till nine," I said.

Wrangler said, "You know something?"

"What?" I asked.

"Time flies," he said.

"You're right," I said. And it did.

About the middle of the afternoon a man and woman pulled up out front in a New Jersey car. They had two kids with them, a boy about six and a little yellow-headed girl a year or two older.

They fooled around out in the curios for a little while and then moseyed into the bar. They sat down and ordered a coke apiece for the kids and a bottle of beer for themselves.

"Sure hot outside," the woman said.

"Oh, it's not bad," Mary said, "for this time of year."

"Oh," she said, trying to get her hunkers to fit on the bar stool all at one time. The old boy glanced through his glasses at me like he knew me. He sat there pushing his long-billed canvas cap back and forth on his head and rubbing his belly, which was bigger than Wrangler's. His wife seemed worried about her looks and kept staring at herself in the back mirror, twisting her head like a one-eyed hound at a treed coon.

The little girl walked over to us and said, "Are you cowboys?"

"Well," I told her, "I ain't yet. But if I keep practicin' and get rid of that horse out there in the pickup I might make it someday."

"You look like cowboys to me," she said, turning around to stare out the window at Old Fooler.

"What a beautiful horse," her mother said.

"Yes, lady," I said, "that horse is just like a patch of locoweed."

"What in the world is that?" she said, squinting out over her overfed cheeks.

"It's a purty little green weed that once in a while comes up in the springtime before anything else."

"What's so bad about that?" she asked.

"There ain't nothin' bad about its purty color," I went on. "It's just that after a long winter, the stock is starvin' for somethin' green. Well, naturally they tie into this locoweed and that's what's bad."

"Why?"

I said, "It gives them the blind staggers, headaches, bellyaches, the shaky trembles, and the scared boogers. Besides that," I said, "it drives them plumb slap dab crazy."

"Goodness!" she said.

"Well, lady," I told her, "that is exactly the effect that beautiful horse out there has on mankind. That is why I have quit my job and turned my pardner here to strong drink."

She looked out the window with new interest.

The little boy was looking up at me with his ears flopping in the wind. "Where's your gun?" he said, looking right hurt because I didn't jerk it out and shoot a hole in the wall.

"I ain't got no gun, son," I said. "My pardner here has one in his war bag. But he's a little loco hisself, and we can't take any chances on him."

Wrangler snorted through his busted nose and took a half bottle of beer down his gullet with one swallow. The kid promptly lost interest in me and tied into old Wrangler, but he couldn't get him to talk. Pretty soon he said, "Aw, you ain't cowboys anyway. Bat Masterson would run you out of town in five minutes."

I said, "Son, if he will ride Old Fooler for five minutes first, I will be glad to take him on in a gun battle and spot him seven seconds' head start on the draw."

"Aw-ww," he said, and walked out into the curio and bought himself a Roy Rogers, the King of the Cowboys, comic book. He kept reading this out loud until his pa said, "Sonny, go on out to the car and read."

This boy looked at me and Wrangler again and said, "Roy Rogers would shoot you so full of holes so quick you wouldn't even have time to turn around."

I said, "Give that boy a coke, Mary, before he gets us bums killed."

Wrangler said, as if I'd included him in the coke business, "I want a beer."

I got up and played the jukebox. While I was standing there the little girl walked over and said, sweet-like, "I don't care what Ronny thinks; *I* believe you're real cowboys. You're just being modest. I bet you can outdraw anybody."

"That's right, honey," I said, patting her on the head. "I am the best hand in the world at drawin' the rough string. Ever' outfit I go to work for turns 'em over to me."

Ma and Pa got up and left. They had to drag little Ronny with them. He was practicing his fast draw and cocking his thumb back, filling me and old phony Wrangler plumb full of holes like a *real* cowboy would have done.

That jukebox was making my feet itch. I jumped up and did a fast jig. Old Wrangler clapped his hands and yelled like an opera singer with her bloomers on fire. Things were getting better all the time.

I went out and tied Old Fooler to the side of the pickup and fed him some oats. After while I took him around in the back of the store to water him, and saw a little catch pen. So I put him in there and he nibbled around on some weeds and old hay.

I said to him, "Eat while you can, you son of a bitch. It won't be long till the hungry dogs will be eatin' *you.*"

He looked up at me kinda funny-like. I shot him with my finger like little Ronny and went back to the bar, feeling good.

Now nine o'clock came and things got even better. Kate closed up the restaurant and came in and sat down between me and Wrangler and ordered a screwdriver—whatever the hell that is. She had two more before old Wrangler decided it was moving time. He jerked her off that stool, and you talk about dancing! Well sir, those two really put on a show. Of all the jumping and hollering and fancy stepping, that was it. I got Mary to take a few shots with me and we joined them out in the middle of the floor. You talk about a couple of good sports, we had them. As time moved on, the dancing slowed down, and the first thing I knew we was stopped—not saying nothing, just holding one another like a couple of schoolkids on a midnight hayride. It was a right nice place to be.

We all went into the back rooms where the girls lived. We took us along some bottles and the girls pushed a button on one of them fancy victrolas and the party was started. These gals wanted to know all about me and Wrangler, but all I could think to tell them about myself was to cuss Jim Ed Love and Old Fooler. They said they knew Jim Ed and thought he was a nice feller. I didn't answer that because I knew what a hand-shaking, ass-kissing, goody-goody he could be when he was out and about among the citizens. It wouldn't have done me or them any good either if I had told them what a slave-driving, dollar-hoarding old son of a bitch he really was.

But when it came to Old Fooler, I wouldn't back down, and then finally Wrangler said something that made me turn back to the party.

"Dusty," he said, holding Kate in his lap and feeding her whisky out of the bottle, "you keep goin' on about what you are goin' to do with that horse when we get into Hi Lo. I'll bet you a month's wages that when the Good Lord sends you to hell you will be ridin' Old Fooler, and he will be buckin' to beat sixty."

"There is a number of ways to look at that," I said, "but I am going to take your bet." With that I gathered Mary up and said, "Honey, it's motel time. What do you say?"

Here's what she said: "I like you, honey, and whatever suits you just tickles me plumb to death."

For a minute I was about half jealous, figgering she had been out with my pardner, even though we did share and share alike. Then I laughed out loud—for old Wrangler was saying the same thing to Kate.

It was a short night.

TWELVE

IT WAS AROUND NOON before anybody tried to get up at Hine's Corner. The first thing I heard was old Wrangler stirring around hunting a drink of water. It took some doing, but we all made it in for breakfast. Now, the more of that water I drank, the more I felt like I did the night before. It wasn't long till we decided we needed a cold beer to sober up on. Then after that we took another to get to feeling better. Then one more to keep the last one from fizzling out. And so it went.

By about mid-afternoon I asked a mighty big question. "Girls," I said, "it is too late to open this business up now. Why don't we all just crawl in that old pickup and lope on over to Hi Lo for the Fourth?"

At first the girls didn't think that would be a good idea, seeing as how they were just getting started in a new business, but after about two more beers and a screwdriver apiece the mood changed.

Mary said, "Hi Lo is the best town in the United States. We haven't been to a good rodeo in three years. Dusty, darling," she went on, "I don't think you have had a better idea since you were a baby boy."

It didn't take us very long to load Old Fooler and get a case of beer and two fifths of whisky for medicine. It was somewhat crowded in the front of that pickup, but a man that would gripe about that would gripe about having to stand up on a train headed straight for heaven.

The girls wanted to know about the bell, and I said we were delivering it to a church in Hi Lo.

Then we got to singing. Now Wrangler sometimes gets it into his head that he has got quite a voice. Well, he has. It makes up for good with loud. It was not so much that we were singing different songs that made it sound so wild, but that goddam Fooler had to join in and nicker to beat hell once in a while. It kind of threw the whole thing off key because he was even louder than Wrangler.

Along in the shank of the afternoon we could see Hi Lo shooting up out in the middle of a big country full of green grama grass. I spotted a clump of brush just off the road at about the same time.

"Let's stop here and have a picnic," I said.

Wrangler said, "We ain't got no sandwiches."

I said, "There is lots of things you can do on a picnic besides eat."

So we all bailed out and took our bedrolls to have something to set on and started opening up them beer cans and taking a slug now and then out of the fifths.

Well, the first thing I knew it was dark and we had to gather up a little wood and build a fire. It was right pleasant to set around that fire and tell lies and sing songs and snuggle up to that good-looking Mary woman.

When the fire went out I was too drunk to gather any more wood, and Wrangler and Kate had drug their bedroll off a ways to be by themselves. I didn't want to bother them. Mary said she didn't know much about what who was doing what and felt like we ought to retire for the evening. I sided right in with this line of thinking.

It was another short night.

About thirty minutes before daylight, I rared right straight up in bed. "God a'mighty," I said, "today is the Fourth of July! Get up!" Then I went to jumping into my clothes. It took some more yelling and a little bedroll-shaking before I could get anybody else to open their eyes. They were all acting drunk-like.

Mary sat up and said, "We haven't been in bed over ten minutes. I'm still tanked."

"It don't matter," I said. "You will have time to sober up before the rodeo."

It was darker than an apple cellar, and Wrangler was having a hell of a time getting Kate to stir. We finally got loaded in the pickup and took off in a big hurry.

I didn't have my eyes open very good, and since Wrangler wouldn't drive I was having a hard time herding the pickup down the middle of the road. I just aimed right down the white line and tried to keep her there. It was getting daylight, and we weren't very far from Hi Lo.

About that time Kate's eyes flew wide and she screamed, "I saw a black cat run across the road!"

Wrangler grunted and said, "Don't let it worry you, honey; he wasn't all black."

"Yes, he was," Kate said.

"Naw," Wrangler said, "he had a white butthole."

This seemed to satisfy Kate, and all of them but me went back to sleep. Well, the sun came up and I could see the dust boiling up off the ranch roads all around Hi Lo where the people was coming in pickups and wagons for the Fourth of July.

I had to drive slow considering my condition, and the sun was up pretty high when I pulled into Hi Lo.

Now I had forgotten about the bell. Just as we started down the main street we hit a bump and it began to ring like every church in the world was right here in Hi Lo. I reckon the clapper had flopped back and forth until it had worn through the gunnysack. Old Fooler began to buck and kick, and I mean kick. The pickup was rocking to beat hell, and I thought he was going to turn it over. People was stopping and staring like a bull at a bastard calf. It made me nervous.

I whipped off into a little vacant lot between two buildings, and by the time I had pumped those sorry brakes enough to get them to take hold I had run plumb across the lot out onto another street. There wasn't near so many people here, so I brought her to a stop.

Old Fooler was still trying to kick the pickup to smithereens, and every time he let fly the bell would ring.

I looked around. My pardner and the two women were damn sure awake now. I said, "Let's get to hell out of here before the law arrives."

Then I noticed something that made my eyes smart something terrible. We had left the picnic grounds in such a hurry and everybody kind of numb from all that drinking that the girls hadn't put on all their clothes.

Wrangler was awake enough now to know he had a half-dressed woman in his lap. Just then who came walking over toward the pickup but Shorty Wilson, the horse buyer.

I jumped out, telling my friends to stay put and I would think of something. Wrangler jerked a bottle out of the glove compartment and they all took a drink. I ran out to meet old Shorty with my hand outstretched. When I got ahold of him I shook hands like he had just saved me from cannibals. Every time he would try to break loose and get over close to the pickup I would shake some more and say, "It sure is good to see you, Shorty. By god, I really miss my old friends. How's the horse business, Shorty? How's the old lady and the kids? Shorty, my friend, come with me, I want to buy you a drink."

He got kind of wild-eyed and tried to break away. "I want to say hello to Wrangler," he said.

"Aw, he's drunk," I said, "and needs his sleep bad." I drug him off toward the Wild Cat Saloon with him looking back over his shoulder every whipstitch. Old Fooler was still bucking and kicking and falling down.

"What'll you take for the outlawed son of a bitch?" he asked.

"We'll talk trade later. I just can't wait another minute to get me a drink."

It wasn't easy, but I finally got him over to the Wild Cat. We had a couple of fast ones and I told him to wait right here. I would be back after a while and have a visit.

I stumbled down the street trying to figure what to do. If we went back after the rest of their clothes it would be too late to get my entry fee in for the rodeo, much less have time for any breakfast. If we didn't eat, me and Wrangler was sure going to make fools out of ourselves at that rodeo. It was not a very pleasant thought.

I saw the Hot Biscuit Café across the street. Arlee Barton, the feller that ran it, was a friend of mine. I stumbled in, and Arlee ran over shaking hands and asking questions.

I said, "Arlee, we have been friends a long time. I want you to do me a favor and not ask no more questions. You see that last booth way back there in the corner? Well, cook up four orders of bacon and eggs with coffee all around and loan me two of them aprons like the waitress over there is wearing."

Arlee said, "What you want them aprons for?"

I said, "Don't ask me no questions, you son of a bitch; just get 'em for me like the good friend you are, old friend."

Arlee went back and got me two aprons from the kitchen. "This is all I have," he said.

Well, I hotfooted it back to the pickup. Old Fooler had calmed down some. Kate was taking the last swallow out of the bottle. I handed them the aprons and said, "Here, put these on."

The girls did and stepped out. Well sir, their fronts was covered up pretty good, but the glare from the backs was about blinding in the morning sunshine.

Now, as I have said before, there is times that old Wrangler shows a faint glimmering of intelligence. This was one of those rare occasions. He pulled off that big old hat of his and slapped it over Kate's rear end. I didn't say anything, but I took mine off and did the same for

Mary. Now it looked like if we worked fast we could make it over to the Hot Biscuit without getting throwed in jail.

We marched along, stepping out like Old Fooler does when he's just throwed me straight up. People was stopping and staring all up and down the street. They weren't looking at the girls but was just wondering what in the hell two cowboys was doing with their hats off so early in the day. The sun was getting pretty hot too. It kind of gave me the staggers.

We got in and I could hear stools turning like rusty wagon wheels all along the counter. We came to a stop at the last booth where the waitress was just putting our grub out. I sure thought she was slow about it.

"Now, girls," I said, "I'm going to count three, then me and Wrangler will not waste any time. I want you to jump in them seats like a ground squirrel dodgin' a fox."

Off came the hats! Down went the fannys!

"We done 'er," Wrangler said.

We wore our hats all during breakfast. Arlee kept looking over at me. He acted like he never seen a girl in an apron before. I walked over and whispered in his ear, "Keep your big mouth shut, or I will stomp you right smack through the floor."

"Take it easy," he said. "Take it easy."

"I will," I said. I walked back over to the booth and finished my breakfast.

"Wrangler, I am goin' down and enter us in the rodeo. Then I'm goin' over to the mercantile and buy these girls some dresses. What color do you like?" I asked.

Kate said, "Blue. Any color, just so it's blue."

Mary said, "Red will just be fine, but hurry. There's a draft."

"What do you want me to enter you in, Wrangler?"

"Bareback bronc ridin', wild-cow milkin', and bull ridin'," he said.

"Don't you want in the calf ropin'?"

"Nawww," he said, "I ain't got no horse."

"That's right," I said. "I'm goin' to sell Old Fooler to Shorty Wilson." I stumbled out of there feeling some relief at just being away from them *associates* of mine, as the town fellers say.

I stopped an old boy on the street carrying an entry blank and asked, "Where do you sign up?"

He pointed across the street to a vacant store building. It was old L. C. Work furnishing the stock and taking the entry money.

"Howdy, Dusty, what in the hell you doin' in town? Don't you know you're gettin' too old and broke up to rodeo?"

"Yeah," I said, shaking hands with L.C. and Glen Frazier, one of his helpers. "But you know me, L.C., my middle name is ignorance."

I got Wrangler entered in the events he wanted. I signed up for the wild-cow milking and calf roping.

"Ain't you going to get in the saddle-bronc ridin'?" he asked, looking kind of puzzled.

"Hell, no!" I said. "There is an old bald-faced roan horse over in my pickup that has done nothin' but take me for a bronc ride for the last eight or nine months."

"Maybe you'd ought to sell him to me for a buckin' horse," L.C. said, only half joking.

"I would," I said, "but that would be too good a fate for him. I'm goin' to sell him to Shorty Wilson for dog meat."

I peeled out the money and paid off. I told the boys adiós, and I would see them at one o'clock out at the arena. A bunch more young hands came in to sign up.

I went over to the mercantile and walked back to where a bunch of dresses hung on a rack. A woman about fifty years old with a grin as big as Telio the bartender's came dogtrotting up and said, "What can I do for you?"

I said, "With no offense intended, lady, but if I was to tell you, you would just haul off and knock me in the head."

She kind of reared back on her heels, stuck her belly out, and folded her arms over it. "Would you like a dress? What size? What color?"

"I can't remember the size," I said, "but I want one red and one blue. Better make them pretty big," I said. "These are growed-up, filled-out women."

She got them all wrapped up, not saying much, and I paid her off. Then I scooted back to the restaurant.

"What took you so long?" Wrangler wanted to know.

"Time flies," the girls said together.

Kate said, "This booth has got splinters."

I said, "Your troubles are over," and handed the package to Mary.

I asked Arlee if it would be all right to run the cook out of the kitchen a minute so our friends could get dressed without going outside to the two-holer. I stared him hard in the eye, and he nodded.

The girls got up. Off came our hats and we covered for them till

they went through the swinging door into the kitchen. I sat down and
swallowed a big bait of that pure clean, fresh café air.

"What did you enter yourself in?" Wrangler asked.

I told him.

He said, "Calf ropin'? I thought you said—"

"By God!" I said, "I forgot I didn't have no horse. Now I'll have to
rope off Old Fooler. God a'mighty, isn't this goin' to be some Fourth
of July?"

The girls came back out and I was damn sure glad they were drunk.
If they had been sober they would have brought the meat cleaver out
of the kitchen with them and split my head down the middle plumb to
my goozle. The dresses was way too short, coming just to their knees.
And when you talk about fitting around the middle, why they had to
make three wraps to get them to stay on. They had tied a big bowknot
in their belts and came prancing out of there like they was dressed to
go to a wedding.

I said, "Let's go over to the Wild Cat. I have got to see Shorty
Wilson and tell him I can't let him have Old Fooler till after the
show."

I wanted to get them over there and buy them some more drinks.
It was a worrisome way to start the Fourth of July.

We stepped out on the street and heard a band playing. I could hear
Old Fooler kicking again and that bell ringing. I hoped nobody would
notice.

Here came the parade. First the school band, then horsebackers of
all kinds, from the brushiest cowboys to the fattest, softest businessmen, kids on broken-down plow horses and some whey-bellied ranchers like Jim Ed on good-looking quarter horses.

Then there was the rodeo queen in a big paper-hung float, and I'm
telling you there was some fancy cars and wagons following.

It was a sight to see, but I couldn't afford to stand idle and watch it
all.

I said, "Come on, folks, Shorty is waitin'." And we went in the Wild
Cat and ordered a drink for the house.

The Fourth of July was on!

THIRTEEN

AFTER THE PARADE everybody started filing out toward the Hi Lo arena. On one side of the arena is a grandstand, and on the other side folks just park their cars right up against the fence and get out and set on the fenders. Under the grandstand is a hamburger and soda-pop booth. A half-mile racetrack runs around the arena. The bucking chutes face north with the holding corrals for the broncs, wild cows, and bulls just behind. The calf pen and chutes face east, and it's a good long run from one end to the other.

The cowboys get down to the rodeo grounds earlier than the spectators. When we drove up in the pickup there was horse trailers parked all over the place. Ropers and bulldoggers were brushing, saddling, and reining out their horses all around us. Some of them was standing around throwing loops over their rope cans or a bale of hay. The bronc riders was testing out the fit of their stirrups on association saddles, and the bareback riders were checking over spurs and riggin'. A lot of these boys had enough ability to go right on into professional rodeo. Most of them wouldn't, though, because of having to stay on the ranch or doing something else.

We unloaded Old Fooler and I saddled him up. The girls opened us a can of cold beer. Now, usually I don't like to drink before a show. But this time I was in such a shape that it didn't make a whole lot of difference one way or the other.

Old Coy Beasly rode over on his big brown roping quarter horse and asked what I was going to rope off of. I told him, "This here horse right here."

He looked at Old Fooler and said, "Well-put-together horse, but he looks like he has recently been in a wreck."

"He has," I said. "Several."

I hated to see old Coy show up. He was always beating me out of first money everywhere we went. Seems like he never beat a feller bad —maybe one, two-tenths of a second, but that was just as good as five minutes.

I got on Old Fooler, quivering all over, and rode him easy-like down to look at the calves. I had drawn Number Twelve—a big gray flop-eared brahma. I would really have to jerk him down hard if I was going to make any time on that big booger.

Several of the other contestants rode up looking for their calves. Finally I went off, trying to get up nerve enough to break Old Fooler out of a walk. I knew if I busted out of that roping box in a dead run before getting him warmed up there would be a whole lot more of a bronc ride than a calf roping. I rode over to where Wrangler was climbing up on the fence to look at his bronc.

"Which one did you draw?" I asked.

"That little black son of a bitch," he said. "They say he really turns it on."

"That's good," I said. "You wouldn't have no chance on a runaway."

The girls said they was going over in the grandstand and would see us after the show. It suited me because I couldn't get my thoughts on them anyhow, seeing how nervous I was about Old Fooler.

Well, the grandstand was beginning to fill up and the music was pouring out over the loudspeaker. Cars was lined up solid along the south fence. Cowboys and horses were everywhere, and the dust was beginning to powder around the arena.

Then the music stopped and Sy Wheeler, the announcer, began blowing in the mike, testing it out. He said, "All right, all you cowboys gather down at the east end of the arena and get ready for the grand entry."

We all lined up behind a couple of local boys carrying flags. One carried the U.S. flag and the other the State of New Mexico flag. All of a sudden the music started up and we all spurred out into the arena. We circled in a good lope behind the two flag-bearers. After about three times around the arena, we lined up and faced the grandstand. They played what Wrangler calls the Star-Spangled Bandanner, for a joke. We all took off our hats. When it was over we made one more circle and rode out of the arena.

Then Sy Wheeler started welcoming everybody to the annual Hi Lo Fourth of July celebration and hoped they enjoyed the show and had a good time. Then he introduced L. C. Work, who was furnishing the stock, and Bill and Angus Blair, the pickup men.

The show was on!

The bareback bronc riding led it off. . . .

"Grady Decker on the bucking horse Sundown comin' out of Chute Number One!"

The big bay ran a little ways, ducked his head, and threw poor old Grady on the second jump.

"Hard luck, cowboy. Give him a hand, folks; that's all the pay he's going to get."

Grady got up, dusting himself off, and stumbled back toward the bucking chutes, trying to get his hat back in place.

One after the other the broncs poured out. A little Mexican from Española kicked the mane out of one and looked like he had first money cinched.

Then I heard the announcer say, "Wrangler Lewis on Black Devil comin' out of Chute Number Three!"

I spurred over so I could watch. Well, it was good. That little black bastard came out with his head down, bucking the first jump out of the chute. Old Wrangler was setting way up on top of the gloved hand where he was holding onto the handle of the bareback riggin'. He had his spurs up high in that black's neck. The black went up and came down twisting. He never hit twice going in the same direction. It looked once like Wrangler was going off, but he righted himself and kept raking them spurs back and forth. I could see where he had loosened the last two snaps on his chaps so they would flap and make it look like he was spurring a lot harder. Lots of cowboys think this fools the judges, but it don't.

Well, the whistle blew to signal the end of his ride. Old Wrangler jumped off and landed on his feet. It sure was pretty. The crowd clapped to beat hell. I figured Wrangler had sewed up second money if the next and last rider didn't beat him.

The last rider was Sowbelly Jenkins. He must have been forty-five years old, an age when most bronc riders are either dead or crippled. Sowbelly was tough but he drew a runaway horse that bucked just enough so he couldn't get a reride and not enough to put him in the money. By God, things had started off all right.

Sy was calling the ropers and telling the next man he was up and the third man to get ready. I was way down the line. Well, the first boys was a little overanxious, and missed. Then Art Walker sailed out there and fit it on one before he hardly started.

Coy Beasly says to me, "There goes the money."

But it didn't. Art's horse didn't keep the rope tight, and the calf got to circling on him and it took eighteen and six-tenth's seconds to tie his calf. Well, there was a twenty-second catch and tie and another miss. Then an eighteen-two. Then a seventeen-eight and so on down the line.

The seventeen-eight was still first money when Coy Beasly rode in the chute. He came out of there fast after that calf. But he really had himself a runaway. The brown horse built to him and Coy reached out with his rope and fit it on, and he come off his horse running and wrapped that calf up in seventeen flat.

Sy Wheeler said, "That's the fastest time of the day, folks."

Well, here it was. I was next up. At least I knew what I had to beat. I reined Old Fooler out into the arena in front of the roping box. I want the world to know that my gut was sucking wind. There was just no telling what kind of ungodly stunt that Fooler horse would pull out here in front of all these people.

I rode him into the box and turned him around. He backed right up with his tail against the back end of that box, his head up and his ears throwed forward. I could feel him quivering all over just a little. Then I knew that son of a bitch had been here before, too. I was beginning to wonder where he *hadn't* been.

I had my piggin' string in my mouth. I took a deep seat in the saddle and tucked the upper strand of my loop under my right arm, so it wouldn't drop down and hang under a stirrup. Then I took part of the loop in my right hand and gathered in that saddle horn. I looked out at the man working the calf chute and could see the rope barrier stretched tight across the roping box and the barrier man standing with a flag in his hand holding the pull-rope, waiting for my signal. Now, when the calf was turned loose and his head came to a line fifteen feet in front of the chute, the barrier man would jerk that rope away. If I broke the barrier before the proper time, I would be fined ten seconds' penalty, and no matter how fast I tied I would be out of the money.

There was no use waiting any longer. I nodded my head at the chute man. He jerked the gate open, and the calf came out running at full speed for the other end. I waited just that half-second so I wouldn't break the barrier, then leaned over on Old Fooler. God a'mighty! He tore out of there so hard I thought he was bucking at first. It took me a little longer than I wanted to be able to turn loose of that saddle horn. A calf roper has got plenty to think about anyway, besides whether his horse is going to buck and run off.

I brought that loop up and whirled her about three times and there was the calf, right where I wanted him. Old Fooler skinned up to him fast with his ears laid back. The calf headed off to the right just a little. That's where he made his mistake. I let that loop fly and it whipped around the calf's neck like that's where it belonged. I jerked the slack, pitched the rope forward out of the way, grabbed the horn in my right hand, laid my left on Fooler's neck (which was his signal to slam on the brakes), and bailed off.

Old Fooler stopped with his hindquarters low and his hind feet tucked way up under him. I hit the ground running and got there just as the calf came down hard on his side. There had been a sudden stop on the calf's end of that rope. Just as I reached him he got up. It was a good thing because the rule says, *You have to have daylight under a calf's belly before you throw and tie.* I caught him just right as Old Fooler was pulling him toward me with a tight rope. I picked up the calf's right foreleg, lifted, pushed, and kneed him in the belly all at the same time. Over and down he went. I jumped over, holding that foreleg up straight next to my face, pulled the piggin' string out of my mouth, and latched the small loop over the foreleg just below the ankle. I pitched it out of the way while I reached back and gathered up the two hind legs. I had my right knee under those legs, helping to hold. I got the three legs bunched together and held them with my left hand. With my right I gathered up the piggin' string about sixteen inches from the leg and made my first wrap. It's the first wrap that holds, so I made it tight. Then I made two more fast wraps and jerked a hooey in the rope and threw my hands out, signaling the timers to stop the clock.

"Nice job, Dusty," old Sy was saying. "Just a minute, folks, and we will give you the official time."

I walked back to Old Fooler where he still held the rope tight and mounted him. I spurred him forward to take the slack out of the rope. A cowboy took the loop from around the calf's neck and turned him over. I held my breath but the tie stayed. Then the judge waved to the timers that the tie was okay. The arena hands took my piggin' string off the calf and handed it back to me. I turned and rode for the gate

out of the arena, hoping and praying every step that Old Fooler
wouldn't change his mind at the last minute.

"Here it is, folks," said Sy Wheeler, "the best time of the day—
sixteen-two."

It was a nice thing to hear. I rode on out and turned around to
watch the rest of the roping. I still had a long way to go before I won
the money. There were five ropers left to go. Well, one missed, one
got tangled up in the rope, two of them tied in slow time.

There was only one roper left. I heard his name called, Walter Hall
from Canadian, Texas. I almost swallowed my dry tongue. There is
always a bunch of good rodeo hands from that part of the country.
This kid, maybe eighteen or nineteen, rode in the arena. He had a
high-powered buckskin quarter horse. His equipment was the best. I
could tell he was one of them rich ranch kids that had never done
anything but practice roping. He rode in there, turned around, and
before I knew it he had signaled the chute man and was out of there
after his calf. He had crowded the barrier just right—touching it as it
broke. He rode out there with a little old bitty loop that wouldn't fit
around a wild steer's horns in a hundred years, but it sure did fit
around that calf's neck. He got off and threw that calf and tied him so
damn fast you couldn't hardly see it.

I turned to Coy and said, "There went my first money. There has
always got to be a smart-aleck kid around."

"Yeah," said Coy, not feeling too good because I had at least beat
him.

Sy Wheeler damn near choked when he made the announcement:
"Twelve point four, folks. The best time of the day."

Well, I had got second money, and that wasn't much to kick about.
Besides, for once I had beat old Coy Beasly. Then, too, I was not only
relieved but kind of proud about Old Fooler.

The saddle-bronc riding came next, and then the announcer yelled
for all cowboys to get ready for the wild-cow milking.

Now, at most rodeos they line up two cowboys on horses as a team
and turn a wild cow loose. After she passes a line out in front, the
cowboys are allowed to rope and milk her. One cowboy will rope, the
other will jump down and mug her. The roper will take a coke bottle
and squeeze just enough milk in it so it will barely pour, then race
back to the judge.

At Hi Lo, they do it different, though. It's a lot more reckless and a
lot more fun. They take the whole herd down to one end of the arena

and the ropers all line up at the other end. There is only one loop allowed, so there is no use for the mugger to be horseback. He can wait out there afoot and get to his cow faster that way through this tangle of cows, ropes, and scared horses.

Wrangler stood there waiting, rubbing his hands together above his little round belly. I built a big loop and got all set. I had picked out two head of cows from the bunch that was horned. I knew that a cow stands a lot better if she's roped around the horns. She don't choke so bad.

Sy said, "Get ready."

The cowboys at the other end had started the whole herd right at us as fast as they could make them move. I only know of two other places in the country where they hold a wild-cow milking like this—Cimarron, New Mexico, and Calgary, Canada.

The whistle blew and the cowboys all spurred out, trying to be first. I knew a lot of loops would be wasted right quick, so kind of easy-like I loped Old Fooler out and worked in beside the cow with the horns. It was plumb easy. I had her! Wrangler was right there and mugged her. She stood like a Jersey milk cow. I ran around behind her and took her tail in my mouth to keep it out of the way while I milked. It wasn't any too tasty, but I didn't have time to think about it. I squeezed them tits a couple of times and got some milk in the bottle. Then I ran back to Old Fooler, stepped on, and rode him up, giving Wrangler slack in the rope. The rule said, *The rope has to be removed from the cow.*

Wrangler jerked the loop off and yelled, "Ride, you bastard, ride!"

I did. We had beat the second best by a full fifteen seconds. It was a very nice feeling, but I couldn't help wondering what in the hell had come over Old Fooler. I was feeling about half let down because I'd expected him to blow up all along. Otherwise I felt as good as a fat hog with his belly in the mud and his back in the sunshine as I rode toward the gate out of the arena. Then I glanced up in the stands for no particular reason, and there sat Jim Ed Love, beaming and waving down at me like a preacher at a tent meeting.

I forgot for a minute that me and Wrangler had gathered in two second places and a first already. I forgot everything except how I would like to bash that grinning face in. How could that bastard still act friendly after the cussing we had give him while we was quitting his outfit for good? It beat me.

The arena hands set three oil barrels in a triangle for the girls' barrel race. Then a bunch of young girls and women ran their horses around them one at a time against the clock. It was a popular event. Nineteen seconds flat won it, and everybody clapped real loud.

The horse races went off pretty fast, and then the final event came up. The brahma-bull riding. There was a feller dressed up like a clown, and he was out there cracking jokes and doing crazy tricks, keeping the crowd laughing. When one of those bulls unloaded a rider, that clown was right in the bull's face, luring him away. He saved lots of lives and took lots of chances with his own life doing it.

A rodeo bull is twice as big as one of those faced by a Spanish bullfighter. He is just as quick and charges with his eyes open instead of shut. He will turn like a cat and is completely unpredictable. That clown, or bullfighter as the rodeo hands call him, makes a joke out of the whole thing, but he faces a lot more danger than those tordors or whatever they call them.

Old Wrangler drew a twisting, running bull that threw him the first four or five seconds. The bull went for him, and the clown ran up and put his hand on the bull's forehead. He ran along in front of him like that, cutting up to beat hell. Then he sidestepped and let the bull go by. The crowd got a big kick out of this, and you could hear them holding their breath and then gasping all at the same time. Then the show was over for the day.

But the Fourth of July still had a lot of hours to go!

Mary and Kate came over and grabbed me and Wrangler around the necks, telling us what a hell of a fine job we had done. It made a feller feel right proud. We walked over and got our money and then stood around drinking beer while the crowd cleared out. Some of the hands that hadn't made any spotted our free beer and it wasn't long till it was gone.

Shorty Wilson came over and said, "Well, you got away with it today, Dusty, but you'll never make it through tomorrow."

"Make what?" I asked.

"Why, that horse, that's what. He'll come unwound tomorrow for sure."

"How do you know all this?" I said.

"I been talking to Jim Ed."

"To hell with Jim Ed," I said.

Shorty saw this conversation was making me mad, so he changed the subject. "Where you staying?" he asked.

"Hell's fire, I don't know," I said, taking a drink out of the last can of beer. "Reckon we'll get a motel room."

"Can't," said Shorty. "They're all full. Listen," he said, "you need a place to put your horse. Come on down to my outfit. I've already let all the beds out, but seein' as how you've got bedrolls you can sleep in the barn. It's better than nothing."

I looked at Mary. I called her off and said, "You feel like another night in a bedroll?"

"Why, honey," she said, looking up at me like a suckling calf at its mama, "anything that suits you—"

"Okay," I said.

I went back to Shorty and said, "Thanks, Shorty, we'll take you up on it."

I knew Shorty still figured he was going to get Old Fooler for the dog-food maker. He was sure as hell right, too, but I was going to hold out for a little more money now. We loaded up Old Fooler and took him out to the edge of town and turned him loose in Shorty's corral. Then we headed for town to get something to drink.

There is a lot of dust around a rodeo arena, and it has a tendency to make a feller choke up and his eyes water. They had several places in Hi Lo just made to cure such ailments—the best one being the Wild Cat Bar.

There was people of all kinds in this place—businessmen getting in a few extra licks with their year-around customers and trying to latch on to some new ones. Ranchers stood around talking about cow prices and grass conditions. The working cowboys was drinking like they invented it, and beginning to brag. The jukebox was going full blast, and every now and then somebody would jump up and go to yelling and dancing. One of them was old Wrangler.

We had a lot of talk about different things that happened at the show, and finally everybody got sure-enough drunk and settled down to some real honest-to-God deep-down bragging!

There was old Sowbelly who was still griping about his bad draw on his horse. He kept saying as how he could ride anything that walked, crawled, or flew. Some of the others agreed that he was right but they could do him one better. They could do all that and roll a cigarette at the same time.

It just kept getting worse until I joined in. I didn't brag on me or Wrangler because I had a plan. I got to telling those bronc riders that I didn't think there was too many good riders left around and I went on to say, "Hell, my ropin' horse can throw any rider I saw out there today."

Well, I had so many bets called before I knew what happened that I had to put a limit on it. I took on Sowbelly and two more boys at twenty-five apiece. Then we asked L.C. if it would be all right if we put on this special exhibition just after the calf roping the next day.

He said sure. Then he called me off to the side and said, "Dusty, what in the hell is the matter with you—matching that ropin' horse against three good riders in a row?"

"It's like I always said, L.C., I was just plain dumb to start with, and have got stupider since. But here's fifty more says I am right."

L.C. reached for his money and then stopped. "Naw," he said, "you know somethin' I don't. That old horse is too bad scarred up."

There was a big dance after the show down at the schoolhouse. We didn't make it, though. We changed over from beer to whisky, and the girls got off on screwdrivers again. We held a little dance of our own in the Wild Cat, and besides, I still was getting bets that Old Fooler couldn't down three top-notch riders in a row.

Finally the bar closed and we went down to Shorty's barn and crawled into our bedrolls. We was tired but happy.

FOURTEEN

THE SECOND DAY there was a bigger crowd than ever. We got the grand entry and all over with pretty fast. Wrangler made a fair ride on a little sorrel mare called Twist. But I didn't believe he was in the money. I was the third roper out. I drew a little blue calf that ran like a scared rabbit. Old Fooler built right on top of him. It was an easy loop. I got down and took him even quicker than I had the day before. But I made a bobble on my tie, and the announcer called the time at seventeen point one. I had a hell of a lot of sweating to go through—almost two dozen ropers to come.

Well, when it was all over I had taken third money. The kid that had beat me out of first money the day before missed his loop, but another tied one in thirteen-five. Coy Beasly took first in the two-day average, and I had second. It was the best I had done in six or seven years. Our luck was sure running.

Then Sy Wheeler made the special announcement. "Folks, we have got a little bonus for you. Something a little out of the ordinary. You just saw Dusty Jones win third in the day money and second in the two-day average on that bald-faced roan called Old Fooler. Well, now get this, folks. He has bet a considerable sum of money that this very ropin' horse can throw three good bronc riders one right after the other."

I could hear the crowd buzzing and heads was turning all over the place.

Sowbelly, Doak Andrews, and Sandy Washam was all lined up over at the bucking chutes ready to ride. L.C. yelled for me to bring Old Fooler on over and get the show on the road.

Sowbelly was the best rider of the three, so he was going to go first. I led Old Fooler into the bucking chute from out in the arena. He acted real gentle—like I was fixing to turn him out to pasture. Sowbelly threw his saddle on him and cinched her up tight. Old Fooler just stood there half asleep, like he had done me the first time I ever saddled him up.

Sy Wheeler was saying, "Now, folks, this has to be a contest ride just like any other rodeo horse."

I was a little scared, but when I heard this I got my confidence back. To make a contest ride a feller has got to come out of that chute with his spurs in the horse's shoulder and keep spurring all the time. He has to keep that right hand up so it don't touch the saddle anywhere.

All of a sudden I was wishing I had more money to bet. Hell, there had been plenty of times I couldn't ride the old bastard pulling all the leather there was on the saddle.

They got the rigging ready, and Sowbelly crawled up over the chute and got set in the saddle. He tested the length of the rein to be sure it wasn't so short he would get pulled off over the horse's head when it went down. If it was too long he wouldn't have any control either. That rein had to be just right.

When he was all set, Sowbelly looked around grinning and said, "Turn this plow horse out of here."

Well, me and Wrangler opened the gate, and I can guarantee the world that there wasn't anybody there disappointed except maybe Sowbelly. Old Fooler hung up just a second, then he felt the spurs in his shoulder, and he tucked his head down between his front legs and jumped about ten feet right straight out into the arena. I'm pretty sure Sowbelly never saw anything but the top of Old Fooler's mane after that.

It was all very familiar. Old Fooler flew way out and sucked back and Sowbelly's hat left his head. Then he went up whirling and came down with his head where his rump had been. Sowbelly lost a stirrup. Then he switched back with a long jump, bawling like a castrated bear and kicking with his hind feet. Sowbelly's head snapped back and then he was sailing up into that cool, pure fresh mountain air looking for a soft place to land.

Old Fooler bucked on down to the other end of the arena, where the pickup men gathered him in. Sowbelly didn't know it, but he had made a damn good ride. The other two boys hit the dirt so fast they didn't even know what happened.

The crowd went wild, and Sy Wheeler kept yelling in the mike, "Folks, that's the damn'dest ropin' horse I ever saw!"

Me and Wrangler ran around collecting our money. I never saw so much money in my whole life. I had every pocket full and it was still pouring in.

L.C. came over and wanted to buy Old Fooler for his bucking string.

"No," I said, "L.C., that is too good for the son of a bitch. You don't know what all he has done to me. I am goin' to let Shorty Wilson have him, providin' he will sign a paper guaranteein' to sell him to the dog-meat company."

A big crowd gathered around wanting to know about this horse. Now, no matter what kind of horse you got (he may be a combination roping horse and a champion bucker), you never want to mention how fast he is. Somebody will call you on it.

Old Ed Foster said he would bet me all I could raise that his black five-year-old stallion could outrun Old Fooler for a half mile.

I said, "Make it a one-mile race and you've got a bet."

Wrangler called me off and said, "Dusty, you have matched a race with a racehorse."

"I don't care," I said. "Remember how Old Fooler caught that coyote? Why, he can run like a turpentined greyhound."

"By God, that's right!" Wrangler said, and commenced counting his money, getting ready to bet.

I said, "Wrangler, our luck is running. Look at all we have made. If we can win this race—which you know damn well we can—we won't have to put up with fellers like Jim Ed Love any longer. We can buy a little outfit of our own or just go over to Santa Fe and lay around for a year restin' up and livin' high off the hog. Hell's bells," I said, "this ain't the Fourth of July, boy; this is Christmas!"

"That is right," said Wrangler, and went off waving a fistful of money. We bet every dime we had. All our winnings and damn near a year's wages.

Sy Wheeler told the folks about the matched race that would be held immediately after the final event.

I saddled Old Fooler up and led him around till he got any bucking ideas out of his head. Then I got on him, talking soft.

"Fooler," I said, "after all you have done to me I am goin' to make you a deal. Now, listen close, Fooler. You win this race and I will sell you to L.C. All you will have to do then is eat and drink and sleep. On weekends you can come out of them chutes and buck for four or five seconds and that is all the work you will ever have to do. Don't you realize, Fooler, that a buckin' horse has got the easiest life there is?"

He didn't act like he was paying much attention, but I knew he heard every word.

"Now," I went on, "if you let me down, Fooler, old Shorty Wilson is just dyin' to take you to Denver to that dog-food outfit."

Well, the show was over. I was so nervous I didn't even go out for the wild-cow milking, my favorite event. I couldn't take any chances on Old Fooler throwing a fit just before the race.

The show was over, but there was still a hell of a lot of the Fourth of July spirit around. Everybody stayed for the race and there was a lot more people trying to get bets down against Old Fooler, but me and Wrangler had run out of money. Mary and Kate bet all they could scrape up and said they knew we would win.

Now, me and Ed Foster had agreed we would ride the horses ourselves. We lined up. The judges got ready, and a big hush came over the crowd. Then the feller shot the gun in the air and around that track we flew! Everybody was yelling and going crazy. Hell, all I had to do was lean over on Old Fooler and he went by that stallion so fast I could smell the hair scorch. We took a big lead and I knew we was going to gain a lot more before we circled that track twice. It was money in the bank!

Just about the time I had settled down for a winning race and was wondering how in the hell I would ever be able to spend that much money, Old Fooler quit the track. He just sailed out over the rails like it was a little old hump in the ground and took off toward town. I reared back on them reins with all my might. I sawed and pulled back and forth hard as I could but it just didn't do any good. That crazy bastard ran down between a bunch of scattered houses and then headed for the main drag. There wasn't a damn thing I could do but go along.

He hit the pavement at full speed and damn near fell down making the turn. Then he lined out right down the highway with his ears laid back flat against his evil skull.

I was cussing and yelling my throat raw. Tears would have been dripping down my cheeks except we was going so fast the wind was drying them up before they could hardly get out of my eyes. We went through a red light at the intersection like it was a signal to run plumb around the world.

It was a good thing everybody was out at the rodeo grounds or we would probably have had a hell of a horse-and-car wreck. Then I heard this wailing noise coming closer. It was a siren. The louder it blew, the faster Old Fooler ran. They pulled right up beside us and yelled for us to pull over. Red lights was flashing all over that police car.

I yelled back, "If you can pull this son of a bitch over I will give him to you."

They drove along beside us getting madder all the time. Old Fooler turned off up toward the city light department. There was a fence, made out of double-strength steel, all around it at least ten feet high. Old Fooler ran through an open gate past the plant, and when he came to that big high fence he tried to jump it. Now that Old Fooler horse is quite a jumper, but he ain't no bird. He got about two-thirds up toward the top, and into that fence we crashed. It bent and laid over quite a ways but we didn't make it through.

By the time I got untangled and the world had stopped dodging around, there stood two great big state highway police. They was saying all kinds of things, some of them not very nice. It seems I had run a red light and broke the speed limit doing it.

I said, "Fellers, I could not help myself. I was just along for the ride. Besides, I didn't know that speed limit took in horses."

They let me know it didn't make any difference if it was a bicycle or a giraffe, a speed limit was a speed limit. Besides, I had failed to pull over to the curb on orders.

I stood around arguing for a while because I didn't have any money to pay a fine. They said we'd have to go see the judge.

About that time some feller working for the light department came running out and wanted to know what I intended to do about his fence.

I said, "My friend, I'll tell you. You ride this horse back to town and I will fix that fence." It kind of set him back and gave me a chance to mount Old Fooler.

Then the police backed up and got into the patrol car, eyeing Old Fooler kind of skittish-like. "Foller us."

"With pleasure," I said.

That goddam animal fox-trotted back to town like a regular parade horse. The crowd was already in town. Some of them had come looking for me, and they was yelling things like, "When are you gonna enter Man o' War in the Kentucky Derby?" and such-like. Everybody laughed but me. I bet Old Fooler was laughing hardest of all.

The judge charged me with running a red light, avoiding arrest, and speeding in the city limits. There wasn't a thing to do but appeal it over to district court, for I didn't have enough money to buy an all-day sucker.

When it was all over, I rode down to Shorty Wilson's. Him and Wrangler drove up.

Shorty said, "What happened?"

I said, "Nothin' much. We just loped over to check the light plant. Can't take any chances on that red light at the crossing goin' out. Might cause a wreck."

"Oh," he said. "You ready to sell that horse?"

"Hell, no!" I said. "I am goin' to buy me an ax (then I thought how broke I was), or rather I'm goin' to steal me an ax and chop this son of a bitch up in little pieces and deliver him to the meat company myself. Hell," I went on, "I doubt if they'll buy him, though. A dog wouldn't eat *this* horse."

Then I asked Wrangler, who was looking kind of sad and droopy, "Where's the women?"

"They caught a ride back to Hine's Corner. Said for us to be sure and stop by and see 'em again sometime. Seems like they had enough Fourth of July and figgered they had better get back to business."

"Smart girls," I said.

Well, I can say, and not lie an ounce, that we took a lot of kidding that night. It got so I begun to grin a little myself, though, and we was setting in at the Wild Cat signing them IOU slips just as fast as they would let us.

They had moved the dance over to a vacant building about three doors from the Wild Cat Saloon. We moseyed over and the music was going full blast.

Me and Wrangler picked us up a couple of dark-haired girls. They was painted up in the prettiest colors you ever saw. They was sure nice girls, and when we would leave the dance to go down and have a drink they always paid for the first one. Then I would sign another one of them slips. I signed them all over town.

It didn't seem to matter to the girls, Emma and Dora. They was good dancers, but when I asked Dora if she would like to go down to my bedroll she said it was a mighty nice thought but this was her day off. It was three days later before I figured out what she meant.

We had gone back over to the Wild Cat for about the fourteenth time when a bunch of those Diamond-2 hands came in drunk and raising hell.

Old Wrangler was out on the floor doing a jig and yelling when I heard one of them boys say something about that bag of bones that Dusty Jones thought was a racehorse.

"Girls," I said, "things has gone too far." I got up and went over and looked them hands right in the eye and said, "Did I hear anybody here mention my horse?" *By God,* I thought, *I will cuss him all I damn please, but nobody else is going to very long.*

One feller opened his mouth to say something, and I let go and rammed my fist down his throat just as far as I could. A bunch of teeth went along with it. Then I kicked him in the belly and turned around to see if anybody else wanted to cuss my horse. Evidently some of them did, for about four of them cowboys began to beat on me at once. The air was plumb full of fists, and every damn one of them was connecting with me. I would have gone down a dozen times but every time one would hit me on one side and knock me off balance, another would hit me from the other and straighten me up.

Then things got a little better. There was not any way they could get worse. I heard old Wrangler hollering and began to notice that the pressure was easing. Now just because Wrangler's legs is bowed so bad that he looks like he's squatting does not mean he is weak or puny. Far, far from it. He has got arms like a bull's hindquarters, and his neck is thick as a pine stump. He was thumping them cowboys in the belly, then kicking them in the face when they doubled over.

We was beginning to see daylight and I had got to where I could actually take aim again when those same state police hit the door blowing whistles and pulling guns. It took them quite a while to get things sorted out, and one of them had to give orders from the floor. He had run in between me and the feller who I had first hit in the mouth. This feller was swinging one of them long, get-even punches, and it caught the policeman in the side of the head and down he went. The other one started shooting in the air. Things gradually died down some.

When the policeman saw it was me he said, "You again?" He put the handcuffs on me so fast I didn't have time to salute.

Wrangler was still jumping around swinging and kicking and snorting through his nose—plumb loco. The other cop got up off the floor and hit him under the ear with a pistol barrel. Poor old Wrangler lost all his interest in the fight right then and there. While they was arresting us, the Diamond-2 boys hightailed it out of there and left town.

They took me and Wrangler over to the county jail and threw us in. It was a long night. It was hot and my nerves was frazzled. I couldn't sleep. Besides, no matter which way I turned there was sore spots and my face was swelled up like a bloated cow's belly. One eye was tight shut. Wrangler was not in much better shape.

About nine o'clock in the morning the jailer came around and fed us some oatmeal and prunes with two cold biscuits and a cup of week-old coffee.

I said to Wrangler, having a hell of a time working my sore jaw, "Wrangler, we are in a hell of a fix. They will have every charge in the book against us and we owe money all over town. What in the hell are we goin' to do? If we don't pay this fine we will have to lay it out in jail."

Wrangler did not give me much satisfaction. He grunted and rubbed one of his swelled-up fists. I was aching all over, inside and out.

The Fourth of July was sure enough over.

We groaned and worried for what seemed like a month. About ten o'clock the jailer came back and took us down before the judge.

I started right in. "We ain't got no money, Judge," I said. "We'll just have to lay it out."

After that horse race yesterday I would have stayed in jail the rest of my life before I would have asked one of these Hi Lo citizens for bail.

The judge didn't pay any attention to me. He picked up the phone, leaving us to stand there twitching and worrying. He called the bank and asked for Mr. Salter, the vice president. Then he put the phone down and smiled at us. That is the first time in my life I ever had a judge smile at me. I looked down at my boots to see if there was any cowshit on them.

Then old Salter walked in and laid a stack of little papers out on the judge's desk. It was that bunch of IOU's I had signed. Even with my sick and bloodshot eyes I could see my name wrote there.

Well, I thought, *they are going to send me to the penitentiary for life.* I could just see me and Wrangler using that big sledgehammer and making little rocks out of big ones till we was so old we couldn't lift our arms no more. Then I could see them standing us up against the wall and shooting us full of holes.

I'll be damned if old Salter wasn't grinning. Maybe the same thoughts had occurred to him.

Salter said, "Boys, you are sure lucky to be working for a man like Jim Ed Love."

Then I remembered Jim Ed was a director in his bank.

"Yes, you sure are," the judge said, still smiling.

I remembered something else. Jim Ed was county chairman of the same party that had elected the judge.

I didn't say a thing.

Salter went on, "Jim Ed has picked up and paid all these IOU's. He has paid your fines here, too, and said he was glad to see you boys had a good Fourth of July, but to get on back to the ranch now just as soon as you could. He has a new string of broncs ready for you to top out."

I still didn't say a thing. I couldn't.

"Shorty Wilson is waiting outside with your pickup loaded and full of gas, all ready to go," Salter finished.

Me and Wrangler swallowed back that day-old whisky and walked out into the dazzling sunshine, as them town fellers say.

Shorty had unloaded Old Fooler and was writing out a check. I went around and opened the end gate and Old Fooler jumped in.

"What's the matter?" said Shorty. "What you loading that horse up for?"

"If I am goin' to have to worry about Jim Ed, I might as well worry about this son of a bitch too," I said, and climbed in the pickup and took off, leaving Shorty standing there waving that check.

We drove out of town just as fast as we could without breaking the speed limit. Pretty soon we was out on the open road. Wrangler hunkered down in the seat so only the top of his head was showing. In a little while we was getting ready to pass Hine's Corner, and I remembered the girls had asked us to stop by. I scrooched down just as low as I could and still see out over the radiator and really pushed down on the foot-feed.

Just when it looked like we would get by without being seen, that goddam bell started ringing again and Old Fooler went to kicking and squealing. I felt like I was naked in church.

I had forgot about the bell, but I wasn't going to stop till we was well out in the country. Pretty soon Old Fooler stopped kicking and went to nickering, keeping pretty good time with that bell.

I wheeled off on that country road. Them bumps sure felt good. I never wanted to hear of another drink of whisky as long as I lived, and I was sure glad it was a full year till another Fourth of July.

"Wrangler," I said.

He grunted.

"Jim Ed ain't such a bad feller after all. He feeds good, don't he?"

Wrangler grunted.

"There ain't but one windmill on his outfit, and he feeds good," I
repeated.

He grunted a little louder, almost talking.

"He don't never interfere and try to tell a man how to break out a
string of broncs. All he wants is results. Ain't that right?" I said.

Wrangler sat up a little and said, "Dusty."

"Yeah?"

"You know what a bronc rider is?"

"What?" I asked.

"It's a cowboy with his brains kicked out."

"I reckon you're right," I said.

The Great Wedding

ONE

HE WAS AT IT AGAIN. Jim Ed Love was smooth-talking hell out of me and poor old Wrangler.

"Now, boys, I had a tough time gettin' you fellers out of that Hi Lo jail. Why you was charged with everything but rape, and if I hadn't seen the kind of gals you was courtin' I'da figured you guilty of that . . . drunk, disturbin' the peace, assaulting an officer of the law . . ." Then he rubbed his great big whey belly shaking that gold watch chain and said, like he was talking to a couple of runny-nose orphans, "Tch, tch."

I knew we were trapped. Everything he said was true and then some. He had picked up a bunch of hot checks and fixed it with the judge to get us sprung.

I looked down at little squatty Wrangler where he stood on his bent-out legs picking his nose. Right at this minute I was wishing so hard my corns ached that old Wrangler was married to a rich woman, but it was head-hurting clear that getting him married was not going to be the easiest job I ever had. Like the town fellers say, "Where there's a will . . ." and it was the only way I could figure out to get away from Jim Ed and get me a decent job for once in my life.

Jim Ed interrupted my thinking with, "Now, fellers, I know you had a reasonably hard winter down at the lower camp, what with spending the whole year gatherin' wild cows and such. I know you missed out on a lot of fun around the ranch here—poker games in the bunkhouse, drinkin' bouts ever' other Saturday in Hi Lo. Well, that ain't goin' to be no more."

I was beginning to believe him till he started rubbing that sirloin-manufactured belly and caressing the brim of that cloud-white fifty-dollar hat.

"No siree, fellers—" He laid one diamond-covered hand out on my shoulder so heavy and friendly if I'd had a tail I'd have wagged it hairless. "No siree, you're going to stay within a day's ride of head-quarters where you can be in on *everything*. Now, we're startin' the roundup in a few weeks. You boys know that's the highlight of the year—sort of the sugar in the coffee so to speak."

Well, guess what? That is right, we shook hands and agreed to stay on at the slave-driving JL Ranch. We walked out of the house feeling kind of numb. There in the back of the pickup was Old Fooler.

I said, "Wrangler, at least this'll give me a chance to get even with that good-for-nothing-but-trouble horse on my own terms. I don't mind the fact that he's tried to kill me ever' way known to horse, man, and maybe God, but when he jumped the rail and lost us all that money in the horse race at Hi Lo, well, the right words are goin' beggin'."

Wrangler grunted out of his somewhat caved-in face and Old Fooler seemed to actually smile at me. It caused another one of them uneasy feelings, that smile. If he'd showed his teeth I would have known what to do—take a fence post and bust him between the ears.

As usual Jim Ed had a big heavy calf crop that spring, and all the other ranchers sent "reps" over for the fall roundup to see if any of their cattle were mixed in with the JL brand. There wasn't much time for visiting among old friends. Jim Ed saw to that. I will say one thing, he gave me and Wrangler the great honor of assigning us the outside circle. Now that is the longest and hardest ride and takes the best cowboys to handle it. I don't think that had much to do with what kind of cowboys we were but more to do with the long hard ride.

They had a Dodge Power Wagon all rigged up like an old-time chuck wagon with a chuck box on the back and a cranky cook up front. Roundup was like Jim Ed said, "sugar in the coffee."

I mounted Old Fooler for the first circle and Wrangler roped him a brown out of the remuda. We worked up through the brush making a wide circle, jumping out little bunches of cattle now and then. We shoved them back down to the holding grounds on the flats. Old Fooler was working smooth and right. A cow no sooner tried to turn back than that old devil blue roan was biting her right in the rump.

By noon the horses were tiring so we rode back down to the re-muda and roped two fresh mounts. I knew tomorrow we'd be working in rougher country and I wanted that crazy Fooler horse under me.

We rode back out for the brush under a sure enough blue sky. The grass on Jim Ed's outfit looked riper than yellow corn and thicker than hair on a skunk's tail. It was what is known among some thoughtful folks as a mighty fine fall day.

We reined up to roll ourselves a smoke and I said, "Wrangler, there comes a time in every cowboy's life when he needs to hang up his spurs for a spell. Sort of set in the saddle without movin', so to speak," and I gazed off into about nine hundred miles of space.

Wrangler grunted in what sounded to me like drunk Navaho and took a drag on his smoke that made her burn halfway to his jaws right before my eyes.

"Now for us old, broke-up cowboys they ain't too many choices."

He looked at me, those little rat-shaped eyes just asking "How?" right out loud.

"First, we can't draw none of this here unemployment pay. Cowboys ain't never had any of that. Second, it's mighty hard and costly to get insurance on a cowboy. So collecting that is next to impossible. Now we could go on relief. You know, get hungry enough a feller'll do anything."

"Oh, it's against the law to starve to death in this country," said Wrangler.

"How do you figger that?"

"Well, if you get so hungry and weak you cain't stand up, some damn fool will drag you in off the street and feed you."

This last, one of the longest speeches in history made by Wrangler, kinda defeated my purpose so I whipped up and got to the main point.

"Course a man could save all that embarrassment and injury to his pride by marrying a rich woman."

"That ain't easy," Wrangler said with great wisdom.

"Ain't nothin' easy," I said, battling right back. "Besides a feller could do a lot of good in the world, like takin' care of his old bunged-up friends by givin' them good jobs on an easy-to-run outfit."

"Well, why don't you marry one?" said that dumb Wrangler.

I swallered hard and studied that nine hundred miles of space again, then I said, "I just ain't got the charm, that's all. If I had what you have, Wrangler, I'd of been hooked up years ago."

He sort of stiffened in the saddle and I could tell this last had taken hold. Course, if a man had to admit to who was the best looking between us, old Wrangler wouldn't even be sucking hind teat, he'd be dragging right by the end of the tail. But I figured it best to keep him thinking the other way.

TWO

I DID SOME HARD THINKING. If I was going to get Wrangler married off the best thing to do was discourage him towards punching cows every way I could. So to start with, I make the widest circle that day I ever heard of. A cowboy may have a rawhide hind end, but that won't keep it from getting numb.

That evening we finished filling up on beans and biscuits just as the sun turned off. Most of the boys hit their bedrolls early. Old Wrangler didn't even say good night.

The cook was cleaning up and the boys riding night herd out in the flats were wishing they were back in camp. I eased back on my bedroll and tried to think some more. I stared up at those zillion stars, nothing helped. It's pretty hard to think with a numb ass.

The next day we caught up our horses. Wrangler's had a hump in his back like a snake-bit hog. He saddled him, led him up a few steps, and climbed on. The brown broke out in a dead run, swallered his head and went straight up about six feet. When he came down he hit the ground with all four feet bunched close together. I felt like my neck was broken just watching, but it didn't even seem to bother Wrangler because he just headed him off in the direction we were going to work.

I mounted up and followed. But just before I did, I grabbed a bottle of Hi-Life the cook used to get rid of stray dogs, and shoved it in my chaps pocket. By the time I caught Wrangler he had pulled the bronc's head up where it belongs.

"Feels good, don't he?"

Wrangler grunted.

We rode on a piece before the horse settled down enough so Wrangler would tear his hand away from the saddle horn.

"This here is some life, ain't it, Wrangler? Get up in the morning with nothing but smoke in your eyes to warm by. The coffee's so thick and bitter it tastes like cedar bark. The biscuits harder'n cinch rings and the bacon is salty and tooth-breakin' tough. Nice gentle horses, too. Easy on a man's old broken bones. You know what I heard the last time we were in Hi Lo?"

Grunt.

"Well, I heard that ever' time an old boy rode a bucking horse it meant one less drunk he could go on!"

He twisted his head around on his shoulders, staring with his eyes wide open. He didn't say anything but I could tell I'd penetrated to the quick.

The sun was up and shining on the mesas and we could see a few fresh tracks now. We reined up.

"Look," I said, pointing way off to the west, "ain't that a bunch of cattle in that opening between them rock bluffs?"

He looked.

I slipped the Hi-Life out and poured it right plentifully on the root of his horse's tail. Now when you pour this stuff on a dog it soaks down around the hair roots and he will run a mile in two minutes, yapping his head off—and he won't be back to visit. It has a funny smell, something like chloroform, so I thought I'd talk fast and keep Wrangler's mind off this horse's intentions.

"Do you see 'em?"

"Naw."

"You sure?"

"Yaw."

Blooey! Away they went. Two jumps out and one back. Wrangler went east and the old pony south.

I took off after the horse feeling mighty sorry about Wrangler having to walk. I just wasn't going to let that happen to my best friend. Way up on the mesa I could hear brush popping and hoofs pounding against rock. It took me quite a spell to hem the brown up in a blind draw and catch him. Then I rode out in a patch of brush where I could look back down at Wrangler. He was up limping around, twisting his head one way and another trying to hear my return.

I sat there about an hour, real still, feeling it my duty to let Wrangler have a chance to get over his embarrassment.

When I finally rode up and said, "Feels good, don't he?" I thought Wrangler was going to choke on all the cuss words he was spitting out.

We finally moved several little bunches of cattle down towards the main herd.

It had been a hard day but nothing like the night. Breakfast came just after midnight it seemed to me. Old Wrangler was sure limping. Of course, he's not much of a walker at his best.

We rode out about a mile from camp when I got itchy to go on with my plans. But I was afraid to pull the cattle-spotting stunt again. Pretty soon old Wrangler pulled it for me. He thought he'd located some stock.

"Yeah," I said, "I believe there's a couple of head, but what is that spot off about fifty yards to the right?" Then I poured on the Hi-Life.

Before it could soak in, old Wrangler spurred up a couple of steps, yanked back on the reins and jumped off. Their heads went down together as Wrangler bit down on the horse's ear. That ole pony was shaking all over trying to make up his mind which end was hurting the most. Wrangler just held him there with his ear clinched between his teeth. After a while Wrangler turned loose and the Hi-Life effects must have been gone because the horse just kind of scooted around, snorted at Wrangler a couple of times, and settled down.

I said, "What'n hell's the matter?"

"I ain't sure," he said, "but this ole pony smelled just like that one did yesterday."

We rode back to camp late that afternoon with me and Wrangler feeling just about the same, sort of let-down and mean as bloody-nosed bears.

We finished the roundup and all I could say when they hauled all those fat, profitable calves off to market in those big long red cattle trucks was, "It sure would be nice if those were yours, Wrangler. Just think, you could go on up to Denver with 'em and stay drunk all the time you was countin' your money."

"They ain't mine," he said.

I had to agree.

THREE

OLD JIM ED sure hadn't lied to us. We could play poker any night we wanted with the boys in the bunkhouse. The trouble was, our hands were so bent and sore from lifting bales of hay we couldn't shuffle the cards.

Haying was a big thing on the JL. South of the house were acres and acres of hay fields, all irrigated from springs. Jim Ed always kept a lot of extra hay so he'd have it ready in case of a big blizzard. I'd heard that one winter he'd come into thousands of acres in Texas and Colorado by controlling the feed market, and made a fortune selling hay to stricken ranchers. Nice feller, our boss.

I really caught Jim Ed off guard when I volunteered mine and Wrangler's services for this hay gathering. Of course, Wrangler didn't know this and I decided it wasn't my place to tell him.

Now this hay was cut and crushed into bales weighing about eighty pounds apiece and there were thousands of them. We pitched bales all day long onto a flatbed truck, then we piled one on top of the other into a pyramid-shaped stack. This was just the first cutting. There'd be another for us later.

"Wrangler," I said, stopping to take a breath and a smoke, "if a man was married to a rich woman he wouldn't have to put up hay. As far as that goes his number one foreman wouldn't either."

"How come?"

"Why, we'd either hire it done or buy it from some other fool. A man needs to be in shape to rodeo and go dancin'. He shouldn't be gettin' out of trainin' by crackin' his back on this hay."

"Sounds fine," he said.

I was encouraged by his enthusiasm.

"Now soon as we get a couple of paydays together, I think we ought to go in and see Rosie at the General Mercantile. It's been two years since her old man died. She must be gettin' lonesome for some male company."

Grunt.

"Now think of this, Wrangler, she's got a big store paid for, a twenty-section ranch running along the main highway with plenty of improvements and water, and no tellin' what else."

"She ain't gonna marry no cowboy."

I hadn't thought about this part of it. It was true that Rosie had known at least three thousand broken-down, worthless cowboys in her time. We'd just have to figure a way to make old Wrangler appear different. I had plenty of time to think about it the next few days.

We put up the hay and I told Jim Ed on the sly that I felt me and Wrangler had had it too soft and wondered if he couldn't find us a fence-building job. He did the next morning.

One of his big springs had turned into a bog. Cows were commencing to get out in it and sink down so far they had to be roped and pulled out. It would take a strong fence to enclose it.

Now a posthole digger is a mighty mean-looking thing to get hold of just standing still, but when you raise the handles as high as you can reach and drive it into the hard ground all day long, it is something most cowboys won't even think of, much less talk about. After the holes are dug, the posts have to be lined up straight and tapped into the ground solid. Then you stretch the wire and staple it to the posts. On top of all that you build gates and hang deadmen (rocks tied to the corner post and buried in the ground) so it will stand upright.

It might be an interesting change of work for a rock-busting prisoner, but it was beginning to tell on us cowboys. This was what I wanted. I was willing to go through any sacrifice to show my friend the bright and sparkling righteousness of hooking up with a rich woman.

I said, "You got to admit that things would look better to us if you was roastin' your shins out at Rosie's ranch house knowin' that she was in town selling them beans and bacon, and your best friend was out in the pasture looking after your cattle. Why, right now instead of holding a bunch of blood blisters in both hands you could be caressin' a fat bottle of bourbon. Not only that but you could bed down tonight full of fine steak and whiskey right next to big-teated Rosie. As it is, you'll sleep in a cold bunkhouse full of cold, dirty cowboys."

"There's some difference there," Wrangler admitted.

Well I figured he was far enough along for me to make my real sales talk—the one I'd been studying over and saving up.

"Wrangler, if Old Fooler was a genuine gentle horse, one you could trust your life with . . ."

"Wouldn't even trust him with Jim Ed's life."

"I know, but what I mean, supposin' he *was* gentle."

"Yeah."

"Would you bet on him in a horse race against anything around Hi Lo?"

"Hell yes. Why?"

"I'll tell you why, because I've got a plan to make you look really great in Rosie's eyes. Not only that, but you'll appear to be the smartest cowboy this side of Canada."

"That's lots of country."

"You're a smart cowboy."

"How come?"

"Listen now, listen like you was goin' to be *given* a thousand dollars worth of Vince Moore's bootleg whiskey if you don't miss a word I say."

FOUR

I WAS STILL TRYING to explain things when we drove up in front of Vince Moore's house.

Now I'll say this for Vince's place: even if the windmill is generally broken, corral poles split and falling all over, panes out of half the windows, the chimney leaking smoke from a loose joint, the porch leaning way to the north, there is plenty of action—chickens scratching about and doing things all over the yard, dogs barking and wagging tails at the same time, dirty-faced kids peeking around the porch, the corner of the house, and between their mother's legs, and Vince throwing the door to the outhouse open yelling, "Don't leave, boys. I'll finish in a breeze."

"Howdy, Mrs. Moore."

"What do you mean, 'Mrs. Moore'? Now, Dusty Jones, you know my name is Marthy."

"That I do, Marthy."

"Howdy, Marthy," said Wrangler.

"Why howdy, Wrangler Lewis," she said, pushing the straight cords of hair back behind her ears, and trying to shove her chest out and lift her suckling glands just a little. It was too late for that—round fifteen years too late. Kids just plain have a habit of swinging down on them instead of up, and when you've had as many kids as Marthy . . . but even so Marthy was always plumb purty to me.

"Coffee?" she asked as we stepped inside. "Er . . . something else?"

"Something else sounds mighty fine to me," said Wrangler, suddenly snapping to.

She got some big tin cups from the cupboard, set them out in front of us, and said Vince would be there in a minute to get the *goody* for us.

"What you boys been doin' besides Jim Ed's dirty work?"

"That's all, Marthy. That's all."

Wrangler nodded.

Jim Ed had been able to take over everybody's ranch that jogged into his but Vince's little outfit. He broke Vince as a cowman, but Vince had come on strong as a bootlegger—of course, strong to Vince might be weak to other people. If he had a new batch of whiskey made up, a half sack of beans, and the same of flour he was pretty stable. Besides he liked chasing coyotes with his old skinny dogs better than he did cattle anyway.

Vince came busting through the door just knocking kids seven ways, shaking hands, pouring whiskey and talking like a radio all at once. He set the jug down on the table, threw a bunch of grease shaped like a hat on the floor, and said, "It sure is good to see you. It sure is." Then his face sort of fogged over. He whammed his cup down and ran to the door. "I knew it," he yelled. "By God I knew it. The mean-eyed son of a bitch is still alive. You ain't tradin' him to me again! He tore up my corrals, fences, everything!" His hair had fallen down over his milky eyes but he was too mad to see anyway.

"Now calm down, Vince," I said. "Why, I wouldn't trade you that blazed-face roan for your whole outfit, kids and all."

Vince sorta whoa'd a minute, breathing like he had to and even if his eyes were covered I knew they were bugging.

"Liars, liars!" he said through clenched teeth as he glanced at Old Fooler standing peaceful-like in the back of the pickup. "I . . . I . . ."

"Now here, have another drink and listen to what we've thought up."

Vince's hair was kinda like Marthy's only thinner and rattier looking. I was glad when he pushed it out of his eyes so I could tell if it had come in his mind to grab the shotgun from the wall and blow my cockeyed head off.

"Here's the plan. Ever'body knows that Old Fooler can outrun anything in the country. He proved that last Fourth of July when he was leading the best horse around by four jumps."

"I tell you I wouldn't have that damn horse if you gave me Jim Ed's ranch to take him."

"Now, Vince, I ain't giving you no sales talk. Just listen." He poured us another drink while I went on. "At the same time ever'body knows that horse jumped the rail and had a runaway."

"We lost," said Wrangler.

"That's right, we lost," I agreed. "We lost ever'thing we'd won in the rodeo and a whole year's wages. Taking ever'thing into consideration I want to ask you boys a question."

"Shoot."

Wrangler said, "Uh."

"Will you fellers agree that you can depend on Old Fooler to mess up no matter what?"

"Hooray, hell yes, and I should say so right out loud in church," said Vince.

"Ever' goddamned time," said Wrangler.

"That's all I need to know," I said, smiling into my cup. "Now, I'm goin' to wind this up fast, so hang on and listen close."

Vince leaned forward across the table. Wrangler humped up with his cup stopped dead still an inch from his mouth. That's listening, brother.

"Well, if Old Fooler was to suddenly turn black . . ."

"Oh good! You're goin' to kill him and let him rot," Vince said hopefully.

"Will you fellers let me do the talking. Now if he was to turn black on the outside . . . say that somebody rubbed some of that charcoal you use all the time to make this wonderful stuff we're drinkin' all over that roan, he'd turn black wouldn't he?"

"Blacker'n a bear's butt," said Wrangler, snapping to a little more all the time.

"Blacker'n Jim Ed's heart," said Vince.

"Now, don't get carried away," said Marthy from over in the corner where she was patching a shirt.

"Now, if some folks around Hi Lo was to see this here beautiful black horse at a distance—just see him runnin' loose and free they would know he was a runnin' fool. Right?"

"Right."

"Right."

"All right, then. In that case if somebody was to match a race on that little bay of yours, Vince, then ever'body would bet on the black."

"Right, by God."

"Whoopeee," Wrangler agreed strongly.

I stopped for breath and poured us all another cup of that perfect thirst quencher from the crock jug.

"If we was to have five hundred dollars bet on the bay we would be sure to win, huh?"

"Couldn't miss," said Vince, "because that Old Fooler horse would jump the rail, fall down, start bucking or running the wrong way before you'd get a quarter of the way around the track."

"Well, me and Wrangler here ain't been to town, Vince, in several paydays, and we've got her right here in cash!" I threw it all out on the table, and Vince tried to swaller the tin cup.

"Now all you got to do is co-operate a little and we'll clean out that Hi Lo so fast it won't know what county it's in."

On the way over to Vince's I told Wrangler that if we'd tip Rosie off so she'd get down some good fat bets, she would sure appreciate the winnings. Not only that, but she'd just bust her big fat drawers wanting to marry old Wrangler when I told her it was *all* his idea. A smart man like that is hard to find.

Vince stood up and sloshed out another round.

"Dusty, you're a go-gettin' son of a bitch!"

"Wrangler," I asked, feeling kind of embarrassed at all that praise, "what do you think?"

"Whatever suits you just tickles me plumb to death."

I knew from past experiences I had Wrangler sold to the gut hollow.

FIVE

WE GOT OLD FOOLER out of the pickup. It wasn't easy to do, but with
the help of Vince's jug we got her done. Vince brought out a keg of
charcoal and we started rubbing it on him.

"Ain't that purty?" I said.

"Yeah," said Wrangler.

"It ain't gonna stay put, fellers," said Vince.

"It don't have to stay long," I said.

"Just long enough to clean out Hi Lo," said Wrangler.

Right there, I, Dusty Jones, started using this head of mine for smart
purposes again. I never felt so cockeyed smart in my whole life.

"Vince?"

"Yeah, Dusty."

"You got any varnish?"

"Sure have, by doggies, a whole gallon of it. Had it for years. Been
aimin' to use it on somethin' like the floor or maybe a wagon bed."

"Your problems are over."

"How's that?"

"Just get it, Vince. Just bring it to old Dusty."

While Vince went to get the varnish I went back in the house to see
Marthy on important business.

"Marthy, do you have a fly sprayer?"

"Yeah, but we ain't had any ammunition for it in three years. Flies
ain't bad out here anyway, not enough fer 'em to eat."

"Well, let me borrow it for just a spell."

She handed it over.

"Now, boys, watch this," I said as I poured the varnish in the fly
sprayer. They sure did watch.

Then I reared back and mashed the handle with the machine aimed
right at Old Fooler. Nothing happened. I tried her again. The same.

THE GREAT WEDDING   145

"It's too thick," I said, and grabbed the jug away from Wrangler. He put up quite a fight till I explained I was only going to use a shot or two.

I poured half the varnish out of the sprayer and filled it up with whiskey. Then I gave her a good shaking and mashed that handle again. The trick was done. That stuff sprayed out of there and settled the charcoal down just like it had grown that way.

"By God, fellers," old Vince said, "I done said it, that Dusty's a go-gettin' son of a bitch!"

I didn't even have time to agree. I said, "Get your bay horse, Vince, we're headin' for Hi Lo."

Wrangler said, "Whooooopeee and hurrah," and jumped just as high as he could right straight up in the air. At that he just barely got off the ground.

We crowded both horses in the pickup bed, Vince fetched another jug, and we all yelled good-bye at Marthy and the kids. When they answered back it sounded like a jail full of drunks. Away we went.

Just before getting into Hi Lo we turned off down a little wagon road and hunted some brush. We unloaded the horses. I tied Old Fooler with a double catch rope to a stout cedar.

"Now, Vince, give me and old Wrangler about an hour in town. Then you come ridin' in like you hadn't seen us in a year. You know what to do from there on."

"Sure do," he said. "Here, fellers, give me that jug. It's gonna get lonesome out here the next hour."

When times were better, Hi Lo had several saloons. Now there were just two, the Double Duty and the Wildcat. It didn't take a man long to make up his mind. Today we picked Nick Barnes' Wildcat.

"Well, looky here," he said, "if it ain't Dusty and Wrangler. Ain't seen you boys since the Fourth of July."

"We ain't been anywhere to be seen," I said.

"Whiskey," Wrangler said.

"Whiskey," I said.

"Comin' up. Doubles or singles?"

"One of each," I said.

"Too bad the way that old roan horse double-crossed you in that race, Dusty. You boys could have bought old Jim Ed's whole outfit with those winnings."

"Well, I ain't aimin' to lose another." I wanted to thank Nick for

bringing up the right subject at the right time. I ordered us another
drink figuring that was thanks enough for any bartender.

Then I went on, "I've got a black horse, gentle as an old blind dog,
but faster than that Old Fooler horse ever thought about."

"Is that a fact?" Nick said, wiping the sweat off his forehead and
rubbing spilled whiskey on his hatbox belly.

"That's a fact."

Wrangler said, "I don't believe he's that fast myself."

"Now, Wrangler, I've told you and told you that I've run him
against Old Fooler and it was a dead heat."

"That's good enough for me," said Nick.

"Sure wish somebody'd come along with some sporting blood," I
said, and in a few minutes somebody with that very kind of blood rode
up singing and yelling to beat hell. I'll be damned if it wasn't Vince
Moore.

"Wonder what he's doin' in town?" I said.

"Looks drunk to me," said Nick.

"Naw, just headin' that way," said Wrangler.

It didn't take Vince long to tie that good-looking bay to a telephone
pole, come in and have three drinks on me and Wrangler. In the time
it takes to do that very thing a bunch of people had started to gather.
Delfino Mondragon was in town with six months' back pay from sheep
herding. Cowboys, farmers, and all gathered around knowing there
was something going to happen. It did.

Delfino said, "Dusty, I feels like a leetle poker game."

He rubbed his black curly hair and said again, "A leetle games of
chances."

Vince Moore whammed his glass down and said, "I'll match that
bay horse right there, for five eighths of a mile, against any horse in
the country!"

I said, "Why, Vince, I've got an old black horse that is just havin' a
fit to run. In fact, if he don't get hisself in a race soon I figger he's just
goin' to fret his poor self to death."

"I'm gonna give you the opportunity to save a horse's life. Cause I'll
bet five hundred he cain't run as good as you think he can."

Well, all hell and things that were more fun broke loose. Everybody
wanted to see this black.

I said, "Now just a minute, boys. When the time is right I'll have
him ready. But first let's toast Hi Lo and all the fine people around it.
To all the rich and all the poor, and let's go ahead and say that we

hope some of them folks get to change places now and then, so they'll
know how the other side feels."

I was so damn near out of breath it took me about a minute to tell
Wrangler, "Get over to Rosie's and tip her off!"

Out he scooted.

Now old Vince had our five hundred and he was willing to bet it for
us. Every dollar of it was to go on the bay.

As soon as I saw Wrangler and Rosie Peabody standing on the
porch of the mercantile, I said, "Now, fellers, all of you line up down
at the racetrack bleachers and I'll show you that black."

A big yell went up and everybody headed for the track. I took off
for the brush. I saddled Old Fooler and told him, "Now, I've given
you a reprieve from soap factories. I've kept you from being turned
into dog food time after time. Now's your opportunity to pay me
back. Just don't buck till I turn you loose at full speed."

Old Fooler looked at me and it was almost a kind expression that
came on his face. I picked up the nearly empty jug Vince had left and
settled its fate in one swaller. I had confidence.

As I rode out onto the track, the black hair gleamed where the
varnish was on it. In the late fall like this, the other horses around had
started putting on long winter hair. This black looked like he'd been
combed and prepared for the Kentucky Derby. When we headed
down the track I opened Old Fooler up, but at the same time I didn't
let a millionth of an inch of slack come in the reins. If I had he'd have
thrown me clear over the bleachers. That's exactly what I wanted him
to do later.

As soon as I got around the track, where nobody could get close
enough to examine Old Fooler, I looked over at the crowd. I could
just hear them sucking in their breaths at this beautiful-moving, shiny
racehorse. They were all gathered around Rosie and Vince making
bets. I knew the odds had jumped a mile as soon as they saw the horse.
I circled once more holding him back.

Vince rode out and we lined up a little ways back from the bleachers. It was agreed that Rosie would say *go*. She gave me a big wink
right out over them big teats Wrangler would enjoy so much, and I
could feel my shins roasting by her fireplace already. I could just see
Wrangler getting up around ten in the morning and saying, "Dusty,
sometime this month we've got to get out and look for a stray cow."
Why, after this race he would actually be able to buy and pay for the
wedding ring. Wonderful, wonderful world!

"Go!"

We did.

I have been on some fancy-moving things in my life when you figure it all the way around, but it seemed like Old Fooler was going to outdo them all. He sure did. He passed the bay so fast I didn't have time to wave good-bye. When we hit the first turn, I pitched him the slack. I knew he would take rail and all when he left the track. Well, I damn near fell off because I was expecting to go one way but he kept running the other. *That* is right. Straight down the middle of the track we went.

Well at the end of the five lengths he was way, way ahead. But that was nothing—on his second time around he caught up with the bay from behind. Then, *that* is right, *then* he jumped the fence.

He was beginning to slow down some when we hit Shorty Wilson's backyard. I'm sure glad it wasn't fenced. I could see a clothesline full of diapers coming right at us. I yanked on the reins as hard as I could and spurred even harder on one shoulder trying to turn him. It did. It turned him from a runner to a bucker. I ain't sure he meant to do it but he saved my life right there. That clothesline would have cut me right in half but Old Fooler, bless his heart, jumped so high that he hung the saddle horn over it and when he came down the line broke at both ends. I reached down trying to get hold of the horn, but it was too late. I prolonged fate about six or seven more jumps and away I went.

As soon as I could get the gravel brushed out of my eyes I looked up to see where Old Fooler was headed. That black-ass bastard was headed uphill for heaven, with two wings of wet diapers flapping the breeze.

It was almost dark before we finally caught Old Fooler and got him loaded in the pickup with the bay and the rest of us. I didn't ask Wrangler how Rosie felt, I knew. I didn't ask Vince how he felt, I knew. There was one of those silences that only the deaf or the dead can know.

We hit the highway and I thought it best to bypass town because Shorty Wilson's wife might want her diapers back and it would take me twenty-five years to gather them.

Finally Vince said, "You know what?"

"What?" old blabbermouth Wrangler asked.

"That Fooler horse is a go-gettin' son of a bitch!"

SIX

I CAN TELL YOU one thing for sure, Jim Ed would just naturally see to it that we got in plenty of work. But old cunning me—I decided to help things along. The way I figured it, old Wrangler just had to get sure enough fed up with this ranch life, at least on the hired hand's end, before he'd get serious about marrying a rich woman.

A second hay cutting was about ready so I bobbed up and volunteered our best efforts. Now Jim Ed acted kind of surprised, but he acted a little bit tickled, too. It ain't the easiest thing in the world to get a couple of broke-up cowboys to put up hay twice in one year.

We took to riding a tractor; that is right. Hard to believe, but sure as hell true. Hooked to that tractor was a long hay-cutting blade that sliced her down slick. Then we came along and raked it up into wind rows and let it dry a couple of days in the hot sun. After that we drove a hay baler over it and the next thing you knew the fields were covered with pretty green bales.

Getting that hay into bales is just the first item; the second ain't quite so easy. It has to be loaded on a flatbed truck, hauled to the stack lots, unloaded, and stacked bale by bale in the form of a long pyramid. Lift. Lift. Lift. It takes some doing. Me and Wrangler were the doers.

After about two weeks of this I could tell my pardner was beginning to weaken. It was also getting boring doing the same thing over and over. That's just the way I wanted it. He even started talking *first* for once.

"This here work ain't fit for nothin' but mules," he said.

"You're right," I agreed.

"Well, how come we're doin' it then?"

I came right back at him since the whole thing was my bright idea. "Mules are too smart."

He grunted once and farted twice as he lifted a great big bale up to me on the stack.

We stacked right on into winter. And I might say there were times when I felt a little bit stupid for getting into this myself.

When we finished the hay-stacking, it was getting cold—plenty cold. In fact, we had washed and hung out a bunch of Levi's to dry and when Wrangler went to gather them in he had to turn them all upright to get through the bunkhouse door. He just leaned them up against the wall like sticks until they thawed out.

I slipped over to Jim Ed's that night and had a little talk.

"Jim Ed," I said, hoping his wife wouldn't come in the living room and examine my boots for foreign matter, as the town fellers say, "a lot of them posts around the stack lots are rotted so bad a feller cain't tighten the wires. If it comes a bad blizzard the cattle are just liable to walk right through that fence and tear down all them haystacks."

"You don't say?"

"Sure do."

"Well, Dusty, I'll put a couple of the odd-job boys on it right away."

"No need for that, Jim Ed, just sic me and old Wrangler on it."

He looked at me kinda sly-like and said, "Well, all right, but hadn't you rather ride fence, drive a truck and feed, or something a little more suitable for saddle-raised men?"

"No," I said, "by God you've saved me and Wrangler from goin' to jail and I'm goin' to see that we take on ever' dirty job you've got around here till we're even."

"Suits me," he said.

We had a couple of long iron bars and a couple of posthole diggers. I might as well say it now that I wanted to back out before the first day was over. The ground was already frozen down about eighteen inches as solid as Wrangler's skull. That meant that it took about an hour to bite out the first half of the hole and about two minutes for the rest. They had to be almost three feet deep to hold right. It was like digging in cement, and the unhandy part about posthole diggers, as I've mentioned before, is the fact that you have to pick them up every time you drive them at the ground. Otherwise they don't dig. Now if the soil hadn't been so rocky we could have used the automatic posthole digger on the back of Jim Ed's tractor. But if that had been the case I'd never have volunteered in the first place.

Our hands got a permanent bend in them. They looked just like hay hooks. It would take four or five gallons of Vince Moore's whiskey before I could pick up anything bigger around than an apple.

One day Wrangler tried to roll a cigarette. He finally gave up and just turned the sack up in his mouth and started chewing. He ain't so dumb sometimes at that.

Then it sure enough got cold. The ground was frozen plumb to the bottom of those holes.

"Progress we ain't makin', Wrangler. All we're doin' is wearin' out some good iron bars and posthole diggers."

He tried to answer but all I saw was a bunch of frost come out of his mouth. His little old razor-back eyes were watering so fast they looked like two fresh bullet holes in a bucket of water.

Jim Ed finally saw the waste and gave us another job. An indoor job at that.

"Now by God," I told Wrangler, "ain't we the two luckiest bastards this side of Hi Lo and the other side of hell?"

"It's all in the way you look at it," said Wrangler bitter-like.

That's what I wanted him to say. It's all that gave me the courage to carry on.

Now Jim Ed has got some mighty big barns. On different occasions, such as blizzards or heavy rains, during calving season, he keeps cattle in these same barns. He also feeds these cattle to keep them strong and healthy. There was soon no doubt in my mind but what they were healthy. That is as far as constipation was concerned. I'm flat-ass certain that Jim Ed never owned a cow that was bothered with this. In fact, after me and Wrangler had worked in the barns awhile I'd have bet my last saddle blanket that they all had the thin dirties.

Jim Ed had said the barn was big and airy. This was true. There was so much air and it got so full of manure dust that a feller had a hard time getting a fresh breath. We backed a truck into the barn and started out digging and shoveling.

Wrangler said, "This stuff is froze just like the rest of the world."

"Yeah," I said, "but it'll break off in layers." It did, by the millions.

One of us was swinging the pick while the other was swinging that scoop shovel full of frozen you-know-what on the back of a truck. When that truck had all it could handle one of us would drive down across the pastures and the other would scatter it out behind. Jim Ed said this fertilized the pastures. I figured the cows would have done a better job of it than we did.

Now Wrangler wasn't exactly complaining. It was more just stating facts. But it gave me hope.

"Dusty," he said, standing there with a scoop shovel full of fertilizer.

"Yeah?"

"Jim Ed lied."

"He did?"

"Yeah, he said it'd be warmer in here. Hell's fire, the sun don't never shine in here."

"Well, I think you misunderstood him, Wrangler. He said we'd be indoors out of the wind and weather. And that's true."

He grunted.

Several months and millions of shovels later he stopped, holding the shovel in the same half-ready position, and said, "Dusty."

"Yeah?"

"It's damn near spring and you know what we've been doin' for a livin' nearly all winter?"

I knew all right. I stopped and tried to see out of my blurry eyes and over my runny nose, fighting to keep that hellacious taste from getting any further down my throat than it was. Just the same I said, "What?"

"Shit," he said, swinging the shovel kinda mad-like. "We're makin' a livin' shovelin' shit."

I could hear them wedding bells ringing clear as a police siren in spite of the half inch of you-know-what packed in each ear.

Hope had calved again.

SEVEN

YES SIR, things were looking up. The grass was sprouting green and tender, the birds were telling everybody about it, and Wrangler, like all the other animals on earth, had his mind on love. On top of that, we'd soon be working the spring roundup and branding—having some real fun.

Then it happened. Jim Ed came snorting and blowing up in front of me and said, "That goddam horse! That goddam horse!"

"What goddam horse?" I said, feeling the question unnecessary but doing my best to be polite.

"That Old Fooler. Who else?" he said, jabbing a finger about the size of a pool cue in my chest. "He's run off with five of my best registered quarter horses!"

"Five?"

"Five!"

"How'd he get out of the big horse pasture?"

"Opened the gate hisself," said Jim Ed.

"He wouldn't do that," I said, swallering my Adam's apple as fast as it jumped up.

"Naw," Wrangler said, not helping much.

"He sure did," Jim Ed said, "and he's gone into the wild horse country. You know damn well I aimed to show all those horses at the state fairs in Dallas and Albuquerque and the Grand National in Denver next January. That son of a bitch will cripple them horses till they won't be fit for coyote bait. That is if we ever get 'em back. Get 'em back," he said again and raised his great big buttermilk belly almost even with the third button on his vest. "You'll get 'em back or no pay, no town, no nothing."

Well just when things looked good, like I might get Wrangler in town while it was still spring and we had several months back pay to boot, and give us a chance to hunt up that rich woman, Old Fooler had sure enough fouled up our world. I might say this was not unusual, just disappointing.

Jim Ed went on, "Now, you're going to be held responsible for them five horses. By the time you work 'em out you'll be a hundred and ten years old."

This was not a good thing to hear. Me and Wrangler were trapped again. It was none of our doing, but there wasn't a lawyer in the whole damn state would take our case against Jim Ed Love. That's the way lawyers are. And even if we had won the case, the judge would have ruled in Jim Ed's favor no matter what. The power's where the money is and me and Wrangler were short as hell on that last item. Besides, everybody knows money's more important than people.

Another thing I knew bothered Jim Ed about those horses, it was his way of showing off, keeping his name on people's tongues and being a big shot all over the Southwest. He liked to read in the paper: Sammy Bar, registered quarter horse owned by Jim Ed Love of Hi Lo, New Mexico, Andrews, Texas, and Stony Stump, Colorado, takes grand prize blue ribbon.

Now I can't say as how I blamed Jim Ed for that, but from my viewpoint I would like to see the name Wrangler Lewis shoved in that sentence at the right place.

As of now it was going to take some doing to get her done.

Now ordinarily Jim Ed would have made us camp out on the hard ground while we tried to gather those horses, but this time it was different. Jim Ed was going to lose face if he didn't show up at those scheduled horse shows. If I hadn't had love and marriage on my mind so strong, I would've spent the rest of my life hunting those horses just to mess up Jim Ed. As it was he let us have the pickup and all the saddle horses we could use.

Every morning we got up before daylight, caught our horses, loaded them in the pickup, and drove about six miles into wild horse country. Then we mounted and rode our hind ends plumb raw (and that is hard to do with a cowboy's hind end) looking for signs of those strays.

There were only about twenty-five wild horses left up in the brush, and with Old Fooler and Jim Ed's five that made a little over thirty. Now figuring that they were scattered over something like fifty thousand acres, and figuring that there are one hundred and fifty trees to

the acre—not counting all the bushes under them—it don't take no
town feller to savvy that the odds were against us.

Every once in a while we would jump a little bunch. Away we'd go
tearing through timber, ducking tree limbs (part of the time), dodging
holes and crevices, and piling up over big rocks. We were working
down lots of saddle horses and getting nowhere.

After about three weeks of this I told Wrangler, "Now, we've finally got Old Fooler's range located and we know where they're watering most of the time."

"Yeah," he said, humping up in the saddle and pushing his hat back.

"So, let's build a wild horse trap around the most used waterhole."

Old Wrangler said for an answer, pushing his hat back, "That sure is
a skinny cloud up there."

I pushed *my* hat back and looked. "That ain't no cloud, that's a
vapor trail."

"You mean there's a bird that leaves a trail in the sky?"

I just couldn't believe he was that dumb. On the other hand, he'd
spent his whole life looking at the ground for cattle and horse sign.
And this was the first time I could recall Wrangler looking at the sky.
All he'd ever got from up there in the heavens was a leather-scorching
sun, high winds, and freezing blizzards. I gave him the benefit of the
doubt and told him about jet airplanes.

"Oh," he said, and I couldn't tell whether he believed me or not.

Well, we built a wild horse trap that would have made the best
carpenter in the world proud of us. It was eight feet tall, the wire
stretched tight as a whore's girdle, and the bottom two wires set back
so we'd have a place to scramble to if the horses went on the prod. We
covered this all over with heavy brush so you couldn't see the wire
leaning on it. Then we swung the gate open and covered it just as
good but with lighter material. We were pleased.

We hunted and we hunted. Twice we saw Old Fooler for a minute
as he led the horses out of sight into the badlands. We were both
peeled and bruised from top to bottom. And I might add our tempers
were in the same shape.

Then the insult of all insults took place. It appeared to me to be as
dirty as if somebody had slipped the President a mickey just before he
spoke to the nation. Jim Ed called his Texas ranch for an airplane.
They used them down there to scare cattle out of the brush. Not only
that, but Jim Ed said we would have to pay for the pilot's time and
gasoline. This was damn near too much.

Now our job, according to Jim Ed, was to stay up on a hill kind of concealed from sight, as far as the horses were concerned, and wait until this airplane drove them down into our trap. Then we were to dash bravely down and close the gate. That sounded real fine, but so does a church bell at a funeral.

For three days we hunkered down holding our horse's reins, watching that tin bird fly around the hills.

"Now, ain't that something," I said, "a flying cowboy. I never thought the time would come I'd have to even get in the same county with one of them things. God-uh-mighty, the world's ruined, Wrangler. You ain't goin' to allow that on your ranch, are you?"

"Hell no," he said, "I'd chop the wings off that damn thing and make an outhouse out of it."

That was the way I liked to hear my pardner talk. Just then I damn near died. Here came that hombre and right under him was Old Fooler and a bunch of horses. The plane circled, sounding like a runaway rock crusher. But just when he was bending her in to shove them into the corral, Old Fooler turned and headed right up the side of a steep hill.

Now this is where the remains of the Wild and Woolly West brought sudden defeat to the modern age. That cow-pilot turned his plane and tried to climb in the air after Old Fooler. He topped out just behind him, but something got in his way. Two pine trees. The wings ripped off to each side and what was left of the plane rammed into a thick clump of oak brush and everything was out of sight—horses and all.

We rode over almost as fast as we could. I think if I'd hit my horse with the spurs just once we could have speeded things up. But me and Wrangler are both very tenderhearted cowboys and we never take advantage of dumb animals—just dumb people.

"By God he ain't dead," I said as I saw this pilot crawling out of the splintered plane.

"Oh hell," Wrangler said; then he corrected it when the pilot looked at us with spinning eyes. "Oh, hell is no place for airplane pilots."

"Where am I?" he asked.

"Well, now, I'll tell you, feller, you're a long ways from where you ought to be."

"Correct," Wrangler said.

"Shall we take him in or wait till Jim Ed comes after him, Wrangler?"

"Whatever suits you just tickles me plumb to death."

I knew he meant it, so I helped the pilot on behind the saddle and we started the first stages of delivering the lost to the fold. We found out that a cow-pilot's ass is not as tough as a cowboy's.

But I learned something that eased my pain a little bit. That plane was insured, so old Jim Ed couldn't make us pay for that, too. The way I looked at it we had saved the price of an airplane that day. That's lots of money even to bartenders and bank clerks. Oh, for the wild free life of a cowboy!

We kept right on hunting, and Jim Ed left us alone for a spell. Besides, he and all the other hands were having a big time down at the spring roundup and branding.

Then it began to rain. Those black clouds built a roof over the mountains and sprung a leak. It rained enough to run an ocean over. It took us three hours to drive up to the hills with chains on the pickup and two to drive back home. That meant we had just a little over two hours a day to hunt wild horses. That's not much time in this big country.

The horses were slipping and sliding all over. A preacher uncle of mine told me he saw it rain so hard in California that a strong man could row a boat straight up in the air. I called him a liar. Now I wish he was here so's I could apologize.

"Wrangler, I didn't know a man could breathe water, did you?"

"There's lots of things a man can do we don't know about."

This wisdom was way over my head, so I shut my mouth before I drowned. I knew we were really in for it now. There would be water holes everywhere. Our chances of trapping that bunch of horses were about the same as a cowboy getting rich. Those are mighty long odds.

I decided since we were going to have to leave the JL without our pay, and since the cause of it was Old Fooler, that I'd shoot the low-lived son of a bitch. I started carrying a .30-30 on the saddle for that purpose.

Then the clouds busted up and the sun came dropping down on the land. The grass was stretching up and our backs drying out.

The fourth clear day, we rode up on a canyon so deep it must've been the roof to hell. And down in the bottom something was moving. After a long hard look we agreed that it appeared to be Old

Fooler with a bunch of his slaves tagging behind. They were moving towards a shallower part of the canyon and towards our trap.

I said, "Let's ride like hell and get up ahead of 'em. They have to come out within a quarter mile of the trap. If we can't booger them into it I'll at least get a shot at that rottenhearted bastard of a roan horse."

Wrangler grunted.

We rode like hell. The wind was in our favor. We waited and waited a whole bunch more. Then old Wrangler just pointed. His jaws were working silently like a single stem of grass in a high wind. I looked where he looked. My jaws worked, too. Old Fooler was slowly, as if it was his everyday job, leading that bunch into the trap. He walked right on in lazy-like. The others kinda hesitated, heads up, ears forward, snorting and trembling, but they followed him in.

Well, old kindhearted us fairly shoved the steel in our horses' sides. I headed for the gate itself and Wrangler for the opening. We had a downhill run but even so four head broke out on us. But when the gate was shut tight we counted up and there besides Old Fooler and Jim Ed's five head were seven wild ones.

Old Fooler stood sleepy-like out in the middle with his eyes half closed. The rest just ran, and jumped and farted and turned like a bunch of airplane cowboys would've done. Plumb foolish-acting animals.

It took us quite a spell to rope each and every one of those seven wild ones and put a garter on them. (That is, we twisted a piece of rope so tight on one leg it cut off most of the circulation.) A three-legged horse is easier to drive. Then we turned them out and headed in. We left the pickup there. We could get it later.

It was damn near dark when I turned into the home gate with Old Fooler coming along nicely right behind and all the other horses scattered out between Fooler and Wrangler. Jim Ed was amazed. It was hard on him but he admitted the seven extra head would take care of everything.

We had a good night's sleep and he even sent another cowboy after the pickup. Then he paid us off the next morning.

We stuck the money in our pockets, loaded Old Fooler in the back of our own pickup, and headed for a wedding. We didn't say good-bye to Jim Ed Love, but I sorta waved one finger out in front of my face as we passed headquarters.

EIGHT

OLD WRANGLER really fought his head to get me to stop in Hi Lo. He said, "I want a drink."

"That, I can understand."

"Well, stop."

"Cain't do 'er, Wrangler."

"No brakes?" he asked, looking at the floorboard.

"No time," I said. "We got to get into Santa Fe before night. We've done wore our welcome out in Hi Lo, and besides there ain't no rich women available since Rosie has deserted us."

Wrangler saw the truth of this, but he was still plenty thirsty.

Now nearly every time I'd been in town since I was eighteen years old I'd either been drunk, in a fight, in jail, or gone broke. Sometimes all four. It was all done in the interest of having fun, even though other folks seemed to think different. But for once I was going to try to handle these situations a little better—really use my thinker. I knew we had to get a pretty fancy hotel to meet rich women. That expense was okay, but this idea of gambling and giving all our money away the first day was out. Why, if we were careful, we could last a whole month, and that ought to get the job done. Another thing that always set us back was those damn jails. It didn't matter how you got in, whether it was your fault or not, the judge was going to say *guilty,* and fine you all the law allowed. That was considerable.

"You know, Wrangler, we had a hell of a time collectin' our wages," I said cautiously.

"Jim Ed's the *takin'* kind."

"That's what I meant. Now, when this is gone we may never get that big amount together again."

"It ain't likely."

"So, we got to be careful till you find that ever-loving woman with the big, fat purse."

He grunted.

I drove on, and then I saw the place. I knew it had to be the one. There it was, off the road a piece. And it said, COCKTAIL (I knew this was fancy talk for whiskey); PHONE (no need for them far as I could tell); TV (hell, Jim Ed had one of those but I'd never got to watch it); SWIMMING POOL (might come in handy for sobering up and taking a bath); DINING ROOM (kinda nice to have in an emergency). Yes sir, the Towne Lodge had it all. Not only that, it was plumb out on the edge of town so there was lots of scrub oak and cedar to tie Old Fooler until we could find somebody to pawn him off on.

I signed up for both of us at the register and paid a whole week in advance. The lady gave me a key and pointed out the room.

The Towne Lodge was a big, old place made out of adobe bricks and there was so much glass in the main building two hundred people could have looked out all at once.

We drove the pickup out back and unloaded Old Fooler. Then we tied him to the pickup and gave him some oats. We'd have to feed and water the bastard every day until Wrangler got his marrying arrangements made—that is, unless we were lucky and he choked to death or something.

Then we went over to our room. It was the fanciest damn thing you ever saw. Two great big old beds, green rugs, just like a cow pasture after a good rain, a bathtub, a phone, and one of them TV sets. There was a picture on the east wall of a naked lady standing there looking at a lake full of water. I walked over real close and took a better look, but the woman was still too far off to tell much about her features.

Wrangler said, "Let's go get a drink."

"Not till we take a bath," I said, "and get on some clean clothes."

"I cain't wait," said Wrangler, and I could tell he meant it.

"Wait here just a minute," I said, "I'll go get us a bottle."

It was all right to get a little drunk the first night here, but to be dirty and drunk both was not going to better our chances of starting a romance.

I went to the bar and brought back a bottle. Old Wrangler was glad to see it. I guess this marrying idea had him a little upset. He took a big drink and said, "Ahhh." I could see that I was going to have to pioneer on this bath deal.

It didn't take me long. I'm a fast bath-taker. I ran a tub full of water for Wrangler. He took another slug of hooch, undressed, and dived in.

"Wowwweeee, oh, oh, woowee."

I ran in to see what was the matter. I must have got the water a little hot. Old Wrangler was about to drown and it looked like when he got in he'd slipped and driven his big toe into the water faucet. I pulled his toe out and threw him out on the floor so he could get his breath. He was getting plenty of that, in fact the way he was choking and going on I believe he was getting too much air. His toe was all bloody and bent. I ran and handed him the bottle, feeling I had done my duty and more. Wrangler was going to be a problem.

I put on clean Levi's and a new shirt and told him, "I'm goin' on over to the bar. Come on over when you get ready."

I went up to the bartender and said, "A double," then I remembered my idea on making that money last and I said, "No, I'm too dry for that. Give me a beer."

He was a friendly feller with a belly as big as Jim Ed's but with a hell of a lot pleasanter look on his round, flat face. He smiled and said, "Whatever suits you is my pleasure."

I looked real hard at him a minute to see if he was kin to Wrangler. He talked some like him, but I knew he wouldn't admit it if he was.

I went over to the jukebox. Sure enough there was my favorite by Banjo Bill but I played some of those tunes by that Sinatra feller. I decided that was the kind of music old Wrangler ought to get married to. Then I got me a seat halfway between the jukebox and the bar at a great big table. That beer was so good and that Sinatra feller so romantic-sounding that I plumb forgot about Wrangler, the time, and everything else. All of a sudden the jukebox went off and I threw my head up and there was a three-piece orchestra scattered out there on a little platform.

One of them started pounding hell out of a drum, another did the same to a piano, and one of them was blowing into a horn with a lot of latches on it. It wasn't as good as that Sinatra feller but it wasn't bad either.

Then I realized the place was damn near full of people. I wanted to get up and go get Wrangler, but I was afraid I'd lose my table. I told the waitress just to bring me three beers so I wouldn't have to move for a spell. Time passed.

Then the waitress came up to my table followed by some women. Four of them to be exact.

"Could these ladies use your table? We're crowded. Miss Hopwell has a party of four."

I jumped up and started to run.

Miss Hopwell (I could tell she was the ringleader) said, "No, please, sit down. We'll just *join* you."

I plunked myself back down. Miss Hopwell pulled a coyote hide or something furry from around her neck and leaned forward. Her bosom slid out on top of the table like a couple of well-watered cantaloupes. If she'd been two inches shorter she couldn't have got within a foot of that table.

"I'm Miss Hopwell, Myrna Hopwell," she said. "And this," she said, pointing a finger just plumb overloaded with rings, "is my niece Gloria, and these are her friends from college, Miss Devers and Miss Rollaway."

I nodded and said, "Howdy. I'm Dusty Jones."

"How is it you're called Dusty?" Miss Rollaway asked, rolling great big green eyes like a hungry calf at a full bag of milk.

"I don't know," I said. "Maybe it's because I'm such a fast bather."

They all laughed to beat hell. I had been dead serious, but it didn't take me long to find out two things about town women, they either sneer or laugh no matter what you say. This bunch was laughing. I tried to tell them about one of my uncle's dogs that thought he was a horse and ate grass till he starved to death. They laughed so damn hard I decided to shut up and dance. I asked Miss Rollaway first.

She was a mighty fine dancer, just snuggling up like a rubber hose and sliding round so easy I could hardly feel her touch the floor. Old Dusty was enjoying himself.

"Are you really a cowboy?" she asked. "I mean *really*. You dress like one, but so many people do, you know."

"Well, Miss Rollaway . . ."

"Jane," she said, and so did I.

"Jane, it's like this. If I said I was I'd be telling the truth, but if I said I was I'd be lying, too."

"I don't understand."

"Well, I used to be a fair hand and I reckon I could have been called some kind of a cowboy. You see, there just ain't no use for us anymore. They've got jeeps and airplanes, and tractors and pickup trucks," and I just went on and on.

"Oh," she said, "I think I understand."

I was glad she was a smart girl and had enough sense to shut up and dance. I danced with them all. Though I might say Myrna was some-what of a problem. The way she was put together kind of made it impossible to scrunch up and get going. She was almost as tall as I was and I'm just about six feet.

I was doing my best when I heard a yell blast out across the dance floor that could come from only one person—Wrangler Lewis.

It wasn't hard to see that he'd finished the pint. He had his hat pushed way back on his head. The only time he did that was when he was sure enough drunk. He had wrapped his sore toe up in a pillowcase and there was sure as hell no boot on that foot. This made him walk a little short-legged but here he came just hollering and dancing a jig. I don't see how he could stand it on that sore foot, but it looked like he jumped higher on this one than the other. Me and Myrna quit dancing and so did everybody else. People on their way to the bathroom just clamped down and stopped to watch. Drinks were held an inch from the swaller hole without moving.

Wrangler ran right up to me and Myrna, circled about three times and then ran right under me and grabbed her.

"She looks just like Toy Smith, only better," he said. (Toy was a woman Wrangler had once had a big affair with.)

At first Myrna looked like she might booger and run, but when Old Wrangler threw his hat plumb across the bar and crowded up under that bosom and began to waltz her around slow and easy I knew we had something going. I slipped over to the bar and said to Dan (that was his name, Dan. I have always liked bartenders named Dan), "Dan," I said, "Dan, what's that woman do?"

He leaned over close and said, "Nothing."

That's all I wanted to know, because if she didn't do nothing she was either a whore or rich and I knew this one was rich. Wrangler would soon take care of the other part of that sentence.

Well, we all finally got settled back down at the table and Wrangler just moved in between Myrna and Gloria. He was talking low and fast. I didn't want to interrupt, but felt that now was the time to order a round of drinks on us. I could see that this crowd couldn't take many more. I was still being careful with our money.

Myrna said, "Martinis," to the waitress.

I'd never had one of them and I didn't figure Wrangler had, but I said, "All the way around."

When the waitress brought them, old Wrangler acted as if he was going to pour his out. Then he said, "I ain't never had none of them before—none of them vegetables or nothing." And he whipped her up and polished it off with one and a half swallers.

We had another. This time Myrna bought. Now I kind of appreciated that. Not only because we were being thrifty but because I never figured why a woman shouldn't buy a drink if she had the most money.

I liked that Myrna, but Wrangler liked her a hell of a lot more. That was fine with me, he was the one we were trying to marry off.

Myrna took out a mirror and sort of powdered her round, pretty face, patted at that short curly brown hair, and stood up. Old Wrangler let out another yell and grabbed the silky-looking coyote hide. Myrna kind of jumped back.

Wrangler said, "I wasn't goin' to steal it or nothin'. I was just goin' to help you put it on."

That just about broke Myrna and the other girls up. The romance was on. They said they'd call us the next day and make a date for cocktails.

"By God," I said, "that's fine," and shook hands all around. We walked out to the car with them. It was a fancy-looking son of a bitch. I'd never seen one just like it before. It had "RR" wrote on it. Just the same I had already figured this was the kind she'd drive.

Wrangler told Myrna to bend over and he gave her one of those hungry kisses and I could see her wiggling in her lace pants. I couldn't make up my mind which one of the girls to tell good night, so I just kissed them all.

NINE

IT HAD TAKEN about an hour of knob-twisting before we could see that TV. It sure was loud, but I was afraid to turn anything again because nearly every time I touched one of those buttons the scene would change to a West Texas dust storm, or a long line of barbwire fence without any barbs.

A little feller was jumping up and down swallering a soda pop yelling "Drink Pep, it has the pepper to make you peppy!" Then a man dressed up something like a cowboy—I could tell he was faking it by the way he laid his saddle down on the skirts, no real cowboy would ever do that—took a long drag on a cigar. He was stretched out by a campfire and he gazed off at the moon just like he'd put his brand on ten head of his neighbor's calves. Then a coyote howled and another look came on his face. This time like a man who had just slept with his first woman. That feller had lots of different looks. I never figured it out for sure but I think he was really a cigar salesman.

Then a program started where a bunch of women got up and bawled and shed tears and a real kindhearted feller gave them iceboxes, electric stoves, and such like. He sure was a generous man. It sorta surprised me. I thought they killed all that kind off.

After a while, a woman called Lolane was interviewed by a man dragging a bullwhip around. He talked with the handle right up next to his mouth. When Lolane talked he held it up next to hers. I don't rightly believe you can say she talked. She just sort of grunted the words and it seemed like she spoke with her chest instead of her mouth. I couldn't place it but something about her reminded me of Myrna.

We watched some of those westerns. I'm still confused about that. It seems that these fellers are called cowboys, but they spend most of their time in town drinking whiskey—which just goes to show that they are a heck of a lot smarter than most real cowboys. When they are out in the country, they never do any of the work cowboys do, they just lay behind rocks and blow people's heads off. It's pretty silly, but kinda fun to watch. This TV is an amazing invention.

The phone rang. We both jumped up and I said, "Answer it, Wrangler, that's Myrna."

"I don't talk over them damn thangs."

So I picked it up and tried to be *proper,* as the town fellers say, and said "Hello" instead of "Howdy."

"Wrangler?" came oozing out over the phone so sweet I could feel the silver melting off my belt buckle.

"No. This here's Dusty."

"Oh, hi, Dusty. Could I speak to Wrangler?"

"No."

A silence came over the phone and she finally said, "Well, why?" sort of short-like. I knew I had to make things right quick.

"Well, it's like this, Myrna. Wrangler's got one of them things about telephones. You know, what do you call it where a man's afraid of something without knowin' why?"

"A complex," she said.

"Yeah, that's it," I said, "he's got a boogery complex about telephones."

"Oh, how delightful," said Myrna. "Just tell the little darling that I'll be over to the Lodge in about an hour."

"Are the girls coming, too?"

"No, they've gone shopping. Jane said to tell you she'd see you tomorrow."

I was a little let-down at first; then I really perked up. This was going to speed hell out of things, her coming over by herself. It sure looked good. Our luck was on the go.

She got there about three-thirty that afternoon. We were the only ones there. We had some more of those vegetable drinks and I gave that singing feller I'd liked so much the day before a dime every time he opened his mouth. It seemed like he knew a big romance was busting out. He really did do a good job, Myrna had already reached over and laid her left hand—the one with all them blue-white rings on it—under Wrangler's beat-up old fist and she was rubbing it like it was made of gold. Wrangler just went on drinking left-handed. I was just getting ready to leave them alone when a feller in a fine-looking speckled suit and a hat that didn't have hardly any brim at all came buttin' in. He was sucking on a pipe and rubbing a little bitty mustache. I could tell he was the vice president of something or other. It seems to me that those vice presidents all walk and talk alike.

"Hello, Myrna, darling," he spouted out like a big bird. "Where have you been, my dear? I've looked all over for you, precious. You look just divine, my pet. Simmmmppply divine!"

By God, I never heard anything like it. Less than thirty words and he had already called her darling, my dear, precious, and divine. That man was a flattering fool. If he stayed an hour I wondered if he'd repeat himself.

I was surprised at how impolite the bastard was, considering his raising and all. He sat down at our table without even being introduced, much less asked. He just kept asking questions and answering them himself.

"I bet you've been to another of your flower shows. Of course you have, sweet. No, no. Let us see. Were you playing bridge at Esther's? That's it. I knew it, dumpling."

Myrna tried to say something but there just wasn't much use. I saw her pull her hand away from Wrangler's. I could tell she didn't want to.

On and on he rattled. New York and Hollywood, London and San Francisco kept coming up over and over.

Finally he kind of half covered his face with his hand and said, "Why, Myrna, you little rascal, leave it to you. Wherever did you find these quaint gentlemen, my love?"

Myrna tried again. "Well, I . . . ."

"Why on earth haven't you introduced us?" But before she could answer, the son of a bitch ordered *himself* a drink.

Well, I'll tell you this, I hated to spend the money, but I ordered three more vegetable drinks. This man, we finally found out that his name was Limestone Retch, kept right on blabbing.

"I wish the Monroes would improve their tennis court. They've talked about it for years. Louise is probably too busy in town, you know what I mean?" he said, looking sideways and flaring his nostrils like he'd just been told he was more of a dude than the Duke of Windsor. I could tell by that little "you know what I mean" business that somebody's throat was bleeding.

We had some more drinks. The sun was about to set. Some other people had come into the bar by now. The blabbing went on. He was getting a little drunk now and started telling dirty jokes. I heard every

damn one of them when I was a kid. He was the only one who
thought they were funny. He laughed so hard every time he finished
telling one I kept hoping he'd bust something.

All of a sudden Wrangler said, "Do you swim, Limestone?"

"Wha . . . er . . . sure, but of course, all over the world, the fin-
est places, Capri, Morocco, the Isle of . . ."

"Well, it's a damn good thing," old Wrangler said kind of humping
up, "because I'm just fixin' to stir my drink with you."

Limestone swallered.

I swallered.

Myrna grinned sick-like.

I could see our ranch going to hell one way or the other right here.
It was obvious that Limestone had just enough sense to understand
that Wrangler was making headway with Myrna and it was just as
obvious that Limestone had the same plan.

Wrangler was getting up on his sore foot, and I could tell he was
going to do some damage to this vice president's mustache.

I jumped up and ran around and said, "Come on, Limestone, I want
to show you my horse. You ride, don't you, Limestone? Well, that's
good. You'll like the looks of this ole pony. He's a dandy. Just wait till
you see him." By God, it was my time to talk and I was doing it.

In the shank of the day I could still see Old Fooler's steel-muscled
hind end sticking around the edge of the pickup. I let Limestone
stumble out ahead of me and the damned fool walked around behind
Old Fooler without speaking to him. Seems to me that as brilliant as
this bastard's conversation was he'd have learned something in school.
Damn near everybody knows you have to speak to a horse when you
walk up behind him, otherwise he kicks. This is a throwback to the
millions of years of time they spent being slipped up on by lions,
tigers, and such.

Blooey.

Whop.

Ooommmp.

Thud.

There wasn't much talking going on now. Limestone was stretched
out there holding his belly and looking for some air. Old Fooler was
jumping around, snorting and kicking right out over Limestone's
head. But Limestone didn't know it. All he knew right then was that
two cannon balls in the shape of horse's feet had whammed him in the
belly.

I poured a half bucket of water on him that was too dirty for Old Fooler to drink and he kind of woke up. I just couldn't get that feller to talk to me. I tried and I tried. So, I thought to keep him from getting lonesome I ought to voice an opinion or two.

"Now, Limestone, you might think that hurt, but that's just like a loving mother rubbing powder on a week-old baby compared to what old Wrangler'll do to you. Leave Myrna alone. Do you hear me?"

He nodded and I could tell that the dumb bastard understood, so I helped him to his feet and he left, stumbling off without his pipe. He still wasn't saying anything. The quietened type, I reckon.

I heard him drive off in one of those little peanut-looking cars. Then in a minute I could see Wrangler and Myrna heading for our room. I got my bedroll out of the pickup and told Old Fooler, "You have now been granted another week of life, you matchmakin' son of a bitch!"

TEN

THE SUN WAS UP when I crawled out of my bedroll. I fed and even brushed Old Fooler down. This made him suspicious. He watched me close.

I said, "No, sir, Old Fooler, today we are friends. This here day will be celebrated sometime in the great future just like the Fourth of July, as the day the cowboys won. Whiskey'll run like spring rains, bands'll play, and bribed judges and crooked lawyers will all make patriotic speeches."

I could tell Old Fooler didn't much believe me. Besides I decided I'd better shut up before I got to sounding like Limestone Retch.

I heard a noise so I looked around the edge of the pickup and saw Myrna leaving. She stepped off down to that big RR car like a madam with a full house. By God, I was nearly as happy as she was.

I dogtrotted over to the room. I just couldn't wait any longer.

By God, old Wrangler was learning fast. He was singing in the tub and soap was spilling out all over.

"Come in, Dusty, you no-good son of a bitch." That was the best thing Wrangler could say to a friend. I was happy.

I started to ask him how it went, then I saw the horrible condition of the bed and knew the deal was cinched.

"Did she get excited when you proposed to her, Wrangler?"

"She sure did. The poor thang fell out of bed!"

Things picked up from then on. Wrangler and Myrna went around everywhere together. She bought him a bunch of new tailor-made suits, shirts, and boots. He even went so far as to wear a new hat when he was with her. They took in the opera, art shows, cocktail parties, and such.

I made myself scarce during this period. Knowing they had plenty to do alone. In the meantime I had me three college girls to escort.

The trouble was, for some reason, I liked this Miss Rollaway better than the others. The reason was hard to come by, because they were all pretty and paid their way.

I was learning fast just like Wrangler. I got to where I could operate one of those phones like a regular mechanic. I'd call her up and have her meet me somewhere without her friends. This helped to keep my spirits up while I waited for the great wedding to take place.

Finally Myrna had us all out to her house. It was out on the opposite side of town from the Towne Lodge. She called it "the suburbs." Now the first thing I can say is that the house covered a whole lot of country. The rooms were all on different levels so it was hard to get from one to the other without falling down. This was impossible after a few of them vegetable drinks. It was one of those old Mexican adobe houses all smarted up with newfangled stuff—pictures, statues, pianos, bathrooms, and bars. There were enough Navaho rugs on the floor to stock a curio store.

The outside was something to tell about too. In the backyard was a big swimming pool all hemmed in with sandstone rocks. The same kind of sandstone I'd spent my whole life riding over and falling on, and here they'd found it useful. Paths wound around everywhere. Little fields of flowers were scattered all over. Myrna really loved those flowers. We were introduced to every plant on the place.

"Look at my little darlings," she said, and reached out almost touching them. She talked to them like they were her kids.

All I could think of to say was, "Sure pretty."

Old Wrangler improved some on this. He said, "Mighty pretty."

I had heard she was an expert flower woman. I don't know if this meant she was an expert grower, smeller, or raiser. It wouldn't have surprised me if she was good at all three.

We were sitting out by the swimming pool after our tour in the warm sun.

"Wrangler," I said, "when I was a kid all the poor folks lived on the edge of town; now it's the rich part."

"Everything changes," he said, firing up a cigar as long as a ruler and putting his brand-new kangaroo boots up on the table.

"Yeah, it sure does," I said, feeling happy at Wrangler's quick adjustment, but at the same time a little uneasy, too.

Myrna had the maid bring us a pitcher of drinks. I didn't know what they were and I damn sure wasn't going to ask. A man that would question free drinks ought to be hung in an outhouse like Wrangler said.

Myrna said, "Dusty, dear, would you like to bring your horse out here? We have the stables, you know? They're terribly empty. I just haven't had time to ride the last few years with the flowers and all to look after." She gazed out at all those short, tall, bunchy, skinny, red, yellow, white, and purple flowers with the same look she had in her eyes for Wrangler. I knew the only competition he'd ever have would be those flowers.

"I sure would appreciate that, Myrna," I said. "It's some trouble over there at the Inn."

"You won't even have to worry about caring for him," she said. "I'll have the handyman do it."

Now by God ain't that a dinger. In a way I was already a foreman. Life sure enough looked good.

My main worry had been about Wrangler's conduct but like most of the things in the world I had strained my poor brains for nothing. In fact, if there was any worrying to do it was about him overdoing it.

One morning I saw him pick up a can of stuff and mash a button. Something sprewed out. He shot it under both arms, then sprayed some of it on his hair and combed it back slick and shiny. I slipped over directly and stole a look at the label. It was the same stuff they'd been advertising on TV: MASHO, FOR SMELLY MEN. PROTECTS ALL DAY. That's what it said on the can.

This might be all right for old society-climbing Wrangler but I'll be damned if I was ever going to admit I smelled that bad. But just the same he was doing better than all right. She was running by to pick him up in the RR car every little bit. And when she wasn't there the cockeyed phone was ringing. But the best sign of all was when she started handing him out a bunch of those brand-new hundred dollar bills. Then I knew old Wrangler had her as helpless as a tail-swinging monkey in a forest of sharp-spined cactus. That's to put it plain.

One day Wrangler came running in with a newspaper, yelling, "Look here! Look here! I got my name in the newspaper."

It said: "An engagement party will be held announcing the coming wedding of Miss Myrna Hopwell, Dime Store heiress (her third) to Mr. Wrangler Lewis (his first) of Hi Lo, New Mexico. Miss Hopwell lives on her estate near Santa Fe, New Mexico, and is a specialist in mountain-grown flowers. Mr. Lewis is engaged in the cattle and horse business."

"I never thought I'd see the time I'd get my name in the newspaper."

"Me neither," I said, but I was just about to bust a gut with pride. This here made it official. Nothing but a plague could keep me from being Wrangler's foreman now. I could just see the fat cattle and fine horses all over our ranch, and me riding around on the best horse in the country telling other people what to do. Oh, I'd be a decent son of a bitch about it. No dirty stuff like Jim Ed Love, but it would be a whole lot better boot to wear. I'll swear it looked like the improvements in this world would never end.

ELEVEN

THE ENGAGEMENT PARTY brought on a pack of new experiences for me. I've never seen such a thing in my life.

At one end of the living room, on a flower-covered platform built for the occasion, was a four-piece band Myrna had—as she put it—"engaged." The other side of the room was nearly filled up with a twenty-foot-long table running over with turkeys, hams, and plate after plate of grub I never saw or heard of before. And besides a bowl of punch as big as a horse trough, she had two bartenders behind the bar working themselves plumb rattle-headed trying to empty all those whiskey bottles. They did a good job, but it took them all night.

Yes sir, this was sure as hell going to be a party of engagements all right.

People were as crowded as fingers on a closed fist and more kept coming in. Myrna had Wrangler by the arm introducing him to all the people around the room.

All these new faces made me nervous. I was really wishing Miss Rollaway and her friends could have made it home from school for this blowout. I finally eased my way over and told the bartender to fill my glass.

"Soda water?" he asked.

"No, whiskey," I said. I turned that old glass up and drank'r so empty it looked like a brand-new one.

"Again?"

"Again!"

It wasn't a very big glass but I felt more sociable and I had learned why they sometimes called these get-togethers cocktail parties.

A feller walked up to me and said, "How do you do, old chap? I hear from Myrna you are in actuality a real, working cowboy."

I didn't want to get into any more discussions trying to tell this Englishman I was an ex-cowboy, so I just said, "That is right."

"Well, it is my pleasure to introduce myself. I am Sir Shambles, Ambassador at Large for Her Majesty. I'm now stationed in the Islands. I flew over for Myrna's party. Good girl. Old friends, you know?"

I didn't know, but I nodded my head and took a sip of whiskey.

"When I heard she was marrying one of the cow people I could hardly contain my interest. You see we English pioneered the cattle industry in America."

This here did sort of set me back on my hunkers. I'd never really thought about how it started. It seemed like to me it had always been here, long as I could remember, at least.

"Is that right?" I said.

"Indeed, it is, my dear fellow. The old XIT Ranch in the Texas Panhandle is only one of the rather large estates instigated by English capital."

I took a liking to this feller right then and there, but before I could get some real friendly talk going a herd of fat old women ran off with him, just introducing one another so fast I thought they were going to tear the poor feller in half.

I learned something else I didn't know—just get you a drink and stand in one place. All kinds of folks will come up and talk to you. If you move about it becomes *your* responsibility to start the talk.

This feller walked up to me and said, "I'm Jack Garfield."

"I'm Dusty Jones."

"I'm vice president of . . ."

I knew it, by God, I knew it. Another one of them. I started to bust him right off and then I remembered I was on good behavior till after the wedding.

"I was just over at Judge Malhead's yesterday. Know him? Fine man. Great person. We're just like this. He said to me, 'Jack,' he said, 'we've been friends a long time, haven't we?' 'Yes, we have, Judge.' 'Well,' he said, 'I'm going to let you in on a big thing. Something *really* big. Get me? You have to swear by the utmost secrecy not to let this out.' I looked the judge straight in the eye and said, 'Judge, you know me better than that.' 'All right, Jack,' he said, 'here it is. They're going to build a new electronic plant here in Santa Fe. It's going to be put on the Smith property.' Well, I'll have you know, Mr. Jones, that *I* just this morning closed a deal for all the surrounding property for *our* company. How do you like that? Fast work, eh?"

"Well, I'll be a goddamned chicken-stealing, lamb-killing coyote," I said.

This seemed to please him because he said, "Mr. Jones, if you ever need anything, any little favors, just let me know. I can get to the judge anytime. Of course there are certain little favors one has to give in return. Convention, you know. Just business. Plain business."

For a minute there he had me thinking he really meant it. But when he got to that "certain favors" part I knew I was out.

He was going on about another one of his smart deals when this woman came up and started talking to him.

I slipped over sideways but before I could take another drink one of those fat women grabbed me. Her eyes bugged out like two tiny burned-out light bulbs. She was wearing so many necklaces they pulled her forward. I had the notion to give her a push and get her straightened up.

"My darling" (by God the world was full of darlings). "I'm so glad for Myrna. She's really been lonely these last years. Of course, she has her flowers and uh, of course, all those millions to comfort her. And uh, you will be good to her won't you, darling?"

"Yeah," I said.

"She needs someone she can trust, you know? And uh, someone to lean on in time of tribulation. Of course, we all do," she said and kind of shook like something was binding her.

"I ain't the one," I said.

"Whatever do you mean?" she said, and gave me a look that would have scared a natural-born coward flat to death.

"I mean, I ain't marrying Myrna. I ain't the one."

"Well!" she said and hustled off twisting all over.

I decided it was time I changed locations. I went to the bar. Then I squatted down behind a little tree planted in a great big bowl. Three or four people were talking at once. Finally one of them got louder than the others.

"I tell you the evils of the world are rooted in organizations: communism, religion, marriage, and yes, even capitalism."

"Capitalism an organization?" somebody said.

"Exactly. You know we all know. We're afraid to admit it. Look at all the organized good we've done to all the primitives in the world. They were happy until the capitalist and the communist started show-

ing them the difference. Death, pain, love, and beauty were all accepted for what they are—simply part of the universe. But now we've
ruined them. We've educated them. Ha!" He was getting louder all
the time. "The only truth, the only government worthwhile has been
found in a monarchy."

Since I didn't savvy a thing they were talking about I got up and
made another move. Across the room, poor old Wrangler was still
going strong on that handshaking. Marrying a rich woman wasn't
quite as simple as I thought.

I saw a lonesome-looking feller sitting on a window seat. I ambled
over and said, "Howdy."

He looked up at me out of sneaky, sad eyes, rubbed his beard, and
nodded.

"Nice party, ain't it?" I said.

"It will do, I suppose."

"You live around here?" I asked, trying to get something going.

"Oh, temporarily. New York is my home. I'm just here on, well,
shall we say research."

He waited like he wanted me to ask him what kind of research. But
I didn't.

So he said, "I'm a poet."

Well I'll be damned if he didn't look and act just like I thought a
poet would. Course I don't know any poets.

There was a commotion outside around the swimming pool. People
had started pushing one another into the water with all their clothes
on. They had to get pretty drunk to do it, but it was happening just the
same. They were laughing real loud like this was the funniest thing in
the world. I was getting a little worried about my sense of humor.
Maybe I was losing it.

I turned back to the poet and said, "Come on, let's grab us a girl
and dance and holler and have some fun."

He looked at me another minute and said like it was making him
sick, "You call *that* fun?"

Well before I could grab me a girl, a great big husky man with a
bow tie on walked up and said, "There's no use. They are just no
good."

"Huh?" I said.

"Thass right. They are *no damn good*. She's gone to her aunt's.
Sheesh taken the kids. My kids," he said, and started crying and rubbing his round face.

"Who?" I asked.

"My wife. She won't be my wife any longer. I just can't understand it. When we first got married we were so happy. I didn't get to stay home much. The business was just starting. Had to make a go of that. A man's got to make a go of that, hasn't he?"

"I reckon he has," I said.

"Well, he does. You just can't get along unless you make a go. You're left out. I worked sixteen hours a day making it go. It went," he said, sniffing and looking up at the ceiling. "Yeah, it went. I just don't understand it. I gave her everything. Clothes, cars, one of the best homes in town. She had a maid. We made all the clubs in town. Look," he said, and pulled out a billfold that unfolded like an accordion. "Look. You see these?"

"Uh-huh. What are they?"

"What are they? Credit cards, that's what they are. Look. I have five different gasoline cards. Three diners, two . . . one . . ." and he just kept rattling. "This is my country club card and I belong to the Masons, Kiwanis, and Lions. Now, if that isn't proof, where is it?"

When he said "proof" I thought maybe he was in some kind of trouble with the law. But that wasn't it at all. It was his wife he was trying to prove something or other about.

All that whiskey I'd drunk made me feel helpful, so I said, "You have to make love to 'em ever' day."

"Every day?"

"Ever' day."

"I don't have time for that."

It was my turn to talk so I said, "And that ain't all you've got to do. You've either got to beat hell out of them or make 'em ragin' mad about something at least once a week."

"You do? Why?"

"I don't know why and I don't care why, but that's the only way they love you." I was just talking bullshit, but he didn't figure it out.

"Oh! Oh, I couldn't do that," he said, "she'd sue me. Why she'd take everything *I* own!"

I wasn't doing this feller much good so I just walked off looking for someone else to help. It didn't take long. This little woman, or girl I reckon you'd call her, just latched onto me and turned the most pitiful set of eyes up to me I nearly ever saw. She looked kinda like a kitten that had just been spanked by a mouse.

"He's done it again," she said.

"Lorda mercy, what?"

"Got himself tied up for another five years. Says he'll be president of the company in another five years."

"What is he now?"

"He's vice president now. First vice president."

"There you go," I said.

"There you go where?"

"Oh, nothing."

"Well, I told him that I'd like to hear something just once besides business and promotions. Just once. And another thing I didn't tell him about is all those silly dinners he makes me go to. I'm supposed to smile at some numbhead all evening and listen about his conquests of the business world. Of his clever little subtilties to get and keep the advantage over his cohorts."

"His what?"

"His associates."

"Let's go get us a drink," I said.

She patted her smooth hair and said, kind of surprised, "Well, all right."

I no longer had to tell the bartender how I wanted my drinks. And I said, "The lady will take one just like it."

She said, "How do you know I'll like it?"

I said, "I don't, but if you're goin' to drink with me that's what you'll drink."

She smiled, "I'm game."

We had another drink. I don't hardly think she was used to this kind of cocktail hour, so I just eased her around and danced with her.

She said, "My, that was nice."

"It sure was."

Then she started blabbing again. "It's to the point now that we're sleeping in separate bedrooms."

I said, "I just can't believe it. Why I never heard of such a silly thing."

"It is true," she said, and tears started running down on her pretty little cheeks.

Here was somebody I could help. I led her around through all those drinking, talking, arm-waving people and down aways to a dark room. I couldn't find a bed in it but it didn't hold things up much. I just grabbed her and kissed her and eased her down on the rug. All she ever got to say was "No . . . noooo. Yesssss."

It wasn't long till this woman was feeling a whole lot better. I even felt some better myself.

She told me, "Thanks."

And I said, "Glad to do it."

I let her go back to the crowd first, then in a bit I followed.

Everybody was looking over towards a sure-enough fancy woman. I'll be a chicken-stealing, lamb-killing coyote if it wasn't that Lolane I'd seen on TV the other day.

Myrna was introducing old Wrangler to her. In a minute he threw his head up and looked around until he spotted me. He waved one of his short, heavy arms for me to come over. I went.

That Lolane's hair was so blond her shadow looked bleached, but everything else seemed real. Real good, in fact. Everything except the feller that was with her. He was about a foot taller than me. His hair was slick and black and so shiny in places it looked like he had deep barbwire cuts in his head. He just smiled and smiled and smiled.

"Hello there," he said to everybody he met, and he flashed that row of white teeth till I thought he was going to split a lip.

Well, sir, the next thing I knew I was dancing with Lolane. It was a real pleasurable thing to do. She was a little silly at first saying such things as . . . "My, it's hot in here, isn't it? I just think Myrna's house is too too. I'm starting a new picture next week. It has the most divine cast, and the script is just too too. I'm tired of it though. Some day I'm going to settle down in a little city like Santa Fe and just do nothing but read."

This last kind of made me taste the steel bits in my mouth. There were so many things a woman like this could do to have fun besides read. Damn near anybody could read. Even old Wrangler knew almost half the words in the Union County Leader.

Poor girl. Everybody stared at her except her husband; he was over talking to the poet. They were flinging fingers at one another in what looked to me like an insulting manner. Course you couldn't tell about that cause one of them smiled all the time and the other one never did.

When the music stopped, everybody gathered around us. They kept wanting to meet her or say something to her or in some way be recognized.

"By God," I said right in the middle of the next dance, "come out here. I want to show you my horse." I'd heard about these artists and fancy folks showing their etchings. Well, I show my horse.

"Reckon your husband'll miss us?"

"Oh, he's not my husband. Why I haven't been married in weeks. Ray's gay. It just looks good for us to be seen together."

"Yeah," I said, "he does seem kind of gay. Smiles all the time."

"You're kidding," she said.

I couldn't figure how she figured I was kidding so I just dropped that subject.

She held tight to my arm and snuggled up a little as we walked down the path to the stables. Now I'm not one to carry on much about scenery, but man, what a night.

Old Fooler was standing near the middle of the corral in the bright moonlight with his head down and he didn't bother to look up.

"There he is," I said.

"Is he a good one?" she asked. "Is he spirited?"

"Yes, Miss Lolane, you are looking at one of the most spirited animals on earth."

"Oh, that's just too too," she said, and kind of shook all over. "I made a western," she said. "Did you see it?"

"No, I don't reckon so. What was it called?"

"*We Fit,*" she said. "It flopped."

A coyote howled off in the hills behind the stable. "My goodness," she said and crowded up closer. "He sounds like he's crying so so sad."

"No, ma'am, that animal's laughing."

"Laughing?"

"*That* is right."

"Well, what on earth does the poor thing have to laugh at?"

"Why, he's laughin' at us people."

"Why would he do that?"

"He's smarter, that's why."

"You're kidding," she said.

Now I was beginning to like Lolane, but I could see right now I was going to have to get her over the idea I was always kidding. So, I took her in the corral to get a closer look at my spirited horse. Then I showed her my saddle where the moonlight shot through the stable door. Then I threw the saddle blanket down in that pale blue shaft of moonlight.

She said, "What did you do that for?"

Bless that old coyote's laughing heart, he howled again before I could answer. She made another one of those shaky snuggles and I gathered her up right against my Levi buttons.

She made out like she was going to pull away, but I could feel her hoping I wouldn't let her. I didn't. I took hold of that little pouty red mouth with mine. She wanted this. I felt up and down her back until my hand found that dress zipper, then smooth as silk I slid it down.

Stars above! When I stepped back, that low-hung dress just dropped off on the ground. That dress had been her entire wardrobe. We dropped right down beside it onto the saddle blanket. Now I knew why she reminded me of Myrna. They were so big it took both hands to give one of them a good feel. But no problems, I have two hands.

"Ohhhh," she said, and by doggies we made love.

At first she acted a little like she was in the habit of doing it just to be nice, but in a minute more she was loving because she liked it.

It was a beautiful, soft, warm place so we lay awhile longer and let the goodness soak all through us.

After a little, she put her mouth to my ear and whispered, "That horse is watching us."

I looked around and sure enough there Old Fooler stood with his ears pitched forward. I whispered back, "It's all right, he won't tell anybody."

All of a sudden I jumped up, grabbed her by the hands and pulled her to her feet. Then I just turned her around in that beam of moonlight and looked. She was a hell of a lot prettier than her pictures.

I walked around and took a look at her rear. It was about the prettiest thing I'd ever seen. Old Wrangler is a milk-cow man. He likes big-chested women. Well they're just fine, but I'm more of a quarter-horse man myself. It's those hindquarters that set me to going.

Then I circled her while she trembled and shivered all over. She was breathing so hard I got worried and thought I better get her bedded down again.

It was better than before. By God if this woman had been out of the spotlight awhile and had the right training she'd have been the champion lover of the whole United States.

We rested again.

Then she said, "Darling, hand me my dress." When I did, she kind of straightened it out and started trying to put it on while still sitting down. She did it!

I said, "I'll be a goddamned chicken-stealing, lamb-killing coyote!"

She said, "Nothing to it. Experience in the dressing room."

Just like I figured, all she needed was experience.

We got up and told Old Fooler good night. I could have sworn he had an evil grin on his face. She walked along holding my arm, her head kind of over on my shoulder. She said, "That was nice. It was real."

I didn't say anything.

The next thing we heard was old Wrangler taking on out in the patio. I kind of hurried up, getting a little scared. Here we were just a half mile from heaven and I didn't want anything to happen.

A crowd was gathered around the pool. Almost everybody had already either jumped in or been thrown in. I reckon this foolishness is what gave Wrangler the idea. He was standing at the edge of the pool with Myrna hanging on to his arm. She looked a little drunk, so I don't think she was being loving or comforting at the moment, but mainly trying to stand up.

The Englishman was standing close by with a big wad of money in each hand taking bets. "Now," he said, "since my countrymen were the pioneers, yea, the very creators of these cow people, and since Mr. Wrangler Lewis is one of that fast-vanishing breed, I will say with all sincerity and implicit faith, I believe he can do what he says! Step right up and place your bets!"

Everybody was looking for gambling money. The vice president was trying to make a bet on the strength of his credit cards.

All of a sudden Wrangler downed a big vegetable drink, threw the glass up in the air, and started singing:

> Jesus loves me this I know
> For the Bible tells me so.
> He will wash me white as snow
> Dirty, dirty job for Jesus.

Yes sir, this society bunch had given Wrangler religion.

I grabbed the Englishman's shoulder and asked, "What's he goin' to do? What're you all bettin' on?"

He looked at me and said, "My dear fellow, your pardner maintains he is going to walk across the pool."

"My God, he thinks he's Jesus!" I yelled, and tried to get through the crowd to stop him. I was too late. He had bent down and picked up one of those loose sandstone rocks right out of the patio floor. Then he walked to the edge of the pool and stepped off. What with holding that big rock and the fact he couldn't swim, he went right to the bottom. And in the deepest part too!

The crowd was quiet.

Myrna screamed, "Save my love!"

I grabbed her and said, "Look!" For there in that pale green water stepped old Wrangler. He walked clean across the bottom of that pool, and when he got to the shallow end his head came out like a turtle's. He was blowing to beat hell. But who wouldn't be, he'd been walking uphill.

The deed was so full of courage that nobody argued any technical points. Instead they hauled him out of the water and a great shout rose from their drunken throats.

Myrna cried, "My hero!"

The Englishman gave Wrangler half the winnings and I just walked over and patted Lolane on her beautiful butt.

It couldn't have been a finer world.

TWELVE

ON THIS PARTICULAR MORNING, we got up by inches.

I said, "All the time I thought I'd been pourin' them drinks in my stomach, they'd been goin' in my head."

"I feel like I've been pulled through a half-inch water pipe a mile long," Wrangler answered, sitting up trying to get the hair out of his eyes. "Anything to drink around here?"

"Nothing but about an inch and a half of stale wine in that bottle over there," I said, pointing to a dresser.

He got up, weaved over and stared at the bottle. "I'd rather drink carbolic acid than that stuff," he said, and picked up the bottle and drained her dry with one swaller. I thought he had a funny-looking face till now. But the one he made after that wine was just too damn bad for even his best friend to look at.

I got up, put on my pants and boots, and stumbled down to the coke machine. I felt bad. I had enough of this drinking to do me for nine years. Maybe forever.

I put a coin in the machine and got my coke. When I got back to our door I said, "Wrangler, want a coke?"

"Hell no, what time is it?"

I looked at the sun. "Oh, about eight-thirty."

"The bar opens in thirty minutes," he said.

"You ain't goin' to drink again today, are ya?" I said. "Hell, the wedding's tomorrow."

"Well," he said, making good sense, "we've been celebratin' the engagement for nine days now, we ought to toast the weddin' itself for at least one."

I couldn't argue. The best thing I could do was see that he didn't get too drunk. Now that was going to be a grind.

We started out by having a couple of beers in the Lodge. Then we ordered three eggs and a big chunk of ham with some black coffee. The world began to look a little bit like it had the day before.

I knew Myrna was busy getting ready for the wedding, and if she wanted Wrangler she'd look for him at the Lodge. I didn't want to take a chance on anything happening so I said, "Come on, let's hunt another bar. This'n here is tired of us."

"Whatever suits you just tickles me plumb to death," he said, being agreeable as long as I was looking for a bar.

Well, by ten o'clock that morning we had found one a lot closer in town. It was dirty and dark. I figured old Wrangler would kinda like this. It's the only kind of joint he's used to. But he wouldn't say much when I talked. Maybe this high living was spoiling him.

"Well, tomorrow it'll all be over," I said, feeling better by the minute. "You'll have a good-looking rich woman. One you can truly love. That's cake with icing, boy. In a few days we'll buy that nice cow outfit and I can go to work running it for you. I bet you never thought that would happen to us, did you, pardner?"

At the word "pardner" he threw his head up, grunted, and motioned to the bartender to bring us another round.

"Tell you what we better do, Wrangler. Soon as we get our ranch tied up, we better start building us a rodeo arena. On Sunday afternoons we can invite the local boys over for calf roping and maybe a little wild-cow milking and bronc riding."

"Had all the bronc riding I want." He was staring at a Mexican gal that must have been the sister of the bartender.

I saw she was fairly good looking. I thought I'd better really move in fast. Old Wrangler might just blow everything. I played the music and asked her to dance.

She stood a minute, looked at the bartender, shrugged her shoulders, and said, "Why not?"

We danced and we danced. Then I'd set her down at the bar and we'd have another drink. I didn't let her out of reach. I could read that look on Wrangler's bulldog face too damn well.

Then I saw him heading for us. It was too late, he'd already set his mind on dancing with this little gal. I can't say as I blamed him. I reckon he figured this would be one last fling before he married. On the other hand he might not be thinking any such thing. He might just like her because she was a girl.

I thought fast. "Wrangler," I said, and it was the truth, "Myrna told me to be sure that you got a blood test today. She said it would ease her mind about the Rh factor."

He stopped, blinking his little snake eyes, and said, "What's that?"

"Well, I don't exactly know, but she said it ran in her family, and it has something to do with having kids."

I'll be damned if it didn't work. He went back to the table and just stared.

A great big noise boomed outdoors. I jumped about three yards. The bartender said, "It's raining."

It sure was. I could hear that water just splashing all over.

"Wrangler," I said, "you better take the pickup and run on in and see Dr. Price. That's who Myrna said was to give you the blood test."

"It's raining," he said, and just went on staring at a place on the side of the bar.

Finally I could see that Wrangler was afraid to go to the doctor, so I walked up to a ragged-looking toothless old boy who was drinking the cheapest wine in the house. I asked him a question.

"Do you know where Dr. Price's office is?"

"Sure," he said. "I ain't never met him but the old lady goes there all the time fer her rheumatiz."

After a little explaining, two more drinks, and a ten-dollar bill, he agreed to go to this Dr. Price and tell him his name was Wrangler Lewis and get a blood test.

Anything to please the new wife of my new boss.

I went back up and had another drink with the girl. Just in case his mind swung around to her again. Several people came in and all except one said, "It's raining." This one feller (he was about as big as me and Wrangler put together) came in, his arm swung around the shoulder of a half-pregnant woman. I'm sure they'd been celebrating something or other, for he said, "Who's raining?"

He had on a brand-new green shirt and she wore a loose flopping red dress. Where the rain had dropped off the shirt onto her dress there were green stripes. By God, she looked like a battle flag. They ordered muscatel wine, a sure sign of their condition whether they were drunk or not.

Wrangler was still staring at the bar, but this woman had filled up the spot he was hypnotized by. Pretty soon this big bastard with the big ears and big mouth noticed Wrangler staring. He walked over and said, "Hey, quit lookin' at my woman!"

Wrangler didn't even look up.

"I said, quit looking at my woman!" and he leaned over with his fists spread out on the table.

"What woman?" Wrangler asked.

"That'n," he said, pointing at the big-bellied red dress with the green stripes over the shoulders.

"I ain't staring at her," Wrangler said, scooting his chair around.

Now it makes no difference where you go in the world, there will always be one of these smart bastards to ruin a man's fun. But he might upset a lot more than that if he happened to land that wad of bone he used for a hand in the middle of Wrangler's face. We might have to postpone the wedding.

I got up, walked over, and said, "Wrangler, this man is a head taller than you are, so I'm goin' to even things up."

I grabbed the son of a bitch around the neck and tried to pull his head off. It wouldn't come. I took another run across the room with him. I could see Wrangler was trying to help. He was pulling in the other direction. But one of the old boy's shoes came off and Wrangler fell backwards. Without this added weight we really began to move. The only thing that stopped us was a cement wall. I couldn't pull his head off and I couldn't drive it through the wall, so I just dropped him there and yelled, "Let's go."

On the way out, I could see the bartender calling the cops on the phone and I asked him, "Why didn't you stop that bastard from picking on my little friend? Then you wouldn't have to call the cops."

I didn't hear what he said because we stepped out into the rain. Our tough-necked friend failed to follow.

We jumped in the pickup, and I want to say that my lightning brains were still working. "Now, where will the police expect a couple of half-drunk cowboys to head?"

"Out of town," Wrangler said.

"*That* is right, so *up* town we're goin'!"

THIRTEEN

WE MANAGED to get uptown without having a wreck.

I even got the pickup parked fairly close to the curb. Wrangler wanted to head for another bar. I figured I ought to try to delay this.

"Listen, Wrangler, do you realize you ain't even bought Myrna a wedding present?"

"Never thought of it."

"Well now's the time. Come on, let's look around town here and see what we can find."

The rain had stopped and everybody was out on the sidewalk looking around. First we went in a store called a Five and Dime. I'll say this though, that sign was a big lie. The only thing in there for five cents was a paper-clip. We walked around looking at all those things: bottles of everything on earth, hairpins, hairnets, hair spray, face powder, hand powder, and powder for other places, shoes, dishes, drawers for both men and girls. They were pink, blue, yellow, red, and all the colors in Myrna's flower garden. This brought something to mind.

"Wrangler, what does Myrna love more than anything on earth besides you?"

He kind of twisted his face around and said, "Them vegetable drinks." He acted so dang pleased with this that I hated to disappoint him.

"No, you're wrong. It's flowers."

"You're right," he said, getting the idea.

We walked over and bought a large, dun-colored flowerpot with a little baby lemon tree in it. They wrapped it all up and told Wrangler to be careful with it.

"I will," he said.

We barely left the store when he spotted another saloon. I knew I

couldn't stop him from going in but maybe I could talk him into
leaving soon. Seems like he was more shook up than ever before.

He downed three double shots while I coasted along on two singles.
That brain of mine, that was getting so lightning fast lately, started
working again.

"You know, Wrangler, Myrna is goin' to ask us the first thing in the
morning how we spent our day. Now wouldn't it be nice if we could
say we spent it at the moving pictures."

"All right, that's what we'll tell her," he said, motioning for another
double shot.

"It ain't quite that easy," I said. "What if she asks what we saw?"

"That ain't no problem," he said, "the picture show's right around
the corner."

"You ain't gettin' what I mean. What if she has seen this show
herself and starts pumping us about it?"

"Oh."

"Drink up and let's go."

He gathered up his flowerpot easy-like and we walked around to
the show. It had a big sign out front:

THE IRON SPIDER
A MONSTER DROPPED FROM OUTER SPACE
TO DEVOUR THE WORLD

I bought us a couple of tickets and we went in. They had a little old
place that looked like a bar where they sold chewing gum, candy, soda
pop, and popcorn. I ordered us a bag of popcorn apiece, but when I
handed it to Wrangler he said, "That ain't enough. I'm hungry." So he
ordered two more bags.

I said, "How're you goin' to handle three bags of popcorn and that
lemon tree?"

He didn't answer. He just took off his hat and emptied all the
popcorn in it. We went to the show.

It was hard to see in there and we both had the blind staggers. A
little feller carrying a flashlight without any light in it, took us down in
the middle of the place and we finally got settled.

The show was just starting. A great big flat-looking thing was flying
over the top of the world. Inside it was a bunch of green men who had
a face in front and the same face in back. Their feet were the same
way. They reminded me of some of those little peanut cars you see
around these big towns. I watched and I watched but there wasn't any

way to tell the front from the back. I kept thinking that maybe if one of their women would show up a feller might get a clue.

All of a sudden a lot of loud, scary music started playing (I never did see where the band was but it played during the whole show) and a great big iron spider dropped out of that flying machine. It came down on a thread like any spider would except it was about seven jillion times bigger. On the ends of its iron legs were some bucket-looking things. Soon as it landed it started sticking out those iron legs and sucking everything right up into that big belly. It was sure enough boogery.

Then the scene changed to a wad of scientific fellers talking to the army, and one of the army fellers wasn't no feller at all, it was a woman who looked a little like Lolane. They were calling out army tanks, and thousands of soldiers and airplanes by the hundred. But this spider just went right on through this city knocking over buildings as big as mountains, swatting airplanes out of the sky like sick mosquitoes, and sucking people up those iron legs as fast as he got to them. One of those science fellers said that human food was like fuel to this monster. He really had plenty, looked like to me.

Wrangler was chewing popcorn so hard and fast that folks all around were turning to us and saying, "Shhhhh." They gave us dirty looks too.

After a while that spider took in after a handsome soldier and this pretty woman. He stuck out one of those iron legs and slowly but surely that poor woman was pulled right up into that bucket.

It was too much for Wrangler. He jumped up and yelled, "Kill the mean son of a bitch!" Popcorn went everywhere. People got all upset, and the little man with the flashlight came down and told us to be quiet or leave. I finally got Wrangler settled enough to watch the picture.

The woman was completely gone and the soldier was fighting like hell trying to hang on to the edge of the iron leg. Then all of a sudden the spider sort of fell backwards trembling and began to weave and sink lower and lower. Finally he fell over, kicked a time or two and died. It sure was a relief.

I was really surprised at how smart that soldier was. Come to find out that wasn't a real woman at all—just a dummy made of wax. The wax choked that spider to death and thereby the world was saved.

Wrangler just sat there pumping his lungs after the show was over. We finally got enough strength to get outside. I expected it to be dark but the sun was still two hours high. Wrangler didn't say a word. He was shaking all over and his eyes were kind of glazed like melted glass. He could see good enough though to read a sign that said HARRY'S SALOON.

He commenced pouring those drinks down and the most I could get out of him was his usual grunt. This didn't look good. The more he drank the more I could tell that spider was on his mind. I played the jukebox, and told all sorts of lies trying to get his mind off the show. Nothing worked.

After a while I said, "Let's go to another saloon."

He got up and followed me out. We walked down the street without talking. I was hoping I could get him to the pickup and haul him back to the Lodge. Then I figured I'd get him in the room with a full bottle and just let him forget all these things that seemed to be on his back.

Well we passed a doorway and on the window next to it was a sign that said:

BETTY'S BEAUTY
SALON

Now Wrangler's not very tall when he's stepping his highest, and I reckon the only word he saw was the bottom one. He just automatically turned in. I followed.

There sat eight ladies under eight hair dryers. Some were cleaning their fingernails, others were reading.

Old Wrangler stiffened like a frozen post. Then he hauled off and threw his flowerpot at one of the hair dryers. His aim was good. The dryer banged, the pot broke, and the dirt and the lemon tree all came down on top of the woman's fresh-washed head.

Then with a wild yell he attacked one of the dryers. The women jumped all directions, overturning things. The ones who didn't faint ran out in the street screaming "Police! Police! Madman!"

Wrangler didn't seem to notice anything like this. He had one of the hair dryers down choking hell out of it and when that didn't seem to make any difference he began to beat it against the floor.

He was yelling, "Don't worry ladies, I'll kill this goddamned iron spider!"

Well, he killed several before the police got there. I just stood and watched. I'd already given up. It was just too much for old tired Dusty.

The police grabbed him and I said, "Here now, this man's a hero. He's drunk and he thought those dryers were spider legs."

With that they just loaded me up and took me along with the hero. Right in jail they threw us and locked the thick iron door. Now an old uncle of mine (the one that wasn't a preacher) once told me that if you were on a party and didn't get in jail, you hadn't had any fun. This was one time he was wrong. What really got me was that before I could chew Wrangler's tail out, the little ugly bastard had gone to sleep.

There ain't no use whatever in telling all about the night. It was long.

The next morning after one of those sorry jail breakfasts, we went before the judge. I tried like hell to remember the vice president's name who'd offered his help at Myrna's party. I just couldn't think straight all of a sudden. Then I thought about calling Myrna and realized that my lightning brain was slipping a little there, too. If she didn't find out about this we'd have old Wrangler hitched today and then it would be too late. Yes, sir, today was the day.

Well, the judge let us know right off that he was God and owned the world and could do anything he wanted to with us. I agreed with everything he said. I'd learned long ago that there's no justice with judges. Especially if you talk back.

He then proceeded to fine us the limit, for drunkenness, disturbing the peace, fighting, and destroying several inanimate objects. Namely hair dryers. Then on top of that we had to pay for those hair dryers. Our rate of payment was based on the price of brand-new ones, even though they were several years old. We paid. The price for being a hero really comes high these days.

I was glad to get out of there even though we only had six dollars and eighty-four cents left out of all our pay, all Myrna's hundred-dollar bills, and all that gambling money the Englishman had given us. It was a damn good thing it was the day of the great wedding.

FOURTEEN

I'LL SAY ONE THING, *that* Myrna doesn't do *any*thing halfway. People were driving up in Cadillacs and RR cars from just about everywhere. Out by the swimming pool three cooks wearing great tall white hats were barbecuing a whole beef. They kept turning him over the coals and on a windy day you could have smelled it as far as Hi Lo. It made a feller's taster act up. Four or five waiters were running around with their hands turned upside down carrying trays of vegetable drinks.

It was sunshiny and the wind was still. People were seated all around the swimming pool, talking and drinking and waiting. Every little bit a car would drive up and unload an armload of flowers. It made me kind of sad that our lemon tree hadn't survived the picture show.

Old Fooler was standing with his head up over the corral looking wild-eyed. He was getting fat and mean.

Myrna called me into the house to try to help Wrangler get ready. It sure was a job mashing him into that tuxedo. In fact, we never did get him in it completely.

The phone kept ringing and Myrna would answer, "Oh, I'm so sorry you couldn't make it, dear. Well, thank you, dear. How are things in New York? Tell Joe 'Hello' for me, darling. Oh yes, he's a sweetie pie. We'll be so happy. Yes, dear, we'll see you in Mexico in January. I will. I will. Bye now."

It just kept on—one thing after another. Then the preacher came in and made a big show out of what was going to take place. It seems we missed some kind of rehearsal.

Myrna's personal maid loped in with the daily paper all spread out and her finger pointing to a certain spot on the front page. I got the cold feeling a baby mouse must get when he's just been swallered by a rattlesnake.

Myrna said, "Not now, Celia, I can't read now. What is it that's so important?"

I made several signs at the maid but she smiled back exactly like Old Fooler after he's kicked you in the belly.

"Madam," she said, "it's *very* important."

Myrna stopped what she was doing and said, "All right, I don't suppose a minute longer will hurt, will it, honey pie?"

Old Wrangler grinned back kind of silly-like, "I reckon not, Myrna baby."

I had already read over her shoulder all I wanted to see and that was this:

HEIRESS'S BRIDEGROOM SPENDS PRE-WEDDING
NIGHT IN JAIL

Myrna turned white even through that suntanned makeup. She glared at Wrangler and spit out, "The cinema my foot!"

Before Myrna could say more, the maid handed her the phone, halfway shouting with excitement, "It's Dr. Price. He says its extremely urgent."

Myrna took the phone. She was shaking so hard it rattled against her golden earrings.

"What? An alcoholic? And it showed positive on . . . on . . . !" and right there words failed her. Whatever was positive must've really been bad. She dropped the phone right across Wrangler's head, screaming, "You filthy beast, you've given me that horrible disease." Then she threw the mirror, and a big bottle of lotion. She tried to throw the dressing table. Then she just stopped and screamed and pulled her hair. "You beast, you vile beast!"

I gathered up the little beast's boots, Levi's, and his shirt. He grabbed his hat and we retreated. I will say this, Myrna's screams had only slightly interested the guests. I heard one of them say as we broke out of the house, "Seems the groom is taking advantage of his marriage privileges somewhat early." But when they saw the groom barefooted with a big, old, greasy cowboy hat on and his little potbelly hanging out over those shiny black britches, a lot of voices stilled, but not Myrna's. We could still hear her screaming.

"Listen," I said, thinking lightning fast, "she'll calm down in a minute and you'll just have to tell her the truth. That we sent somebody else in your place. That wasn't *your* 'positive' blood at all."

Wrangler just stood there shaking. He had a ten-day hangover to help him, but I believe his courage would have snapped anyway.

She was at an open window now still pulling her hair and yelling. For a minute she kind of choked down. That's when we heard the music.

Around the big circle driveway came a truck—a large truck—and it was hauling a whole band. As it came on around the circle, the driver started squeezing the horn and a man was beating a drum like he was trying to kill it. Every man on that truck started blowing or beating something.

I heard a loud crashing noise down towards the stables and saw Old Fooler booger and jump right through the corral. He was plumb wild and didn't know where to go. He ran this way and that but there was always some wedding guests in his way. Finally I reckon he must've spotted me and Wrangler because he came tearing around the swimming pool scattering people everywhere. He ran right up beside us. He was shaking as bad as Myrna.

Suddenly he kind of settled down and went to gobbling some prize-winning dahlias out of the flower bed, raising his head, snorting and shaking dirt off the roots every time he got another mouthful. Then he did it. There wasn't any hope now. It was all done. I don't really think Old Fooler meant it as an insult. I just think he was plain scared into it at the sight of all this society. He lifted his tail and took a big dump right out on the patio with a pure white flower hanging out each side of his mouth.

There is not another thing to tell about old Wrangler's wedding day except this—we left.

FIFTEEN

NOW SIX DOLLARS and eighty-four cents is lots of money if you're well fed and know where you can get another meal. But it ain't much in four days without either. As soon as the word got to the Lodge they kicked us right out. We moved to the edge of town, slept in our bedrolls, and ate cheese and crackers every day like it was pure honey.

We went into town and started asking around for a ranch job. Seemed like everybody was well supplied.

One feller asked me why we didn't draw welfare payments. I didn't exactly understand what it was and I knew less after I talked to the Welfare people. We were offered a job in a filling station, but we didn't even have a social security card. I tried to find that vice president to borrow one of his. He must have been out of town.

Finally we went to an employment agency. The man said, "Tomorrow's Friday. We have a client coming in who needs a couple of cowboys to break out a string of broncs. Will that be all right?"

I said, "Listen, as hungry as we are, I'll fight six wild tigers barehanded if you'll let me eat the remains."

"All right then, be here at two o'clock tomorrow afternoon and we'll see what we can do."

It was a long time till then. That night I tried to eat some of Old Fooler's oats. It wasn't that he was stingy. It was just that I couldn't get them down with him looking at me.

Wrangler said, "You've heard that song, ain't you, about the hobo who was so hungry he could eat grass. Well, I'm so empty I could eat the ground it grows in."

"This here ground's too full of rocks."

"Yeah," he said, "I done tried it."

Two o'clock finally did come. It took all the strength we had left to climb the stairs up to the second story. We went in and sat down. At two-thirty this rancher still hadn't showed. I was too weak to ask the smiling secretary if something had gone wrong. In fact, I could only smile back at her with one side of my mouth.

Right about three o'clock the man who ran the office walked in with the rancher.

That is right! It was Jim Ed Love!

Weak as he was, Wrangler jumped and ran to the window. The only thing that stopped him from jumping out was the fact he got tangled up in a bunch of those venetian blinds.

I dragged him away from the window saying, "It wouldn't do you no good to jump, Wrangler. We ain't but two stories up. All you'd do is break a bunch of bones."

He stopped kicking. We both looked at Jim Ed. He smiled and stuck his belly out over his fancy silver and turquoise belt buckle.

"You boys look like you've had a fine time. A *fine* time."

We just stood and swallered air.

"How about us going down the street here and getting a great big juicy sirloin steak with potatoes and hot gravy to boot?" Jim Ed said.

Us two ex-city slickers just followed him down the stairs rubbing our growling bellies and licking our lips.

Orange County Cowboys

IF A PERSON'S WHOLE WORLD was going to end within two weeks, very few people would spend this precious time tying barbwire around sandstone rocks and dropping them into a gully, but that is exactly what the two weathered, battered cowboys, Dusty Jones and Wrangler Lewis, were up to. They were repairing a water gap, three or four strands of barbwire strung across a draw to keep the cattle in a certain pasture. Instead of being firmly anchored to fence posts, the bottom wire is tied to suspended rocks so they swing freely instead of breaking in a minor flash flood.

Dusty made a wrap around a ten pound rock and secured it with a tight twist of the wire. As he dropped it, he turned to Wrangler saying,

"Ever since those Japanese people looked at this ranch with the idea of buying it, I've felt like one of these rocks was barbwired to my balls."

"Awww, I think they'll probably like George Haley's place better than this'n."

Jim Ed Love, owner of the Hi Lo, New Mexico, ranch was definitely serious about selling it to a group of Japanese investors. He had shown his usual wisdom in allowing his foreman, Dusty, to be their escort guide. The interested buyers were led by Mikio Reynolds. She was the divorced, thoroughly Americanized sister of Mr. Yakahami of Tokyo and other worldly places. Dusty had given the tour all he had even though it hurt him deeply knowing that his bragging about the ranch might cost him the only home he'd known as an adult.

Dusty pushed his hat back on his head and said, "I'll tell ya, Wrangler, I never wanted to lie so bad in all my life, but this is a great ranch and . . . that Japanese lady, Mikio . . . well . . . nobody could ever lie to her and get away with it."

Wrangler grunted and said, "Maybe they won't like it a tall. Maybe they're just kinder shoppin' like folks do in town. Maybe Jim Ed don't really want to sell. Maybe if you'd run off with that purty Mikio lady, that'd stop the deal. Maybe if . . ."

Dusty interrupted a little tautly. "Like they say down at Lubbock, Texas, maybe if the dog hadn't stopped to shit he'd of caught the rabbit. If . . . if . . . if . . ."

Wrangler only grunted this time.

Dusty rambled on as they finished repairing the water gap. "Two weeks. That's what we got left to make a too-late, brand-new beginning. If you'd just married that rich old Myrna Hopwell over at Santa Fe that time we wouldn't be havin' these worried notions."

"Now let's don't start that agin. I can't help it if she thought I had that terrible epidemic disease."

"You couldn't help it?" Dusty snapped his head in Wrangler's direction, then said through clenched teeth, "If you hadn't been so damn drunk you wouldn't have sent that poor old, toothless wino to take your blood test for you. What 'da you mean you couldn't help it?"

"Sounded like a hell of a good idea at the time." Wrangler began gathering up the tools. Then he smoothly added, "Seems like that Japanese lady took quite a likin' to you, Dusty ole pard." He waited for a smart-ass answer, but when it didn't come, he continued, "I can see plumb through a mountain of malpai that she's the marryin' kind." He snorted a couple of laughs through his flattened nose, and added, "I reckon it's your turn next."

They tossed the wire stretchers, wire pliers, staples, and hammers into the back of the pickup and drove off down a rocky, rutted, bumpy road in a cloud of powdered dust.

Dusty rubbed his sleeve across his dry mouth and suggested, "Why don't we stop at Vince Moore's and have a cup of his bootleg belly burner."

Wrangler cheered up. "Yeah, why don't we? I never seen a drink of whiskey I didn't like."

TWO TALL BUSINESSMEN, dressed up to play cowboy, sat in the John Wayne Airport lounge in Orange County, California, and raised full glasses of Scotch, toasting one another.

"Here's to fourteen days of freedom," said Ed Mason.

"Here's to escape," said Al Goodspeed, smiling for the first time in a week.

They were on their way, this time without Al's family or Ed's girlfriend, to Al's vacation ranch in northeastern New Mexico. This vast, rolling, canyon-gashed land was called the Hi Lo country. From the high mesa top, twenty miles east, three other states could be seen on a cloudless day. It was an ideal place for Al to build a ten-room log cabin.

Goodspeed's land was surrounded by large, working cow ranches, but he didn't run cattle on his spread. Deer, bear, cougar, and an occasional stray elk had that privilege. They wandered freely across his place and drank from the small trout lake formed by a thin stream. The coyotes howled nightly, and during the day the hawks circled the sky looking for rabbits or rodents. It was a choice place to entertain clients in the fall with big game hunting. In the spring it was good for trout fishing or just watching the grass grow and the neighbor's newborn calves leaping and frolicking in a nearby meadowland pasture.

Al Goodspeed, an international manufacturer of precision machine parts, headquartered his company in high-tech Orange County. He had just turned a heavy-framed fifty-five. Ed Mason, his best and longest-lasting friend, owned a small but elite advertising agency in the same county. Ed was about to finish out his skinny forties. Because of Ed's independent nature he operated the agency alone and had, by his own choice, limited his clients to only three—but they were good ones. Al Goodspeed was his best. They looked forward to talking things over out at the ranch—heavy things that had been bothering them—but right now they had just enough time for one more fast drink before catching the plane to Albuquerque where they'd rent a car and drive north.

Al said, "Do you think these people here"—he motioned around the airport bar—"believe we're real cowboys?"

Ed answered, "Well, last time we were up there, your rancher friend George Haley said we looked 'purty much' like the real thing, but I have a feeling he was being very, very kind."

Al laughed aloud now, his blue eyes beginning to visualize things other than his factories and sales offices in Orange, Sweden, Germany, Belgium, and Switzerland.

"Hey," Ed said, "it's time to go, and this is one plane we don't want to miss."

If the two had just joined the first wagon train to pioneer the Santa

Fe Trail they couldn't have felt more excited or adventurous. When the plane finally reached thirty thousand feet, and each had a drink of Scotch in hand, the friends knew they were finally "away."

Ed said, "I can already feel the freeway bullshit dropping off my back."

"I'm somewhat lighter myself," Al said as he settled in for the ride.

Ed Mason and Al Goodspeed weren't the only part-time residents on their way to the high altitude ranches of Hi Lo. Jim Ed Love's shiny, twenty-six-year-old secretary-companion, Shirley Holt, drove him in his Cadillac along the highway between Clayton and Raton as if she owned it. She and Jim Ed had left the ranch headquarters near Andrews, in far West Texas, early that morning.

Jim Ed had inherited the shinnery, sand, and mesquite-covered Texas ranch in the mid-thirties from his father, along with a foreclosure mortgage, the Great Depression, and a searing drought. He would have lost the whole forty thousand acres except an oil company leased the mineral rights and drilled, bringing in a thousand-barrel-a-day well on the first location. Now two hundred and fifty pump jacks, looking like great steel blackbirds, pushed their bills deep into the earth and forced his liquid wealth to the surface. The drop in oil prices shouldn't have bothered Jim Ed much, but it did, even though all it meant was his income changed from three and a half million to two million a year. He'd also diversified into high-tech stocks, real estate, and businesses in San Diego, Beverly Hills, and other expensive places. Even so, Jim Ed had decided to trim his huge holdings and take life a little easier. He was somewhere in his seventies—the quiet country years—but was in good shape physically and his mind could slice up granite.

He picked up the car phone and called his son, Jason, who had privately jetted to the Hi Lo ranch two days earlier from Midland, Texas.

Jason answered, "How you doin', Dad?"

"Fine, son. I woke up this morning with nothing to do and I believe I got about half of it done."

"Glad to hear you've been so busy. Did you get any of that good rain at the ranch that we got up here?"

"Awww, maybe four drops and a squirt."

Jason knew that it had, in fact, rained an inch and a half just two days back, but he wanted to hear what his dad would say about it, knowing that if one of these old ranchers had just received two feet of moisture they'd swear a dust storm was already blowing the grass dead.

"Well, Dad, the Tokyo people are still here. I got your price within three dollars an acre on the Hi Lo ranch."

"Hey, that's sounds okay. What about the cattle?"

"Market price on the day of closing like you said."

"Mineral rights?"

"They want three quarters of those."

"Oboy, they know there's a huge coal deposit under the north half of that ranch, don't they?"

"Yes, and they're also aware of those hundreds of C2O gas wells Amoco has drilled all around us."

"Well, that's the big trap. There's always a trap to watch out for. Always."

"And that's not exactly all. I've been dreading to tell you this. They want George Haley's ranch too, because our coal deposits extend over on his land. And . . . if they can't get George's they say they don't want ours."

"What's the hang-up then? Have you talked to George?"

"Yes, and so have they. George swears he'll never sell."

"Ever'body says that, son. We'll have to see what we can do to change George's mind. Won't we?"

"Guess so. Say, Dad, there's something else that's bothering me. What are we gonna do about Dusty and Wrangler? They've been up here on this outfit for over half their lives."

"Well, we can move 'em back to Texas on the Big Lake Ranch. They oughta like that."

"But then we'd have to demote Dusty from foreman to just plain cowboy, and that don't seem fair to me."

"Hell, maybe the Japs'll keep them both on. They'd sure be smart doin' it. Nobody alive knows that spread like ole Dusty and Wrangler."

"Yeah, but . . . they're gonna feel like . . ."

"Listen, son, don't go gettin' sentimental on me here. There's nothing in this world as pitiful to gaze upon as a broken-down cowboy with ambition." He gave a quick chuckle, then added, "We'll be there soon. Bye."

Jim Ed hung up the phone and was thoughtful for a few minutes. Then he reared back in the cushioned seat and said to Shirley, "They're trying to hang us out to an early frost on the mineral rights and they're making the deal subject to Haley selling his outfit under the same terms, and he doesn't want to sell."

"You'll handle it, Jim Ed. That's for sure," she said, smiling warmly at him.

Jim Ed was quiet a spell as the car moved over the graveled road. He thought to himself how many generations the Love family and the Haleys had been friends. Fine people, the Haleys, but just as tough as they were kind.

"Tell you what I'm gonna do, Shirley. We'll toss a party for those Oriental folks that they'll never forget. We'll invite ever'body in the entire Hi Lo country. Hell, we'll have us a big fiesta. We'll throw so much bullshit, booze, and music into the air that old Haley can't help but *discover* he wants to sell. I know the Japanese are smart traders, but they haven't lived through a Jim Ed Love fandango before."

"See? I told you, you would handle it."

"Awww, Shirley, you know this ole boy don't know thin brush from firewood." He gave her a sly wink and the two Cadillac jockeys shared a comfortable laugh.

GEORGE HALEY was watching his wife, Doris, comb her auburn hair with the streaks of gray at the temples. To him, she was even more beautiful now at forty-five. Her figure was slightly fuller, but better, and her blue-green eyes seemed deeper and more caring. He found it hard to believe they'd been married twenty-seven years. Sometimes it seemed like last week, and at other moments it seemed a thousand years. Where in hell was time, anyway, and what was it to deceive them like this?

Haley forced his mind out of the past back to the present and said to his wife, "Well, Goodspeed was supposed to come in from Orange yesterday and here we are taking off for Albuquerque."

Doris replied, "Don't worry about it, hon. He's bringing Ed Mason with him and they'll probably appreciate being alone to rest up for a few days. We'll have plenty of time to visit them when we get back from the Cattleman's Convention."

"You're right. Anyway, we really don't have a choice. I feel like we have to go. There are lots of issues on the docket this year besides the low cattle prices. There's the high land taxes and those fees for the grazing permits sure have to be talked out, and I darn sure want to be there to put in my two-bits' worth." He paused for a minute, thoughtfully, and added, "Besides, I'll be kind of glad to get away from here for a few days. It'll give us a little time to think. We've got quite a bit to sort out in our heads."

George was, in part, referring to the prospect of selling their ranch to the Japanese investors. It would be a difficult decision to make.

Life on the Haley ranch had been tough, but full, and they liked it here. Together they had fought all the natural disasters that befall ranchers—droughts, blizzards, and currently it was low cattle prices and mounting debts. Somehow, up to now, they had kept the place afloat.

George and Doris were partners, and Doris had done more than her share. Without her, Haley could never have made it go. Besides making her family a comfortable home, keeping them well fed, neatly dressed, and healthy, she also helped George with a lot of the ranch work—branding and fencing. The bringing up of their two children, sixteen-year-old Terri and their twelve-year-old son Dodge, had been mostly her responsibility. She was proud of the results her dedication had brought.

The Haleys loved their land and the lives it gave them, even though the years of increasing debts were wearing them both down to the marrow. They fought on, still losing ground by the day. Now they could change it all if they chose to. They could get out with a livable nest egg, enough that the monthly check they were now receiving from Al Goodspeed to look after his place wouldn't have the same importance. That money had kept them off the edge, and they were grateful for it.

George found himself wondering if Doris would, in her heart, really want to change everything, or would she just go along with what she thought he wanted? Guess he'd never really know that for sure. Anyway, they wouldn't deal with the Japanese unless Jim Ed went along as well. He'd be in from Texas anytime now and they'd have to decide, but they could think about all that later.

"Well, while you're gettin' ready, I'm goin' down to the barn and talk to the kids."

Today his daughter and son, and some of their friends, were going to move a herd of cattle from one meadow to another. George believed in rotating his stock regularly in the lower country. Then in early summer he'd turn the cattle out into the high-timbered pastures until fall. This kind of rotation would let the meadows near headquarters grow lush and tall to make hay for the winter.

He found Terri and Douglas warming up a couple of quarter horses. In an hour or so, five neighboring ranch kids would arrive and they'd move the three hundred mother cows and their calves from the Francis meadow to the adjoining north pasture. It wasn't much of a cattle drive, but the young cowhands would be doing it without their parents, so it couldn't have been any more exciting if they were driving thousands of head from Texas to Dodge City.

George checked things over, gave a few last instructions, and said good-bye. He felt completely trusting of the youngsters. All of them had been working cattle since they could climb on a horse.

He and Doris were ready for town!

ED MASON AND AL GOODSPEED arrived at the playhouse ranch on the kind of summer day God would have bragged about. The early afternoon clouds had gathered, rumbled, rained, and moved away east. The slanting sun drank the moisture from the meadow grass so swiftly that damp ghosts of steam rose lazily into the freshly washed air.

Three hundred head of George Haley's whiteface cattle grazed in the meadow about a half mile west of Al's place. The biggest-boned, best-conformed, five-year-old "boss" cow nursed her three-week-old calf and chewed nonchalantly on her cud. The bull calf was so full from the plentiful milk that he slobbered and gasped for breath. Even so, he hunched at her bag so hard she kicked at him from the pain. His tail whipped back and forth like a contented puppy. Then he heard, and saw, the blur of a frolicking little heifer race by.

He let the teat slip from his mouth, and turned his head to watch as she ran away, jumping and twisting. She whirled and charged straight at him only to veer off at the last second. The young bull pursued her, kicking and bucking even higher. They circled and chased one another, stopping to playfully butt heads. They were so full of life on this one perfect day that they had to expend it in joyous celebration. They went running, weaving, teasing across the meadow, strengthening their muscles and improving their agility.

A few years back, this meadow had been cleared of timber except for one huge pine tree. George Haley left the giant as a remembrance of how mighty the forest had been. Since it had no others of comparable size to act as buffers against the strong winds, a violent gust had toppled it. There it remained with its roots in the air higher than a horse's withers and a hole in the earth as big as a cellar.

The two calves, faces as white as the top of Pike's Peak and their deep-red body hair complementing the emerald green grass, raced almost side by side now, heads stretched out, tails arched. The baby bull jammed his front feet into the ground to whirl back and away, but one hind leg slipped off into the hole left by the fallen tree. His momentum whirled him like a top and he fell thumping on the bottom dirt.

He was addled, but swiftly recovered and attempted to climb out on the only slope possible. It was still muddy from the rain and his hooves cut and churned at the earth as he struggled upward and slid back down over and over. Soon the ground was smoothed slick so that it was impossible for him to climb out. He was trapped.

He smelled around its sides. At one end where the topsoil reached down to clay, a small basin of water drained in and was captured from the recent rain. He dropped his muzzle down into the puddle, took a couple of sips, and then found he couldn't turn around in the narrow end of the hole. There was nothing to see but the water, the banks of brown dirt, and blue sky above where a couple of buzzards circled floating on updrafts, looking and smelling for anything dead or dying.

THE YOUNG COWHANDS did a good job rounding up the modest-sized herd. The cattle were moving along smoothly now, with the kids yelling like old-timers, popping hands on chaps and snapping the ends of catch ropes at the slackers. They were making a lot of noise, but they were also being careful not to chouse the stock too much so the weight loss would be kept a minimum.

There was only one problem. The "boss" cow, who usually led the bunch, kept cutting back out of the herd, bawling. Terri noticed that her bag was so full it was dripping milk from each teat. It was obvious that she was looking for her lost calf.

Terri searched among the cattle for the little bull. Not finding it, she left the herd and loped back through the meadow. She made a wide circle in the well-fenced pasture, but there was no calf to be seen.

She finally decided it might have been killed earlier by a mountain lion or a bear, or even a coyote, and dragged off into the brush. After a while she accepted the loss of the calf as ranchers always do, with a minute of pain and a necessary forever of forgetting. She'd tell her parents the moment they returned, but for now there was a job to finish, and after that came the picnic, the flirting, and the "horse bragging" with the other young wranglers.

MASON AND GOODSPEED were finally relaxed. The winds of the Hi Lo Country had blown the particles of concrete and plastic from their bodies and erased the computer programs from their heads.

Yesterday they fished, and feasted. Last night they enjoyed a relaxing meal of venison and quail out of the freezer and the fresh trout they'd caught by Al's lake. Now, today, after a good night of sleep, they sat out on the porch sipping drinks and nursing a semi-hangover.

Al got up and focused the powerful telescope, perched on its tripod, down on the meadow where they'd heard the cattle bellering and the kids yelling the day before. He moved the scope around, as he loved to do, looking for wildlife. He moved it up the slope, through a forest of rocks and then back down. He saw a sudden movement. A badger was chasing a ground squirrel. He watched as the little squirrel twisted, turned, and leaped, avoiding the jaws and claws of the predator. It dived into its burrow four inches ahead of death. The badger rammed his head down into the hole, backed out, looked around, then jumped down and started digging—the thing badgers do best.

Al was hypnotized by the life and death action occurring across the quiet, resting valley. Ed was reading a book by William Manchester on World War II—a somewhat larger, but no deadlier, struggle than Al was watching.

The dirt flew out behind the badger's claws like he had shovels on his legs. He was digging down out of sight now until he backed up for a moment to kick the surplus dirt away. Al could tell by the excited posture of the animal's body that he felt he had his prey ready to pluck from the deep dirt trap. Then, to his eternal amazement, Al saw the squirrel's head rise from a tiny escape hole a few feet from the main entrance. The squirrel looked swiftly around, leaped out, and dashed frantically for the large rocks above.

There was a blur as a hawk dived from the air, scooped up the ground squirrel in its claws, and flew to its nest on top of the pillared rocks where she ripped it apart and fed the pieces to her young.

Al's thoughts flashed back to the nursing home and the last visit he'd had with his Uncle Carl. He was devastated when the old man didn't recognize him. Al's mind just wouldn't accept that this man he loved so much, who'd been so vital, so full of spirit all his life, had in two short months lost the use of his brain, his body, and possibly his soul. It didn't matter that Uncle Carl was ninety and had enjoyed a full life. No, it just wasn't right. After all, he didn't retire until he was eighty-five, when he was still going strong. Al was only fifty-five now, and Carl had gone on producing for decades after that age, but still the visit had really turned Al's head around. All he could recall was the vacant stare from the man in the wheelchair, and in his mind he put his own body there. He was thinking like the song says, "Is that all there is?"

He stood back from the telescope and stared off at the mountains. He ached to describe the drama in the dirt to Ed. His feelings had been filtered to their purest form. Words would have to wait for the proper progression of time. Instead, he quietly moved into the house and got them each another drink.

The two old friends talked about the good times for a while. They reminisced about the camping trips to Baja before the tourists discovered it—when they had once driven for hundreds of miles without seeing a human. How they'd loved the desert, the camaraderie with a couple of other friends, the Mexican beer, the long empty beaches, and the quail chirping their cheerful sounds across the precious stillness. They spoke of their drinking and business bouts on Sunset Boulevard twenty, even twenty-five, years ago. Ah, how their youth had laughed at hangovers, business setbacks, and how swift the recovery from broken love affairs. They elaborated on the trips to Europe as Al's business expanded, the great museums they'd seen, and the grand hotels they'd stayed in. My God, they'd had a lot, and now, this moment, they felt incomplete. They believed their clocks had stopped and the winding keys had been lost.

Ed tried to convince Al that he had pulled it all off. "Hell, old pardner"—he reverted to the local way of speaking—"you've put it all in a box and tied a bright red ribbon around it. You've got a pretty wife, two healthy, educated kids, and business around the world. You have the ballets, the clubs, the boats, money, position, and power that goes with it all. Seems to me, you've done damn well."

"That's just it," lamented Al. "It's not what I thought I wanted. Now I feel vacant . . . and . . . ah, hell, I don't know. There's just got to be more. Something . . . something else that really matters."

Ed Mason looked out across the meadows where the late sun had turned the green pastures to soft gold and said, "There is, Al, if you want to pay the price."

"What's that? Just tell me how I get out of this . . . get rid of this feeling of doom. Go ahead, tell me."

"Think of all the things you can enjoy when you have the time. The time, that's the catch," Ed said. "That's the one thing you can't buy. You love art. You love reading good books and watching fine films. You love the outdoors and sometimes the isolation. There are dozens of things, except the time to do them. Sell the goddamn factories and go do all the things you love. You've got enough to take care of you and your family from now on. What in hell is holding you back?"

Al's face turned deep pink as he rubbed at his greying blond hair and said, "I know you're right, but I just can't call up the guts to do it. I can't seem to make the break no matter how much I want to. I keep thinking of all the reasons why I shouldn't—my wife, my kids, my employees."

"Okay then. Okay," Ed said, shrugging his shoulders, "Go ahead and work yourself to death. What will anyone really care—and which will be remembered the longest, you or your properties? Everybody'll start fighting over them in about three seconds after you're gone anyway, so everything you've worked like hell to put together will crumble and turn into a beautiful pool of diminishing, confused crap."

Suddenly Al decided he resented the very thing he'd asked to hear.

"Okay, look at yourself," he said. "You've sold out to a comfortable house full of paintings and books. You never work on the novel you constantly say you're going to write. Why don't you just quit and follow your heart like you're telling me to do?"

"You got part of it right. I could have stayed up on Sunset Boulevard with that advertising agency and lived in a castle in Beverly Hills, but I chose to come down here and do just enough work for you and my other clients so I can live well, but some good books, hang a Couse and some Icart paintings on my walls, and now old friend, just like you, I want to get to work on my novel and the Hollywood and European stories I've dreamed of writing. I feel just as miserable and cowardly as you do, believe me."

"Well then, why don't you follow the advice you gave me? Just quit and do it," Al said smugly.

"That would be about as fruitful as irrigating concrete. I don't have any income except what I earn each and every month. None. So don't try to put me in the same Rolls Royce you're in, old buddy. I'm coming on fifty, you know?"

"You're just a kid," said Al with a grin, and then they both laughed and touched their drinks together. Al added, "You know, Ed, the truth is, we built our own big trap and jumped in it with both feet."

"And eagerly . . . too damned eagerly, if you ask me," Ed agreed.

"Let's go into Raton tomorrow and celebrate the fact that we've got the problems of the universe solved."

"No, no. Raton has about ten or twelve thousand people. Why don't we drive over to Hi Lo where the population is about a manageable three hundred?"

"Of course," Al agreed, "that's what Uncle Carl would have done."

As the sun set they heard the yapping of what seemed like all the coyotes in the world—but there were only six. The coyotes stayed up, but Al and Ed went to bed early.

THE OLD MOTHER COYOTE sat on the hill and stared down at the calf in the hole. She was confused. So were her pups. If she meant to attack right now she'd have spaced her three pups out like a military formation, but they stood and squatted by her sides because no definite signal had come from her. Now, two grown dog coyotes had joined them and also sat staring down at the baby calf. It stood motionless except for the occasional nodding of its tired head.

The coyotes had never experienced a setup like this and their genes had no guidance to give. The sun said good-bye behind the western mountains and a half moon came up. They howled at the sky and at the top of the earth. Now, however, the wind was moving just right to blow the scent of a mountain lion down to them from where it had gorged on a freshly killed deer. It was dragging the victim's remains to some brush to hide it for recovery later when it, in turn, caught the scent of a four-hundred-pound black bear shuffling along, clawing at rotten logs for insects. Because of the wind's direction the bear didn't smell the lion, the lion didn't smell the coyotes, but the six coyotes were getting it all—as well as the blood-scent of the dead deer. It gave them enough to puzzle over so that they delayed, for a while, their attack on the calf in the hole.

The Hi Lo wind had once again altered life and death here this night.

THE NEXT AFTERNOON Mason and Goodspeed drove optimistically
down from the rim of Black Mesa towards Hi Lo. This entire vast area
had at one time exploded into a flaming, searing, molten hell. Scores
of malpai mountains had formed, most of them spaced apart and of
greatly varied shapes. These vistas and historical happenings always
stirred their receptive minds.

Off to the west, eighty or a hundred miles, the Sangre de Cristo
Mountains shoved thick, white, spear points into the tender turquoise
sky, and just on the other side of them was the old art colony of Taos
and the multi-storied Indian pueblo that was still very much inhabited.

Ed pointed southwest toward the distant Eagle Tail Mountain. "It's
sure plain to see why that was the main lookout point for the Coman-
ches, and all those other tribes, who were planning attacks on the
wagon trains and all the white settlers that were invading their land
along the Santa Fe Trail."

Then he switched his attention due south, toward the national mon-
ument, Capulin Mountain. He waved his arm in a circular motion at
the hollowed-out edge of the recently extinct volcano. "It's so perfectly formed it looks like it might explode any moment just for the
hell of it. It kind of takes you back in time, doesn't it?"

Al agreed. He enjoyed the atmosphere of the surrounding country
almost as much as he liked hearing Ed expound about it every time
they came. They always arrived in Hi Lo almost transported back into
the Old West.

About twenty miles easterly was one of the largest lone mountains
in the world, Sierra Grande. It would take a rancher in a pickup truck
from sunup to sundown to encircle its base. Highway 85 wove around
its edge approximately halfway between Clayton and Raton. There,
hovering like a neurotic child pulling its mother's skirts in the pres-
ence of a stranger, was the village of Hi Lo.

The Orange County friends could observe, from their present position, over a million acres of land. They wheeled down to the little
town of Folsom where that important archeological discovery of primitive man's remains had taken place.

Shortly, south of Folsom, they drove close to the railroad where it
made a very sharp curve next to a huge volcanic cinder mine.

Ed pointed with elation: "Now there's where a bit of Western history took place. See? Right there."

Al glanced at the railroad.

Ed continued, "That's the very spot that Black Jack Ketcham, the famous Western outlaw, jumped on to rob the train."

"Yeah, I've read all about it. That's where he got shot up and was later hanged over at the county seat of Clayton. Right?"

"You got it." Ed spoke with enthusiasm. "And when they dropped him through the trapdoor it jerked his head clean off."

Being in the core of such a mighty circle of bandits, train robbers, pioneers, and cowboys hastened their natural desire to reach the village of Hi Lo and associate with those who presently lived and survived right in its middle. They speeded up the car, humming down the eternally corrugated road.

THE WIND was laying the grass flat outside the Hi Lo Bar, but inside the jukebox was playing, the cowboys were drinking, and Dub, the bald-headed, ex-horse-shoeing bartender was a little edgy. Even though he was built to take care of any trouble, this grizzly man with his belt-stretching belly and forearms like fireplace logs knew in his lower brain that the ceaseless winds did more than bend trees and drive tumbleweeds against the fences; it bent people's minds as well, and on a high-wind Saturday night in a cowboy bar it could get dangerous.

"Shut the goddamned door," Cowboy Dusty Jones yelled when someone opened the front entrance. "The wind's blowin' the whiskey outa my glass."

Wrangler looked at his glass and said through his flat nose, "Shoot, with the door shut tight the wind's still makin' waves in my whiskey."

The two had been telling tales about their long-gone horse, Old Fooler. They never got tired of talking about him, or so it seemed to Dub. He'd heard so much about that danged horse that he wished Old Fooler was still alive so he could kill him, even though he had been the "greatest" roping horse, the "greatest" cutting horse, and the "greatest" rock working horse that ever lived.

In reality the old roan horse had done everything he could in his twenty years to disable these two cowboys. He'd run under tree limbs with them, banged them against tree trunks, bucked them off in the middle of nowhere miles from headquarters, bitten, kicked, and otherwise declared all-out war on the whole human race.

It puzzled Dub that they never talked about how Old Fooler died.

Wrangler had been riding him as he and Dusty worked a small bunch
of cows off a rimrock. Old Fooler thought he'd caught Wrangler nap-
ping and he started pitching. Wrangler grabbed the saddle horn with
his right hand and locked his right elbow over his hipbone and rode
him. It made Old Fooler so mad and mean he bucked off an eighteen-
foot bluff, breaking his neck and dying instantly. Wrangler ended the
fall with a cracked arm, a broken leg, and a fractured skull. It was
several months before he could mount a horse.

Still, Old Fooler remained their favorite topic. In desperation to
change the conversation before it drove him berserk, Dub bought his
two best customers each a double shot. It worked. They were so
shocked by this unheard of event they forgot all about Old Fooler.

After downing the precious gift in a couple of swallows, Dusty said,
"Give us another'n jist like it."

Wrangler raised two fingers and said, "Make that two to save time."

Dusty tried to get serious. "I was just wonderin' if we've been so
busy keepin' up with the changes in the way to handle horses and
pickup trucks that we got about three steps behind the violin. That,
and the VCR Jim Ed bought for the bunkhouse, is enough to make a
man lose the path to the barn forever. Don'tcha think."

Wrangler didn't really want to strain his jumbled grey matter, but
realizing that Dusty had something bothering him, tried to help.
"Seems to me like you done saddled the mule."

"Yeah . . . well, I was just uh wonderin', too . . . that maybe,
just maybe, them new owners . . ."

"Them Japanese don't own it yet," Wrangler insisted.

"Yeah, well, what I was thinkin' was that maybe they'd leave me on
here as foreman. Whatta you think? Reckon we both oughta try stayin'
on here? Wouldn't it be better than goin' to Texas where Jim Ed
would be looking down our collar all the dang time?" He wasn't
getting the response from Wrangler he was expecting. He straightened up his chair and rearranged his whiskey glasses and the ashtray
and continued: "Well now, Wrangler, when you get right down to it,
no matter how the deal turns out, it's either Jim Ed Love or the Japs.
Take your pick. It's like my ole Uncle Slim once said, We got our asses
between a landslide over here and a flash flood over there. Soooo,
what do you think?"

"Whatever suits you just tickles me plumb to death." Wrangler
answered in a low voice like ball bearings rolling over velvet. "I

didn't come here tonight to wear out my thinker. Let's get to dancin'
and havin' fun."

AL WHEELED THE CAR to a dusty stop in front of the white stuccoed
building. They had arrived at their happy destination—the Hi Lo Bar.
Several older cars and pickups were already there.

Ed and Al opened the front door and were blown inside just as
Dusty was on his way to the jukebox.

They all three stopped, shook hands, and said how glad they were
to see each other again.

"Is Wrangler here, too?" Al asked, looking around the dimly lit
room. About that time Wrangler let out a yell that made the paint
want to peel off the walls.

Dusty answered, "Yeah, I believe he is."

Wrangler waved at Delfino Mondragon, from Folsom, and ambled
over to the table to ask if he could dance with Mrs. Mondragon, their
two daughters, and Mrs. Mondragon's widowed sister.

Delfino said, "If you're loco enuff to try 'em all four, I'll pay you by
the hours."

They all finally got seated around the table and Ed asked Dusty,
"How's everything going over at the Love ranch?"

"Purty good fer now. Got some early rain, but we'll have to have
more moisture quick or we'll start turnin' to desert. How's big ole
California treatin' you fellers?"

Ed and Al gave each other a look, trying to figure out an answer.
Finally Ed said simply,

"All right."

Al ordered another round of drinks in lieu of a proper reply.

About that time, young Eddie John from Kim, Colorado, made his
entrance into the room. He took his time shutting the door. He was so
big that the wind barely made him weave even though he was already
drunk. He walked up to the bar and said in a noticeable voice,

"Give every other person in the joint a drink, cuz I'm gonna whup
all the rest."

All that prevented the front wall from being torn apart by about
twenty escaping people was the fact that Eddie John was laughing
when he said it.

Dusty leaned over the table and quietly relayed vital information to
Al and Ed. "Them Kim, Colorado bastards are sure-nuff bronc riders,

bull doggers, and fistfighters. And right there's the toughest of 'em all. I seen him take on a whole bar in Raton. A bunch of 'em got him down and kicked in about six ribs and other things and drug him over in a corner. They left him for dead and went on with the party. But Eddie was hurting too much to die, so after a while he got up and whipped all their butts."

"I'm glad he seems to be in a good humor right now," Al said.

At that instant Eddie John spotted Dusty. "Hey, Dusty, I ain't seen you in seven hundred years. You still shoveling cow shit for good old Jim Ed Love?"

Dusty swallowed and said, "Naw, Eddie John, I'm about caught up for the summer."

"Bulls beller and cows bawl," Eddie yelled for no apparent reason and then introduced himself to Ed and Al, asking them, "Where you two fellers from?"

"California," they answered.

"California, huh?" he repeated, and he went back toward the bar muttering "California" over and over.

Dusty Jones never claimed to be the world's brightest cowhand but he was smart enough to know that Eddie John coming back to their table with a full glass of whiskey in one hand and the grin gone from his face meant trouble. He said quietly to Ed and Al, "Get ready to turn on the tough."

Dusty knew there was nowhere to go. If he was going to get killed it might as well be indoors out of the wind.

Eddie John stood towering and glowering above the table. Ed grasped a heavy ashtray. Al had moved one hand around to clutch the back of an empty chair.

Just as Eddie John said, "California, huh," again, Dusty stuck his whiskey glass in Eddie's free hand, saying, "Here, hold this a minute, please."

Eddie stared first at one glass, then the other, and somewhere within that open space, Dusty rammed a fist. Eddie went back and down. Wrangler jumped over and kicked Eddie in the ribs and then stomped up and down on one hand until he figured there was no way he could close it into a fist. That still left him with one hand to hold a pain-numbing drink. This time Eddie accepted his loss. He even bought every other one that he was going to whip a drink.

Wrangler and Dusty rejoined Al and Ed at the table. They were trying to get their breath back and have a drink all at the same time.

Dusty said, "Course ole Dag Oakdale might've taken Eddie John by himself."

Wrangler said, "I wouldn't've known who to root for."

Dusty agreed. "Me neither. You ever met him, Al?"

Al answered, "I know his outfit joins Haley and me on the south, but I've tried *not* to meet him."

Wrangler said, "Mighty good judgment. The first time I ran into'm was nose first," and he rubbed at the flattened appendage in painful remembrance.

Everything returned to normal fun. Everybody there, including Delfino, danced with all available women. The party was on.

"Black Jack Ketcham and the Wild West live again," Al yelled at Ed as he whirled Teresa Mondragon off her feet.

Ed returned the shout. "We're home, pardner. Hotdamn, we're home."

THE NEXT MORNING the Orange County boys decided to walk off their hangover. They wore their cowboy duds proudly today. Hellsfire, they'd survived a real Western showdown last night and were about to go to another one coming up soon. Shirley Holt had called and invited them to Jim Ed's big *do*. They would have to get back in shape for that one.

Al wanted to show Ed an old cabin beyond George Haley's cow meadow. A shoot-out had occurred there in the late 1880s between Indians and late-blooming mountain men who were trapping the Indians' furs. There were a few artifacts lying around and the bullet holes were still visible in the cabin walls.

They got into their Old West attire and mood. Bears had been prominent in the area recently so they had a good excuse to strap on a couple of pistols. Al chose a collectors old Colt .45. Ed wore a new .357 Magnum.

Today the wind had let up, the clouds didn't come, and the sun had a free shine at this part of the earth. By the time they'd crawled under or between the wires of several cross-fences and stumbled over the main meadow, they were soaked in their own brine. The thick grass looked like the carpet in the Royal Suite at the Dorchester, but in reality it was a rough, ankle-twisting, tendon-stretching jaunt.

Ed stopped a minute and said, "Al, when are you going to get some horses on this ranch?" That, of course, was the missing element of their "cowboying."

"The cabin's not too far now," Al said, stopping to catch his breath.

Ed didn't move, but said, "Ah shit, I can see it good enough from here."

Al was not difficult to convince. They took what looked like an easier and more interesting way back. As they walked within perhaps a hundred yards of the great downed pine, they saw six coyotes lope off over the hill out of sight. Both men wondered what so many were doing together.

They walked toward the massive fallen tree and looked down into the hole at the swaying back of the calf. They were suddenly confused by the helpless feeling permeating their beings.

"My God, it's trapped," said Al.

"I can see that."

They both stared for quite some time until Al broke the silence.

"That poor little thing must have been down in the hole since the kids moved those cattle. It's been standing there for four days." His voice was filled with disbelief and admiration. He took action. He leaped down into the hole with the intention of lifting the calf out to Ed.

He picked up one end, but the other dropped back down. After a short struggle, he tucked both arms under the calf's middle and, with Ed's grunting help, they hefted him out of his four-day torture chamber. They felt an elation now. So did the calf, but he was starving. As nature intended, he tried to nurse. He rammed his muzzle between Al's legs first and shoved upwards. As Ed stood wondering why Al was bent over moaning, he found out. The calf would take any mother it could find. Ed was bent over, holding his crotch, gasping for air. Finally he choked out, "That little bastard is a karate expert."

When both men regained most of their composure, Al said, "We better take him to his real mother."

They moved across the rolling, cedar and pinion-spotted hills towards the county road to Haley's ranch. The calf followed behind like a puppy, except it kept rooting them in the back of the knees, occasionally almost knocking them down.

"Ed, do you realize that we can build up a herd with this bull? He's high quality, you know."

"A one-bull, no-horse ranch sounds about right for us to handle."

Then they got serious about the little creature. There could be no doubt about it; it was fate, their finding him at the last moment before his demise. By the gift of life it must become theirs. They wondered how much money their neighbor would want for him and pondered on the cost and care of several head of cows with their new companion as the number one herd bull.

They had walked at least two tortuous miles, with blisters forming in boots that were made for riding, when they spotted a road-grader growling towards them.

Al said, "That noise is going to scatter our herd."

Ed, by now completely unsound of body and mind, agreed, and offered up the supreme sacrifice for their ranch. "I'll go ahead alone and have a showdown with that herd-buster."

Al was relieved, but another thought flashed into his head. "Oh Lord, what am I going to do with this Colt .45 when I get there? It'll embarrass me to death for that driver to see me wearing this thing."

Ed was now so involved in his "western" part that nothing could deter him. "Here," he said grandly, "give it to me." He strapped it across his own gun belt and started walking valiantly down the road. This very tall, slim man with very long legs tied to very sore feet walked straight at the iron monster moving relentlessly towards him cutting wide swaths in the earth with its massive steel blade. Ed, just for a fleeting moment, thought that not John Wayne, nor any other gunman for that matter, had ever topped this. The "walk-down" music thundered in his head and the palms of his fast-draw hands itched for action. Man and machine edged closer and closer together for the final confrontation. Ed stopped spread-legged in front of it.

The driver braked the machine and leaned out, asking politely, "What can I do for you?" Who wouldn't be polite to someone armed with two pistols and all dressed up like he was playing cowboys and Indians for the first time.

"You can stop that goddamned noise for a few minutes," Ed the gunslinger said.

There was no doubt in the driver's mind that this person was deranged, and he instantly agreed to move the machine from the road until the "herd" had passed.

Ed motioned for Al to proceed. "Move 'em out," he waved and screamed.

When they neared, Ed took up the "point" position while Al held up the "drag." The three-part trail drive didn't last long because the calf just couldn't go any farther. All attempts at verbal persuasion—

"Here, baby. Come pretty calf"—failed, as did whistling, finger snap-ping and hand clapping. The calf's wobbly legs finally gave out and it sank to the ground.

They cautiously, tenderly, lifted him up several times, but nothing worked, so Al sat down on the road and held the calf's head in his lap, stroking its neck and telling it encouraging stories while Ed bravely walked the two miles to the ranch for help.

George drove Ed and his blisters back to Al and the calf, marveling that it was still alive and agreeing with Ed that it was saved by the trapped rainwater.

When they reached the ranch, Doris fixed a big bottle of warm milk for the calf. He drank and drank, even though he was so weak they had to hold his head up. Soon he was miraculously looking around for a mother again.

Al rode in the back of the pickup and held him while they drove to the new meadow to reunite mother and child. Jim had warned them that the "boss" cow might not accept her offspring because her bag would be swelled tight and sore now and be about ready to start caking before finally drying up.

All the cows ran away except the "boss." She stood and waited. Even with the excruciating pain, she let her excited, tail-switching calf nurse as she licked at his red-haired coat.

It was just part of a lucky day's work to George and Doris. To Al and Ed it was a miracle. It was part of both.

When talk finally moved on to other subjects, they discussed Jim Ed's fandango. The Haleys told Al and Ed about some of the other parties that had taken place at the Love ranch. It was definitely not to be missed.

The Hi Lo country was rapidly weaving together its basket made of minerals, cows, cowboys, cowgirls, and varied and sundry other wet and dry things.

AT ONE POINT OR ANOTHER, Wrangler Lewis had bucked off horses onto rock piles, cacti, concrete highways, barbwire fences, pole cor-rals, and other similar things. He'd broken legs, arms, ribs, one nose, one neck, two hands, and mashed his balls ninety-nine times, but he'd never had even a minor twitch in his ankles. These appurtenances had been magically immune from harm until this very morning.

Walking blind sober from the bunkhouse to the corral, on smooth, rockless ground, he'd stumbled, farted, and fell in screaming agony at a brand-new pain. He had sprained his ankle at last . . . and just one day before Jim Ed's big celebration. It was cause for a quandary.

Dusty saw the whole thing. "You want me to tail you up?"

Wrangler answered without getting up. "Why don't you quit your blabberin' and saddle me a horse. I want to get up off this dangerous ground."

Dusty saddled two horses and after much moaning and cussing Wrangler pulled his stocky body into the saddle and they rode off for the day's duties. Checking out the windmills nearest headquarters was at the top of the list. There had been only one windmill when they'd first started working here. Everything, even the earth, had changed on them.

It was unheard of in recent Hi Lo history—the wind had been still for two consecutive days. The temperature, however, was normal—very hot. So far all the windmills were pumping because Dusty had to climb them every one and whirl the wheels by hand to test them. As much as they hated the usual three-hundred-and-ten-days-a-year blow, they could have made use of a little breeze today, but the fact was, they spent so much of their time justifiably bitching about the mind-zapping winds that it would have seemed ill-mannered to do so this morning. Wrangler didn't mind the stillness nearly as much as Dusty because he was badly wounded and hadn't dismounted all day for fear his friend the foreman might suggest he climb up on one of the wind-mill towers.

They always kept a coffee can tied to each windmill to drink from. Because of his climbing exertions, Dusty dipped a can full of water for Wrangler and then one for himself at every stop. After several wind-mills Wrangler felt a desperate need to get down and relieve his kid-neys of the generous and bountiful liquid that his old pardner had been supplying him. However, if he dismounted before they arrived back at the home corral it would look as if he'd been slacking off all day. At the last windmill he could control it no longer. He felt like the liquid would soon start draining out his ears.

He waited until Dusty was up on top of the crow's nest of the mill. Then he suddenly had only three choices left—go in his Levi's, get down and risk endless ridicule, or stand up in the stirrups and relieve himself while still in the saddle. Like any sensible cowboy, he chose the last, twisting and aiming the best he could, while trying to achieve the greatest possible distance. He sure didn't want to get anything on the horse, the saddle, or himself. He certainly didn't want Dusty to observe the carefully calculated procedure.

The first part of the plan worked. The wet jet did arc out to the side of the horse's head by about six inches and for just a fleeting second he'd kept the saddle and himself dry. It will probably never be known why the horse dodged sideways at such a harmless little stream, nor why he ducked his head way down to look at the spot where it splashed, but he did, and he didn't raise his head for about twenty belly-whomping, ground-pounding jumps.

One can't fault Wrangler for turning loose of the vital instrument that had sent the horse up and down and round and round, and grabbing the saddle horn instead. Of course, there had been no time to put it back into his pants, so it just kept spewing on the horse, on the saddle, and on himself. Some of it even sprayed out into unoccupied space.

Dusty was observing this from the top of the windmill, but his vision wasn't as clear as his fine eagle eyes would dictate for they were full of laughing tears. As he leaned over to hold his hurting belly, he tripped on a loose board and fell off the windmill into the water tank some thirty feet below. It didn't kill him, but did knock the laugh out of his lungs and replace it with pure mountain water.

The horse quit bucking and Wrangler got the rest of his middle self back into his Levi's. He just sat there on the winded horse praying for a fast, burning wind to come dry him out before his good and jovial friend Dusty rode up. He looked out across a peaceful green valley carpeted with deep, rich, buffalo and gramma grass where sixty-five head of Hereford cattle grazed and lay about contentedly chewing their cuds. A calf bawled, a squirrel chirped, and a bird warbled, but Wrangler Lewis didn't see or hear any of them. His ears were sensitive only to the sound of an approaching horse to his rear. He felt that the recent dampness he'd absorbed had shriveled and shrunk him down to the size of a baby skunk. He seemed so naked between his shoulder blades that he wondered if there was a bull's eye painted there.

Dusty, still dripping, rode up behind him and looked across the draw at the peacefully grazing cattle for three or four years and then said in an extremely soft and pleasant voice, "Not a cloud in the sky. Looks like we're in for a looooong dry spell."

They reined off into a valley on the trail heading back to headquarters and the upcoming grand get-together. It had been just another average romantic day in the life of a working cowboy.

DELFINO MONDRAGON got his tall, powerful body up early, checked the sheep, goats, and cattle in his hay meadow, fed the pigs and chickens, took a bath with rainwater from a cistern, shaved, combed the hair on his corrugated skull, put on the only pair of blue dress slacks he owned, a white Western shirt, and a silver and turquoise bolo tie. By Jesus and his disciples, Delfino was ready to go have some "parties."

He sat out on the porch of his rock house taking a sip of homemade chokecherry wine out of a fruit jar. He was getting conditioned for Jim Ed's big day while he waited for the women. He could hear them chattering excitedly in Spanish and was struck for the thousandth time with wonder at how they could all talk at once and still understand one another.

Delfino had heard rumors that the Japanese, and even the West Germans and British, were trying to buy up some ranches around Hi Lo.

He petted the black and white, bushy-tailed old dog stretched out by his chair and said to it, "Well, thees place is probably too leetle to even interest them, but eet doesn't matters, ole dog, because, eet ain't for sale. Never. You don't have to worry your leetle head about thees, Pedro."

His ranch was fully paid for. He had subirrigated meadows as well as a variety of livestock and he didn't mind milking a few cows, feeding chickens, and slopping hogs like so many modern day ranchers. His wife could raise a lush vegetable garden every year, and they had some fruit trees. All these thoughts ran through his head.

"What a paradise we have here, huh, amigo?"

Pedro raised his dark eyes to let his master know that he was completely aware of the importance of his words. His soft tail brushed the porch in affirmation.

Delfino was a very secure man. He was a skilled rock mason and could pick up extra money building tanks, fences, barns, and sometimes even a small house.

To hell with these business thoughts. He wanted to get on over and grab a taste of Jim Ed's generous hospitality, sing a few songs, do a dance or two, and raise a little hell if he got the smallest excuse.

DELFINO WASN'T ALONE in his thoughts that day. Al Goodspeed had
gotten up at dawn and gone fishing at his lake. The trout were biting
salmon eggs this morning, and by an hour after sun he had six browns
from ten to fifteen inches long. He was surprised when he got back to
the lodge and found Ed was up drinking coffee and reading the World
War Two book by Manchester.

While Al cleaned and cooked the trout, fried some potatoes, and
baked a can of refrigerator biscuits, Ed finally finished the book he'd
been reading. He closed it with a look of satisfaction.

"Well, I got that done."

Al said, "You make it sound like a difficult job."

"No, no. It was a great pleasure to read and I'm sorry there's not
more. It's just that I wanted my head free to enjoy Jim Ed's party."

Al served the hot food and poured each another cup of coffee.

"I tell you what, Ed, fill your belly now, and then again after we get
there. That's the way to prepare for Jim Ed Love." Al took a sip of the
brew, halted his cup in midair, and said, "You know, it rips my guts
out to think of the Haleys having to sell their ranch, and it also tears
me apart to think they might keep it and risk losing it all. They're the
kind of people we're damned short of in this world."

Ed was surprised at the depth and sincerity of his friend's feelings.
He was mute for a moment and then replied with what he instantly
felt was an inadequate statement, "Yeah, it's a tough decision for them
to make. It seems everyone and everything gets in a trap. You just
have to figure a way out."

Al nodded his head in agreement. "Right, look at us."

PEOPLE from all over the Hi Lo country were talking and preparing
to attend the grand happening. Others had already landed out-of-state
jets and prop planes at Jim Ed's private airstrip. They were all moving
towards the center of the circle, from the air, in limousines, cars,
pickup trucks, and a couple of neighboring cowboys came horseback
even though they'd had to sleep in their bedrolls the night before.
The entire area would forever be changed in this day and upcoming
night.

By noon, droves of people had arrived. They were simply as-
tounded at what they saw and heard. There had never been anything

to touch it around here before and it's doubtful if there ever would be again.

Jim Ed and associates had the grounds set as large and colorful as a state fair carnival. Brightly colored tents with the sides rolled up were scattered over a three hundred yard circumference. There were whole beeves and pigs turning on spits over barbecue pits. Great iron pots held steaming pinto beans, red and green chile, and posole. Long tables would soon be filled with chickens cooked in a variety of ways. There were even imported seafood delicacies, fruits, vegetables, and melons.

The music was as varied as the food. The entertainment groups were set far apart so the audience could choose their favorite. A maria-chi band, dressed in colorful native clothing, strummed and sang all the old Mexican favorites. A country western group from Austin sup-plied the cowboy atmosphere, while a pop band from Albuquerque kept the younger generation entertained. A special section was re-served for Indian dance groups from Laguna, Zuni, and Taos pueblos.

Near each musical group, bars with several attendants were set up to serve drinks. The beverages ranged from plain whiskey to the fanci-est liquors found at the Algonquin or Polo Lounge.

People were feasting, drinking, dancing, and visiting. Every age group was represented, from babies in strollers to great-grandparents who could barely toddle around. The wide spectrum of nationalities provided an international flavor to the gathering. The totality of the colorations of their clothing, the tents, and decorations added up to a kaleidoscope of rainbows.

As the cacophony of sound grew, the musicians unknowingly played louder to compensate. At first the children were in awe and fairly quiet, but soon with their bellies full of food and soda pop they sensed that their parents were occupied with many different wonders, and they proceeded to invent their own amusements and to run wild as outhouse rats, as the Kansas wheat farmers used to say.

By two o'clock in the afternoon everything was at full volume. The number of dancers gradually increased with each song and drink as the stomachs negotiated the alcohol into the bloodstreams and hearts pumped it on to the brain, and the steps grew faster. Jim Ed Love had certainly pulled off a grand shindig, but he would have a lot of anxious hours before he would know the final result of his calculated munifi-cence. Right now, though, his luck was running—the weather was just right. It had been practically windless for the two previous days and now it was about seventy-eight degrees with just enough breeze to keep the sweat down, the men's hats on, and the women's hairdos in place. Yes, if there was one thing important to the mood swings of the Hi Lo inhabitants, it definitely was the weather. The gods had smiled, however briefly, for Jim Ed Love.

There was so much more going on, besides the party, that was unseen to most and hidden by the knowing few.

Mr. Yakahami and entourage had come out of Jim Ed's large guest house with all the men in dark dress suits and their women wearing high-fashion apparel. However, after mingling awhile and sampling the rich, varied foods and beverages, they had quietly retired to change into more casual, comfortable clothing.

Mikio was the exception—she came dressed in Levi's, boots, and a custom-tailored silk shirt right from the beginning. She was different from the rest of her countrywomen. She had been married to Jackson Reynolds, a wealthy land developer from the San Francisco Bay area, while she was there lecturing at a university about the changing cultural phenomena between Japan and the United States. On the night of their twentieth wedding anniversary celebration, Mr. Reynolds fell dead. Mikio inherited the entire thirty-eight million dollars' worth of bonds, stocks, cash, and real estate. Since they had no children, she also inherited an awful lot of free time.

Mr. Yakahami, knowing that his sister was thoroughly Americanized, and experienced in business-world transactions, gave her the challenging job of handling all his U.S. investments. She had happily and admirably delivered. It was Mikio who first brought the geologist, agriculturist, and several other kinds of experts to inspect the Love and Haley ranches. Her report had been thorough and confident. Her decision—buy at the proper price. Since the yen was so low against the American dollar, and cattle, oil, and hard minerals were depressed, she suggested that they utilize carefully directed haste to gain the full benefit of proper timing.

The preliminaries had come off without a flaw. Jim Ed's son, Jason, had fronted for his father, as Mikio had done for her brother. Dusty Jones had been sensibly appointed official guide and driver of the large van. It was all perfectly logical and well organized.

Mikio walked over to talk with Dusty. He was happy to see her again and flattered that she treated him with such warm respect as she introduced him to all her people. She thanked him again for the kindness and efficiency he'd extended on her last exploration trip. Dusty felt a pleasant glow as she and her friends moved on towards the mariachi bandstand.

Jim Ed was everywhere, shaking hands, slapping backs and rears, succeeding at making the guests feel wanted and pampered. He had several people seeing that Mr. Yakahami and his associates were looked after properly. They had reserved seats at each event.

While all the merriment was taking place on the grounds, it was quite a different happening in Jim Ed's redwood-paneled office. Jason and Mr. Yakahami's lieutenant, Akiri, and their secretaries were missing the party altogether, except they had enough food on the table between them to feed a highway building crew. There was no alcohol. Only soft drinks and herbal and Indian teas filled that void. They were politely trying to cut each other's throat while smiling and without the blood showing. The final results could possibly create far greater ripples than a contest to the death of two great Samurai warriors.

The first major plans for the final battle were taking place in these rooms, but those who would sharpen and hand over the swords were outside mingling with the uninvolved, and acting as if they were on their first picnic.

When the Taos Indians did the war, wind, buffalo, and eagle dances, the Orientals were ecstatic with applause. Their appreciation was genuine. Then Alfred Two Lions, age seven, did the hoop dance to the rhythm of a drum beat, passing more than twenty hoops up his legs and back down, then up and over his arms, back, and shoulders in whirling, twisting, smooth, complex moves, without a moment's pause. The audience stood fascinated and with a measure of awe as they unknowingly felt ancient vibrations through this Indian child.

When the performance ended, Ed, Al, Doris, and George strolled back toward the bar for refills. The Haleys were talking casually about the party as if their entire world wasn't on the sales block. The two friends respected this and left the subject alone.

Dusty, walking unusually stiff in all joints, and Wrangler, limping noticeably, moved into the circle of friends.

Haley asked, "What happened to you boys? Did you both get run over by a hay bailer?"

Dusty answered, "I think ole Wrangler got on a horse he couldn't get off of, but me," he hastened to explain (he wasn't about to confess falling off a windmill to anybody), "I'm just walkin' like this so it'll make him look better."

Wrangler snorted with what authority he could through his flat no and said, "If I looked any better they'd cast me in bronze and stand me up in a beauty parlor for all the ladies to admire."

Delfino Mondragon walked up overhearing this last and said, "My eeears they are so full of bullsheet it weel take a gallon of wheesky to wash 'em clean again. Give us all a two shotter for starters."

The bartender complied. Al asked for another round. Dusty politely duplicated the procedure. Business was improving rapidly at Jim Ed's *free-* drinks bar.

Jim Ed, the big man himself, arrived on the scene. "Now, it's good to see you fellers enjoying yourselves. That's what we're all here for. A man's got to pour a little gold dust on the rust of life once in a while out of appreciation for this bountiful earth and the wondrous opportunities it offers us all. Right, friends?" Jim Ed took only two bourbons in the evening, but he raised his hand cupped around a ghost glass in a toast to his own words. Everyone else did the same with the real thing without even noticing the illusion.

Jim Ed took Haley firmly by the arm and steered him away from the crowd at the bar. "It's lookin' good, George. Mr. Yakahami and his sister know that the price of oil and cattle has started easing upwards. It gives us an edge. They're gonna want to get this deal over with before the prices go too high and while the dollar is cheap against the yen. I tell you, George, if we'll hang tough another hour or two we'll get four more dollars per acre and get to keep three quarters of the mineral rights. I tell you what, George, we're not just sittin' in plain clover, we're harvestin' *four-leaf* clover and making pure honey out of it."

Haley dug a toe of one boot in the dust, pushed his hat back and scratched his head with the same hand, saying, "Jim Ed, I know you're tryin' to make a good deal for us, but I've told you twice I just can't bring myself to sell at any price. Even at four dollars an acre more, all we'd have left is enough to barely squeeze by on. That ain't no good and you know it. We ain't made that way."

"I know how you feel, George, but it's a whole lot better than starting over with nothing. Nothing, you hear? That ain't gonna sound, or feel, too good to your family, George. Think about that now. What're you gonna tell them when it *all* goes under?"

Haley left Jim Ed and returned to the bar. None of his friends had heard a single word that had passed between the two but they somehow sensed the essence of the conversation. Jim Ed didn't have a deal
without the Haleys, and they all knew that Jim Ed would drop his only

son out of an airplane into an erupting volcano if it would help make a deal.

Ole Wrangler yelled out, "Give us another glass of that hero juice and save the last ten dances for me."

With some noise and a great deal of joy the group of friends totally agreed with Wrangler's whopping wisdom.

Ed and Al had talked earlier about the difficulty of George Haley making a decision that would alter his family's destiny on land that had passed through several generations. Ed had reminded Al of the agony that must be going through the souls of Dusty and Wrangler. He was so right. This day was filled with multiple, hidden emotions for many people. Dusty and Wrangler were at the top of the list.

The two old partners had been with the Jim Ed Love ranches since they were kids in far southwest Texas. They started work on the Big Lake Ranch. Then they were moved to the Andrews, Texas outfit right after the first big oil well was hit on that sand and mesquite bush land. As soon as Jim Ed bought the Hi Lo ranch, they were transferred again. At that time they were still in their teens, but they made good ranch hands. They'd been here on the JL since then. Ever so often, they'd get their "neck hair up" at Jim Ed and take off. But they would either wind up broke or in jail. Jim Ed would *always* bail them out and they would *always* have to come back to him.

It had been home to them for most of their lives, and they'd made Jim Ed a considerable profit over the years. There was no question about what they had given to the JL Ranch. They had left a lot of freezing breath in the high-wind blizzards of the Hi Lo winters, along with dust-burned eyes and scratched lungs from the blowing sands of many dry eroding summers. Pieces of their flesh had been left on rocks, trees, barb wire, and the hard land itself for decades now. Most of their bones had been broken and a lot of their joints almost welded solid from the strings of bucking horses and the jolts of working cattle in both thick brush and sharp boulders. They had dug post holes in miles of hard rock and fixed windmills and put up hay. They'd fed cattle in snowdrifts taller than a Jeep in below zero weather and chopped ice from water tank after water tank so the cattle could drink instead of dying. All this and more—not to even count the various times they had left their blood on barroom floors trying to get out of the goddamned wind and forget the constant pain, of which they seldom spoke, that wracked their battered bodies.

They had no retirement funds or insurance plans and they were getting old for working cowboys. Today. Today, they could be cast out into the street like any wino, the plain shiftless, the government spongers, or the truly unfortunate. Their lives had been spent in the wide open outdoors. The streets to them would look like Dante's next dream. They'd put in a long, rough time, and now they had absolutely nowhere to go and nothing to say about it.

Dusty gathered up his cowboys for a meeting. He knew they had heard all the rumors concerning their futures, but hadn't been told anything to give them any reassurance. So, being their foreman, he felt it was time they were told the true situation.

They were a select group that could handle the old, or modern, ways of cowboying. Besides Wrangler, there was Sonny Jim, a Modoc Indian, a Mexican named Pat Flores, and Big Timber Smith, a one-eyed black who was the greatest outlawed horse breaker in the entire country. They all stayed at the lower camp. Dusty had spent a lot of time there when he was young and knew that few men could handle the loneliness and isolation, much less the real ranch work. Elliot Calhoun was the headquarters fix-it-up man. At one time he had been a top rodeo cowboy. Dusty had always thought that Sonny Jim could easily have taken those honors, even bigger, better than Calhoun, if he'd wanted it badly enough.

Dusty explained as best he could about the Japanese negotiations, adding, "If the deal goes through, fellers, we may all be pecking shit with the buzzards. If the deal falls flat I reckon we'll go on just like we are for Jim Ed."

"Is there a hell of a lot of difference?" Sonny Jim quipped.

Big Timber Smith said, "Well, I shore don't want to go back to pickin' cotton."

They all laughed and then Sonny Jim got serious again. "How does it really look to you, Dusty?"

Dusty said, "I can see a cow on the other side of a mountain, but I'm plumb blind on this. One good thing about it though, we ain't gonna have to hang around frettin' about it after tonight." Then he added, "Now don't you boys say one goddamned word about this till I tell you. Hear?"

Pat Flores said, "We ain't opening our mouths for nothing but brown whiskey and red chile."

Dusty felt better and walked the whole bunch over to the country western bar and ordered them a free drink. He didn't feel like they were free—he'd already paid for them a thousand times or more.

Dusty spotted Mikio and her companions in the crowd. All day long he'd been watching her from afar. However, he tried to hide his interest from everyone else. He'd been a little in awe of her from their very first meeting. There was something else there that he couldn't explain, especially to himself. The way she walked with little short steps, or the delicate way she moved her hands and tilted her head slightly to the side, affected him. She made his hands and feet go cold and the rest of his body feel like it was melting and running down into his Tony Lama boots.

He turned his attention back to his cowboy helpers, lifted his glass gesturing a toast, and said, "You fellers have fun. I'll see you later." He looked in the direction of Mikio's group but now she wasn't among them. He strained his eyes through the hundreds of moving people but he couldn't see her. Then, like a good cowboy spotting cattle in brush, he saw her coming from the bunkhouse. She was pulling a straw hat down on her head.

Dusty watched her. Even in cowboy boots she walked as gracefully as a professional dancer. She wove her way through the erratically moving crowd. Dusty realized with a start that she was coming straight toward him. If he'd been horseback he would have reined around and spurred for the highest mountain and the thickest timber. Instead he grew roots.

She came right up smiling with her entire face and said in unaccented English, "Mr. Jones, could we have a private visit?"

"Dusty, that's me. Call me Dusty," was all he could get out.

Mikio took him by an arm with such a gentle touch that he could barely feel it, yet he was guided as firmly as if he'd been tied by the neck to a bulldozer.

"Is there somewhere we could have privacy? There exist some matters I'd like to discuss with you."

Dusty's brain waves flashed around like a ricochetting bullet. She had said "private." He couldn't take her to the bunkhouse. It might be misconstrued, and if Jim Ed and Mr. Yakahami failed to deal they would blame it on Dusty, claiming as sure as hell that right in the middle of the trade Dusty was trying to slap the make on Mr. Yakahami's beautiful sister. And that is how it would look. On the other hand, he wanted desperately to be with her even if all she needed to know was how long it took a cow to raise a calf.

There was only one choice. It was a big risk. He took her by the arm and guided her to his pickup. He started to open the truck door for her.

Mikio thanked him, but refused. "I may have to get used to opening my own truck doors. So I will start now."

As they drove past the horse pasture, Dusty slowed the vehicle to a crawl, pointing out special mounts and explaining each one's specialty. An old Indian camp was the next stop. They picked up a few potsherds and she found an almost perfect arrowhead. She was childishly thrilled with this. On the rock bluffs he showed her the petroglyph carvings of deer, mountain sheep, cougars, medicine men and women, the sun symbols, and more. Mikio suddenly became very solemn as she studied the pictures and said there must be a link somewhere between the American Indians and the Orientals because the drawings on the rock face somehow reminded her of old Japanese textiles.

Dusty didn't exactly understand the last, but was happy she was observing and absorbing part of his private world.

As they drove along now, he became more comfortable. He showed her spots where he had bucked off horses and had many assorted adventures.

They were talking and laughing where the only other noise was the muffled hum of the motor in the quiet stillness.

Dusty and Mikio weren't the only ones to stray away from the fiesta. Terri Haley and Luke Fremont were secluded in a patch of brush on some thick vega grass about a half mile below Jim Ed's headquarters. They had grown up on neighboring ranches and had always cared for each other. Luke was eighteen and would soon be enrolling as a freshman at Highlands University in Las Vegas, New Mexico. They were desperately in love, and today he was going momentarily blind as he touched her. But his mind would soon be cleared by her reluctant, but successful, repetition of "No. No. No."

The revelers at the party weren't saying "No" to very much of anything. Their enthusiasm seemed to be growing.

Al and Ed walked slowly through the mob in the direction of the Indian drums. On their way there they caught pieces of conversation as varied as the nation they lived in.

"Oh, darling, there is just no place in Mexico except Ixtapa, don't you know," said a blonde with a distinct Southern drawl. Ed gave Al a "What do you think?" look.

Two housewives were exchanging ideas. "Well, I don't care what you say; the vegetables are always fresher at Safeway."

"It won't matter before long. Wal-Mart will probably put in a grocery department and put them all out of business, anyway."

Several seasoned-looking cowmen were talking about horses. One said, "That ole sorrel horse of my boy's can turn on a penny an' give you back twenty-nine cents change."

"Boy, I'd like to have a look at *him.*"

Al and Ed smiled as they passed someone saying, "Listen, I'm trying to tell you gentlemen a truth. There just isn't any choice. The United States, Mexico, Canada, Great Britain, France, and Japan must form a solid alliance now. I mean now, while there is still time. We're all so interlocked by history, art, intermarriage, inter-trade, borders, banks, oil, and the absolute and final need for one another that the blindness not to do so will lead to all of our eventual destruction."

Al said to Ed, "We might ought to join that group."

One jovial fellow slapped his leg and said, "I had to buy me a country club. That's the only way I could join one."

As Ed squeezed past a couple of wildly dressed women one of them was saying, "I desperately need a cyanide . . . and . . . a root beer."

Then out of nowhere came, "Well then, if you're so damned smart, who gave birth to God?"

"Hey, bartender, give that man a shot for rabies."

They were almost to the circle of Indian dancers, then were stopped by thick crowd congestion.

"It'll never work. You see it's too round on this side and too square on the other. Besides it'll swell up and burst in cold weather and tip over in a high wind, and you couldn't even see the damn thing in a thick fog. That's not all. It has so many holes in it the darkness will leak out."

Ed turned to Al, "Well, like the man said, it'll never work."

A female voice drifted out to them: "Well, Jim Ed sure knows how to throw a party, even if he is making a fool out of himself over that Shirley Holt. Why she couldn't be a day over twenty-five."

And in the same group, someone said, "I don't care what everybody says about Jim Ed trying to take his money with him when he goes. I've never seen a Brinks truck at a funeral."

The drum stopped just as Al and Ed arrived at the dance circle, and the dancers started mingling with the guests. The Indians were being very polite and answering, with myths, the stupid questions, and laughing quietly to themselves. They didn't need, or want, sympathy from anyone. They were professionals and had received adulation all over America and Canada. And they really didn't like all the interference from the outside "do-gooders."

The business procedures were gaining in momentum as two jets landed on the airstrip. One carried two lawyers from Midland, Texas and one from Dallas, to represent Jim Ed. The other contained two lawyers from San Francisco and one from Tokyo to take care of Mr. Yakahami's legal needs. Numerically the Samurai were evenly matched. The dice were still spinning.

Wrangler had been discovered by Charlene, an Odessa, Texas oil widow who had gone to school with one of Jim Ed's kin. As they danced less and drank more, she somehow got the facts mixed up. She decided that Old Wrangler was Jim Ed's cousin instead of working for him. So anybody kin to Jim Ed was her flesh, blood, and full partner.

Wrangler had favored his twisted ankle so long that he had now numbed the other one. So, he walked Charlene over to the bunkhouse without a limp and got her bedded down in the lower bunk. The trouble was his ankles had swelled so much that he couldn't pull off either boot. Therefore he couldn't pull his tight-legged Levi's off either. He got them down about halfway over his hips where they rolled into a jam. He went back to his boots, pulling and straining till it looked like his eyeballs were going to fly out and smash the wall.

"Goddamned, son of a bitch, bloody-nosed bastard, stupid pukeheaded, frog-eyed, badger-nose, skunk-assed, shit-eatin' dog." Even though he used the correct vocabulary for removing tight boots, they wouldn't come off.

Charlene was getting a cramp in her thighs from trying to hold the waiting position on the narrow bunk.

She made a practical suggestion. "Darling, why don't we just do it with your pants on. It's fine with me."

This was one wonderful shortcut in what was left of poor Wrangler's mind. He said, "Whatever suits you just tickles me plumb to death." Whereby he attempted to stand up, turn around, and jump on Charlene all at the same time. What he did was step, stumble, and fall, ramming the top of his head into the leg of a heavy oak table, knocking him as cold as an Arctic night. Charlene waited a spell for him to regain his composure and finally realized that her anticipation was being wasted. She pulled her dress down, got up, and staggered past Wrangler on the floor, saying to herself, "I keep hearing what great lovers these cowboys are and that one there can't even get his pants off."

As Charlene bounced out of the bunkhouse, Delfino came around the corner where they collided into a hugging match. He gathered her up and took her to the tack room at the barn. Delfino's ankles were in perfect condition.

Al was now sitting at a table with all four of Delfino's women. He had been dancing with one right after the other. The Latin music, along with a bottle of Scotch, had made him nostalgic about the old days in Baja, California. He was telling his dance partners some Baja stories and they were laughing and having fun.

Ed had been captured by a supposed lady clothing designer from Santa Fe and they were regaling one another with sharp and cynical quips between dances at the pop-group location.

The party showed no signs of slowing down nor was anyone considering abandoning it for the peacefulness being enjoyed by Dusty and Mikio.

Dusty drove the truck as far as he could into the rocks and timber. He told Mikio they'd have to walk a short distance to get to something he wanted to show her. She reached out and took his hand as he wove his way carefully through the trees and brush, protecting her from spring-back of branches as he pushed them out of the way. Then they were there.

They looked down on a horseshoe-shaped cliff formation of reddish-brown sandstone surrounding an emerald pond about sixty feet across. Its overflow formed a stream that ran down a steep slope of rock and created another pool perhaps a hundred feet below.

Dusty carefully led her down through the rocks to the edge of the water. In the soft mud along the bank he pointed out the arrowhead-shaped tracks of a coyote, the bearlike prints of a raccoon and the round impressions of a bobcat. He showed her the pronged prints of several wild turkeys.

Mikio was touched by their sharing of a lifetime of knowledge and the special private pool. They moved back up from the sun-jeweled water to a rock outcropping with a grassy spot underneath. They sat next to one another and looked out across the quiet, far-spreading spaces over the top of the Rockies where great castles of clouds climbed so high they became lost white wonderlands that faded into the mists of eternity.

After a while Dusty said, "What was it you wanted to ask me?"

"You've already answered," she said softly. "There is one thing though . . . if you'll forgive me . . . why didn't you present these special things to me when we were here before?"

"I only showed you the parts that make money. Besides"—he paused before he confessed—"I didn't really want you to buy it then. It's the only real home old Wrangler and me have ever had. I didn't want to leave it. Not ever."

He wanted to tell her they had no other place left to go at their ages. No place worth living on, anyway. He didn't have to.

She took his hand and said so quietly he had to strain to hear, "If we acquire this ranch, I'll need you . . . need you very much. You know so many more things than I."

This time he was speechless. He looked at her and she turned her head half to him, but her black eyes were on his. He reached over with one battered-up hand and touched the back of her head, and then they both fully and completely touched the earth together.

ED, AL, AND DELFINO had wound up together at the country western bar, and, of course, the band was playing "On The Road Again." They all three felt "plumb keen," as Delfino would say. The sun was only an hour high and the party had mellowed to fewer and fewer cowboy yells.

Ed observed, "Free booze gets the festivities going fast, all right, but it also thins out the tame ones rather quickly."

Al added, "The musicians are getting a little woozy from all the booze these kind and thoughtful music lovers have been bringing them."

Jim Ed and Mr. Yakahami had now moved inside along with the lawyers. The closing, or the "cut and run" period, was coming to a collision point soon. All of America was condensed here at Jim Ed's this day. The rich, the poor, the strugglers and stragglers, the big winners and the little losers. All colors and combinations, all attitudes and affections. All. It was judgment day as well and the major decisions were about to be handed down.

WRANGLER HAD BEEN SO BUSY pursuing his own sources of R and R that he hadn't noticed Dusty's absence, so he wasn't surprised when

Dusty returned to join everyone. He was surprised to find that Dag Oakdale was sitting with the group.

Dag was big and dumb and mean. A dangerous combination in any society. He owned a ranch to the south of both Al and Haley. He was a natural-born greedy son of a bitch and he was jealous and furious because no one had contacted him about buying his ranch. It had been on the market for three years without a taker. Dag didn't express any of this verbally, but he said something else in a loud and penetrating voice:

"The thieving Texans came in and bought up all of Eastern New Mexico, and now the car-makin', computer-punchin' Japs are movin' in and buying out all the egg-suckin' Texans. Wonder who'll come and kick-ass the goddamned Japs."

Dusty and Wrangler started to attack the offender because there was a group of Japanese and at least thirty Texans within insulting distance. They all were hoping that the hands on the grandfather clock in Jim Ed's office were approaching the moment of final and momentous decision.

Al said, "Gentlemen, shall we do our Boy Scout deed for the year?"

Delfino had waited patiently all day for an opportunity such as this. At the same instant that Ed and Al each grabbed an arm belonging to Dag Oakdale, Delfino got him by the crotch, and they led him away to avoid any more embarrassment than had already occurred.

Ed yelled back at a stunned but grinning Dusty and Wrangler, "We owe you one from the Hi Lo Bar."

Dag would have been screaming like a parrot with his tail feathers on fire from Delfino's powerful, rock-mason grip, but Al Goodspeed had his free hand clamped over Dag's mouth. All Dag could do was snort like a fresh-saddled bronc.

They marched him behind the main barn and Delfino said, "Turn thees mad dog loose." They did. Delfino stayed with Dag's crotch but added a new and helpful move with his other hand. He grabbed him by the throat, charging the barn with him, bending Dag's head down as they gained momentum. Delfino had hoped to run Dag's head all the way through the barn wall, but since it was made of corrugated steel, he failed. Delfino didn't give in easily, though. He tried to accomplish his mission three times before he dropped Dag to the ground and gave up.

Back at the bar, Dusty was saying to Wrangler as they got a new glass of brown 'hero' juice, "Nice fellers, those three."

Wrangler grunted. He asked few questions in his life, but now he just couldn't hold off any longer.

"How . . . how're we doin', ole pardner?"

Dusty grinned real big and said, "The barbwire with the rock tied to it has finally been removed from my balls."

Old Wrangler forgot all about his twisted ankle and jumped right straight up in the air yelling, "Jesus wept, Moses crept, and Peter came a crawlin'. Hallelujah and wild horses!"

They toasted their plastic glasses together so hard it squashed out all the contents. It didn't matter because Jim Ed had a plentiful supply of whiskey and everything else.

Delfino, Ed, and Al returned triumphant. Delfino casually remarked, "Dag Oakdale ain't gonna bother nobody till mornin' no more. Savvy, amigos?"

They did.

Goodspeed saw Jim Ed and Haley walking along in a close-headed discussion. Haley reached out and touched Jim Ed on the shoulder, signaling to be left alone for a minute. He walked over to meet Doris, struggling within himself. Then he looked up and saw Al. Haley's eyes said, "Help."

Al walked over wordlessly. Then George cleared his throat and strained out, "They've come up the four extra dollars an acre Jim Ed was trying to get. He said they would. Of course he's got a hundred and twenty thousand acres and that adds up to lots of money. It's not that much with our place. Not anything like that . . . but . . ."

Al interrupted, "Would there be enough left over to have all your debts erased and all the cattle and horses paid for?"

"Yeah, and a little bit more . . . but . . . what good is that without land to put 'em on?"

Al said, "Well, George, I've put considerable thought into this. I've got a deal for you. But you can't stall around like you've done with Jim Ed and the Japanese. You'll have just ten seconds to make up your mind. That's all."

George Haley looked at Doris and then back at Al like he was witnessing the Resurrection.

Al said, "I'll buy Dag Oakdale's place and lease it back to you until you're in a position to purchase it."

Haley stared at Al about three seconds. It took two more to ask, "You mean it, don't you?" Then at about the nine-second mark he looked at Doris for her answer. She nodded, "Yes." George and Al shook hands.

Al said, "It's done." Then the industrialist leaned over and whispered a private thought to his rancher friend. "You're doing us all a big favor, George. We've got to get that chickenshit Dag Oakdale to hell and gone from *our* part of the country."

Haley laughed out loud for the first time in days and he and Doris walked toward the main house to make the Jim Ed Love and Yakahami families—as well as a few working cowboys—very happy indeed.

THE FUN LASTED until the sun shone new again. It turned out to be the greatest party ever held in the Hi Lo country, and it was certain that people from many diverse worlds would look back on it with some fondness and eventually noble nostalgia for as long as they could remember.

ALL ARRANGEMENTS had been made for the purchase of the Oakdale ranch. Al and Ed drove up to the old Haley place, as it would be known from now on, to tell them good-bye. They were invited inside but declined, wanting to get on the tedious road home.

George said, "Say, I sure want to thank you boys for saving that calf. I'd already picked him out to butcher this fall."

Al was shocked. "You're going to kill him? We'll buy him from you. Why, he'd make a great breeding bull."

"Not now he won't. We've done cut him."

At Al's puzzled look, Ed got to show off his Western knowledge once again. "They castrated our calf, Al," he explained. "He's a steer now and forever."

"Oh," Al said softly.

They said their goodbyes and solemnly started south. Soon they were on I-25 headed toward Albuquerque and an airplane that would take them back to Orange County. Ed looked off left towards Eagle Tail Mountain and said, "Quite a trip."

"It sure was. We'll have to do it again before long."

"Yeah, and if we ever do get horseback . . . hell, Al, there's just no telling what we might do."

"Right," Al said, suddenly in very high spirits.

They drove on through bluish-brown hues of the immense jagged, undulating Hi Lo country with a surprising feeling of gratefulness for having been there.

Al said, "Old Dusty and Wrangler sure were a lot of fun."

Ed didn't answer for a long moment. Then he grinned and said in a solid tribute, "Yep."